WHAT THE SCOT HEARS

Agents of Change, 3

AMY QUINTON

CONTENTS

Acknowledgments   ix

Prologue   1
Chapter 1   9
Chapter 2   17
Chapter 3   22
Chapter 4   35
Chapter 5   46
Chapter 6   50
Chapter 7   59
Chapter 8   67
Chapter 9   73
Chapter 10   81
Chapter 11   89
Chapter 12   94
Chapter 13   99
Chapter 14   112
Chapter 15   125
Chapter 16   139
Chapter 17   144
Chapter 18   156
Chapter 19   163
Chapter 20   170
Chapter 21   178
Chapter 22   184
Chapter 23   190
Chapter 24   194
Chapter 25   201
Chapter 26   206
Chapter 27   210
Chapter 28   215
Chapter 29   220
Chapter 30   229

Chapter 31   238
Chapter 32   242
Chapter 33   250
Chapter 34   254
Chapter 35   257
Chapter 36   261
Chapter 37   267
Chapter 38   271
Chapter 39   279
Chapter 40   284
Chapter 41   288
Chapter 42   291
Chapter 43   294
Epilogue   299

About the Author   305
What the Duke Wants   307
What the Marquess Sees   309
What the Rake Remembers   311
Also by Amy Quinton   315

Published 2017

Manufactured in the United States of America
This is a work of fiction. The characters, incidents and dialogues in this book are of the author's imagination and are not to be construed as real. Any resemblance to actual events or persons, living or dead, is completely coincidental.

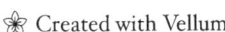 Created with Vellum

What the Scot Hears

England 1814: *Reticent Scottish Lord pursues Mouthy, Independent, American Woman...* She is an outspoken American orphan with a questionable past and a dubious purpose. He is a man of few words on the lookout for a traitor. How could they NOT get along?

Mrs. Amelia Chase is a highly-opinionated, 23-year-old woman from America on the run from her past with a penchant for self-preservation and a healthy love for Shakespearean insults. Much to a certain Scotsman's dismay:

She isn't:

- Quiet—not with her tendency to talk to everyone about anything...
- Demure—highly overrated if one cannot wear red and show off one's curves...
- Equine-savvy—she once fled some currish, toad-spotted, coxcombs—er, villains—in a stolen carriage at a pace slower than a meandering walk. Oh, and mistook a common mule for a thoroughbred. But other than that...

And she is:

- Brave—Smart, Loyal, Witty. Er, charming. Plus, Modest, Lonely, Secretive—Um, forget that last part...
- And In love—with a distrustful Highlander of all things...

Lord Alaistair MacLeod is an agent for the Crown and a man with secrets. He doesn't speak of them, he doesn't dwell on them, and he certainly doesn't let them define his future. Much. One thing is for certain, he definitely doesn't share his confidences with a peery, outspoken American woman who is obviously trouble, acts highly suspicious, and is far too nosy for her own good... No matter:

He is always:

- Focused—men who cannot stay to task are foolish...
- Pointed and Reserved—enough said...

And he isn't:

- Cheeky—like a certain American firebrand...
- Led by his... ahem...even when following on the heels of a curvy, red-wearing... ahem
- Or In love... especially not with a Troublesome, Meddlesome, so-called Independent American Woman...

Can he trust enough to embrace such an enigmatic woman? Can she awaken the passions of such an intensely private man?

Acknowledgments

I would like to thank my editor and cover artist, Jessica Cale, for the superior editorial work and beautiful cover art. Jess, you are an amazing person and a phenomenal editor.
Thank you!
I appreciate all your hard work and assistance in helping me bring this story to life <3.

I would also like to acknowledge my friend and fellow author, Angela Mizell, for all her help brainstorming this story. Angela, your assistance made this story better than I could have possibly imagined.

Thank you!

To all you Ladies, Lasses, and Sassenachs who love a great Scottish Romance, who swoon over a kilted man, and who enjoy the sound of a deep, Highland Brogue...this one's for you...

Prologue

March 1809: Southern France

It was time to face the day, though Lord knew, he wasn't ready.

Eyes still closed, Lord Alaistair MacLeod reached out and slid his hand across rumpled, silken sheets seeking the familiar shape of his lover. Where warm woman should have been, his hand met nothing but cool silk. Och, after five hours of loving, he was surprised she could even move, much less get out of bed.

He certainly couldn't.

Aye, he was thoroughly knackered. Pleasurably so.

After what felt like mere seconds, MacLeod was startled awake once again. He blinked once, twice, surprised he'd managed to fall back asleep at all, much less so deeply. Worse, he realized he might...*might*... have been roused by the rumbling, earth-tremoring sound of his own snore.

And that certainly wouldn't do.

MacLeod reached for the headboard, forcing himself to stretch his weary arms and legs and savoring that loose-limbed, post-coital feeling. He rolled over and sat up, only to lean back on one elbow.

He found his lover standing naked in the open window, absentmindedly playing with the pendant of her necklace. Her face, strikingly dark, was set in quiet contemplation as she stared off into the distance. A moment later, her face lit up and turned a soft golden hue as the sun's rays breached the horizon, bathing her in delicate morning light. She tilted her head back then, as if cherishing the warmth of those gentle beams.

He waited until she opened her eyes. "Och, come back to bed, love." He patted the empty space next to him. "I need ye."

Delilah turned and smiled, a sultry, fixed expression, while he tried his best to ignore the haunted look that crossed her face before she did. She all but sauntered over, as confident as he in her nudity, then crawled upon the bed and reached straight for his cock which jumped eagerly in agreement. But MacLeod didn't want her for that. Or not *only* that. He needed more from her. He wanted her. The woman. A companion who would be more than a lover.

"Nae, lass. Come up here, where I can hold ye in my arms a spell before we must rise to face the day."

She pouted, her lips turned down in a petulant frown, "But I want to play with this fellow right here..." and squeezed his cock.

"Nae, lass. Not now."

She stoked him again and a corresponding shiver chased up his spine, but still...

"'Lilah..."

She frowned her displeasure, but obeyed nonetheless, the insatiable minx.

"Alaistair, darling, you know I tease," she purred, "yet still, you don't laugh."

She didn't wait for him to answer, and he didn't intend to; she knew he didn't find humor easy. Instead, she walked her fingers up his chest and added, "Darling, must you leave? You never tell me where it is you go. I worry, you know."

He stroked her back while he held her close, pleased to know she cared, but uncomfortable with her continuous pressure to talk about his work. "Aye, I know it, love, but you know I canna."

She tweaked his nipple and threw him a mischievous grin, while she ran her fingers through the hair on his chest. "How about a hint, Alaistair? Tell me something...you know you talk about your trust, our trust. Trust me now. Tell me something, so I can imagine you doing what it is you men do all day."

He sighed; they seemed to have this conversation daily. He supposed it wouldn't hurt to give her something, and besides, she was right. He needed to have more faith in her if he was to expect her trust him in return. "If you must know, I'll be seeing my brother, Alain."

His heart accelerated a moment over revealing even that much, though surely he was overreacting. He ignored the anxiety that threatened and kissed her nose, while desperately searching for his earlier peace.

She pouted when she realized that was all he was willing to say. He found it adorable, mostly, and soothed her ruffled feathers with, "Och, love, you will stay busy as you always do and before you know it, it'll be tomorrow. Then, you'll have me all to yourself. For days."

Her eyes watered. "You promise?"

"Aye, of course."

"Well, then...let us get moving. The sooner we start, the sooner tomorrow will come." Already, she was pulling out of his arms and leaving the bed. He stifled a surge of disappointment. After all this time, she still resisted being physically close for anything other than fucking.

What a pair they made. His seriousness, her mercurial moods. His physical need to touch, her distance and distrust. For that matter, he wasn't precisely an open book. As a British spy for the Crown, he couldn't afford be. And in truth, her own emotional distance should make her his ideal partner.

Further, she trusted him enough to agree to be his wife. Considering he was the only man to gain such trust in her twenty-six years of life was saying something.

MacLeod climbed out of bed and began to dress, though it was apparent Delilah was still annoyed. She glared in the mirror of her vanity while she brushed her hair with hard, angry strokes.

When he was ready, he placed his hands on her shoulders, giving them a brief squeeze. He tried his best to make amends. "Lilah—you know what I want to see you wearing when I return?" He kissed her on the neck and once behind the ear. She stilled, waiting. "Wear the red cloak tonight, you know the one?"

She smiled with wicked intent. He could always get through her fits of temper with passion. "You mean the one I was wearing the first time we met?"

"And nothing else..."

"Ah, darling." She clasped his hand. "How could I forget?"

He squeezed her shoulders once more and dropped a final kiss to her shoulders. "Guid. Until tonight, my love."

It was warm for early spring in the south of France. Warm and damp and dark.

Tempestuous winds whipped through trees and rustled fallen leaves, proclaiming the approach of an early summer storm. Moisture hung on the air and lighting sliced the ebony sky with streaks and flashes of brilliant blue light. The tempest itself was far enough away that the accompanying sound of thunder could not be heard and no rain yet wetted the ground. But still, the storm's angry vitality was decisively felt. It saturated the very air, inundating every living thing in the vicinity.

Including Alaistair MacLeod.

MacLeod stood beneath the branches of a massive oak and balled his hands into fists as he inhaled the warm, humid air. He closed his eyes and listened to the wind as it raged and battled with the earth. His blue and green kilt lashed his legs, his shirt sleeves whipped his arms. He wore no coat, for he could not afford to have his movement restricted in any way.

MacLeod drew power from the turbulence surrounding him, its raw energy and intensity fueling his senses. Enhancing his strengths. Underscoring his mood.

Preparing him for what lay ahead.

But this night, despite employing his usual meditations, his normally focused thoughts were as unsettled as the oncoming storm, for he waited beneath the branches of this immense oak for his twin to arrive.

Along with his enemies.

His twin, Alain MacLeod, was the other half of his very soul. Light to his dark. Boisterous to his calm. Droll to his gravity. No one in the world was more openly friendly and gifted with putting others at ease than Alain. Unlike himself, who only ever seemed to make others uncomfortable. Except for Alain.

And Delilah.

Yet Alain was the only person who knew him completely. The only person he could speak to about anything and everything: good, bad, or indifferent. They communicated without words, as if connected by some invisible force on every level of their being. They felt each other's pain, each other's joy...hell, each other's boredom.

The last time they'd talked, Alaistair had opened up to Alain about his secret passions and dreams, for even though he was innately serious, he did have both. And Alain had encouraged him to step out of his habitual existence, to embrace his fondest desires.

But despite all that was best about his twin, Alain simply wasnae a spy. He had no training in the art of espionage. No guile. No skill for subterfuge.

Again, unlike him.

But Alain was so verra useful as bait. And he wasnae weak, either. Merely...honest. Almost *too* trusting and gregarious.

It was all in service for the Crown, of course. Their actions tonight would save lives. Many, many lives. And what was life without a small amount of risk and adventure?

A twig snapped in the distance and MacLeod froze, listening for further sounds to identify as human in origin. It was too early for his brother to be here. Far too early.

A low hum began to buzz in his ears and rumble beneath the surface of his skin causing the muscles in his neck and back to twitch.

Damn. No' yet. No' yet. God, no' yet.

It was nothing. It had to be. With this wind, it could be anything. A fallen branch was far more likely.

MacLeod took another deep breath and rubbed one hand along the back of his neck.

Yesterday, he and the Marquess of Dansbury had been cocky and arrogant, certain of their abilities and their genius, for their plan surely was brilliant. It had taken no effort at all to convince Alain to do his part. He merely needed to befriend a few of the locals, lead them out here, and the enemies they sought would play right into their hands.

Their scheme was simple and perfectly inspired. How could they not succeed?

The hum intensified.

Shite, they should no' have contacted Alain...

But alas, wishing for change didn't result in it.

They had thought their scheme foolproof. Foolproof! That sort of overconfidence should have given them pause. Should have compelled them to reconsider...

Och, it was too late.

MacLeod sucked in another deep breath and counted to ten. He exhaled slowly, forcing himself to take a full fifteen seconds to expel all his air. He tried to restore order to his chaotic thoughts.

He never doubted himself. Never. And he would not begin now.

Another streak of lightning lit up the sky, causing the trees around him to appear to shift malevolently. A trick of light and shadows.

And again, a twig snapped, but this time the sound was followed by the soft murmur of several voices, scarcely distinguishable above the howl of the wind and the swishing of fallen leaves. One voice in particular was a touch louder than the others. That man spoke slowly and laughed openly, freely. MacLeod knew that cadence and that laugh as well as he knew his own.

Alain...

His brother was here. Early.

Suddenly, the wind died down as if Mother Nature herself held her breath in warning. As if she knew.

Och, no, Alain...

Alain's laugh, so unfettered and gay, was interrupted mid chuckle.

MacLeod didn't miss a beat as he sprang into action and ran, full on towards that sound. He was as silent as a cat and as fast as the wind.

He pumped his arms and legs, practically flying across the ground, as he sprinted ever closer toward his brother.

Alain. Alain. Alain, he recited with each pump of his arms.

His twin's mounting anxiety was palpable. He could taste anxiety on his tongue, feel it in the back of his throat.

Alain. Oh, God, I'm coming, Alain.

Alaistair pushed harder, his heart racing in terror, running faster than he'd ever run in his life. He heard the first crack of thunder, as a particularly bold bolt of lightning streaked across the sky overhead. In the ensuing light, he caught sight of a familiar red cloak as it disappeared through a copse of nearby trees. An overwhelming feeling of betrayal almost brought him to his knees, he stumbled a bit but remained on his feet.

And still, he kept running.

Another bolt exploded nearby, a warning. And then, utter silence.

With a burst of speed, MacLeod ran faster.

Alain. Alain. Alain.

A shout in the distance sounded like cannon shot in the deafening calm. Then a bellowed plea, "Alaistair!"

It was the last thing his brother said before the sound of a lone gunshot pierced the air, a deafening silence ensued.

MacLeod roared his fury, his horror. "Alain!"

Chapter One

1814 - Five Years Later: The Quiet Witch Inn, England

The woman did no' belong.

It wasn't her bold, colorful attire—*red* of all things— which stood out like a brace of candles in a darkened room. Nor was it her loosely pinned, golden-brown locks, which danced upon her shoulders with every turn of her head, threatening to fall apart and spill down her back at any moment. Hell, it wasn't even the flamboyance behind her every move: her over-bright smile coupled with the way she flung her hands about while she spoke to *everyone,* without an apparent chaperone in sight. The women of his acquaintance would never be so bold. More's the pity.

She laughed and smiled and appeared utterly carefree—at least, on the surface.

But it was what *else* he saw...the strain behind her smile and the subtle anxiety peeking out from the depths of dubious eyes...that suggested all wasn't as it seemed.

MacLeod narrowed his eyes, and as he beheld her striking presence, one word pierced his mind like an unexpected shot in the dark:

Trouble.

Aye. She wasn't just troubled. She *was* trouble.

Then she glanced his way, and in that unplanned moment, their gazes collided and locked. An unexpected stab of heat scorched the back of his neck and skated down his spine. He could have sworn an echoing shiver danced its way down hers, the signs were all there—a subtle twitch of her shoulders, a slight hitch in her next step.

But then she looked away, and he found himself able to breathe once again. Christ, he hadn't even known he'd stopped.

Aye. Major Trouble. The kind that wise men avoided if they knew what was good for them.

Still, he followed her with his eyes as the rest of the patrons at The Quiet Witch Inn faded comfortably into oblivion. He no longer saw the accumulation of grime that characterized the tap room's interior décor. Nor the sound of boots treading across the dusty, wooden floor, or the cackling laughter of the pair of old biddies at the far table. It was all a muted backdrop to the colorful magnificence of this woman's presence within the room.

Alaistair MacLeod was not accounted a poetic man, and he was old enough at thirty-six not to allow his cock to make the decisions in the general course of his everyday life. But as he watched her, he couldn't help but note she was a vision in red, with curves as rounded as the bend of a twisty mountain path in his beloved Highlands.

Poetic, indeed.

As his eyes devoured every inch of her, an unsettling feeling pooled in his groin. Like a recalcitrant teenager, his ill-behaved cock practically stood up and took note.

MacLeod shifted in his seat, irritated by his body's inconvenient response.

Red walked over to a couple of men seated at the bar, a mug of ale before them as they leaned on their hands and likely contemplated life, or perhaps the loss of their youth. Both men jumped to attention in a most comical fashion, probably unused to seeing such a woman in an inn as remote as this. She bestowed upon those men a smile to light up the room, which had both men grinning like fools, half in love with her already, and left him ready to march across the room, flinging tables and patrons out of his way in the process, before throwing her over his shoulder and carrying her out the door and away from this dusty, godforsaken place.

Which was barbaric, and absurd, and never going to happen.

MacLeod tightened his grip on his mug of ale and leaned to the left as someone, or something, blocked his view.

"Stuff it. Do you hear? Don't say a word," came an angry voice from above.

MacLeod looked up and noted fellow agent for the Crown, Clifford Ross, otherwise known as the Marquess of Dansbury. Dansbury flung back his chair, then sprawled out in his seat, his arms crossed...a rare mood for the normally amiable man.

Ciarán Kelly, another agent who was already seated and MacLeod's all but forgotten companion, laughed and said, "Oh, but ye should see the look on yer face, my friend. Priceless. Got under your skin, has she?"

She was Lady Beatryce Beckett, whom Dansbury was protecting from powerful, criminal men, including one murderous assassin. MacLeod and Kelly were both tasked with providing support for Dansbury and Lady Beatryce as they fled these dangerous men.

As Dansbury and Kelly continued their pointed barbs, MacLeod contributed nothing toward their banter. In truth, he was only vaguely aware of his friends continued repartee. Rather, he was far too preoccupied...*still*...with the woman in red as she moved on to a new table and a new conversation.

He scrutinized her every move as she bobbed in and out of clusters of rowdy patrons, speaking volubly to everyone around her. Her voice, deep and husky, vibrated and wormed its way beneath his skin. She laughed loudly and frequently, smiling all too broadly and ensuring everyone took note of her presence.

Aye, it worked. They all noticed.

Including him.

Hell, especially him. Oh, he was doing a fine job of convincing himself it was because her actions were suspicious; he was only doing his duty, right?

But then how did he explain his lack of attention toward everything else going on around him, and in particular, his lack of response to Dansbury and Kelly, the reasons he was here in the first place?

Seemingly out of nowhere, Dansbury slammed his fists on the surface of the table, momentarily capturing MacLeod's attention and making their mugs of ale—and some of the nearby regulars—jump. "That woman will be the death of me if I do not kill her first."

Determined to ignore his friend's uncharacteristic outburst and Kelly's usual teasing replies, MacLeod wiped his hand on his kilt and reached for his drink, his eyes comfortably resettling on *her* once again.

Still, Dansbury and Kelly's ribbing continued around him and served as a distant irritant. And they were becoming more and more difficult to ignore with each passing minute.

MacLeod managed it a few minutes longer, *just*, until Kelly said, "I don't understand why ye despise her so much. She nearly married Stonebridge, so she can't be all bad. And I hear tell yer uncommonly rude to her. She is..."

MacLeod dropped his mug to the table and blurted out the truth as he saw it, hoping to put an end to their grating arguments. "Och, he's rude because he wants to tup her, ye ken?"

Dansbury spewed his drink all over their scarred table, his face registering disbelief at the sentiment. MacLeod wiped his face on his sleeve and scowled at his friend. "Now, cannae we just get doon to business?"

As if *he* weren't utterly preoccupied with something else up until that point.

Dansbury sputtered and held up a finger, "But I feel compelled to address your last point..."

"Deny it all ye want, my friend," Kelly interrupted, "we all know the truth. The Scot is right. I'm telling you, the rest of the room fairly burned in the wake of yer lust. Even I gave *Bertha* an extra look." Kelly shivered in disgust. Bertha was the Innkeeper's wife, a rather large, somewhat soiled woman with a decided lack of interest in bathing; a bacon and biscuits enthusiast to be sure.

Dansbury barked out a laugh, and just like that, the man's good humor was restored. It was a skill that had always baffled—and completely eluded—MacLeod.

Dansbury sought out MacLeod's gaze. "How are you, my friend? Enjoyed your trip here with this here talkative rogue, I take it?"

MacLeod stared at his friend over the rim of his mug. He refused to answer such a baited question. He didn't want to admit that Kelly's nattering irritated him—the man was never quiet—or that their gleeful banter at his expense was growing tiresome. And he really didn't want to admit he felt that way because he was equally frustrated by his inability to ignore the woman in red. Or that there was some truth to the barbs they aimed his way.

Aye. He knew he was a difficult man.

Dansbury shook his head when MacLeod didn't respond. "Right. Out with it."

MacLeod didn't waste another breath. "There were people here, asking aboot ye, before you arrived. It was a good thing ye changed yer clothes, they were asking aboot a pair of aristos."

MacLeod heard the woman in red laugh out loud and couldn't help but look over at her, his eyes drawn to her as if she ensorcelled them to do so.

Damn it.

"Who were they? Do you know? Did you find them?"

"Nae. But it doesna sit well that they looked fer ye here. This place isna easy to find and not the most obvious of places to search, ye ken?"

A flash of red caught his attention, and once again, his eyes flickered across the room. He genuinely couldn't help it.

"You're right. It is a concern, though they could have gotten lucky. I'll be more vigilant, just in case. Any leads on who is pulling the strings?"

"Nae. Stonebridge has everyone in his command on it, though."

"Well, it can't happen fast enough. Lady Beatryce is driving me mad."

"Yea, it sure looked like it a little while ago," taunted Kelly.

MacLeod looked past Dansbury's shoulder once again, ignoring Kelly. "Aye, I hear ye. We'll be trailing ye for added protection, ye ken?"

"Thanks. Now, why do you keep looking over at the American, MacLeod?"

MacLeod jerked his attention back to Dansbury, surprised to be discovered, but with no intention of defending his actions. How could one explain the unexplainable? And even though he'd just been caught out by Dansbury, he looked over to the woman *again*.

To find her walking straight toward them.

MacLeod jumped to his feet, his chair scraping the wooden floor with a loud grinding sound as he did. Och, she walked with a grace that rendered every man mute. Her every gesture...every step...fluid and sensual.

He swallowed hard.

She smiled as she neared, of course. "What's with all the brooding? You gentlemen look like you could use another drink," she assumed. "I'm Mrs. Amelia Chase. From America. You know, the colonies?" She laughed at her quip. "How are you gents this fine evening?"

Her voice, so much clearer now with her proximity, was husky and bright; the sound enveloped every inch of him, hard, gruff edges and all.

Dansbury made the introductions, using his assumed identity rather than his real name. "Clifford Churchmouse. It is a pleasure. This man is Lord Alaistair MacLeod and the man impolitely seated is Mr. Ciarán Kelly."

"Churchmouse? Are you the strong silent type, then?" She laughed, again, and continued, "Lord MacLeod, Mr. Kelly. May I join you?"

"Nae." MacLeod shook his head no, though he desperately wanted to say yes. He wanted to study her, determine all the ways in which she was put together. And he absolutely needed to touch her, ever so gently, to see if her skin was as soft as it appeared. These were patently ridiculous thoughts. They had a job to do; this thing...*she*...was an unwelcome and dangerous distraction.

"Of course, allow me." Dansbury spoke over him and pulled out a chair, damn the man.

MacLeod accepted that he'd been overruled and retook his seat. He ignored the inanities that ensued as he considered the woman before him. Might as well. Besides, Dansbury was the charming one; he could do the talking. MacLeod was content to watch, unable to participate in small talk even at the best of times.

So. Who was Mrs. Chase?

For one thing, she was *not* a typical lady. It might have been the bold way she looked him in the eye when she spoke. It might have been the carefree laugh, rare to hear in his circle of acquaintances... apart from Dansbury, and more recently, the Duke of Stonebridge. Perhaps it was the way she introduced herself to everyone in the taproom, which in itself was curious. It was as if she were looking for something.

Or someone?

Something wasn't quite right and he wanted to know what. Worse, he wanted to ask her things that were too personal for public consumption...even in front of his friends.

MacLeod studied her hands. Her nails were clipped and tidy, her fingers long and tapered. When she spoke, she twirled her hands about in the air; she was quite animated...so very alive. But when she was listening, she fiddled with the strings of her reticule, twisting and turning them around her fingers until they began to knot.

"Dansbury, weren't you..." Kelly began, then his voice trailed off.

MacLeod jerked, then glared across the table at the Irishman. *What. The. Fuck?*

"D-Dansbury?" Mrs. Chase turned to look at Dansbury. *Of course*, she didn't miss Kelly's lapse.

"Aye." Kelly interjected. "We call him Dansbury because Church-mouse is just plain odd. And since he used to work fer the Dansbury estate, we took to calling him that."

Kelly tried to explain away his gaffe, but it was a ridiculous excuse only an idiot would believe.

"You worked for the Dansbury estate? Do you know the marquess well then? Are they...are they nice...people?" asked Mrs. Chase.

"Fairly well, I'd say." Dansbury smiled. "They are extremely nice people. Very giving. And you? Do you know the marquess?"

"I'm a...his...No..." She seemed unsure, which was curious and damning. "...but I look forward to meeting him some time. I've heard great things."

MacLeod narrowed his eyes as he noticed her rubbing her hand along her skirts, an unmistakable nervous gesture.

And like that MacLeod's interest turned from mere...curiosity...to bloody outright suspicion.

She couldn't possibly fall for that tripe Kelly made up, could she? No reasonable person would.

So then, what was her aim with this line of questioning? Why did she not call Kelly out for his gaffe? Was she simply being polite? To his knowledge, that wasn't a trait Americans were known for. Unapologetically bold and brash, yes. Timid and reserved, not on your life.

A few minutes later, Mrs. Chase excused herself and returned to the bar. She sat with her back to the wall, facing the room at large. It seemed she no longer had any desire to flit about and pester the other customers.

MacLeod sat back and observed it all with an apprehensive eye.

He was rewarded for his troubles half an hour later when Dansbury left to retire upstairs. MacLeod watched with an unsettling mixture of satisfaction and exasperation as Mrs. Chase followed Dansbury with her eyes then stood and quietly slid up the stairs after him.

"Dammit, sometimes I hate being right..." MacLeod muttered before tossing back the remains of his drink. Then he stood, adjusted the lay of his kilt, pushed in his chair, and threaded his way to the stairs, following on the heels of an enigma.

Och, trouble was right.

Chapter Two

Upstairs at The Quiet Witch Inn

The faded green door to room #12 closed with a soft click.

Sigh.

Mrs. Amelia Chase blew away the stray hairs from her falling coiffure as she peeked around the corner in time to see the verdant door snap shut. Such innocuous things, doors: simple and useful. Yet this particular door was so much more, for this door might very well open, *or bar*, the way to her future. For better or worse.

Maybe.

Hopefully?

No. She was by nature an idealist despite her *colorful* past, and besides, there was no room in her plans for uncertainty. The room simply had to belong to Churchmouse, or Dansbury, or whatever he wanted to call himself. He was the last person to climb the stairs ahead of her; she knew, for she'd been watching him all evening.

Amelia pulled back around the corner and braced herself against the wall. She closed her eyes and concentrated on the feel of rough wainscoting beneath her clammy fingertip. Small fibers of wood seemed to reach out and thread across her fingers as she brushed them along the wall, following the grain.

But then Amelia's hand slipped and she fell completely against the wall, breaking her concentration.

Arg. What a time to develop a case of the nerves.

She'd never been hampered by anxiety in the past, why now? Perhaps her recent brush with the law...? No. She would not go there. And dash it all, she was close, so close.

So where, then, had her infamous confidence hied off to?

She could read the measure of a man in a matter of moments. Dansbury/Churchmouse: honorable, charming, good-humored. Kelly: a rogue, a flirt, loved women; would never hurt one. MacLeod:

Hmm...MacLeod. Self-contained. But like a banked fire, scratch at the surface and discover an inferno buried beneath. And yet, she had the irresistible urge to poke at him and make him ignite. Yes, it was juvenile but compelling. Too bad she hadn't the time to play that game with him.

But the point was, none of them were setting off her internal 'this way lays danger' alarms.

Amelia wiped her damp hands on her dress and squared her shoulders. Now was not the time to be thinking about broody Scotsmen. She was Amelia Chase: resourceful and persistent. She had a job to do and she refused—*refused!*—to doubt herself now.

Amelia peeked around the corner once more, her gaze drawn to #12 like a magnetic compass pointing north. Her options were:

A: she could boldly knock upon the door to #12, proclaim herself Mr. Churchmouse's long lost sister (all the while accusing him of being the Marquess of Dansbury in disguise—*Ha! Ha! Caught you!*), and hoped he believed her story, or

B: she could try Plan B, the details of which were still somewhat ill-formed, stupid, insane, and quite honestly too ludicrous to mention out loud.

Alas, she was Amelia Chase, a Plan B kind of girl...adventurous, courageous, and a brazen voice for the disadvantaged...but always looking out for number one.

Right. Plan B it is, then.

Now that her little motivational speech was out of the way, Amelia took one last deep inhalation of breath, rounded the corner, and dashed forward on the tips of her toes, stopping just short of #12.

She jerked her head back over her shoulder, her eyes attempting to pierce the shadows behind her, which seemed to swell and twist between spheres of lambent light emanating from the randomly lit wall sconces. The carnage red carpeting and dark, dingy walls added to the malevolent feel and all but shrieked *Danger!* in bold, screeching sounds.

But there was no one. Her unease had her hearing and seeing things that simply weren't there. It was all thanks to that blasted Scot; his intensely daring and constant gaze had put her on edge all evening.

Amelia shook away thoughts of his brooding, soul-dark eyes, filing such reflections away until she had time to examine them.

Amelia turned back around and, once more, wiped her clammy hands on her dress. She was filled with anticipation and a tiny—almost not worth mentioning, really—dose of fear. Because, well, Plan B and all. And then there was what would happen should she fail; she *really* didn't want to think about *that*.

She had to have faith in her disguise: it was utterly foolproof—*foolproof!*—for it gave her license to hide in plain sight.

But if all that weren't enough, she could still be Caught by someone respectable, even though it was quite late and reputable people were meant to be abed. Sleeping. However, based on her limited knowledge of English rules of etiquette, getting Caught equaled a Scandal and the End of Life as everyone knew it, so this was important to note.

She snorted. Ha! Really? How *dreadful.* Such drama for a society that frowns upon drama.

Amelia chuckled softly at the absurdity of it all. In America, people would simply think she was quirky and move on.

On a positive note, her daft thoughts worked better than anything else to quiet her anxiety. Which was fortunate, lest she lock herself in a dark room and hide beneath the covers for the rest of her life.

Focus, Amelia. Sheesh.

Amelia threw herself into a role. She checked the hall once more for good measure, her finger pressed to her lips, her very demeanor all but screaming "I'm lost."

After confirming once again that the hallway did indeed remain clear of other guests, Amelia finally acknowledged her behavior for what it was: a stalling ploy.

So, without further ado, Amelia lifted her chin, faced the door in question: #12, threw her reticule to the floor...

...and dropped to her knees, setting her right eye to the key hole.

Yes, she was Amelia Chase:

- orphan
- newly-minted-spy-extraordinaire (in her mind at the very least)
- Independent American Woman...

...and a woman who peeked through key holes.

So, some might call her a Peeping Tom should she be Caught, but really, she didn't make a habit of this. Honestly. And she was on an important, almost—No. Not almost. She would call it what it was: *desperate*—mission here. Allowances should be made.

She just needed to be certain the room was Dansbury's. That was all, a trifling thing really. Despite being confident she knew his identity, that confidence didn't matter when she knew better than most that mistakes happen. Though some mistakes had far more severe consequences than others, as her recent situation could attest.

In this instance, she couldn't afford to be wrong...not about who he was, and more importantly, not about whether she should reveal who she was in truth.

Unfortunately, all she could see was the shadowy outline of a man— definitely a man—for his shape was far too large to be that of a woman.

Amelia alternated between putting her ear to the lock to listen and then trying once more to see, all to no avail. No sound came from the room and the man standing before the door appeared to be rooted to the spot.

Eventually, Amelia leaned back on her heels, reeling with frustration. She gripped the door knob with her right hand for balance. Now, that she was fully committed to Plan B, she wasn't quite so nervous.

Wouldn't it be funny if Dansbury suddenly wrenched the door

open with her leaning back like this? She'd find herself sprawled on the floor at his feet, probably opening and closing her mouth like a goldfish out of water and at a loss for words.

For once.

Amelia put her free hand to her mouth to stifle a giggle. In truth, she wanted nothing more than to smack the door in sarcastic frustration. She settled for shaking her fist at the door in mock anger.

Blast the man! Why couldn't he cooperate and make this easy? A sign on the door would suffice.

Amelia rubbed her tired eyes, then leaned forward again, trying once more to see anything useful through the blasted key hole.

She held absolutely still.

She was one with silence, her breathing slooooow...

And steady...

And calm...

If she strained to listen, she might hear...

...*Creak*...

A nearby floorboard groaned under pressure...

Then a wisp of warm air wafted across her ear, sending a shiver up her spine just before a deep, gravelly voice with a delicious, thrilling Scottish brogue said, "What do ye think ye're doin', Mrs. Chase?"

Chapter Three

Mrs. Chase jumped.

He had not expected the lass to jump. And he certainly had not expected her to hurdle right into his chin whilst doing so, causing him to bite his tongue in the process. But she had. And he did. And dammit, it hurt like hell. He swallowed the coppery tang that tainted his mouth.

Mrs. Chase spun around, one hand rubbing her head, her eyes watery with pain, and jumped right into her own accusation. "What in the blazes do you think you are doing, MacLeod?"

"What am *I* doing?" *Really?*

"Yes. What are you doing? Don't you know better than to sneak up on a person when she is...um... When she is..." Mrs. Chase licked her lips. "...erm...concentrating?"

He snorted and stepped closer, crowding her before the door, his eyes drawn to her wetted, plump lips.

Nae, dammit. No lips. Especially not from sneaking, spying, temptresses.

He jerked his gaze up to hers, pinning her in place with his regard and searching for the truth in her golden-brown orbs. Against his better judgement, which was normally quite sound, he felt the beginnings of a smile tug at his lips. "Och, is that what you were doing?"

When he'd witnessed Mrs. Chase follow Dansbury upstairs, he'd become convinced her actions were nefarious. All right, maybe not nefarious. Suspicious, at the very least. He had trouble truly believing her a spy, for based on her behavior downstairs, she obviously wasn't aiming for secrecy.

And now this? Real spies didn't spend their evenings peeking beneath locked doors. Obviously. But her reaction to getting caught? Audacious. Preposterous. And utterly suspicious.

If matters with Dansbury weren't so serious, he'd add borderline charming. But they were. He had to remember that.

With the little space he'd left her, Mrs. Chase reached down and felt around for her reticule, her gaze never leaving his. Still, she smiled when she asked, "Well, what else would I be doing?"

MacLeod very nearly snorted once again; instead he forced himself to look serious rather than incredulous or worse, enchanted. "It looked to me like you were spying on the occupants of this room." He nodded his head toward the room in question.

Mrs. Chase fiddled with the strings of her reticule, not quite meeting his eyes now. Still, he heard her clearly when she replied, "Ridiculous."

MacLeod frowned. "So you weren't on your knees just now, spying through that verra keyhole?" He nodded his head toward the aperture in question.

She looked over her shoulder, following his gaze, then back at him, wetting her lips once more. "Well, that would be silly now, wouldn't it?" She grinned as if she found him infinitely amusing, then reached up and patted his arm. "M-my, you have quite the imagination, MacLeod."

Her words of denial were ridiculous. They both knew he'd caught her doing just that.

MacLeod shook his head and found himself once more on the verge of a chuckle. "I can honestly say no one's ever accused me of that before."

That's when he realized what he had to do. Oh, he could play her game; he was here for the night anyway. If she wanted to spend the evening standing in a drafty, smelly old hall while he listened to her invent some imaginary yarn he would not believe anyhow, he could accommodate her and play along. But he was better off questioning her where they were not likely to be seen or heard, especially by Dansbury. And he really should take a more serious, harder look at her motives.

Mind made up, MacLeod stepped forward and leaned down. He was so close, he could hear her shaky intake of breath before she gulped. He waited a second more, then said, "I'm also no' much of a talker." He reached out impulsively and tugged at a loose lock of hair, "I'm more a man of action, you ken?"

And without another word, MacLeod scooped her up and tossed her over his shoulder. His destination: his own room down the hall.

"MacLeod," she hissed.

He ignored her.

"Let me go...*oomph*...you big, oversized, popinjay." She punctuated each word with a fist.

Popinjay? Him?

MacLeod rounded the corner and stopped before his room, one identified by a distressed red door and tarnished brass numbers proclaiming it room #18. He fumbled around in his leather sporran for a moment, then pulled out a rusted old skeleton key and unlocked the door.

The door scraped and screeched as he shoved it open, the hinges in obvious need of oiling. The floor varnish had worn away in an arc fanning out from the doorway due to years of guests opening and closing a door in desperate want of a good planing.

These features did not slow him down.

He pushed the door wide and felt her cringe when it slammed against the wall.

Good. If the lass were rattled a bit, maybe he could get her to fess up sooner rather than later. He prudently ignored the sense of disappointment that hovered about in the back of his mind over her possible perfidy.

MacLeod put Amelia down before closing the door and locking them in. Then he opened his sporran and replaced the key, never once taking his eyes from hers. Fortunately, there was enough light from the setting moon to make out her features. After lighting a few candles whilst they both kept silent, he leaned back against the door and folded his arms across his chest.

"Nou, speak. And the truth this time, lass, if you will."

Amelia rubbed her arm and scowled.

He hadn't hurt her, not really. She was clearly stalling for time while she tried to figure out exactly what to tell him. He could see every bit of her efforts flit across her face in perfect clarity.

He decided to help her along. "So, Mrs. Amelia Chase. Is there a Mr. Chase?"

She shook her head. "No."

He'd suspected she wasn't married—what reasonable man would let a woman like her out of his sight for even a minute—and he was surprised to feel a small sense of relief with her answer.

Amelia took a deep breath, squared her shoulders, and said, "Fine. Churchmouse, otherwise known as the Marquess of Dansbury, is my brother."

Och, not bloody likely.

Hell, she'd even inflected her voice at the end, making it *sound* like a question, not a mark in her favor.

MacLeod narrowed his eyes and cocked his head. "He's no' Dansbury."

Amelia shook her head as if she could not believe he didn't trust her, which was laughable. She paced over to the fireplace, then spun back around. He watched as she marched back across the floor. "Well, I heard Mr. Kelly. He very clearly called Mr. Churchmouse 'Dansbury' earlier in the taproom. No matter what you all said afterward, I know a cover up when I hear one...and not a very convincing one, at that. You all expected me to simply take your word for it and leave the matter alone, so you scarcely tried. But I've got news for you, Mr. MacLeod: it won't work. Do you want to know why?"

He said nothing for he suspected nothing he could possibly say would matter.

Sure enough, she stepped directly in front of him, her skirts tangling with his bare legs, lifted her chin and said, "...because I am an Independent American Woman, and as such, you cannot pull one over on me!"

"He's no' Dansbury."

"Well, I *no'* believe you," she mimicked, putting her hands on her hips for emphasis.

He couldn't stop his eyes from following the movement nor could he hide the flare of heat he knew burned anew in his gaze. Bloody hell...a woman up to no good should not have curves as attention-gripping as hers. He dragged his mind back to the topic at hand with some difficulty. "He's no'..."

"Stop!" She stamped her foot and held her hand up to shush him, "Saying it repeatedly won't *make* it true all of the sudden, Mr. MacLeod."

He tilted his head and regarded her, surprised she had effectively shushed him. *Him.* Didn't she realize he had the upper hand in this conversation?

She shook her head and stepped away. He hated that his first instinct was to grab her by the arms and pull her back.

"Dansbury does no' have a sister," he maintained.

She spun around. "Well, I beg to differ." Then, she spread her arms out. "I'm very real, as you can see."

MacLeod stood away from the wall and dropped his crossed arms, bracing them on his hips. He could not help but look her over; she'd all but invited him to do so.

He took his time, savoring the moment. He started with the tips of her toes. Then drug his gaze up her skirts. Slowly. Precisely. He was *always* thorough in all that he did. Why should this be any different?

Would he see similarities to his friend in her features? He sought the answer in her curves, and as lust crept over him, threatening to overtake his sound reasoning, he was more than willing to find out, all the while praying that the answer was *no.* God, no.

He heard her breath catch as she watched him study her. He missed absolutely nothing...not the hitch in her breathing, nor the shuffle of her feet beneath her skirts, not even the sound of her chewing on her plump, delectable lip.

On the heels of that thought, he realized an uncomfortable truth—understood how far his plan had backfired—for the temperature in the room climbed with the speed of a bullet. He had a tenuous hold on his lust. His attraction to her had only been loosely restrained, waiting for the opportune moment to break free. He refrained from reaching for her by the tiniest thread of control.

She was so beautiful to behold—voluptuous. Strong. With a kind face and a smile that lit up a room. He could tell she struggled not to reveal her own discomfort beneath the intensity of his scrutiny. It was in the way she held herself—so tense, her fists clinched in her skirts.

He looked to her face once more and was stunned by what he saw there. Her golden eyes were wide and locked on him; his own knees threatened to buckle under the weight of her regard.

In desperation, he cleared his throat and maintained, "I would know it if the mon had a sister."

"W-well, he does," she croaked. He could commiserate, for he'd nearly done the same.

He re-crossed his arms, a show of strength to convince her his judgement would not be swayed by her charms. In truth, it was the only way he might have a chance at keeping his own yearning in check. "Prove it," he challenged.

Amelia lifted her chin and straightened her spine. Och, he reluctantly admired her determination.

"I don't have to prove anything to you, Mr. MacLeod, and you know it. Neither can you keep me here without cause."

MacLeod forced a shrug that belied the storm of emotion churning beneath his skin, then paced away toward the fireplace as she'd done moments before. He poked at the fire in the hearth while he gathered the scattered threads of his control. She might be beautiful and voluptuous with a smile he suspected could light up one's soul if given half a chance, but she'd proven herself false, at least on the surface, and he couldn't simply ignore that in order to appease her. Despite her vibrant beauty and apparent flair for life that seemed to reach out to some dusty, dark recess in his soul, he would not now, nor ever, succumb to her charms, no matter how strongly he was attracted to her.

Besides, if anyone could keep her here without reason, it was him.

He returned the fire poker to its stand and turned to stand before her, while keeping her safely out of arm's reach.

Yet she stepped forward, a move that was, again, unexpected, as seemed to be her nature. "Fine."

She took another step. She was close now, once more in his personal space. She looked down for a moment as if gathering her courage, then back up at him through her long lashes. She quirked her lips, and gifted him with a smile that was sultry and all woman.

The change in her demeanor was sudden and unexpected. Now, *he* squirmed...and he *never* squirmed. The desire to loosen his cravat and remove his jacket was nearly overwhelming.

She reached for him and walked her fingers up the sleeve of his coat, two points of heat that branded his arm every step of the way, marking him as hers. He tried in vain to swallow the lump in his suddenly parched throat.

She purred, adding, "Why do *you* think I'm here, MacLeod?" He saw a flash of fire in her eyes. "Am I a spy acting against the British Crown? Is Dansbury my mark?" Her look turned coy. "Perhaps I am a murderess on the run from the law..."

MacLeod snapped. Any softness he'd felt toward her vanished like smoke caught up in a stiff breeze. Her words too closely mirrored his own worries to be accounted a coincidence.

But when he reached to grab her, she spun out of his arms and threw her hands in the air. "Ugh! You, sir, are impossible!"

Again, her response was unpredictable, and he'd never admit he almost jumped in the face of her outburst. His only outward response was to re-cross his arms, but he no longer advanced. He didn't trust himself to advance. Hell, he didn't know whether he wanted to see her jailed or fuck her. And wasn't that madness?

Amelia pressed her fingers to the bridge of her nose. "Look, MacLeod, it's late and I'm exhausted. I'm willing to set this aside for the evening and take it up with Churchmouse in the morning, when clearer heads will prevail."

He frowned, but agreed. "Aye. All right."

He had his reasons for his quick acquiescence, not the least of which was so he could remove the temptation he only narrowly avoided. Besides, he wasn't a fool; he wouldn't allow her to remain unguarded.

She dropped her hand. "Good...till the morning then."

Yet they both simply stood there, entrenched in place. She likely expected him to make it easy for her.

He wouldn't, not when he wasn't entirely sure of her guilt—or innocence—or what to do with his knowledge. She hadn't committed a crime...yet. It all left him feeling edgy, an uncomfortable sensation for him; he was never at a loss for what to do.

Until now.

His life centered around black and white, right or wrong. Yet Mrs. Chase forced an inkling of doubt into his well ordered world; she successfully painted everything in shades of grey. And his traitorous body's attraction to the woman was not helping matters. His barely constrained lust compromised his every consideration of her guilt, which was a problem he'd never experienced.

"Wonderful. Now, would you mind?" She gestured toward the door behind him, then wrapped her arms across her waist.

MacLeod stepped aside, leaving it up to her to make her own way out, for she was, as previously stated, an Independent American Woman.

Amelia squared her shoulders and marched to the door. She reached for the knob with both hands, obviously recalling that the door tended to stick.

But she hadn't recalled he'd locked it, and he was callous enough and angry enough to let her figure that one out on her own. While, he would spend this time productively and master his inconvenient desire.

After a few minutes of tugging and pulling and possibly a muttered curse or two, which nearly made him chuckle despite everything, she remembered.

Mrs. Chase sighed, dropped her hands to her sides, and didn't even look in his direction as she said, "Would you mind?"

He stepped up behind her and reached around her petite form to unlock the door. It wasn't difficult, for the top of her head only grazed his chin as he bent over her.

But when he was finished, he didn't back away. He was compelled to remain there, close. It might have been the intoxicating smell of her, warm and sweet, that he hadn't noticed before. Or maybe it was her stature; she seemed to fit so neatly before him, as if she were fashioned to fit there.

Whatever the reason, he had the inexplicable urge to pull her against his chest to test the theory.

And she seemed to feel...something...in return, for she remained standing there, too. So close. He could hear her labored breathing as if she'd run the length of the hall, not stood inside this dim room talking of spying and a kinship that couldn't possibly exist. And, och, he could have sworn she leaned back into him ever so slightly.

So much for getting ahold of his desire.

He'd barely finished that thought when the moment was broken. Amelia jerked and grasped for the door. It took several pulls before she wrenched it open, but she did eventually manage it.

He followed her out, then leaned against the door jamb as he watched her storm up the hall, her head tilted high with apparent indignation. Absurdly, the urge to laugh churned in his gut yet again. He had to fight to stifle it else he'd start guffawing in great fits, which he hadn't done since he was a mere lad.

So he was undeniably attracted to her, yet she was clearly up to... something...and he had a job to do.

With that thought, he once more cloaked himself in his black and white world, secure in the knowledge that he was right and could make decisions without allowing his emotions to affect his choices.

Before she stepped around the corner and out of sight, he called out to her, "Mrs. Chase..." She stopped, but she did not look back, her shoulders squared and tense. "...be in the taproom at half-five and doona be late."

She did not acknowledge his remarks; she simply dropped her shoulders and carried on her way.

It didn't matter. She wouldn't be making it to their 'meeting' anyway.

At least...not if he had anything to say about it.

30

At the Same Time: Secret Meeting Rooms in an Old Warehouse
along the Thames

"Lords of the Society, our meeting is called to order," Intoned the
Minister of Actions, a heavily robed man wearing an ornately curled
wig and buckled, heeled shoes reminiscent of the last century. He was a
rather short man, and he stood on a box behind his lectern in order to
appear taller. But what he lacked in height, he made up for with his
loud, booming voice.

In an almost trancelike response, the members of the assembled
men replied in unison, their voices echoing loudly in the lightly
furnished warehouse, "We are the Lords of London. Our worthy
mission, blessed by God Himself, is to purify the bloodlines of our
English citizens, from the wealthiest of Lords to the poorest of the
poor. Our actions are guided by Divine Intervention. Our methods,
from bloodshed to the making of common laws, are always justified.
With Deific Blessing, all is forgiven. Amen."

Eyes watering with unholy emotion, the Minister spoke again.
"Amen. Thank you, gentleman for your presence today and for your
dedication and sacrifice to our just cause." He looked over the assembled guests who were seated in rows of pews on either side of a central
aisle. There were forty in attendance, only a fraction of their total
membership, which was an excellent turn out for a group that relied
upon intense secrecy.

The minister smiled with wicked glee when his gaze caught on an
unfamiliar attendee. "I see new faces this evening. In that case, we
shall begin our meeting with recommendations for inductees. Do we
have any initiates who are prepared to take the oath? Might there be
anyone capable of standing strong beneath our intense scrutiny?"

One man, heavy set and draped in furs and jewels, and a marquess
at that, stood at the request. "I submit for your consideration, Lords of
the Society for the Purification of England, Viscount Sharpe." He
gestured to the man seated next to him, who stood at the introduction
and bowed his acknowledgement of the referral.

The Minister nodded and held out his hand. "Very good, my lord.
Viscount Sharpe, please approach the lectern."

Viscount Sharpe was of above average height and dressed quite completely in black. His hair, unpowdered and unwigged, was a rich mahogany and tied back in a queue with a short length of black leather. He walked with the use of an ebony cane, though his stride was confident and he appeared to be no older than perhaps thirty.

Despite all the subtlety of his attire, he wore gleaming rings of silver on every one of his long fingers, more than one on some fingers. A contradiction, to be sure.

But what truly caught everyone's attention, making them squirm uncomfortably in their seats at the sight, was the scarring that covered the left side of his face. No one was bold enough to openly stare. And no one was strong enough to ignore it.

A hunched, balding man, wearing what appeared to be a monk's robe, approached from the side of the room bearing a large bible. He stood awkwardly beside the minister, barely managing to hold up the heavy tome with which he was entrusted, as Viscount Sharpe made his way up the center aisle to the front of the room.

"Viscount Sharpe," said the minister, "You have heard about the Society of the Purification of England from your sponsor?"

The viscount dipped his head, "I have." He spoke with an accent as English as the bluest of England's highest nobility.

"Do you understand all that is required and expected of you?"

Again, the viscount's voice echoed clearly and confidently around the room. "I do."

"And did you willingly submit to questioning by your sponsor, submitting all the necessary documentation as required by the Society of the Purification of England?"

"I did."

The minister looked out to the sponsoring marquess, who confirmed this statement with a nod.

The minister looked to the viscount once again and folded his hands across the lectern. "Very good. And have you, proudly, marked yourself a member of our group?"

Viscount Sharpe rolled back his sleeve. And there on his forearm was an intricate tattoo of an English Oak with the letters S, P, and E entwined among the branches.

The minister smirked once more. "Very good. Now, place your right hand on our bible and repeat after me."

The viscount did so, his eyes locked with the monk-like figure holding the bible. In return, the monk began to sweat and shake as he strove to hold up the bible under the pressure of the viscount's hand.

No one else seemed to notice this.

The Minister began. "I, Viscount Sharpe, do solemnly swear to uphold the mission of our Society by any means possible."

Viscount Sharpe repeated him, his gaze never wavering from the monk before him. "I, Viscount Sharpe, do solemnly swear to uphold the mission of our Society by any means possible."

"I promise to do whatever necessary to achieve our aims, even kill suspected traitors if need be."

"I promise to do whatever necessary to achieve our aims, even kill suspected traitors if need be."

"All for the benefit of our future Society."

"All for the benefit of our future Society."

"God's Will. Our Will, be done."

"God's Will. Our Will, be done."

"And if I should betray this trust, whether by word or inaction, I shall accept my punishment accordingly, including death if it be so deemed."

"And if I should betray this trust, whether by word or inaction," the Viscount looked at the minister then and said, "I shall accept my punishment accordingly, including death if it be so deemed." The minister swallowed. The viscount's eyes seemed to be afire...it was as if he was making his own promise, his own threat with his words. But now, that couldn't be.

"Thank you, Viscount Sharpe, and welcome. You may return to your seat," the minister squeaked out. For a moment, it appeared as if the viscount had no intention of doing so.

But then the man responded, "But of course."

The minister, obviously relieved and starting to appear a touch irritated, looked out to the congregation. "Now, on to new business. Where are we on the attainment of the Marquess of Dansbury to our membership?"

A silver-haired man in flamboyant colors sitting in the back of the room stood and said, "We have our best men working on the problem. It's only a matter of time."

The minister rediscovered his usual smirk. "Good. Very good."

Chapter Four

Entirely Too Early in the Morning: The Quiet Witch Inn

Amelia woke with a jolt; her stomach and sides screaming in protest. She looked around to orient herself, barely able to make out the furniture in her room, despite the bright light of a late setting moon. She still wore her shift and stays, hence her protesting body. For a moment, she could not for the life of her recall where she was, nor how she came to be there. But all too soon, she remembered everything: a green door, an angry Scot, and a thorough perusal of her body by said Scot.

She couldn't stop her mind from recounting, in absolute vivid detail, that most devastating...that most...*memorable*...aspect of their conversation...

After pronouncing herself Dansbury's sister with open arms, MacLeod had stood away from the wall and dropped his crossed arms, bracing them on his hips. He'd taken her gesture as a direct invitation to inspect her form from head to toe.

And, dash it all, he'd done just that...and taken his time going about it.

A warm trail of heat whispered across her skin as she remembered everything... It was the same acute and all-encompassing sensation she'd felt in the wake of his perusal.

God, he'd been so very...*thorough*...

Amelia held her breath as she recalled watching him study her. His regard, so intense and...and...*comprehensive*, had missed absolutely nothing.

She could still feel the intensity about him...such passion and concentration surrounded him and seemed to be ever present, like an aura that engulfed his very essence.

And oh, his dark eyes...they were sharp, lethally so.

Being studied by Alaistair MacLeod was unsettling and acute and...*delectable*...all at once. It had taken an extreme amount of self-control to keep from squirming beneath such scrutiny. She thought she'd managed to hide her discomfort, for the most part.

Maybe.

Eventually, he had looked to her face once more; even that had left her feeling faint.

And, at that moment, she'd realized, with absolute crystal clarity, that she was very, very fortunate he was not an exceptionally charismatic man. As it was, he was already far too fascinating for her curious nature to ignore.

If he were charming as well as enigmatic, she'd be prostrating herself at his feet for one moment of his favor.

Yes, well fortunately he'd destroyed that possibility by allowing her to embarrass herself trying to open a locked door without a key?! Argh...the pig-headed oaf.

And just like that, Amelia was past the sensual review of his perusal. She began kicking off tangled sheets so she could stumble out of bed.

He was clearly a complicated man, one that women across the world were wise to avoid. She would never, ever, EVER find herself at the mercy of someone like that again. Never.

Besides, if he knew the truth about her past, he'd toss her out on her ear in a heartbeat. Or in jail...

Oh no. We are not following that train of thought, Mrs. Chase.

Though the sun had yet to rise, Amelia forced herself to get out of bed. She wasn't fooled by MacLeod's easy acquiescence; he plainly didn't care for her interest in his friend, Churchmouse née Dansbury... or whatever he wished to be called.

Well that was too bad. She would not allow him to leave her behind by stealing away before dawn. He said five-thirty. Well, she intended to be there by four.

"Be in the taproom at half-five and doona be late." She mimicked as she stoked up the banked fire. "Overbearing brute. Unmuzzled, spurgalled, varlot. I'll show you *doona be late*. I'm so not going to be late. I'm going to be so early I couldn't be late even if I crawled down the stairs on my blasted stomach." She poked at the coal in the hearth, imagining she poked a certain highlander in places he'd rather her not.

So she was being childish; that's what happened when she was running on only a few hours of sleep with worry constantly lingering along the fringes of her every waking moment.

Finding Dansbury was too...necessary.

After washing her face with the bracingly cold water found in the washbasin beside her bed, Amelia pulled on her dress over her rumpled shift and stays. She'd slept in her stays to keep things simple...and to ensure she didn't oversleep. Who could whilst wearing such ridiculous contraptions?

The dress she donned was one designed to be put on without assistance. Double plus.

Once her frock was settled over her voluptuous frame, she checked her appearance in the full-length mirror on the wall next to the door, a surprising but welcome feature of the room. Her hair was a bit of a mess, so she tugged on her wavy locks and repinned a few strays until she was satisfied with her appearance. She nodded at her dim reflection.

You look fabulous, Amelia Chase.

Deciding she was ready to face the day, or more accurately MacLeod, she picked up her reticule from her bedside table and fumbled around inside for her room key. She could already taste the steaming hot cup of coffee she'd be sipping in a matter of moments.

To her consternation, her reticule seemed to contain all her usual possessions—minus her room key.

Well, that is odd. I distinctly remember locking the door, and I'm quite sure I put the key right back in here.

Amelia set her bag on the bed and looked around the room, hands on her hips.

Now, where in the world could it be? The table? She glanced that way. No. The washstand? No. The floor? She circumnavigated the bed, checking the floor on all sides and only hitting the corners with her knees twice as she fumbled around in the dim light. She looked under the blankets she'd kicked off the bed. No. Nothing. A sinking feeling began in the pit of her stomach.

He wouldn't dare...would he?

But she knew the answer before she even finished asking the question.

"MacLeod!" She swore as she raced to the door and reached for the knob, hope springing to life in her heart for a few impossible seconds, though she knew better. Oh, yes, she knew.

It was locked.

Argh! Damn you, MacLeod!

Amelia beat the door with her fist once, before sliding to the floor where she leaned back against the sealed barrier...her personal prison gate.

She knocked her head against the door in frustration.

"That beastly, surly man! That errant, ill-bred, lout! How dare he? The next time I see that man...ooooh..."

"Mrs. Chase? Are you all right?" came a muffled voice through the door.

Amelia practically tripped over her skirts as she jumped to her feet, banging her head on the door for real in the process.

She spoke into the key hole. "Y-yes? Is someone there?"

She turned her ear to the door. "Yes, ma'am," came the reply. Amelia blew out a breath of relief a moment before delicious revenge began to take shape in her mind.

MacLeod was in for it now.

But first she had to get out.

She spoke through the keyhole once more. "My good man, I'm afraid I am locked in this room without a key. Would you be so kind as to speak to the proprietor so I might be freed? It is a matter of some urgency."

She picked at and pulled off strips of peeling paint from the door while she waited for her potential savior to consider her request.

Mere seconds, felt like an hour.

"Alas, my lady. I fear I cannot. He said he would return soon enough and that you could...ahem..." the voice trailed off.

Clearly, the man realized he probably shouldn't finish that sentence.

Blast MacLeod, that loggerheaded, plume-plucked, scut! How dare he?!

Amelia beat the door with her fist, then stood back and crossed her arms as she considered her situation.

Her guard sounded young. Well of course, he was. What grown man would sit on the dirty floor of a drafty old inn, likely all night long, to guard a lady's room? Either someone with little smarts to recommend him...or someone desperate enough to need the coin.

Hmmm...

Amelia suspected the latter, and that gave *her* the advantage.

"I'll double...no triple...whatever he paid you if you will set me free."

No answer.

Amelia applied the sweetest, gentlest voice she could employ. "Come on, my good man. We both know MacLeod's bark is worse than his bite. He doesn't *really* want to see me detained, not really."

"He was v-very s-specific and m-most insistent, Mrs. Chase..." The boy cleared his throat, his voice having cracked on the word 'specific'. Aahh, he must be thirteen or thereabouts, she guessed. Even better.

"Well, of course he was, my young friend. But you see, he and I like to play practical jokes on each other. In reality, he has this warm fuzzy side of him he lets few people see..." Amelia could practically hear the boy's expression of disbelief through the door, and she had to choke down a laugh, "He's really a big softy beneath that gruff exterior. Honest to God, 'tis true. I promise. We've been playing jokes like this on each other at every stop since we left London. It was supposed to be my turn for a prank tonight, but I cannot very well return the...the ah...favor if I'm stuck in here, now can I?"

"No, ma'am."

Amelia smiled. She had him now.

FIFTEEN MINUTES LATER, AMELIA STEPPED INSIDE THE INN'S STABLES with a mind to arrange for her carriage to be readied for departure. Her hindered exodus from her room meant she'd missed Dansbury by a matter of moments...something she was more than willing to lay at MacLeod's feet the next time she saw him.

And there would be a next time, of that she had no doubt, for it seemed they both had similar objectives: Dansbury.

Setting aside thoughts of retribution, for now, Amelia looked around for someone in authority to assist her. The stables were dark, but well-ordered and filled with the smell of horses, hay, and oiled leather.

A boy she recognized from when she'd arrived the day before walked up the center aisle, struggling under the weight of a large saddle. Red hair poked up from an unfortunate cowlick on the back of his head. She knew from yesterday that his face was dotted with freckles and his demeanor was as cheerful as sunshine.

Amelia smiled in greeting. "Ah, Timmy, how are you?"

Timmy looked at her oddly.

"Timmy?" she queried.

He stepped closer, then gasped and dropped the saddle. "Oh! Milady. How can I help you?" He pulled off his hat and tugged at his forelock as an afterthought, as if unsure how to greet her.

Then he jerked and glanced down at the saddle on the floor before his booted feet. Amelia and Timmy both stared at the ornate saddle, she in bemusement, he in mute horror.

She distracted him by saying, "I'd like my carriage readied for departure post haste, young man."

Amelia reached into her reticule to retrieve a coin and was surprised when she looked back up to find the boy standing there, saddle still lying on the floor at his feet, squeezing the life out of his cap with his grimy hands. The boy's face held a look of utter dismay.

"Timmy? Is there a problem, son?"

"Well, I-I don't rightly no." He pulled at his forelock once again, obviously nervous. "Yer husband came down an hour ago and took yer carriage to the next posting inn. H-He let your driver go, with a bonus for the... uh...change of plans...said...uh...ye wouldn't be needing your carriage for a few days.... Milady...er, Ma'am."

Husband? She had no husb... Amelia smirked. *Ooooh, MacLeod! You scoundrel!*

Of course, she kept her thoughts well-hidden and graced the young man with a benevolent smile. "Oh, that's quite all right, Timmy. It must have slipped his mind that I needed to use the carriage one more time this morning. Let me ask you? Is my *husband's* horse still here?"

"Of course, milady!" He smiled wide and his green eyes sparkled with delight, a sure sign of his returned good nature.

Amelia couldn't prevent the wicked smile that crossed her lips. "Perfect! Please saddle his horse; I need to borrow it for a quick errand this morning...it's a surprise for my wonderful, thoughtful, darling husband...and I have several coins here with your name on them should you make it quick," she added in a sing-song voice.

Timmy pulled at his forelock a third time, and practically performed a jig in his boots. "Yes, milady! Of course, ma'am!"

"Good man. Thank you."

So, MacLeod thought he could get the best of her, did he?

Ha! We'll just see about that...

AMELIA STEPPED OUT OF THE DIM STABLES, INTO THE REAR courtyard of The Quiet Witch Inn, holding her hand up to her forehead to shade her eyes from the brilliant morning sun. It was a fine day to set off by horseback. She had the inexplicable urge to dance her own jig for she was nigh giddy with anticipation for the adventure that awaited her.

In all honesty, she was far more interested in daydreaming about MacLeod's reaction when he discovered her and his horse gone. She imagined steam blowing out of his ears and out the top of his head.

The imagery would feed her revenge-minded soul with life-sustaining amusement...for a little while, at least.

Until their next meeting, the thought of which added an extra spring in her step.

The stable yard was bustling with activity this morning as regulars stumbled home after a night spent drinking and subsequently sleeping it off in the taproom. Proper guests saddled their horses or loaded their wagons as they made themselves ready to depart. This inn was quite aways off the usual path out of London, hence no fancy carriages or coaches were present nor expected, not even the mail coach.

Amelia stepped through and around all the hubbub and made her way inside the inn, careful not to step in any steaming piles of excre-ment *gifts* left by the many horses being led about along her way. She also kept her mouth closed and forced herself not to stop to talk to the more interesting guests milling about in the yard as was her habit.

She needed to get out on the road posthaste if she wanted to make significant progress before MacLeod returned and learned what she'd done.

Oh, she wanted nothing more than to rub her hands together in unsympathetic glee. What she wouldn't give to be there when he discovered how she so perfectly foiled his plans.

Amelia stepped inside The Quiet Witch and paused, waiting while her eyes adjusted to the dim interior. She squinted and found the bar relatively empty in contrast to the hurried activity outside, and in particular contrast to the rowdy crowd here the night before. Dust still coated every surface and cobwebs, every corner. She rather suspected that dust and those exact cobwebs had seen the last turn of the century.

Amelia wove her way between empty round tables, their surfaces pitted and scraped from years of abuse, and headed toward the main desk at the back of the room. A hefty mustachioed man was standing behind the counter, his beefy hands on the bar.

"Checking out?" asked the innkeeper, his large wet lips nearly spraying her with saliva.

She shuddered. "Yes, I am, but I would like to pay for the room to be held another night, if you please. My husband shall be returning in a few hours to collect my luggage, for I cannot take it with me."

"And you are Mrs. Chase?"

"Yes, yes, I am." She set her reticule on the bar before her, clasping it with both hands as she spoke.

"An' you say Mr. Chase will be along by noon?" Ha! She could just imagine MacLeod's response to being called Mr. Chase.

But she corrected the innkeeper all the same. "Weeelll, actually he goes by Mr. MacLeod. It's a long story, you see..."

"Ma'am I don' care fer yer reasons. I don' ask questions, so long as I'm paid what I'm owed," he interrupted.

How rude...

"Fine, then."

"Right. One night plus one half day...that will be...ten crowns."

"Ten crowns! Are you crazy? You, sirrah, are taking advantage of my situation."

The man smiled, rotten teeth peeking out beneath his full mustache. "Ten crowns, or I put your luggage out on the side of the road by nine o'clock."

Amelia scowled at him, then looked down as she fumbled around in her reticule for the requisite amount. Honestly, the man had some nerve taking advantage. It was a wonder he remained in business with practices such as his; he was slovenly, gone to fat, lazy, and a complete crook...not to mention the state of disrepair present in every inch of this bar and the rooms above.

Were she not in a hurry, she would stay behind and give the man a piece of her mind until he capitulated and suggested a more reasonable amount...and with an apology to boot. Not to mention she was going to have to find a way to get more money...and soon...at this rate.

But, alas, time was not on her side at the moment. She needed to be on the road posthaste.

Thus, Amelia begrudgingly forked over the coins and the room key she'd retrieved from her 'guard' this morning. "Thank you," she said, with more than a little bit of sarcasm coloring her tone. "No, never mind. I don't thank you for relieving me of so much."

Still, she was grateful to be leaving this place behind, even though she wasn't entirely sure where she was headed.

"Ah, ma'am, one minute...I have a message here for ye." *Now, he finds his manners, of course.*

"For me?"

"You did say your name was Mrs. Chase?"

"Yes. I did."

"Then yes, I do."

He handed over the note, leaving a smudged print on the outside of the paper with his dirty thumb.

Ugh.

"Thank you." Manners were as natural as breathing.

But the man didn't respond, he'd already disappeared between two swinging doors, presumably toward the kitchens.

Amelia broke the seal with haste, tearing the parchment a bit in the process...curiosity getting the best of her patience.

Dansbury is headed to the Sorceress and Lusty Hound Inn. I'm confident you will find your way there.

— K

Excellent!

Sure, she wasn't entirely certain who the note was from, but it mattered not. She had had no real idea of where she needed to go next, so a questionable direction was better than no direction at all and that was all that mattered.

Amelia raised her fist to the air. *Take that, Alaistair MacLeod!* She reached over to the bell on the bar and rang for the proprietor with an overzealous amount of relish.

He reappeared through the swinging doors, clearly unamused. "What now?"

Amelia ignored the surly tone of his voice. "How do I get to the Sorceress and Lusty Hound Inn?"

The man stood there and crossed his arms.

Amelia waited with excited anticipation for a minute, then rolled her eyes. "Oh, all right..." and pulled out another coin.

He took it without even looking at it and answered, "Follow the road north. After about five miles, turn east on the B road. You'll find it eventually."

Amelia was unimpressed. "Sir, if you haven't noticed, there is rarely any sun shining through the constant cover of clouds in this godforsaken country, and I have no compass. So tell me, which way is north?" She didn't really despise England but some of her citizens were really beginning to piss her off.

"Where were you before you showed up here?"

"London, but..."

"Don't go back to London." He answered, then stormed off.

Amelia called after him, "You could have just said turn right!"

Ridiculous man.

Now that she knew where to go, Amelia went off in search of her quill and parchment, all but crowing with glee over the provoking note she would leave for her dear, thoughtful *husband*.

Chapter Five

M acLeod sauntered into the dimly lit stables of the Quiet Witch Inn sufficiently pleased with himself. He'd taken care of the Inconvenience named Mrs. Chase, at least for now. Aye, Mrs. Chase was a complication, whose actions, whether innocent or not, put several lives in danger.

Including her own.

But more to the point, who was Mrs. Chase? He'd worried that question in his mind for hours. Was she involved with the Secret Society for the Purification of England, the men behind the attempts on Dansbury's life? He doubted it. Could she be Dansbury's sister? It was possible...hell, many a man had their secrets, particularly family secrets; he and Dansbury wouldn't be the only ones...

Aye, she could be entirely innocent or remarkably calculating. Regardless, given her actions, she was certainly up to no good, but how up to no good was she? His gut told him to keep a wary eye on her. Her actions screamed her guilt. Sure, Dansbury could take care of himself, but Dansbury had enough on his hands dealing with Lady Beatryce.

That left Mrs. Amelia Chase to him. He steadfastly ignored the lift in his chest at the thought of their continued acquaintance.

So his methods weren't exactly above board, but he did what he could to keep everyone safe, and even ignorant if necessary, as was required of his job as an agent for the Crown. People were the reason he shunned society. They commanded you to cater to their demands. Forced you to question the logic of sound decisions.

From his experience, that way lay danger; emotions overriding common sense got you or your loved ones killed...or permanently disabled.

He unconsciously rubbed at the sudden ache in his chest.

MacLeod walked back to where he had stabled his horse, Stonewall. The stall was empty and his saddle gone.

What the bloody hell?

MacLeod marched back to the tack room and found the young stable hand, Timmy, sitting on the floor against the wall. The lad smiled down at his hands, both overflowing with coins.

MacLeod had a bad feeling about this.

"Timmy, lad. Step to."

The boy jumped to his feet, his hands clenching his coins in tight fists. Several shillings stuck out between the dirty, protruding knuckles on his skinny little fingers. Timmy looked at him in distress for a minute, then relaxed when recognition dawned.

"Oi, MacLeod."

MacLeod had a *verra* bad feeling about this. "Timmy, where's ma horse?"

"Oi, yer wife borrowed him for an errand or some such..."

Ma wife? Yes, a verra, verra bad feeling...

"She left goin' on about fifteen minutes ago. But..." The boy reached over to a nearby table and picked up a folded piece of paper. "...she did leave you this message."

He snatched the proffered note and ground out a gruff, "Thank you."

MacLeod turned his back on the boy and tore open the message. His body all but thrummed with anticipation when what he should be feeling was palpable anger. *People.*

Alaistair...dearest,

Thank you, dear husband, for taking the time to see to the return of my carriage and for the use of your fine horse. While you are being so thoughtful and helpful, would you kindly see to the forwarding of my luggage? I did not wish to place such an undue burden upon your fine steed; thus, I left the luggage behind in my rooms.

I've included my new direction below.

I look forward to seeing you at the Sorceress and Lusty Hound Inn. Until then, safe travels, my love.

I Remain...

Affectionately Yours, etc.,

— AMELIA

And then:

P.S. Right now, I am taking particular pleasure in imaging you scratching that scruffy chin of yours while you attempt to discern exactly how I knew where Dansbury would be headed next.

MacLeod dropped his hand from his chin, having been in the process of scratching it as he read her note. He would never, ever admit to almost...*almost*...smiling; she was a cheeky, determined thing.

But how *did* she know where Dansbury was headed next? His mind checked off several possibilities, all of them rendering her guilty in any sensible person's eyes.

Damn, he was in trouble. Already his mind shied away from believing her truly a threat.

MacLeod refolded the note and put it in his inside jacket pocket, proving to himself that he would not let a pretty smile cloud his judgement. It was evidence should she turn out to be guilty. That was all. He certainly wasn't holding on to the note like some lovesick swain.

Och, the more he tangled with her, the more questions he had.

MacLeod exited the stables, more anxious than ever to be away, though he'd never own up to the sense of expectancy that settled over his normally well-ordered mind.

But first he had to see a man about a horse...and then one stubborn, Independent American Woman had better be ready.

Chapter Six

The Next Morning at Ridiculous O' Clock: The Sorceress and Lusty Hound Inn

Amelia dragged her bone-weary body up the rickety stairs of The Sorceress and Lusty Hound Inn. It had taken the entire day and most of the evening to travel here...all of it on horseback. She was tired, grumpy, and utterly and stupendously filthy. Even pigs would turn their noses—er, snouts—up at her.

Amelia chuckled at the imagery.

Of course, as soon as she had arrived, she'd paid the innkeeper an exorbitant sum to have a hot bath prepared for her in her room while she waited in the taproom downstairs; she was NOT going to carry the mud and dust from her travels into bed with her no matter how tired and sore she was.

Yes, *tenacious* could be another candidate for her middle name.

Now that her room, and more importantly, her bath, was ready, she headed upstairs, barely able to wait a moment more to submerge herself in warm, clean water.

Mere minutes later, Amelia closed her eyes as she soaked. The warm liquid soothed her aching muscles. Her mind drifted away with the steam, content and at peace for the first time in a very, very long time.

But of course, all too soon her faithless mind wandered unerringly toward one big, strapping highlander: Alaistair MacLeod.

Amelia smiled as she imagined his reaction to her note. Would he be furious? Would he finally laugh...perhaps, smile...at her audacity? He'd certainly scratch at his chin, a habit of his she'd picked up on the night before as she watched him watch her in the stuffy taproom of The Quiet Witch Inn. Oddly enough, she wondered about his laugh... would it be hearty and drawn out? Clipped and understated? He'd probably have a deep, rumbling laugh that would reverberate across her skin like the rumble of a large, beating drum, leaving her arms and legs tingling with feeling.

Without conscious thought, she imagined the two of them meeting in better, happier times. It was a delightful thought, full of awareness and oddly enough, laughter, which always had the effect of leaving her feeling comfortable and content. Being an orphan, she imagined her mother had laughed often when she was a babe, causing her to be attuned to the action in others.

Refusing to traverse *that* line of thinking, Amelia opened her eyes and glanced around her room, or what she could see of it, from her corner behind the large, moveable dressing screen. It was still dim, almost dark, the sun just beginning to make its presence known to the inhabitants in this part of the world. The fire danced in its grate, having been started by one of the inn's maids as part of preparing her room.

Amelia watched as the flames cast interesting, writhing shadows on the walls and ceiling. She couldn't resist holding up one arm to catch the light and add her own shadowy puppet to the mix but her intended dog came out looking like a squealing duck, and she gave up trying, content to watch the fabulous light display.

Suddenly, she noticed one rather large silhouette, which appeared to climb over the screen and darken the nearby wall, probably a shadow created by the tall bureau she recalled stood sentinel next to the bed. It reminded her of a fairly broad man...

A broad, angry man...

One particular man, in fact...

One over-sized, muscular, particular, broad...

"MacLeod!" Amelia sat bolt upright and shouted his name.

Right away, she winced and reached around to rub her backside, her still sore buttocks making their presence painfully felt with her sudden jolt. She'd been in the saddle for so long, she was sure her bottom was one giant bruised blister, a complaint she was all too happy to lay at the booted feet of one over-sized highlander, which was clearly why her thoughts kept returning to him.

Amelia laid back and closed her eyes once more, encouraging her mind to relax. She'd have plenty of time to think about...and face...her Highlander...later.

She breathed in and out, forcing herself to take a slow, deep breath.

A sudden knock at the door almost made her jump out of the water in one giant leap, proving that she was not very successful at relaxing. Already, her heart galloped in its place.

Could it be MacLeod?

It was certainly possible.

Amelia was practically squirming as she called out, "W-who is it?"

A muffled voice called back, "Emily, the maid, miss. I've brung ye towels..."

Amelia swallowed the obvious shift of disappointment that somersaulted in her chest and called out, "Oh, of course, come in."

The maid opened the door. A few moments later, she stepped around the bathing screen, a couple of towels folded over her crossed arms. "I'll set these on the chair, shall I, miss?"

"That'll be fine, thank you."

A thump against the wall from the neighboring room made them both jump, the maid with her hand to her chest and Amelia setting her bathwater to lapping against the side of the tub once again. It seemed she wasn't the only person on edge this evening.

Both women smiled in relief and nearly laughed at their obvious skittishness. The maid stepped back to the edge of the screen. "D-do you require anything else, miss?"

Amelia started to answer but stopped when she heard the door click, the sound like the crack of a gun at this early morning hour to a mind already jumpy. A heavy tread marched a slow and steady beat across the floor. The maid peeked back around the screen. Her face lost all its color as she reached for her throat. "S-sir. You cannot be..."

"Get oot!" growled the disembodied, gruff brogue.

The maid squeaked and bolted, presumably for the door. It slammed in her wake. Amelia heard it but couldn't see it happen from her corner of the room, concealed behind the screen.

After the maid's loud departure, the ensuing silence was deafening. She heard nothing, now...no one rifling through her things, no one walking across the floor. Only the crack and pop of the fire in the nearby grate. Her heart beat faster with every second that passed as she waited for MacLeod to say something, *anything*. Or at the very least, to appear around the edge of her screen. She stared ahead in anticipation, her body flushed with emotion, her heart galloping.

Amelia willed her hands to stop shaking, while her mind flittered from thought to thought as she considered how best to respond to his arrival. Should she pretend to be surprised? Elated? Angry? Expecting?

Seconds felt like hours.

Amelia held herself as still as possible. Waiting. Anticipating. Thinking.

Her bathwater rippled in time with his heavy tread as he finally approached.

One step. Another. And another. Then, silence...

She was going to die. Honestly. Her heart couldn't take this.

"Who the hell are ye, really, lass?" came a tight brogue from over her shoulder.

Amelia shivered and, somehow, managed to not leap out of her bath. "Oh, MacLeod!" Instead, she took a deep breath as she sank further into the tub, attempting to appear relaxed, as if she were expecting his arrival. She took a swift glance down, thankful to see that her most intimate parts were hidden from view. For the most part, at least. Her breasts hugged the surface of the water despite her best efforts to submerge them.

Amelia stared at the far wall ahead of her, somewhat reluctant to face the man who'd so successfully snuck up *behind* her despite her best attempt to appear as if she'd been confidently awaiting his arrival.

She swallowed, silently clearing her throat. "It's about time you got here." She chastised with a nonchalance she certainly didn't feel. She licked her dry lips. "What took you so long?"

She heard the floor creak. Once. Twice. Softly, he said, "Och lass... ye ken...precisely..." he inhaled a long, drawn-out breath "...why...I'm late..."

He released his breath. She felt the warmth of it flit across her neck.

Oh God, he was so close. She shut her eyes and imagined him leaning over her shoulder, staring down at her; her gaze locked on her breasts. Could he see them in the flickering light of the fire? Could he make out her other womanly parts through the clouded, soapy water? These thoughts tortured her, warmed her. Made her want to reach behind her and grab him, pulling him into the tub with her, her lips locked with his.

Damn it, this was not acceptable! And where had this shocking, sensual, boldness come from?

She sensed movement to her left and opened her eyes as MacLeod stalked by, his kilt swishing and teasing about the top of his knees, confidence and strength oozing from his every pore. Her bath water rippled in time with each of his booted steps, lapping at her bobbing breasts, which peaked with awareness.

She had quite the interesting view from her *disadvantaged* position in the tub.

She relaxed, somewhat, as he continued past her and toward the chair which was placed in the corner facing her tub.

Still, she involuntarily threw her hand to her chest as she followed his movements...six and a half feet of kilted anger in the form of one deliciously broad, ginger highlander was quite something to behold. Her breath caught the tiniest bit at the sight.

He positioned himself at the end of her tub and took one heated look over her entire form. An interesting line to his kilt caused her to recognize that he was not as unaffected by her nakedness as he might like her to believe. He leaned forward and gripped both sides of her tub, an unmistakable heat burned in his gaze.

He leaned forward thus for a moment or an hour? Then, he stood and turned abruptly, tossing the towels on the chair to the floor before taking a seat. His large frame overwhelmed the small alcove created by the bathing screen. He laid out his arms, deceptively casual and open, resting them on the arms of the chair. His face looked strange, almost menacing and was a study in contrasts, deep shadows and highlighted planes danced and intertwined across his half-lit face, brought to life by the flames of the nearby fire.

Yes, he tried hard to appear relaxed and confident, but she knew better. That man was no more relaxed than a winter hare looking straight into the eyes of a large cat. She reluctantly acknowledged that she liked it. *Really* liked it.

He stretched out his legs before crossing them at his ankles, teasing her with a glimpse of strong, hairy thighs in the process.

She forced herself not to stare down *there*. "Is this a habit of yours? Breaking into people's rooms unannounced?" she taunted, knowing that nothing she said would make him leave and wanting to come across as confident in the face of her indignity.

He uncrossed his legs again and leaned forward, his kilt spread suggestively across his knees like an open invitation. She had to stifle the urge to tilt her head and *look*.

"Answer the question. Who are ye?" he growled, a husky note in his tone which was both intriguing and disturbing, but had her pulse taking up a faster rhythm all the same.

Amelia splashed at some of the soapy bubbles in her water, striving for an appearance of insouciance she definitely didn't feel. "Ah. I see you are a sore loser, Mr. MacLeod. No worries, darling, better men than you have tried to best me and failed."

Not really...only truly evil men.

She attempted to gather the fading bubbles of her bath, determined to keep her charms hidden from his fiery eyes, even though a large part of her wished to feel his large hands...and his wide mouth... caressing those very same parts...

She looked up and caught the direction of his gaze. He followed her movements with suggestive interest.

As he zeroed in on her bobbing breasts, her nipples tightened further and she broke out in a sweat; her body, already frightfully aware of his, flushed with lust.

MacLeod sat back again and clenched the arms of the chair, his knuckles white with tension. A pronounced twitch appeared in the side of his jaw as he clenched his teeth. His gaze was hot, palpable. It left her feeling edgy. She clenched her thighs together as an echoing surge of heat and desire pooled at the center of her womanly core. Unquestionable longing raced through her veins.

She refused to allow him to see it. She would not allow it to dictate her behavior.

Amelia searched for her bathing cloth. It was hiding *somewhere* in the sudsy water. Once she found it, she began to wash as she tried desperately to hide her shaking hands. There was no point to her sitting there; she'd waited up for this bath for a reason, and she was determined to see to it, audience or no.

Who was she kidding? It proved a safe and useful distraction from her overheated desire.

"What are you doing?" he bit out, his tone drawn with an edge that wasn't present before.

"Bathing, of course." she said, smiling as she did, completely aware she'd shocked him to the tips of his booted feet. She risked a quick glance and noticed he'd sat forward again, this time dancing on the very edge of his seat, his knuckles still white with tension.

Amelia lifted one arm out of the water and ran her cloth down the length, taking her time to clean every inch of her skin. She was fully aware she was putting on a private show for her Highlander, but continued all the same.

If she kept him distracted and on edge, he couldn't probe with uncomfortable questions. Right? And he was a thorough gentleman. He wouldn't do anything she didn't...want...surely?

Was there *anything* she didn't want?

She dunked the rag between her legs, causing further ripples in the soapy water. She felt her nipples tighten once more as the water lapped at her breasts. It was an evocative dichotomy: the warm water lulling her nipples to relax, followed by opposing forces...lapping water...his heated gaze...both provoking them to tighten once more.

MacLeod cleared his throat, yet his tone was gravelly and strained anyway, but softer, almost shaking with an emotion that sounded an awful lot like desire, but was most likely frustration. Or maybe both. "Are you no' going to answer me, lass?"

Amelia reached out of the water and pulled a stool closer to the edge of her tub. Upon it rested a small mirror. She began to finger comb her hair, checking to see that it wasn't plastered to her forehead unattractively.

It was. But no mind.

"Do you honestly expect me to?" she countered while continuing with her exhibition.

Unsatisfied with the results, Amelia leaned her head back to dunk it once more, closing her eyes as she did so. She sat back up and raised both arms, pushing back the excess water from her hair.

She opened her eyes, startled, when a rough moan emanated from the corner. She jerked her head up and locked eyes with MacLeod. His entire body was wound up as tight as a coil and his eyes glowed with fiery awareness, piercing her through the dim room and diving straight into her soul. She felt his hunger as keenly as if they were connected by a living thread.

Now it was she who was rendered mute.

She froze, simply unable to continue her ministrations with him watching her so intently. He unsettled her; there was nothing else to call it, though perhaps even that description was an understatement.

For the longest time, she could not look away from him; neither of them had that ability as desire, nearly tangible in its potency, arced between them.

They no longer felt the passage of time. Hours could have passed or mere minutes. Nor did they recall the reason for their presence in this room. The outside world simply ceased to exist.

"Mary, we need towels for room twenty-eight!" shouted a maid from out in the hall.

It was enough to snap them out of whatever spell had been cast upon them. Amelia broke eye contact and threw the rag into the water, dunking it a few times before pulling it up to squeeze out the excess. It took her three tries to rehang the cotton from a bar on the stool; her hands were shaking like a leaf in a cold autumn breeze. She nearly threw the rag to the floor in frustration, resenting the fact he'd unsettled her so thoroughly.

"Amelia..."

Her gaze flew to his. He gave her a warning glare, clearly thinking he was in control once more.

Ha! She'd see about that. Now the tension had been broken, she became all too aware of the dangerous line she walked. She could not allow him to continue his earlier line of questioning. She needed a better distraction.

One guaranteed to make him forget...everything. Amelia pulled upon her womanly strength; this was no time to be bashful.

After all, she was Amelia Chase: Seductress and Slayer of Men.

And of course, he was a man and susceptible to her charms. Yes, she knew she was pleasing and attractive to men. She knew it as sure as all capable women knew such things, and that gave her the advantage. So without warning, she grabbed ahold of the edges of the tub...

...and stood, water sluicing down her naked body revealing everything to his ravenous regard.

She was confident in her own body if nothing else. His eyes devoured her with one sweeping glance, supporting the conviction of her self-assurance. Satisfied she'd incapacitated him for the moment and, more importantly, determined not to spill her secrets to this man, no matter how connected to him she felt, Amelia stepped out of the tub with single-minded purpose.

Unfortunately, she'd only taken a few steps before she slipped on a puddle of pooled water...

...and straight into the arms of Alaistair MacLeod.

Chapter Seven

MacLeod was surely dead.

And in heaven.

He scooped Amelia Chase into his arms in one reflexive move, pulling her wet, naked body tight against him; his arms wrapped fully around her back. *Oh God*, he looked up and beseeched the ceiling a moment before he closed his eyes and tucked his head into her neck, savoring the feel of her body molded to his and the fresh, womanly smell of her clean scent. He could feel her plump breasts where they soaked his shirt and pressed against his chest. Hell, he'd forgone his waistcoat and jacket, wearing only a shirt for this... meeting...and with the dampness from her body, he could feel her pebbled nipples as they teased and taunted him, begging him to dine. He wanted nothing more than to lift her up and suckle both breasts until she cried out his name.

He lifted his head. He could do it...right now...just a taste. There was nothing in the way, for she was fully naked in his arms. And as aroused as he. He could see it in her wide, dilated eyes and hear it in her labored breathing. Could feel it in her racing pulse.

God knew he was going to hell for this.

And prepared to enjoy every minute of the trip.

And yet, he knew tasting those delectable nipples, the pink centers pulled taught and pointed, were not going to be enough. He could feel all of her, her heat and the water from her bath seeping through his clothes. He wanted more. He wanted to lift her higher and wrap her legs around his waist, burying himself to the hilt in one swift thrust as she clung to him, arching her back as she bowed with pleasure.

He wanted it all. Right now. Hard. Against the wall. On the floor. In the tub.

Hell, he would happily bend her over the large trunk she owned and take her from behind.

God, he'd slide right in and wouldn't it feel divine?

He'd never been so achingly hard in all his miserable life. What power did this woman wield?

He looked at her, his gaze meeting hers in the dim light. And like the snap of a twig underfoot, he broke.

He pulled her closer, his lips diving for hers and in search of a kiss that had been in the cards since the moment she'd walked in to the taproom of The Quiet Witch Inn. He tasted and devoured her; her mouth as sweet and as hot as he'd imagined a thousand times since that fateful night.

Last night.

God, he was turned inside out. Since when had he lost such complete control of his own desires? It made him forget everything... his name...his job...his...

He was halfway to the bed, clenching her ass and nibbling at her lips, when it all came rushing back to him.

The mission. Dansbury.

"Aw, hell," he ground out a whispered curse.

She might verra well be Dansbury's sister.

It was like the proverbial bucket of cold water had been dumped on his head.

Shite. She might. Be. Dansbury's. Sister.

MacLeod set Amelia at arm's length and held her there while he caught his breath, which was sawing in and out of him as if he'd run the Newmarket Town Plate several times over on his own two feet. She smiled at him, utterly aware of the effect she was having. Hell, his cock was presenting itself front and center for her inspection leaving no doubt whatsoever as to the effect she was having.

Once he felt he was in control once more, he began searching for a towel. Anything to cover her.

Dammit.

He'd momentarily lost his head, lost sight of his honor...hell, he'd all but lost sight of his mission and the note he found shoved beneath his door this morning. The one practically burning a hole in his sporran that read:

MacLeod,
  Don't trust Kelly.

— SPYDER

Spyder—their most heavily used and least understood agent. His mind swam with the implications. Was Kelly a traitor? How in the hell did Spyder know where to find the man? His knowing Kelly's whereabouts in and of itself lent credence to the missive's warning.

MacLeod eventually spotted a towel. He reluctantly left her to retrieve it and looked away as he handed her the length of cloth. It was self-preservation, plain and simple.

The situation was serious and the woman before him was becoming more than a puzzle to solve or an inconvenience to manage, for she clouded his judgement. He could almost accuse her of being in cahoots with the villains. Almost. Yet he was reluctant to do so.

Ha, his mind shied away from convicting her with surprising vehemence.

Though perhaps in truth, he already had but didn't want to acknowledge it, which made this odd, physical attraction to her unacceptable, dangerous, and damned exasperating.

She could be a villain or she could be Dansbury's long lost sister; either way this attraction was a problem. It was as inappropriate as it was galling.

MacLeod turned back and glared down at Mrs. Chase, and she, rather than look worried—*as she ought*—glared at him in return, but at least a towel now covered her nakedness.

He crowded her, walking her backwards until her legs brushed up against the bed, an impenetrable wall of anger the only thing separating them from another inadvisable intimate embrace.

He refused to consider that his anger was over his own behavior, more than hers.

When he spoke, it was only a fraction above a whisper, though there was an unmistakable note of anger in his tone that left no doubt as to his level of irritation. "How did you know where Dansbury was headed?"

Many a man would be ready to piss their breeches at the sound of his tone.

But not Amelia Chase.

She plopped onto the bed, her towel gripped tight to her chest with one clenched fist. Yet her voice was steady as she replied, "I received a note."

"From whom?"

"There wasn't a name." She enunciated each word, slowly and clearly, a sure sign that she was cross herself.

No name. Really? "So how did you know the note was legitimate?"

She lifted her chin a wee bit higher and straightened her spine. "I didn't."

MacLeod was incredulous. He stood back and looked her over. "Let me get this straight...you followed the directions left in a note...from someone you did no' know...and rode my horse to a place you'd never been nor heard of before...on a...what? A whim? Was it a dare?"

She crossed her arms, but gave him a coy look he would have to decipher later. "Well, when you put it that way..."

He clenched his fists and tried to calm his mind lest he find himself tempted to throttle her. "What? What way, Mrs. Chase?"

She walked her fingers along a pattern in the bedding, "Well, it does seem a tiny bit ridiculous when you state it as such." She looked up to him once more. "But honestly MacLeod, I had nothing else to go on, so I figured, what did I have to lose?"

Oh, Mrs. Chase, far more than you could possible know.

MacLeod searched her eyes for the truth. It pained him, this...not knowing. "May I see this note?"

She hesitated a moment, then shrugged. "No."

"No?" He had absolutely no qualms about searching her things for it, but it'd be easier if she simply complied of her own accord.

"I-I no longer have it."

He crossed her arms lest he be tempted to tip her over his knee; she could use a good spanking. Or kiss her again. He could scarcely tell the difference anymore, his passion for her felt remarkably like anger. "Och, convenient, that."

She shrugged, but remained silent, maintaining her story.

MacLeod considered everything he knew so far, but ended up no closer to understanding the truth. However, an idea began to take shape. Perhaps he could call her bluff? Aye...he could bring Dansbury to *her.* They could put a full stop to the narrative of this entire situation once and for all and move on.

Mrs. Chase could be in gaol by midday for her crimes. He absent-mindedly rubbed at his chest; the idea of her in gaol did not sit well with him.

She could also be declared Dansbury's sister...and *that* possibility was the only thing that stayed his hand from applying heavier means of interrogation, as he would with any other suspect who worked against his men.

Och, who was he kidding? He truly only wanted to touch her with passion and nothing else. Still.

And she might be precisely who she claimed. Hell, it was that very idea that had stopped him from fucking her senseless not five minutes ago.

His cock, which had settled, twitched the tiniest bit with renewed interest.

He ignored it. The damn thing apparently wasn't very particular at the moment.

"All right, Mrs. Chase. I'm going to give you your chance."

She looked decidedly nervous at that; he hoped she was. Better than seeing straight through the façade of furious indifference which he hoped he portrayed but knew he didn't, not really. She was far too calm.

"How do you mean?" Her hands drew back into the folds of her towel and started tangling with the fabric. He pointedly watched her do this until she realized what was happening and clenched her fists instead.

He looked back up and caught her regard. "Easy..." he paused and settled his breathing; it was hard to hold her gaze for there was an unexpected depth to be found in her dark orbs. "I'm going to go fetch Dansbury now. You can tell him who you are, and we'll see which of your stories holds true, aye?"

Her eyes widened a fraction. "Well, I'm going with you. You're not leaving me alone again." She lifted her chin in defiance, all but daring him to argue against her.

"Oh no. You can wait right here, and I'll bring Dansbury to you. We would no' want all and sundry to witness *this*..."

She crossed her arms. "Fine."

"Fine," he concurred.

Mrs. Chase lifted her chin further, if possible, her nose practically touching the ceiling. "Fine..." she repeated.

Shite. She was far too confident.

MacLeod opened the door, convinced at any moment she would give away her bluff.

"W-wait, MacLeod?"

MacLeod smiled, satisfied. *Here it comes...*

He stopped inside the doorway and leaned against it with one arm raised and gripping the frame above as he looked back at her. "Aye?"

"Tell me something. Why is Dansbury pretending to be Mr. Churchmouse? Don't pretend he isn't who we're talking about; it's beneath you and insults me."

He looked her in the eye as he said, "I canna answer that."

"Can't or won't? And which part?"

He stood away from the door and shrugged. "Both. All of it."

"Well, then. I-I'm not ready."

He raised a brow in query.

"...to tell Dansbury who I am, I mean," she added.

MacLeod stepped back inside the room and slammed the door. Leaning back, he raked a hand through his hair. "Why?"

She swallowed. "I-It's private."

Of course it is, Mrs. Chase. "Private, aye?"

"Aye...I mean, yes."

Unbelievable. "And I'm supposed to just trust ye, now?"

She squared her shoulders and looked him straight in the eye. "It seems we both have to go on a little faith at the moment."

Bloody hell; this woman.

He turned to leave, yanking the door open with enough force to make it creak. As he left, he called back over his shoulder, "We're not through here, Mrs. Chase."

Aye, far from it.

At the Same Time: In a Blackened, Unmarked Carriage - Not Far From The Sorceress and Lusty Hound Inn

Ciarán Kelly climbed into the black, unmarked carriage a few ticks after midnight. Inside a carriage lamp swayed in time with his steps, but the man waiting inside remained hidden in shadows. The only unique part of his person betraying anything to the light were the glint of silver rings which adorned every one of his fingers. An identifying idiosyncrasy to be noted, for sure.

Kelly seated himself across from his...host...and patiently waited for the man to speak. In the meantime, he looked around and surveyed his surroundings. Inside the carriage, luxury reigned supreme. Plush blue velvet shot through with silver thread and expert tufting covered the seats, which were firm yet comfortable enough to suggest they would remain so even after extended hours of traveling.

The shadowed man rapped on the ceiling with his silver-tipped walking stick and the carriage jerked into motion. He was fiddling with the rings on his left hand when he finally spoke. "You've had trouble apprehending Dansbury, I hear."

The man's accent was unmistakable: Spyder was Welsh.

Kelly shrugged in response, betraying no discomfort. "He's a formidable opponent, as I'm sure you are aware."

The man chuckled softly. "Indeed. Too formidable. But even for you?"

Kelly narrowed his eyes. "I wasn't present on that cockup of a job, now was I?"

The man chuckled again. "Of course not. How could I forget?"

Did he find this farce of a situation amusing?

"No. I do not find this amusing at all." The man responded as if he'd read Kelly's mind. He leaned forward, and his dark, scarred visage was revealed by the swaying lantern. He leaned heavily on his walking stick but held Kelly's gaze without hesitation. "But let's turn our attention to more important matters, shall we? I take it you've had the pleasure of meeting Mrs. Chase?"

"I have." Kelly agreed, somewhat hesitant regarding this line of questioning.

The man smiled, though one side of his mouth seemed to sneer as his lip curled awkward, forced so by a scar that pulled tight across his right cheek. "And do you, by chance, know who she is...who she *really* is?"

Kelly ignored the scar and shrugged once again. "I have a hunch."

The man sat back again and resumed fiddling with his rings. "Do you now? Yes...I suppose you do. Your instincts serve you well, Irish."

Kelly acknowledged the compliment with a nod.

"And I suppose you also realize that there is very little Dansbury wouldn't do for his long...lost...sister?"

Chapter Eight

At a More Reasonable Hour in the Morning: The Sorceress and
Lusty Hound Inn

A traitor?

MacLeod returned to the main room of the inn after talking privately with Dansbury in the stables about the possibility of a traitor amongst their team. It was a damn shame, for he respected and trusted these men...or had, especially Kelly. They were among the few people left in his world for whom he would lay down his life. Hell, he could count their number on one fucking hand.

MacLeod caught himself scratching absentmindedly at his chin and clenched his fists in frustration. It was a ridiculous habit he was determined to break.

To his surprise, he had learned that Dansbury and Lady Beatryce, who were still posing as husband and wife while on the run from a mad assassin, had been attacked en route by four men on horseback lending truth to the idea that there was, indeed, a traitor amongst them. Very few men knew Dansbury's route out of London, which was far off the beaten path.

MacLeod had not told Dansbury of his suspicions regarding Amelia Chase; not when he needed to be more certain in his own mind about who, exactly, she was...friend or foe. Dansbury could ill afford another worry on his mind; he had plenty of his own troubles to deal with.

MacLeod swept his eyes across the room, taking measure of the few patrons up and about this early spring morning. Three regulars were at the bar; he was quite sure they were there when he'd retired last night as they wore the same clothes and sat in the same manner: heads in their hands, a mug of ale on the bar between their elbows. Four women sat at a table talking over each other about God knew what. They were there last night as well. At the same table. In the same seats, even, and still talking, though they were at least wearing different clothes.

MacLeod looked over to the only other occupied table in the long and narrow taproom, expecting to see Mrs. Chase and Lady Beatryce where he'd left them an hour ago. In the far corner, Lady Beatryce sat alone with a cup of coffee cradled in her hands.

He scanned the room once more, but there was no sign of her.

Though she was likely only taking care of her personal needs, MacLeod marched over, concern creasing his brow as he noted Lady Beatryce's expression. She seemed to smirk, chastise, and smile all at the same time, making his gut churn with added tension.

He wasted no time with pleasantries, but braced his hands on the back of the chair across from her and demanded, "Where is Mrs. Chase?"

"La, she's gone." Lady Beatryce replied with a wave of her hand. Then, she took a sip of her drink, casual like, as if she had all the time in the world for coffee.

For a moment, it felt as if his heart stopped. He couldn't have heard her right. "Och, what do you mean, gone?"

Lady Beatryce shrugged. "Just that. Gone. Left. Adieu. Adios. Good bye." And she waved at him as if to demonstrate what she meant by *good bye* to a child in the process of learning to speak.

The chair creaked beneath his grip, and his brogue was thicker than ever when he asked, "Where. Did. She. Go?"

Lady Beatryce waved her hand in the air once again, as unconcerned as ever. "La, how should I know?"

He very nearly threw the chair across the room at her flippant response, yet he remained composed—only just. "You did no' ask? She did no' mention it in polite conversation as she said guid bye? She just got up and walked oot without saying a bloody word?"

If she dares to say no...

"My, my—so many words from a man who guards his words so judiciously." Lady Beatryce shrugged. "Mrs. Chase didn't leave in *precisely* that manner, of course not. She received a note from the barkeeper over there," Lady Beatryce nodded toward a middle-aged man at the bar with wide, hairy side burns and a bald pate, drying glasses with a dirty length of cloth. "Then, she very politely excused herself while she read the letter. All the sudden, she popped up out of her chair and said she had to leave." Lady Beatryce touched a finger to her lips and looked thoughtful for a moment. "Come to think of it, she did seem somewhat startled and agitated by what she'd read...and, of course, in a bit of a hurry."

"And you did no' think to press her for more?"

"Why should I? It's none of my business. Besides, she was in a hurry, as I just now pointed out. Who was I to slow her down?"

Damned difficult woman...no, difficult women; Mrs. Chase was definitely one of their number.

"Has that ever stopped you before?"

Lady Beatryce didn't answer; she simply smiled into her cup. They both knew the answer to that question.

"What did you two talk about prior to her receiving the letter? Did she say anything that might give me a clue as to where she was headed?"

"Now, *that*, I'm not going to tell you."

For the first time ever, he had the urge to reach over and throttle a woman until she confessed everything, a concerning feeling that he did not care for, despite there being what some might consider justifiable reasons for it. Fortunately, he was more of a gentleman than all that. But, damn, the impulse was there, manifesting itself in a clenched jaw, whitened knuckles, and now a cracked taproom chair.

MacLeod patiently clipped out, "How long ago did she leave; can you tell me *that* at least?"

Lady Beatryce rolled her eyes. "Of course, MacLeod. La, believe it or not, I *am* on your side. Let's see...she left about two minutes after you went out to speak to Dansbury. Indeed, the barkeep was on his way over with her message as you walked out the front door."

MacLeod was running for the stairs before Lady Beatryce had even finished speaking.

Shite.

That was over an hour ago. He'd process the rest of Lady Beatryce's baffling statement later; it made no sense to him now. God, how he hated it when women spoke in riddles.

He'd just hit the second tread (he'd skipped the first) when he heard Lady Beatryce call after him, "Good luck catching up with her, MacLeod; she's a wily one," followed by a genuine laugh.

MACLEOD REACHED THE FIRST-FLOOR LANDING AT AN ALL-OUT RUN. He didn't stop for the maid lugging a bucket and a filthy mop behind her as she dragged her feet down the stairs. Nor did he stop for the wiry footman descending with alacrity, his arms laden with a motley collection of valises, bags, and boxes.

And he certainly didn't stop when he reached Mrs. Chase's room, rather he tucked in his shoulder and burst his way straight through the locked door with a loud clash, pulling the hinges straight out of the door frame.

Once through, he stood inside the broken doorway, splinters of wood framing dangling all about him, his breath sawing in and out, and surveyed the room. She wasn't there, which he expected, but still...he felt...uncomfortable, an odd little ache had sprung up in his chest upon the realization that she'd really, truly gone.

He rubbed at his chest and swore up and down.

Hell and damnation, will the woman never stay put where I leave her?

He looked about the room and was surprised to see her luggage still there, stacked neatly against the wall.

Well that is deuced odd...

MacLeod continued his sweep of the room, and then he saw it: a note propped upon a pillow in the middle of the disordered bed...

He wasted no time; he lunged for the missive.

It was addressed to *him*.

MacLeod ripped it open.

Alaistair...dearest,

If you are reading this, you know by now that I received pressing news and had to depart in a bit of a rush. To my everlasting regret, I did not have the opportunity to bestow upon you a suitable...goodbye...yet again. One day, dear 'husband', I shall make it up to you.

As such, it is with profound remorse that I must beseech you to assist me once more: I need you to forward my luggage...again, if you will. I've included my direction below.

The haste with which I had to leave forced me to abandon everything but the essentials. Fortunately, I have you, my strong, capable, adoring 'husband', and I have every faith in your ability and willingness to carry out this task on my behalf.

I shall be at the location indicated two days hence. Until then, I look forward to our reunion with great anticipation.

I remain in your debt and always yours, etc.

— AMELIA

MacLeod couldn't stop his own smile, but he quickly stowed it away and returned to his habitual scowl, which felt far more comfortable upon his face.

P.S. I shall leave you with this taunting tidbit of information: my latest missive was not from the same source as the last one. I'll see you anon.

P.P.S. Stop scratching your chin lest you rub away that scruff I adore so much!

MacLeod shook his head. *She adored his scruff?* He refolded the note, tucked it in his pocket, then turned on his heel and left.

Two days? Aye, he'd be there, waiting.

If he didn't find her first.

Chapter Nine

Outside the Sorceress and Lusty Hound Inn, In a Private Carriage

"Welcome, Mrs. Chase. I must say I am honored to finally meet you in person. I trust you had no difficulty escaping your escort?"

Amelia climbed inside the unmarked carriage and glanced up at the man who'd spoken before taking a seat on the empty bench across from him. She did her best not to seem startled by his shocking appearance, for he was dark and heinously scarred.

The skin of his face and neck was sun darkened, as if he spent a significant amount of time out of doors. And though he appeared to be about ten years her senior, his hair was long and the color of rich mahogany without a hint of gray to be seen. And he was entirely outfitted in black; his breeches, shirt, waistcoat, jacket, and even his cravat were all solid black. Indeed, his entire visage was mysteriously forbidding, yet he was as handsome as sin; she'd never seen a man so visually stunning.

As such, she would have expected the man's eyes to be ebony as well, a match to his shadowy presence, or even a cold, ice blue to match a formidable personality, but no, his eyes were a surprisingly warm, reddish brown. The color of a rich, dark port.

But what really stood out the most was the obvious scarring down the right side of his face. From his hairline to his chin, a myriad of scars crisscrossed his cheek, his brow, his lips. It was as if the right side of his face had been shoved through a large glass window.

And still he was beautiful. Dark as sin, but beautiful nonetheless.

Amelia nodded her head in agreement to his query, but refused to speak. She was a touch too wary to let down her guard in front of this man, though honestly, most would say she hadn't been wary *enough* considering she'd climbed into a carriage with a man she barely knew.

But he certainly knew her and that was the entire reason she had thrown caution to the wind and gone through with it.

Besides, Amelia had met truly evil men before; she knew the type, and this man was not it. He'd helped her when it mattered most, when her life was nigh forfeit. And she was determined to understand why and to do her part to repay his efforts on her behalf.

Amelia looked around, content to survey her surroundings. The carriage was black (*surprise!*) and unmarked on the outside, including the livery, if one could call it that, of the driver and attending footmen, but inside the carriage, opulence abounded. Plush navy velvet covered every conceivable surface with accents of silver and leather. It was sumptuous and extravagant, luxury like she'd never seen before.

The man reached up and knocked on the ceiling with his walking stick, and the carriage jerked forward as they took off. Even the ceiling was midnight blue.

The man sat back in his seat and crossed his legs wide, ankle over knee. He laid his cane across his lap using one hand to keep it in place while he rested his other arm on his lifted knee. He appeared utterly at ease.

Oddly enough, the man had a ring on every single finger, each band cast in silver or white gold. He absentmindedly fiddled with each of the rings on his left hand, one at a time, with his thumb.

"Have you nothing to say, Mrs. Chase? I understand silence isn't your forte."

Amelia shrugged, and watched the man twist his rings. It was all true; she was never at a loss for words. And considering she'd run off from MacLeod, despite her better judgement, *in order to speak* with this man, it was ridiculous for her to keep silent. She was self-aware enough to acknowledge that. Still, she held her tongue as if her life depended on it.

"How about I start by introducing myself? Your new *friends* call me by various names; MacLeod happens to favor Spyder."

Amelia looked up at him, startled. "And what exactly do you do, Spyder? Besides rescue damsels in distress, I mean."

Alas, she couldn't help herself. She was curious. In fact, she was surprised she'd managed to remain mute for as long as she had.

The man called Spyder smiled knowingly. "Let's just say I collect information."

Amelia crossed her arms and nodded her head. "Ah, a blackmailer."

The man half-heartedly shrugged. "Blackmail is such an unpleasant word, though I suppose some would see it that way. Kelly finds it amusing to call me the Puppet Master."

The man smiled distantly, as if he'd recalled a fond and amusing memory.

In her mind, *the Puppet Master* wasn't any better than a blackmailer or Spyder, and she wondered if she'd made a truly grave mistake in coming here after all.

But she owed him.

The man looked back at her and she saw a flash of anger cross his face. "I find it useful not to make assumptions, Mrs. Chase. You do not know me, my past, nor my situation well enough to assess and pass judgement. I would expect you of all people to refrain from doing so."

It was as if he'd read her mind. And he was, in all honesty, correct. Her past was—colorful—to the say the least. What would MacLeod think to know he followed on this heels of a convicted felon?

A spark of fear skated down her spine, but she ignored the sensation as best she could and hoped her voice didn't shake when she spoke.

As for Spyder, she might believe he wasn't evil, but that didn't mean she wasn't nervous when warranted, as any sane person would be. "Well, there's an easy enough solution to that problem. Why don't you enlighten me, and I'll make the decision as to what I think of your character?"

The man smiled. "Ah, but we're not here to talk about me. We're here about you and the man you are looking for, the Marquess of Dansbury."

"Go on." Amelia glanced once more at his fingers as he played with his rings.

"How much have you learned about Dansbury?"

Amelia leaned forward, determined not to be distracted by the damn rings. "Mr....Spyder? Look...Is there something else I might call you? I am not comfortable calling you Spyder, Blackmailer, or the Puppet Master. To be honest, they all sound quite ridiculous to me. It was one thing for me to read it in the missive that saved my life or as a code name for information, but face to face, the entire thing seems ridiculous. And childish."

The man dipped his head. "Certainly, Mrs. Chase. You may call me Lord Sharpe."

Amelia laughed and gave him a look of utter disbelief. "That's not your real name, is it?"

Lord Sharpe simply smiled, which was fine; her question was rhetorical anyway.

"Well, Lord Sharpe...I thought I was here for you to enlighten *me*, not the other way around. Yet you insist upon questioning me, which does not bode well for my end of this bargain, now, does it?"

The man nodded in agreement. "How very astute, Mrs. Chase, and you are quite correct. And I will remedy that anon, but first tell me what happened when you arrived in merry old England."

"So I'm just supposed to trust you, then?"

"You question that now? After traveling all the way here on my word and a bag of coins? You're not in a position to bargain now, are you?"

"Well, I presume there is some reason you sent me here, so I must be of some value to you. Or are you merely an obliging gentleman rescuing a lady in distress?"

"I may be a gentleman, but I am not obliging...and you, my dear, are no lady...but you have a point. Shall we alternate, share information back and forth as it were?"

Amelia agreed with a nod.

"Excellent. Tell me what has happened. You arrived at The Quiet Witch Inn as planned and found Dansbury..." he prompted.

"Oh, I found him all right. Precisely where you said he'd be, but what I didn't expect was that he would be pretending to be someone else. And then there was MacLeod, Kelly, Lady Beatryce..." she trailed off, making it clear it was Lord Sharpe's turn to speak.

"There have been some unforeseen complications."

"Such as?"

Lord Sharpe rubbed the bridge of his nose, the first sign of humanity in his carefully orchestrated façade. "MacLeod and Dansbury are both spies for the Crown. Dansbury and Lady Beatryce are on the run from assassins. MacLeod and Kelly are there for additional protection and support." Lord Sharpe paused and eyed her. "Does this information surprise you?"

Amelia maintained a blank expression, determined not to give away what she was thinking or feeling. Remaining aloof wasn't one of her best skills by any stretch of the imagination, but she gave it her best shot, for she was a damned good actress.

She didn't answer his question, for she would give herself away if she even tried to respond.

The man acknowledged her attempt with another dip of his head and a knowing smile, but carried on. "The leader of their band of merry men is the Duke of Stonebridge. You have yet to meet him, but I'm sure that oversight will be corrected in the near future."

It was ridiculous, she knew, but Amelia was relieved to hear the evidence this man intended to release her, though it would be ludicrous for him to save her very life and then kill her after all. She relaxed a bit more, reassured by that knowledge.

"As for the fourth man of their jolly group, Kelly: he's in a *delicate* situation at the moment. Best to leave him out of this discussion for now."

Amelia wasn't sure how she felt about Lord Sharpe's revelations.

All this talk of spies and assassins, including the cryptic descriptions of the men she'd recently met, was almost amusing in its sheer absurdity.

Almost.

Yet, it explained an awful lot. It seemed many men (and women, she supposed) had their secrets.

Lord Sharpe waited in silence, as if he knew she needed time to process all he'd told her thus far.

"Mrs. Chase, we have about an hour ahead of us, and what I'm about to impart is important. When we reach our destination, I intend to leave you with the contact information for Lady Beatryce, or as she was introduced to you, Mrs. Churchmouse. It is important that you follow my directions carefully if we are to see all of this end in the way we wish it."

Amelia was doubtful. "How can you possibly know how to reach Lady Beatryce? Even *she* wasn't sure when or where she could be reached."

Lord Sharpe chuckled, a quick bark of amusement. "I find it difficult to believe that you haven't realized by now. I have my ways. Now, are you ready to hear about the Society for the Purification of England? I assure you they will have a major role to play in all this before we reach the end of our little adventure."

'A little adventure' was not the term she would use to describe all of *this*.

Amelia wasn't sure whether she was honestly ready, but did it matter? If she weren't in such a desperate situation, she might have run away from this mess as fast as her feet could carry her months ago, but really, she had nowhere else to go. And no funds to get there. Besides, she owed this man an awful lot.

Her very life.

Amelia studied Lord Sharpe carefully. "First, tell me this: I cannot place your accent. It's not English, nor is it like MacLeod's Highland brogue. Where are you from?"

"It matters not."

Amelia crossed her arms. "It does to me."

"My, my. So full of questions, Mrs. Chase. I'm betting MacLeod doesn't know quite what to make of you, does he? How *fun*."

"I'm sure he would disagree with that sentiment, but since you've mentioned him, tell me more about MacLeod. He's been particularly difficult. That man is incredibly suspicious and doesn't give up the bone."

"Ah, MacLeod. A complicated man, to be sure, and full of so much distrust. But I have to say, despite his gruff exterior, he's the most honorable man I know."

"Is that supposed to mean something to me?"

Sharpe smiled in return and dipped his head in acknowledgement. "Let's just say that if things don't work out with Dansbury, or if you find yourself in trouble and Dansbury isn't around, you can rely on Alaistair MacLeod."

Amelia nodded in agreement. "All right then, tell me about Kelly. Can he be trusted? Is he truly a traitor?"

"Time will tell, Mrs. Chase."

Amelia crossed her arms, frustrated. This man was playing games with her and telling her nothing in the process. "Well, you're not really giving me a lot to go on, are you?"

"I've given you a lot. Not many people know of these men's work for the Crown."

She raised one brow as if to say, *is that all you got?*

"Are you ready to hear about the Society?"

She *did* want to know. She obviously needed to know, considering. But first she had one question that was burning in her mind. Simply thinking about asking the question made her utterly nervous all of a sudden. She knew what she wanted the answer to be, but...

Amelia took a deep breath and steadied herself as best she could. "Yes, tell me one thing, first. Am I...am I truly Dansbury's sister?"

"Does it matter?"

Amelia looked out the window and answered, her disappointment evident. "I suppose not."

C.K.

Your information proved accurate, but I'm afraid our mutual acquaintance was unsuccessful in acquiring Dansbury and Lady Beatryce while they were en route to the Lusty Hound.

That outcome was rather unfortunate. However, a certain informant has left his lair and is directly involved in our plans. You know him as Spyder...or, as you personally refer to him, the Puppet Master.

Spyder has our friend, MacLeod, redirected at the moment, and he assures me that MacLeod will not make it to the next rendezvous point with Dansbury.

This is your opportunity to redirect suspicion away from you. Make the most of it.

— X

Chapter Ten

Two Days Later: Ye Olde Howling Monkey Inn

here in the hell was she?

WTwo of the longest days of MacLeod's life had passed in the time since he had dashed off from The Sorceress and Lusty Hound Inn on the hunt for Amelia Chase. He hadn't caught a single glimpse of her since the morning he had stolen into her room during her bath, demanding she explain herself. It was like she'd disappeared from the face of the earth in a matter of moments.

He swallowed the inexplicable feeling of loss that accompanied that thought.

From what he could gather questioning patrons at The Lusty Hound, she'd left in an unmarked carriage no one had ever seen in these parts before.

The very idea of her hastening off with some nameless, faceless man when traitors and evil men were afoot had him tied in knots, a sensation he hadn't felt since...well, in quite a while.

There wasn't a soul in any of the neighboring towns for fifteen miles in any direction who had an inkling of who the carriage belonged to, much less where it had gone. It hadn't even been seen by anyone since it'd left the last inn two days ago. He knew, for he'd checked with the locals in every village in the area.

Every. Single. One.

He was exhausted and sullen and ready to brawl with the first person to look at him wrong.

He needed sleep.

He needed to see Mrs. Chase.

Now, MacLeod paced outside Ye Olde Howling Monkey Inn as he waited for her to arrive. He was in a state of agitation such that he hadn't experienced in a long time. He couldn't stomach doing something as mundane as sitting inside to wait for her to pop back up while sipping on a mug of ale. He needed to *do* something, but he couldn't, and it was driving him daft.

The clip clop of an approaching horse had him spinning on his heel, looking to the road, as he had countless times this morning. It was only a man of the cloth on an aging nag. The man was a local, based on the warm welcomes from the men who greeted him as he dismounted. He was unlikely to carry word of Amelia Chase.

MacLeod raked his hands through his hair and resumed his pacing. He felt like a caged beast, tethered to this location as surely as a tiger bound in a steel enclosure.

Next time, I'll put her under lock and key with a more reliable guard—me.

He actually pointed his thumb at his chest as he thought it.

Bloody hell, he was now talking and gesturing to himself.

MacLeod had circled the perimeter of the inn's main courtyard another half dozen times when a familiar carriage pulled into the yard from the south.

Oh, Christ, no' yet.

It was the Duke of Stonebridge, a man well known to him because he also happened to be his boss.

Shite.

Worse, he didn't have a suitable excuse for missing the last rendezvous point with Dansbury, and it was glaringly out of character for him, something he didn't need hanging over his head in the face of an unknown traitor amidst their group.

Instead, he'd been off hunting *her*.

God, who would scarce believe it of him? This strange sense of urgency had flat out compelled him to search for her, fully undermining his usual common sense. He hadn't understood it, yet even as he'd loathed the urge, he'd still heeded it.

MacLeod met the duke's carriage as it pulled to a stop in front of Ye Olde Howling Monkey. He waved off the footman and opened the carriage door himself.

"Duke."

"MacLeod? What the devil are you doing out here?" Stonebridge asked as he disembarked.

"Pacing." There was no point to lying to this man. MacLeod never lied, and he was man enough to own up to his actions, even if they didn't always paint him in the best light.

"Is there a particular reason?"

"Aye." But he wasn't about to explain that a woman had him tied in knots. Especially this particular woman.

It was a revelation to know that his renowned honesty only went so far.

"Come," the duke beckoned. "Let's talk inside."

Once inside, they were lead directly to a private dining room off the main taproom, the duke's footman having preceded them and arranging everything ahead of time.

The furnishings were delicate and rich, incongruous with his mood of the moment. He wouldn't have to put forth much effort to toss a chair across the room and have it splinter to bits. Not that he planned to do so.

Stonebridge crossed the room to stand before the fireplace, but MacLeod chose instead to position himself by the front facing window, away from any unsuspecting pieces of furniture.

Aye, and to watch for *her*, he admitted it, at least to himself.

The duke didn't waste time getting to the point. "You weren't at the last rendezvous point with Dansbury. Are you going to tell me why?"

"Nae." He couldn't. How does one explain the unexplainable?

How does one explain that despite his utter and perfect dedication to his job, one woman had him acting so completely out of character that he'd missed a scheduled engagement with a friend who was essentially fleeing for his life? Doing so without an acceptable reason danced the line of treason, he knew it.

The duke knew it, too.

Still, he didn't answer. He wouldn't answer. Worse, he continued to look out the window rather than at the man addressing him.

So it'd finally happened. Too many rounds of fisticuffs have finally turned me into an idiot.

It was the only reasonable explanation.

But the duke was also his friend, or as close to one as MacLeod could have, considering. The duke trusted him and wouldn't press him on it, though he had every reason to do so. Hell, the man could even threaten to jail him if he so desired.

But he didn't. "MacLeod, I'm sure I don't have to tell you that your timing is bloody awful. It would be all too easy to question your loyalty."

MacLeod had zero difficulty hearing the note of exasperation in his friend's tone. "Aye, I ken it."

Still, MacLeod didn't turn away from the window to look at the duke while he spoke. The fact the duke didn't demand he do so, coupled with his decision not to question MacLeod's reasoning further, was a mark of significant trust.

It left a bittersweet taste on his tongue and a heavy feeling in the pit of his stomach.

How had he merited such loyalty?

The duke sighed in frustration, then sharpened his tone. "Well, this thing that has you so thoroughly occupied is going to have to wait."

MacLeod stiffened, his gut screaming 'No!' though he wasn't foolish enough to voice this reaction.

"Dansbury has disappeared." MacLeod started to turn around at that, but saw the duke hold up his hands in reassurance out of the corner of his eye. "To my knowledge, he's all right; he's abandoned the original plan due to the possible traitor in our midst."

MacLeod nodded, agreeing with the duke's assessment, and returned to watching the chaotic bustle outside the window. "That's wise."

The duke came over to stand next to him. "I agree, though I don't like it. So I have a new task for you."

The duke paused, and this time, MacLeod looked directly at him. The duke's face was grave as he said, "I need you to find our traitor."

MacLeod's hands clenched where he held on to the window frame. His stomach felt sour for so many reasons: he knew the duke was telling him to abandon his search for Amelia Chase. At the same time, Stonebridge was also admitting he trusted MacLeod. It was significant, even in the face of everything else going on.

Unfortunately, MacLeod knew the biggest reason for this unexpected internal—ache—was because he wouldn't be seeing Amelia Chase again, at least for a while, possibly months...

...which was wholly absurd yet woefully real.

"Alaistair, I *am* aware you are looking for the American, Mrs. Chase, but it is of no matter. She is not significant in the face of this directive. You do realize that? Finding our *traitor*—" Stonebridge cleared his throat. God, even the duke had difficulty saying that word, "—is far more important."

"Aye, I ken." Still, it was disconcerting to know that his gut did not agree with his head.

Regardless, it mattered not; he had no choice. The duke was his superior, and this was a direct order. His gut might not like it, but the duke was right.

At that moment, he could have reported his suspicions regarding Amelia Chase. Hell, he should have, but for some reason, even though it was on the tip of his tongue to do so, he didn't. Doing so felt like a betrayal to *her*.

What a fucking mess.

But this time, MacLeod knew what he had to do. He would do his duty and no longer carry with him some measure of regret for choosing a woman—one he hardly knew and worse, barely tolerated—over his responsibility, his honor.

He absentmindedly rubbed at his chest. Who was he kidding? He thoroughly enjoyed Amelia's Chase's vivacious personality, though he would never admit that out loud. Hell, he barely admitted it to himself.

He was attracted to her on a level that utterly shocked him and he found he had a reluctant but earnest respect for her determination and tenacity.

Still, it was not enough to further destroy his career, his respect, and his friendships over.

Unfortunately, everything else inside him intensely disagreed with that sentiment, as did the depressing feeling that blanketed his mind at the thought of doing what he knew was right.

Stonebridge clapped him on the shoulder, jerking him from tumbling further into his miserable and chaotic thoughts. "Excellent, keep me posted, and we'll be in touch soon. And MacLeod? Bring him to me."

There was no need to ask who *him* was. They both knew, and they both hated it.

AFTER THE DUKE LEFT, MACLEOD RACED UP TO AMELIA'S ROOM TO leave her a note where she'd be sure to see it. It felt suspiciously like goodbye and he had to stifle the urge to falter, to change course and disregard a direct order.

Instead, MacLeod returned to the stables to prepare for his departure.

Half an hour later, he walked around his horse for a fifth time, checking once more that all his gear was strapped down correctly. It was a delaying tactic, he acknowledged it.

But after a few more checks, and still no sign of Amelia Chase, there was nothing for it; it was time to go. MacLeod mounted his horse and gathered the reins in his gloved hands. He was turning to leave, when an unmarked carriage pulled into the courtyard, capturing his undivided attention.

The carriage, large, black, and spotless, pulled to a stop on the opposite side of the great, bustling courtyard. MacLeod held his breath, watching. For a moment, nothing happened. It felt like an eternity passed while he waited for something, *anything*, to happen.

Finally, a coachman climbed down and opened the carriage door.

MacLeod's heart moved up into his throat and hammered out a fast rhythm that sounded like a thousand men marching in his ears.

The carriage dipped once and then out stepped Amelia Chase.

As if she were some angel gifted to the people of this earth, she stood tall in a shaft of sunlight, a bright light in an otherwise dreary world.

MacLeod's heart felt as if it flipped in his chest.

A man near to his own age leaned out, his face only visible in profile, and kissed her hand. He took entirely too long to get on with it, leaving MacLeod with the urge to gallop across the courtyard and wrench her hand away, while slamming his fist into the man's cheek.

Eventually, the man returned to the safety of his carriage and it rolled on its way in the opposite direction from whence MacLeod was headed.

Still, he desperately wanted to chase it down.

Instead, he looked Amelia Chase over from head to toe. She appeared unruffled and well.

Amelia hefted her small valise and looked about. There were many people going about their business in the dingy courtyard, but she stood out like a lone bright buoy in a sea of gray.

Then she looked directly at him, her eyes locking with his.

And, as always seemed to be the case with her, the remaining world dimmed and faded into obscurity.

She smiled and lifted her hand to wave. And oh, that smile...it was a smile meant for him and only him. It pierced his heart as surely as an arrow might when delivered by the hands of a skilled archer. She was happy to see him.

Aye, the entire world fell completely away in that moment. The bustling activity, the horses whinnying, the footmen shouting, the children running amok underneath it all. It was just her standing there looking at him and he at her—so close, but so utterly out of reach. It was almost poignant. He wanted nothing more than to close the gap, racing his horse through the crowds until he landed at her feet and swooped her up in his arms.

He felt a mixture of relief to see she was whole and disappointment their moment was over.

He could not go to her.

He *would not* go to her.

His horse stepped back a few paces as he inadvertently tugged on the reins, and in that moment, her face fell. She surely realized he had no intention of going to her.

It broke him to see it, yet he refused to be moved to treason by the loss of her smile, though the world seemed darker with the knowledge this was goodbye, at least for the foreseeable future. He reached up and absentmindedly rubbed at his chest, the pain there sharp and unexpected.

He supposed he knew, deep down in the blackest recess of his mind, he knew: they weren't through. Not at all. They couldn't be.

Aye. They couldn't be.

So with that bit of reassurance settled firmly in his mind, he tipped his hat and winked at her, a move so completely foreign to him that he frowned and abruptly turned his horse about and rode out of the courtyard before he did something truly stupid...

Like pull her onto his horse and across his lap and take her with him on his hunt for a traitor.

Och, he was sure he would replay their numerous interactions over and over in his mind while he was away...and quite effectively redis-cover his anger towards her. It was the way his mind worked.

Impossible as it was, he could have sworn he heard her voice above the bustling crowd as she whispered goodbye. His mind argued the sentiment.

Nae, Mrs. Chase, we will meet again.

Chapter Eleven

A melia Chase was crestfallen.

    Yes. Downright cracked up, mouth frowning, foot stomping disappointed. Dash it all, he wasn't meant to leave her like that! They had things to say to each other. Names to call each other. Things to yell at each other. Or throw at each other. Or both.

She wasn't finished with him, damn it!

Amelia turned on her heel and stormed into Ye Olde Howling Monkey, paying little notice to the odd assembly of patrons enjoying their afternoon libations. But it was difficult to overlook the stuffed monkeys perched on random shelves around the room and at either end of the long bar, all of them posed as if howling with laughter and pointing into the distance at one another or the odd patron seated nearby.

She even stopped completely before the ten-foot-tall stuffed monkey in red livery standing next to the base of the stairs, his arm holding a white tea towel and a ring of keys. But this one was absurdly strange and impossible to ignore, no question about it. He appeared to be silently howling!

She wanted to howl, too. Ye Olde Howling Monkey...how appropriate.

Argh. Stupid, over-bearing brute of a man. That craven, knotty-pated coxcomb.

Amelia harnessed her anger lest she become overwhelmed with despair. Unexpectedly, she paused in her march and gasped in a breath, almost completely losing her composure, then she pulled herself together once more.

She was Amelia Chase, dammit. Independent American Woman.

Amelia marched toward the innkeeper, fully prepared to take out her frustration on him. Yes. She was happy—*happy!*—to have this, erm, little, white-haired old man fill the part of her own personal punching bag.

All right, so maybe she was somewhat hesitant to attack a defense-less old man.

But then again, he was probably used to rowdy regulars kicking up a ruckus. Never mind that his face wore the deep lines of a man who lived the bulk of his life with a smile on his face and far too much laughter. It was so evident it was practically carved around his mouth and in the corners of his eyes.

But no! She would not let that sway her, not one bit. And she would simply ignore the sweet smile he bestowed upon her now. He was a man. One of *them*. Strange and rude and unforgivable creatures that they were.

Amelia glanced down at the man's hands, then looked away imme-diately. Drat, not even the sight of his trembling hands as he held an old key in his gnarled fingers would leash her barely restrained tongue. Someone was going to get a tongue lashing and this man was it.

Amelia dropped her small valise on the counter with a bang. "My husband has a room reserved. The name's Chase. Mrs. Amelia Chase."

Her tone was clipped. And commanding. No 'please' would be forthcoming from Amelia Chase. And the innkeeper had better hope the answer to her implied question was yes.

Or more to the point, *MacLeod* had better hope the answer was yes.

The innkeeper simply held up one quivering hand to cup his ear, the universal sign for 'I didn't hear you.' and his smile firmly in place the entire time. "Eh?"

Amelia spoke louder. "My husband has a room reserved. The name's Chase. Mrs. Amelia Chase."

She was determined and holding on to her justifiable anger with both hands. No please forthcoming, still.

"Eh?" came the innkeeper's reply.

This time, Amelia used her lungs' full capacity, but tempered her shout with a smile. "The name's Chase! Amelia Chase!"

The man's smile widened then, if such a thing were possible. "Yes, ma'am," he hollered in return. "Right this way."

He walked around the bar and turned toward the stairs.

"Thank you," she said by mistake. She *wasn't* being polite, dammit.

He stopped and turned back to her. "Eh?"

"Never mind!" she yelled. It was becoming quite clear that the inn was appropriately named for several reasons.

The innkeeper reached down, grasped ahold of her left hand, and patted it with his right, all with a smile that reached his dark blue eyes, crinkling them in the corners with a merry twinkle of delight. "It'll be all right, dearie. No need to yell." Then, he turned back around to lead the way.

And just like that, she was no longer prepared to make this man her personal whipping post. What self-respecting woman would take out her anger on a sweet old man who was practically deaf? Especially one with a smile as genuine as all that?

AMELIA EXHALED A SIGH OF RELIEF WHEN SHE STEPPED INTO HER room to see her personal luggage stacked neatly against one wall. At least something was going right.

She took a moment to survey the room with an appreciative eye. It was bright and airy and decorated in white with blue flowers

But best of all...it was clean.

Amelia launched herself onto the bed and spread her arms and legs wide. The bed was even soft and comfortable. She'd get a perfect night's sleep here. She wanted to sleep now. And all of tomorrow. Maybe even the next day, she was so very tired.

Amelia sat up on her elbows and looked around the quaint room once more as she fought of the sadness that loomed around the edges of her mind. She would not think of MacLeod leaving. She would not.

Not at all.

All right, Amelia. Focus.

This was the prettiest room she'd seen since she landed in England some months ago. She took in the full-length mirror, the beautiful tiles surrounding the fireplace, the ornate stand for the washbasin, delicate with blue and white flowers.

Amelia bounded off the bed, almost falling to the floor when her feet tangled in the sheets, the minute she registered the note propped up in front of the washstand's mirror.

She raced over to snatch it up.

It was addressed to her and written in a tight, unfamiliar but very precise and neat script.

Amelia walked back to the bed to lie down—or more accurately, to sprawl across the mattress—her petite frame taking up as much room as she possibly could, and held the note high above her to read by the light of the afternoon sun streaming in through the window.

Darling wife,

I had to leave...duty calls. I have paid the room fees for the next week.

Where I go, you cannot follow, so for now, we must part until such time as we can resume our wee game of "Who is Mrs. Chase?", and this time, I will have answers.

I have no inkling of how long; it may be months.

But when I'm finished, I will find you.

Until then, I remain yours, etc.

— *MACLEOD*

Amelia held the note to her chest and smiled. She was ridiculously pleased he continued with their husband and wife charade, as bizarre as it was.

And the note was so completely MacLeod, or at least the MacLeod she was coming to know.

Months, eh?

Well, he'd better be ready. They had a reckoning coming.

C.K.

We have a new mission for you, one we know is precisely suited to your unique...abilities.

Retrieve Mrs. Chase. She is to be our guest.

— X

Chapter Twelve

Three Months Later: Bloomfield Park, Bath: Lady Harriett Ross's House

It was almost time. Finally.

Amelia Chase surveyed the very English study in which she was currently ensconced with more than a little nervous curiosity. The room was remarkable because it was so very unexpected. It had all the usual appointments, of course—a desk, shelves of books, a globe, two green overstuffed chairs in front of a roaring fire—much like many of the men's studies she'd seen back home in both style and function. Yet, it was different, as well. She just couldn't place her finger on why.

Perhaps it was simply the knowledge she was very much alive and here, in England. Though they spoke the same language, Amelia was coming to learn that England was quite different from America in language, custom, and particularly with regards to the rights of women.

But perhaps it was because it belonged to him, her newly discovered brother. The one she was about to *officially* meet in, oh—she glanced at the clock on the mantel—half an hour. (He was busy getting married at the moment.)

But also, and probably more realistically, she was anxious about seeing *him* again. MacLeod. For surely he would attend one of his best friends' weddings?

She had thought of him steadily over the past three months, and a million questions to put to him burned in her mind. But most importantly, she wanted to see him and hear his deep brogue as he teased her.

Would he tease her?

She had to admit she didn't know what to expect when they next met and wasn't that a first? She excelled at reading people. Always. It was a skill she owned; a skill which kept her alive.

And yet she struggled to work out the puzzle that was Alaistair MacLeod, and that made her both infinitely curious and decidedly nervous.

Enter the aforementioned anxiety, which was really an odd mix of excited enthusiasm plus a healthy dollop of apprehension. It made her insides flutter and her mind unsure of whether she should jump up and down with excitement, dance with wild abandon, or jump ship and disappear. For good.

Amelia rose from her position on the desk (long story) and walked the perimeter of the room for the one hundredth time in as many minutes. Maybe it would be best to be seated by the fire when they arrived? She'd already tried standing by the window arms crossed, then arms at her side, then arms behind her back. She tried standing by the globe, sitting behind the desk, laying across the desk...ahem, erm, yeah. She hadn't tried the floor, but even *she* wouldn't go that far.

So, she might have considered, briefly, throwing herself under the desk. To hide.

But really, she wasn't a coward. This meeting was too long in coming and far too important.

Amelia glanced at the mantel clock. Twenty-nine and a half minutes to go. Oh, the agony of a perpetually slow moving clock.

She began pacing the perimeter of the room again, muttering to herself all the while. "Come on Amelia, how should we do this? Hmmm...let's see...'How do you do, Lord Dansbury?' No. No good. How about...'Brother! We meet at last!' No, no...far too informal. How about...'We meet again, Dansbury'? Hmmm...sounds a bit too flirtatious and rather shady, for that matter. Let's see...'Oh, hello, Mr. Kelly?' How about...'Brother mine, how do you...'"

She was so preoccupied with trying to choose how she wanted to address Dansbury, it took a moment to realize what she'd said and consciously note Kelly standing there beside her brother's desk, but then she *was* nervous.

Amelia spun about. "Mr. Kelly, what a surprise! How have you been?"

"Ah...fine?" came the amused Irish brogue of Mr. Ciarán Kelly. All black haired, ice blue eyed, six feet—or thereabouts—of him. He still wore that knowing, roguish smile, as if he was imagining what she looked like beneath her corset and chemise. Just like last time. Honestly, it made her uncomfortable, though she'd never admit it out loud. He was meant to be a friend of her brothers.

"Excellent. Where have you been? You all but disappeared the last time I saw you..."

"Tra..."

"MacLeod was very tight lipped about it all and acting *verra* strange," she interrupted with a laugh while she ignored the pang of wretchedness she felt at the memory of her last sight of MacLeod...or at least, she tried to ignore it. "Well, I suppose that's normal, but I mean for him—wait a minute. How did you get in here? You certainly didn't come through the door."

Amelia crossed her arms and tapped her foot while she threw him a speaking look, then glanced passed his shoulder to the heavy drapes hanging directly behind him—drapes which should have been hanging still, not billowing before an obviously open window.

Amelia threw him a cautious look before marching over to said window and throwing wide the curtains.

She looked out to the ground below and tapped her fingers on the frame while she considered what to say. His behavior surpassed bizarre.

Amelia spun back around and pointedly nodded her head at the open window behind her as she spoke, "You climbed in the window?"

Kelly was leaning against one of the wing back chairs by the fire now, arms crossed, watching her with a smile. He shrugged his shoulders, his grin firmly in place.

"But...but there are *bugs*. And most assuredly snakes lying about in the shrubbery."

Goodness what an idiotic thing to say. But it was the first thing that popped into her mind.

Amelia could have slapped her hands over her mouth at the absurdity of such a thought, but managed to keep her poise. Just.

And still, Kelly didn't answer.

Over the last few weeks, Amelia had categorically decided she disliked uncommunicative men. Never mind she hadn't given him much chance to speak.

Never mind she sounded like a ninny bringing up bugs and snakes.

But really, normal people didn't climb in through the window of their friends' houses when there was a perfectly serviceable front door.

Never mind that she'd climbed out of quite a few windows in her day.

Then again, if you and your friends were known spies...

Amelia brushed off her wild notions and looked askance at Kelly again. "But, why?"

Kelly stood straight and walked over, his steps measured and sure. His arms were outstretched in an open, friendly manner belying the serious look about his face. "Ah, *bean álainn*. I truly am sorry we had to reacquaint ourselves under such circumstances."

"And what circumstances might those be?" She suddenly wanted to be anywhere but here. Still, she was as curious as a cat with only five— make that *four*—lives left. (She was rather known to be a tad too adventurous even by American standards.)

"You see. I have a job to do, and I mean to see it through."

She crossed her arms and studied his face, marking his solemnity. "Sure. Sure. But what does that have to do with me?"

"I regret I must insist that ye come with me."

Amelia chuckled and waved him off, convinced he was making a not so very funny joke at her expense. "Don't be absurd. I'm about to be introduced officially to my brother, and I'm nervous enough as it is. I certainly cannot leave now."

He must be joking. He really must.

"I was afraid you'd say that. Unfortunately, you don't have a choice in the matter, *bean álainn.*"

Chapter Thirteen

At the Same Time

The wedding of Lady Beatryce Beckett to Clifford Ross, 7th Marquess of Dansbury, was a small, intimate affair. Held in the drawing room of Dansbury's beloved aunt's country estate near Bath, the bride and groom spoke their vows in front of ten guests, two birds, several cats, three dogs, and one vicar.

To Alaistair MacLeod's relief, the ceremony itself was short and to the point. Soon after the vicar introduced Beatryce and Cliff as husband and wife, the small wedding party filed out of the drawing room and reconvened in the massive foyer of Bloomfield Park, the ladies exclaiming how colorful and beautiful it all was: the bride, the flowers, the groom, Aunt Harriett...

He had to admit he was disappointed not to see *her* there. He'd convinced himself that after these three long months, this was where he and Mrs. Amelia Chase would face each other once again and resume their...*thing*. He didn't even know what to call it at this point. Their feud? Argument? Game of cat and mouse? Test to see who exactly was Amelia Chase? Attraction? Unbridled lust?

MacLeod pulled one hand through his hair, agitated by the

memory of their certain magnetism and concerned by the fact that he didn't know what to expect or say when he did finally see her again.

If Amelia Chase was who she claimed: an innocent, *Independent* American Woman who genuinely believed that Dansbury was her long, lost brother, wouldn't she be here of all places: her *brother's* wedding? He'd not broached the subject of Amelia Chase with anyone in three months, but surely Dansbury would have said something had he known of their *connection?*

But she was clearly not here, which left him agitated and deeply unsatisfied. He'd been anticipating this moment for months, and her absence irritated him with a surprisingly forceful intensity.

Well, one thing was certain. Once he was free to leave, he would find her. His conviction behind that decision surprised him, nearly stopping him in his tracks.

Lady Beatryce called for everyone's attention and turned toward her new husband. In a loud voice and in front of the entire assembly of guests, she announced, "Now, I have a surprise. A wedding gift for you, my love. One I know you will adore."

Alaistair nearly groaned out loud. He wanted to leave and start his search now. Instead, he was swept along with the entire mob of wedding guests as they followed Lady Beatryce and Dansbury to the library, which doubled as Dansbury's study when he was in residence.

It was painfully evident they were all meant to witness her 'gift'. Personally, he'd rather be in his room reading, or even in the stables mucking out the stalls for that matter, than see this. Never mind his sudden, impatient need to hunt down Amelia Chase right at that very moment.

Sure, there were only a handful of guests, and he knew most of them, but it was still a handful too many to suit his tastes this morning, Amelia Chase's absence notwithstanding.

Which honestly was no different than any other time. He always felt as if he were wearing his skin two sizes two small when out and about in social situations. Even with friends.

Worse, he loathed small talk.

Lady Beatryce paused with her back to the double doors of the study and looked up at her husband. Her eyes softened with emotion. It was clear that she cared about Dansbury. She cared very much.

"You are the world to me, Cliff. My heart. My love..."

Sigh. MacLeod had the sudden urge to sprint down the hall and out the front door, or at the very least, roll his eyes and voice his displeasure with a growl. In his current mood, hearing the newly married couple espouse their feelings brought forth a myriad of emotions, none of them good: resentment and bitterness were foremost present. And perhaps a touch of arrogance as well. For he knew better than them all, happily-ever-afters did not exist. Not in his eyes.

Not anymore.

Lovers could betray you without remorse.

He tried to tune out Lady Beatryce's monologue as he imagined backing out the front door. He wasn't entirely successful, Lady Beatryce was difficult to ignore at the best of times, even whilst being sappy.

Honestly, he preferred the bitchier version. At least, at the moment.

And with his ginger hair, broad shoulders, and six-foot six-inch soaring height, he would hardly be inconspicuous trying to maneuver out from amidst the tightly assembled guests.

"Darling D, I have found your sister..."

But *that* remark got his attention. Her announcement caused a buzz of murmuring amongst the guests. MacLeod zeroed in on those closed library doors, his senses acutely focused. The perpetual darkness that seemed to hover at the edges of his consciousness these days brightened a tad with awareness.

Every one of the other members of the party were as intent, curiosity writ plainly across each face.

His heart started up an unsteady race in his chest and his hands turned clammy. He wiped them upon his kilt and licked his lips as his mouth turned dry.

She would be there.

It had to be her, the very woman he'd tried to put out of his mind for the last several months while he attempted to do his job. And yet despite his efforts, she remained stubbornly entrenched in his thoughts.

He would see her again, at last. They would have their reckoning. Their situation resolved.

With a grin as wide as the Cheshire plains, Lady Beatryce pushed open both doors and hurried out of Dansbury's way before he ran her over in his haste to finally meet his long lost sister. MacLeod could appreciate the desire. He had to hold himself in check to keep from tossing everyone to the side, including Dansbury, to barrel through and reach her first. Instead, he strained his neck as he attempted to see passed Dansbury's shoulders to the room beyond.

It only took one quick glimpse to know that Amelia Chase wasn't there. Though in reality he needn't even see the empty room to know that truth; they would have heard her if she were in there, the woman did tend to talk. Often and loudly.

He rubbed his chest at the sudden disappointment he so clearly felt, bizarre though his feelings were for holding to such a sentiment.

Almost immediately, the crowd began talking excitedly all at once. The noise like the buzz of angry bees to his sensitive ears.

Without examining his reasons for volunteering, he abruptly announced. "I'll find her."

One might have heard a pin drop to the marble floor, the sudden silence was so complete and immediate.

Well, he wanted the opportunity to be away from the chaos and uproar of house, however briefly. They should all know that by now.

And it was as good excuse as any.

Slowly, the others began talking again, the volume growing louder by small increments.

He best not waste time. MacLeod turned to leave.

Before he had taken four steps toward the front door, Aunt Harriett called out, "Try the stables. She loves the animals."

Well, that is a point in her favor, to be sure, but how inconsiderate to wander off at a time like this? Would the woman never stay where she was supposed to?

He only paused a moment to consider Aunt Harriett's remarks and his subsequent thoughts before he continued toward his purpose. He was comfortably ready to embrace anger rather than allow disappointment to fester.

MacLeod stepped outside with more than a small amount of relief, thrilled to be away from the others. Contrary to the pandemonium going on inside, he was convinced Amelia Chase had simply wandered off, and though he was both anxious to see her—he would admit to that, at least—and quite angry at her apparent flighty behavior, he stalled for time to calm his thoughts.

Aye, he was quite irritated by the idea that she had wandered off, which proved a convenient tool. It allowed him to ignore the little bastard voice inside his head that taunted him with the rebuke: *She's Dansbury's sister after all, no' a spy... You were wrong. So verra wrong.*

Instead, MacLeod placed his arms on his hips and arched his back while he took in a deep breath, savoring the purity of the crisp country air as it filled his lungs and restored some of his humor—the little he maintained, at any rate. He could smell a touch of rain on the air. Dark clouds lingered overhead with only a few breaks in their heavy canopy to allow the sunshine to reach the earth. The effect was quite dramatic. And was the perfect backdrop to this growing anticipation.

He would see her again.

MacLeod hoped a storm would linger rather than blow over, for he loved it when the weather was like this, dangerous and foreboding. He felt more alive. He felt dangerous.

He felt at all.

He could have found a million ways to further delay heading to the stables. For some reason, he still wanted desperately to stall for time. He wanted to savor the anticipation. Imagine the moment they would meet. Would they circle each other, two predators stalking their prey? Would they freeze, unable to think of what to say? Find nothing to say? Doubtful.

But his friend was anxious to acquaint himself with his sister, so before long, he stepped off the front stoop and turned down the worn path leading to the Bloomfield Park stables.

It was a short but steep walk to the stables and he had to work to slow his pace, so as not to start jogging down the trail with his descent. The wind breathed a song of rain, while it rustled the leaves of nearby trees and whipped his hair about his eyes. Despite the heaviness of his wool kilt, the wind was gusty enough to swirl the hem and stretch his pleats, threatening to give the residents and guests of Bloomfield Park a public showing of his nether regions should they be watching him through the south-facing windows.

Och, well. Let them see his bare arse. MacLeod couldn't care less. He marched on in annoyance couched as determination, every step deliberate and hard.

His anticipation was rapidly turning to indignation.

MacLeod reached the stables and stepped inside, a shower of leaves followed in his wake and settled around his boots. The deep recesses of the stables were very dark, what with the overhead clouds all but blocking the sun.

Right away, MacLeod knew Amelia Chase wasn't inside. For one thing, it was far too quiet, with only the shuffling of hooves and the occasional whinny or snort to be heard from a few of the older mares retired from service. The stable hands were out exercising the remaining cattle, leaving the inside of the stables disconcertingly quiet.

Maybe she had fallen asleep. He'd check every stall to be sure. One never knew. Especially with someone as unpredictable as she.

He was about to step further into the stables when he noticed the lantern on the floor to his right, mere inches inside the main doors, lit and unattended—a dangerous proposition in a wooden structure filled with dry hay. Usually, a stable boy was on hand to keep an eye on things, and lanterns were never left unattended on the ground.

"Halloo?" he called to the darkness.

MacLeod strained his ears, but no one answered his call. To his left was the tack room. He'd check the in there first, and when he found the stable boy, likely sleeping, he'd thrash the little scoundrel for his negligence in shirking his duties with a morning nap.

He wouldn't really thrash the lad, but he'd give him a good scare for his carelessness.

MacLeod picked up the lantern and turned to his left. Between two freshly oiled saddles hanging from pegs in the wall, was the dark green door of the tack room, complete with a rusty iron door knob, the paint around it rubbed away from years of workmen's hands reaching for the knob. The door was shut tight.

MacLeod shoved open the heavy oak door and stepped inside, holding the lantern up high as he did.

The room was quite dark, both from the many clouds darkening the sky and years of built up grime on the windows. Yet it was spotlessly clean, apart from the windows, and organized, and smelled of a complex mix of leather, rope, and oil, with a touch of liniment and oats. At first, the room appeared to be vacant, but then he spotted two small booted legs sticking out from around the shelves of gear to his right.

Right. As he'd thought. So, the rascal thought to nap on the floor in the corner, did he?

"Och, ye ken not to be napping on the job, lad. Now, step to."

The legs, such as they were, started squirming in a bizarre, synchronized fashion.

Well that was verra strange.

MacLeod stepped forward with his lantern. Closer inspection revealed the lad's legs to be bound with rope.

MacLeod set the lantern down on the desk and marched over to the boy, concern taking residence in his gut. The lad was on his side with his hands tied behind his back and a length of cloth serving as a gag. The boy's tears cut trails of white through the dirt and grime otherwise covering his face. MacLeod did his best to ignore the lad's bright, pleading eyes as he set to removing the bindings. Responding to the plea with pity would only embarrass the boy.

"There now, lad. Let's see what we have here."

Sniffle.

"I take it someone got the drop on ye, eh?"

Sniffle.

"There's no shame in that son. It happens even to the best of us."

It took a moment, but before long MacLeod finished untying the boy and sat back on his heels while the young one wiped his nose and eyes with his shirt sleeves. He had no kerchief with which to assist the boy in his task.

Sniffle.

"E-Even you?" came a small, still trembling voice.

"Aye, lad. Even me."

MacLeod stood up and the boy's eyes widened as he watched, surprise writ plainly upon his face. Aye, he was a big man. A boy that age would find it difficult to believe someone could ever get the better of him. And they hadn't for a verra long time.

He held out his hand to the boy and pulled him up. "Why don't we take a step outside, son, and perhaps you can tell me what happened."

"Yes...Yessir."

The boy followed meekly behind, not quite over his involuntary captivity, but too proud to want that fact pointed out.

They found a bench under a nearby oak tree and sat. MacLeod turned toward the boy, hands by his side, while the boy kicked his legs back and forth in the dirt.

"Go on, son," he prodded, "Tell me what happened."

"T'were Mr. Kelly, sir."

The boy spoke to his feet, and could barely be understood, but MacLeod was used to listening and had remarkable ears for all that.

"You know Mr. Kelly?"

"Yessir." He wiped his nose on his sleeve, again. "I was coiling a length of rope when he walked in carrying that nice lady with the funny accent what's been hanging out in the stables off and on the past fortnight."

The boy ducked his head again, while he drew slow circles in the dirt with his feet now. "I-I saw her ankles..." his voice faded as he spoke until he didn't say anything at all.

After a moment, it was clear the lad was too ashamed to continue.

"That's all right, lad. Och, it weren't yer fault for all that."

MacLeod's show of support seemed to embolden the boy for he continued, speaking quickly as young men were wont to do. "Mr. Kelly told me she'd been hurt, and it was plain she was a-visitin' her dreams. So Mr. Kelly says I was to go in the tack room to fetch some supplies.

But while I was in there, bent over cleaning out a bucket, he walked in and...well, you can prob'bly guess the rest, sir."

Sniffle.

"Aye. I ken."

The boy wiped his nose again, then, "He arrived on a big black horse, with two socks on the forelegs only a few minutes before. I'd barely had time to tend to his horse before he returned. From what I could hear, it sounded like he left on 'im as well."

"Likely. How long ago would ye say?"

"I'm not sure. Prob'bly the better part of an hour, I'd say."

MacLeod stood. "Chin up son, Mr. Kelly is a big man. There's no shame in what happened to you."

Then, he reached up and ruffled the boy's head, the gesture unexpected, before turning on his heel and storming off.

Bollocks.

He set a hurried pace back to the house. He'd done his best to soothe the lad's fears, but he wasn't exactly good at that sort of thing. People, even children, simply weren't his forte.

And it was all made worse as he was utterly desperate to leave the lad and hie off after Amelia Chase.

Argh, Kelly. Damn him. They were supposed to be working for the same team. He, Kelly, Dansbury, and the Duke of Stonebridge—they were all investigating the Society for the Purification of England, a secret society of noblemen who weren't afraid to murder anyone who stood in the way of them achieving their primary objective: ridding England of anyone who wasn't pureblooded English. *Particularly* the Irish.

Kelly was Irish. So what could possibly have motivated him to switch sides?

MacLeod marched into the library to auditory chaos. Aunt Harriett was arguing with Beatryce, who was arguing with Dansbury, who was, characteristically, laughing at them all between whatever points he was trying to make. Stonebridge and his wife, Grace, were merely watching.

"Could you be serious for a moment, Cliff, or I'll walk right out of this room and handle it myself." Ah, there was the Beatryce he knew.

Lady Beatryce was the first person to notice his return. "MacLeod! Did you find her?" She made to look past his shoulder. "Where is she?"

"She's been kidnapped," he replied, blunt as always.

"What?!" everyone exclaimed at once. Dansbury no longer looked his amiable self, his trip to furious took less than two seconds.

Stonebridge was right there with him. They both wore matching murderous expressions.

And they all looked at him. For a moment, they were all silent, waiting for him to speak.

MacLeod remained mute, surely they didn't need him to repeat himself? He'd been perfectly succinct. They didn't have time to discuss this. They needed to leave. Now.

Then everyone, except him, of course, started talking at once again.

"Call the magistrate."

"Fetch the butler."

"We can track her down."

MacLeod wanted to run from the room with his hands on his ears from the cacophony of sound bruising his ears. Instead he added, "It was Kelly."

That quieted everyone for a moment.

The duke said, "He won't harm her."

Everyone else turned to look at Stonebridge, incredulous. The tension around the room was palpable.

MacLeod stormed over and got in his face. "And ye know this how? Are ye willing ta stake her life on it?"

The duke grew angry in return. "Back off, man. There is more to this than you know."

MacLeod held his position. "Well, why don't you enlighten the rest of us, then?"

The duke shook his head. "You know I cannot."

MacLeod threw his hands in the air, but didn't back down. "Well, that's no' guid enough for me!"

"Duke," Dansbury interrupted, "This game of cat and mouse with Kelly has been going on for far too long. You know this. This time, he has gone too far."

The duke nodded his head in agreement but stood his ground. "He won't harm her."

"Ye. Canna. Know. That," bit out MacLeod. But he did take a step back then, and more softly, he added. "And I'll be the one to track her doon."

For the most part, everyone remained silent at his pronouncement, likely stunned.

"She's my sister, MacLeod," argued Dansbury from somewhere behind him.

"You just got married," he shot back over his shoulder, though he never broke eye contact with the duke.

Surprisingly, Beatryce walked out of the room without uttering a word. It seemed it was a day for odd behavior.

For a moment all was quiet, though it didn't remain that way for long. As if on cue, everyone began speaking at once as they voiced their own suppositions of the events leading up to this point.

And for the next half an hour, he and Dansbury argued over who should go after Amelia, with Aunt Harriett and Grace occasionally chiming in with their opinions. The duke maintained his insistence that Kelly wouldn't harm her, stubborn bastard, and Dansbury, eventually, seemed to support his supposition, which simply pissed off MacLeod that much more.

It was the most MacLeod had talked in a month. And it was absurd that he was doing so when they should be marching out the door before the trail turned cold. He was beside himself with the urgent need to walk out on everyone and begin his search, despite the duke's weak reassurances, but Dansbury was correct. Amelia Chase was *his* sister; MacLeod had no right. Not really.

Still, it didn't fucking matter. Nothing and no one would stop him from searching for her, from *finding* her.

But damn, when Dansbury needed to speak his mind, he really

needed to say it. "It's not right for you to go. You're not related. And you don't seem to like her very much. I'll not have my sister treated to your brand of stony, silent *non*-communication, MacLeod. Not after…"

Dansbury's latest argument died in his throat as Lady Beatryce walked in wearing trousers, of all things.

"While you gents were wasting time arguing," she said as she dropped a saddlebag on a nearby chair, "I've saddled the horses. I, for one, am leaving now. You had best hurry if you want to join me."

Beatryce turned her back on them and made to leave.

Dansbury looked over at MacLeod, and with a wink to him despite the seriousness of the situation, said aloud, "Sure darling, you have my permission to join us," and with a final nail in his coffin, added, "This time."

MacLeod winced. Apparently, Dansbury still enjoyed provoking his bride even though they were '*in love*' and now, married. Till death do them part.

Which might be sooner rather than later, knowing Lady Beatryce. She was not one to be told what to do.

Lady Beatryce froze, lifting her shoulders. MacLeod imagined her anger leaping off those squared shoulders in giant emotion-filled waves.

But when she turned around, he knew right away he was wrong. Rather than spitting fire and brimstone, the ice queen had returned— no emotion was to be found in her expression at all.

Which was far worse. He turned to wish his friend a good journey to the afterlife…

…but Dansbury simply grinned like a fool, with a smile that held a certain amount of pride. If anything, he was smiling even more than he had been before he made such a ridiculous, needling statement.

Lady Beatryce walked over to Dansbury, her steps deliberate and steady, and with every footstep she took, Dansbury's grin widened further. "I can see by the smile on your face that you don't really mean what you said. And since it is our wedding day, I'll let your provoking statement slide." She kissed him once, briefly, on the lips, but then her eyes narrowed in warning. "But I'm promising you now…if you ever think to control me in such a fashion in the future, I'll be having your bollocks with my afternoon tea."

Then she patted his cheek with a smile, turned on her heel, and left.

Dansbury looked over at MacLeod with a grin and a shrug and said, "That's my woman," with more than a touch of delight coloring his tone. He followed his wife out the door.

"Aye." MacLeod agreed.

Thank God fer that.

Chapter Fourteen

The Next Day: Possibly in Her Bed at Bloomfield Park, Or Possibly Not

It was dark and the air, stifling.

Amelia Chase took a slow, deep breath as she came to in drawn out stages. She was stiff and ached all over, as if she'd slept hard for a full night without once moving in her sleep. She tried, unsuccessfully, to roll over. Her skirts were twisted and had ridden up to her waist, partially covering her head.

Well, that wasn't so unusual, she was ever a restless sleeper. But why in the world had she gone to bed in her skirts? Again.

The room swayed unsteadily for a moment, and it was a deuced unsettling sensation. That coupled with her groggy head made her wonder if she'd indulged too heavily at her brother's wedding the day before. Her tongue was so dry and swollen, she felt as if she hadn't had a drink of water in two days.

The bed dipped again. "Stop shaking the bed, drat you," she muttered aloud. Someone in her brother's household was downright inconsiderate.

A man chuckled, the sound and the voice distant but fleetingly familiar.

Something strange is going on here. How many glasses of sherry did I have?

Still somewhat groggy and knowing a headache was imminent, she kept her eyes closed and pushed past her personal discomfort as she relied on her remaining senses to orient herself. She could smell leather and feel a touch of wet velvet beneath her cheek. Between that and the constant rocking motion, and she began to suspect she wasn't in a bed at Bloomfield Park after all, but rather a bedroom courtesy of a moving carriage. One that was moving at a reasonably fast clip based on the rapid cadence beneath her.

Amelia shifted again. *Ah.* She was lying on her side, legs bent, probably on one of the benches. She tried to straighten her legs, but hit a wall before she could straighten them completely. She pushed with her legs and slid up the seat until her head touched the other wall. Alas, she was finally able to stretch out completely, although she was still somewhat cramped. She wiggled her toes.

Huh, where are my shoes?

She flexed her stockinged feet against the wall.

Definitely no shoes...

She kept her eyes closed and searched her elusive memories. Right. She'd been at her brother's house. Tick. She reached up and rubbed at her forehead as she struggled to recall the rest. Oh—yes, Kelly had climbed into the room through the window and said something about having no choice but for her to leave with him. She'd laughed in his face, turned on her heal to leave, then, nothing...

Oh, God!

Amelia eyes flew open and she lurched upright onto her elbow as the rest of her memories came hurtling to the forefront of her mind. He'd drugged her, dash it all! Ciarán Kelly had drugged her.

The sudden movement almost made her vomit and she gagged a bit before her stomach settled.

Amelia looked about the carriage and homed in on Kelly sitting across from her. Her eyes felt gritty with sand despite her obvious slumber.

Kelly was somewhat disheveled, the stubble of several days of growth upon his face and no cravat to speak of. His black hair hung in his eyes, making his face appear shrouded with darkness, yet those intense, ice blue eyes seemed to glow from within the recesses of his veiled countenance. He was staring out the window, one hand fisted against his mouth, deep in thought and no longer paying her any mind whatsoever.

"You...you...*kidnapped* me...you villainous, hasty-witted miscreant. What in the Sam Hill do you think you are doing?" It felt odd to say the word *kidnapped*. "Who does that in the real world? This isn't some sort of twisted gothic novel. Really, are you mad?"

"If ye're thirsty, I have a flask of water." He didn't even look at her when he spoke and he ignored her questions. Well, one question. The second two were rhetorical.

The man was absolutely motley-minded, fool-born, crazy.

Amelia pushed herself all the way into a sitting position. It wasn't easy, what with twenty-five yards of tangled silk, but she managed it all the same.

Ha, she was lucky her skirts weren't all the way up around her ears.

Amelia wiped her mouth with her sleeve; she doubted Kelly would have a handkerchief on hand as a gentleman ought.

"A gentleman would have at least wiped the drool from my face," she said to his shadowed profile.

One side of his mouth hitched up in some small semblance of a smile.

"It's really not funny. You should be ashamed. Honestly. Why don't you let me go at the next inn, and I'll forget we ever met?"

"No."

She crossed her arms, though his answer wasn't unexpected. "Well, I happen to find it a marvelous plan."

He snorted. "You would." He didn't so much as look at her when he said it.

Even though he continued to look away, clearly intent on ignoring her—or trying to, at any rate—Amelia smiled baring all her teeth.

Oh, she had found herself in awkward scrapes before; this was nothing new, precisely, so she wasn't scared, per se. But Kelly was a different beast of a man. He was too charming and street smart. She would never be able to persuade him to release her.

He was too much like her.

Still, Amelia concocted several plans of escape in her mind, but discounted them all. Kelly was no fool. And honestly, she didn't think he truly meant to harm her, not really. In fact, as absurd as it sounded, she wasn't scared or angry for any of the obvious reasons.

In fact, she was quite confident the first time they stopped, she would easily escape him and whatever minion he had driving the carriage.

But at the moment, she was stuck with him and her true anger, what made her downright furious, was that he'd messed up her plans to further cultivate her—what did spies like to call it? Her *mark?* Dansbury.

And by that she simply meant that she was to lay low under Dansbury's protection until Viscount Sharpe contacted her. *Snort.* So very adventurously spy-like.

And, more importantly, her reckoning with MacLeod. Which meant her priorities were completely upside down, but she was too angry to analyze what it all meant.

But then a sudden, cunning plan sprang to life in her mind. One painful, but good plan. One unexpected, possibly tedious, but guaranteed to piss him off and make him regret the day he climbed in to that study and took her, plan.

Amelia smiled, ready. Kelly looked at her then, noted her obvious contentment, and said, "You're a little different than I expected."

Amelia's smile widened. "Yes? And how is that?"

He shrugged. "You're charming and intelligent, but you haven't tried very hard to escape. I expected somewhat of a fight on my hands this morning. With you using all manner of methods to convince me to let you go."

"Hmmm. That's interesting. I feel the same about you. You're clever and charming, yourself. I know I cannot convince you to simply let me go; you took me for a reason. But you must know....an intelligent woman always has a backup plan."

THREE HOURS HAD PASSED. THREE LONG, TORTUOUS HOURS. AND now her voice was growing hoarse from her constant, belligerent chatter.

But thankfully, Amelia could see the strain taking its toll on Kelly. A muscle in his jaw ticked as he ground his back teeth together. Even the fine lines around his eyes and mouth seemed to have deepened steadily by the half hour. Both hands were clenched into fists on his knees. He glared at her. His eyes, which had been glazed over for the last quarter of an hour, were now blazing with anger.

She pointedly ignored the warning signs and carried on with her side of the conversation. The *only* side.

"Do you know I find that type of stitching to be incredibly tedious to do? And so hard on the hands? I cannot fathom why anyone would want to spend time learning that technique. I believe it was created as a clever form of punishment by some mean-hearted harpy with nothing better to do with her time."

Yes, she'd talked *at* him constantly. For hours. It wasn't easy to get to this point, for he was known as a charming man—a ladies' man—and so initially, he was somewhat engaged in her attempted monologue.

But Amelia Chase would not be beaten. She was Amelia Chase: Talkative Harpy and Collector of Useless Knowledge.

She would irritate the piss out of him and make his life hell, so long as he forced her to endure his company.

Oh, yes.

She questioned every decision he made...

"Shouldn't we stop for the ladies retiring room now?"

Discussed every subject known to man...

"Did you know that hunting pigs in Hedgesville, South Carolina is illegal? Why on earth pigs? And only pigs. Everything else is fair game." *Snort.* "Fair game. Ha Ha."

And women, for that matter...

"I spent the first hour at the side of the room; not really bothered by the dancing. And the clothes! Let me tell you..."

She spoke of inappropriate things...

"But did you know she kissed him twice every Sunday behind the church?" (He'd appreciated that).

Inane things...

"Have you ever watched paint dry?" (But not that).

By this point, she was even getting on her own nerves.

But definitely his.

Yes, her plan was working beautifully. Which was a good thing, for she was in real danger of running out of things to say. Which was incredible, really.

She never ran out of things to say.

At this point, almost everything she said was entirely made up. And so it wasn't easy to keep a running monologue of stories flowing off the cuff, not to mention making them both believable and dull.

Dull was key.

Another long-winded hour later, and Kelly finally, *finally*, lost it.

"Shut up!" he yelled.

Amelia fought desperately to withhold her smile.

Ha! He expected his command to work. He doesn't know me very well.

Amelia crossed her arms and stamped her stockinged foot, a touch muffled without a shoe to enhance the sound, sure, but effective. "But you haven't let me finish telling you about this latest knitting stitch I learned on the voyage over from America." Her voice suggested she was thoroughly put out by his indifference.

"Mrs. Chase, I mean it. I am ready to throttle you to within an inch of your life."

She doubted that. If he'd intended her harm, he would have done something to injure her hours ago. She knew he had no intention of doing so, and thus she only wanted to piss him off. It was all she had until she could free herself.

A few minutes later, the carriage slowed as they prepared to pull off the main road.

Ah, at last.

THEY WERE IN A FIELD IN THE MIDDLE OF NOWHERE. KELLY AND HIS driver—no, his unarmed-lady-kidnapper-assistant—no, not that either...his cowardly minion (yes, that'd do) had set up camp in a small clearing in the woods. She could smell trees and burning wood. And that was all. Not a sign of life other than what could be found in nature. Birds, bugs, and bees.

And probably snakes. She suppressed a shudder and eyed the men. Both were yawning and rubbing their eyes. She smiled to herself. Yes, it was only a matter of time.

It was dark now, the sun having set about fifteen minutes before. The men had laid out three bedrolls on the ground around a small fire. Outside.

Snort. And they say America is uncivilized. Ha!

But she had a new plan now. She'd stumbled upon it while taking a walk to relieve herself when they'd arrived. She'd heard the two men discussing the fact there was an abandoned cabin nearby, but they had decided it was used too often by others in the area to be a safe place to stay, even for only one night. *That* in and of itself was promising, but what really had her dancing in her boots were the mushrooms she'd spotted. While she might not enjoy sleeping outdoors—the bugs, you know—she did know her way around plants and animals, and those mushrooms would put a man to sleep in about an hour. It was slow acting, but effective. Once those men were asleep, *nothing* was going to wake them for six hours or more.

And they were tasteless in tea.

She'd quickly mashed up the mushrooms between two medium sized stones, collecting the paste in her pocket. It was a sticky mess, but needs must. Then, when she returned to camp, she'd prepared the men their 'tea' over the fire they'd started while they saw to the horses, gathered more wood, and generally set up the rest of camp.

They didn't suspect a thing. She wanted to rub her hands together and laugh in evil triumph...but not yet.

"Mrs. Chase," Kelly began, "I know it's not the Albany Hotel, but this must do for the night. And unfortunately, I'm going to have to secure you. Can't have you running off in the night on us, can we?

"Do your worst, Mr. Kelly," she said with a smile. She tried for cheerful, rather than smug.

Kelly gave her a meaningful look, then tied her arms and feet with some rope. Once she was secured, he said to his driver, "You take first watch."

Within ten minutes, both men were snoring loudly. She tilted her head up to the sky and let loose a stomach splitting half laugh, half yell laugh out loud. The local wildlife did not approve.

But most importantly, the men did not even twitch.

Amelia tried pulling her arms free and found her restraints to be loose enough to get her hands out with a little effort. Within minutes, she was completely free.

She stood and brushed the leaves from her skirts, then walked over and looked down upon Kelly's sleeping form.

She bent down, her nose practically touching his. "Take that, you scoundrel!" she yelled in his face.

Snort. Snore.

"Best response you've had all day, I'd say." She wiped her hands clean over his head, figuratively and literally, and walked off, shaking her hips with impudence.

Besting those men felt good. Dashed good.

I am powerful!

AMELIA PICKED HER WAY QUICKLY THROUGH THE WOODS, HEADED toward the carriage. The moon was quite bright, making it very easy to see. Thank goodness.

When she reached the carriage, she doubled over, and laughed uncontrollably. They'd left the horses in their traces, presumably in the event they needed to ride out in a hurry. Unbelievable!

They were making her escape too easy.

And really, how hard could it be to drive a carriage? Especially in the middle of nowhere with no traffic to speak of? It was one of the few things she hadn't learned to do in her life, which really was an oversight in hindsight.

After racing back to camp to light the carriage lamps with the campfire, Amelia returned to the carriage, loosed the ropes hobbling the horses, and climbed aboard. *That* was the hardest part so far—climbing up to the driver's perch.

Amelia took a deep breath, counted to five, and released the brake. Another deep breath and with reins in hand and her head lifted high in the face of her effortless success, she flicked her wrist with a loud, "Heeya!" while bracing herself with her legs for the first jolt forward.

Nothing happened.

The horse on the right looked like it might have tried to look back at her, but otherwise, nothing. Zero.

She tried again, this time with a flick and a "Woot! Woot!"

This time the horse on the right actually moved.

Yeah. He moved, all right. Moved his head to the side and down and began grazing on the grass growing at the side of the road.

Definitely not the movement she was going for.

The horse on the left looked over and simply watched his feasting friend with indifferent eyes.

Amelia laid the reins across her lap and slapped her legs once before pressing her fists to her hips, prepared to have a woman to horse talk with her four-legged colleagues.

"Alrighty, my equine friends. We need to move along here." She looked pointedly to the horse on the right. "Now is not the time for a light repast, my friend." She gave him her best, stern look.

The banqueting horse did lift its head and flick his ears back to her as if listening, though he carried on masticating his culinary delight.

"Excellent. I'm glad I have your attention. Now, are you going to walk on or...?"

At 'walk on' both horses jerked forward.

Amelia, unprepared, nearly fell from her perch.

Thankfully, only nearly.

After resettling herself, she added. "Right. Well, I'm glad we had this talk, then." She gave the horses a light slap with the reins for good measure, pleased to have asserted her position of authority once more.

Half an hour later, Amelia was ready to scream. She sang inappropriate ditties in her head to keep her mind occupied, but still, the going was...s...l...o...w...

No amount of bribing, cajoling, or yee-hawing seemed to convince the horses to move any faster than a leisurely, fixed clop.

At least they were moving, but at this speed, Kelly and his man would be able to walk and catch up with her by midmorning. And they would be laughing until their sides split the entire time. Honestly, she wouldn't blame them.

She was sure Kelly would be able to easily track her, regardless. Thus, she needed a better plan anyway.

The answer to her prayers came not ten minutes later in the form of a wagon with a broken wheel at the side of the road. It was a one horse set up, and on board was a very concerned man and a very, very, very, oh-my-goodness-call-the-midwife-right-this-minute pregnant woman.

Yes!

"Halloo! Halloo down there. Can I be of assistance, my good man? Oh, and woman?" Yes, one very, very pregnant woman.

The gentleman gave her an odd look for a moment. She supposed it was rather shocking to see a lady driving a carriage, but he shook his head and responded with quite a bit of relief evident in his voice. "Yes, yes, oh, thank you, yes! The name's Jones. Harry Jones, and this here's ma wife, Mary."

"How do you do, Mr. and Mrs. Jones. I'm Mrs. Amelia Chase."

"Oh, Mrs. Chase, we are mightily relieved to see you. My wife. She's near her time, as you can see, and cannot possibly ride Ole Bruce, and the wagon is stuck good. The wheel is broken and cannot be repaired without a trip to town. But of course, I cannot leave Mary here on her own while I make the trip, so yes, we're in a bind, I must admit."

Amelia desperately wanted to ask what in the world they were doing out driving at night with the missus being so very, very pregnant. But that would be rude. Though she might have cajoled them into telling her anyway had she the time on her hands.

But she didn't, of course, and she certainly couldn't make time by going with them to town.

Their horse, Ole Bruce, caught her eye when he shifted to sniff at something on the side of the road and a plan came to her in a moment of skillful inspiration. A brilliant plan. A welcome plan.

"Well, it so happens I have a solution of sorts, if you're amenable."

Mr. Jones nodded his head cautiously.

"Excellent, I propose a swap. You can have this fine, easy to drive carriage. Your lady can ride in comfort inside whilst you drive the team...if I can have your horse."

The man shook his head in disbelief for a moment. "Wouldn't you rather ride into town with us? I can strap 'im to the back of the carriage."

"No need." She thought quickly. "I'm staying near here, it's really quite close." She prayed there was a house near here.

"Oh, staying up at the Stonebridge Park, are you? A guest of the duke, perhaps?"

"Ah, yes. Yes, I am." Stonebridge Park was near? "I was just headed there anon."

"Forgive my impertinence ma'am, but isn't the Park back yonder that way?"

"Of course, it is, my good man. Of course, it is."

He waited for her to elaborate as to the reason she was headed in the wrong direction, but she decided she should volunteer as little information as possible considering she was making it all up as she went along.

"But you're not getting much of a bargain out of this ma'am, if you don't mind my saying. That carriage is worth a lot more than Old Bruce."

Think. Think. Think, Amelia.

"Oh...that's all right. I've been meaning to get rid of this old thing anyway. I'm...erm...I'm terribly tired of the color. And I have plenty of horses. I'm sure we won't miss these two."

The farmer still didn't look convinced. And both horses looked back at her as if to raise an objection to her insult. She could hardly blame the farmer for his skepticism when she secretly agreed with the sentiment.

"You do realize that Stonebridge's friends are rather eccentric and not at all spend thrifty. What I mean is, we love to put on airs and throw our money around as if it's nothing. And...erm...honestly, I made a bet with the...erm, duke that I'd get rid of this carriage in some irregular fashion and come back on a lone horse, so, really, you'd be doing me a favor. Honest."

"A bet, eh? That doesn't sound like the Duke of Stonebridge. That man isn't a betting man. Plays things straight on account..."

"Well, of course he does, but he and I are close friends. We go waaaaaaaaaay back. Way back. Yes, since we were super young. Good ole...erm...*duke* and I. And our little bet is a trifling thing, really. No money involved, no. Just sort of a dare and some good-natured ribbing among friends."

Goodness, what a load of malarkey.

She silently prayed for forgiveness for her many falsehoods this night.

The man still gave her a skeptical look, but then looked over at his wife, who caught his eye and started furiously shaking her head.

Mr. Jones cleared his throat. "Well, then I guess that'd be fine. If you're sure?"

Oh, thank God.

"Oh, I'm sure—*oomph!*—all right," she said as she climbed down from the carriage. This was the best plan. If Kelly was tracking her, he'd follow the carriage straight into town. She'd be headed in the other direction via horse. It was perfect.

"My lady..."

"Oh, I'm no lady."

"Ma'am, are you really sure? Ole Bruce, he's really quite stubborn, and I have no saddle."

"Oh, not to worry, my good man. I excel at dealing with stubborn. Stubborn should be no trouble at all. The duke sometimes calls me Amelia Stubborn Chase. Or Mrs. Stubborn. Or just plain Stubborn."

She really should quit while she was ahead.

The man looked at her dubiously. She clearly wasn't dressed for riding bareback across the countryside and her story was wildly farfetched. Meanwhile, his wife had already ensconced herself in the carriage and was leaning her head out of the open doorway to beckon her husband. "Come on, Harry. Best not to look a gift horse..." she hissed.

"As you say, Mary." He turned to Amelia and reached out to shake her hand. He grabbed hers with both of his and shook enthusiastically. "Thank you, ma'am. Thank you so very much. May God bless you and see you safe this night."

She patted his hands with her free one. "Thank you, my good man. Now do hurry on and see your Mary home safely. I'll be quite fine." He released her and she turned to her new ride. She reached up and patted her new horse on his withers. "Horace and I will get along famously. You'll see. Well, I guess you won't, actually. But it'll be fine. Really."

"His name is Bruce, ma'am."

"Bruce, then. Do hurry, Mr. Jones."

"All right, if you're sure."

"I'm sure."

He climbed up to the driver's perch of the carriage. "We'll be on our way then, if you're sure," he called down.

"That's fine."

"I'm releasing the brake..." Clearly, he was giving her plenty of opportunity to change her mind.

"That's probably a good idea."

"Do you...?"

Sigh. "Just go, my man. I'll be fine."

His "Right-o," was followed by an unmistakable sound of relief from within the confines of the carriage, and then *finally* he turned to the horses with a loud "Yee Ha," a whistle, and a whack of the reins.

And those horses—those large, naughty, fickle, equine fiends—launched themselves forward with great speed.

Pfft. Picky, temperamental beasts with no sense of loyalty.

Amelia turned from the sight and looked up at her new companion, Ole Bruce. He appeared to be watching his owner leave, though he seemed wholly unconcerned over the prospect.

"Well, Horace, it's just you and I, my horsey friend."

"Haw Hee..."

"Er, my donkey friend."

Amelia patted Horace absentmindedly as she looked to her right. She'd head that way; hopefully toward safety and not more enemies disguised as friends.

Chapter Fifteen

The Next Morning: A Familiar Abandoned Tenant Hut

Alaistair MacLeod arrived at the abandoned tenant hut by horseback a few ticks before six in the morning. The place still looked as abandoned as it had the last time he'd seen it. More so, for this time, not even a single waft of smoke drifted up through the chimney that would otherwise suggest someone's presence within its walls. Och, it would be deuced cold inside.

At this time of the morning, patches of fog still hovered near the ground, while numerous wisps of it climbed the outer walls of the hut like ghostly fingers rising up from the ground, augmenting the already eerie gloom that characterized such a dilapidated dwelling.

Alistair tied his horse to a nearby tree and crossed the remaining distance to the hut on foot, the morning dew wetting the toes of his boots as he shuffled across the damp ground. He could feel the humidity creeping up his kilt.

The front door was held secure by planks of wood stretching across the width of the frame, the hinges having been removed ages ago. He laughed to himself as he remembered the last time he was here with Stonebridge.

Alas, there was simply no way Mrs. Chase had entered through that door. Wooden planks were nailed on both sides of the door to keep it from falling in our out.

Och, he'd look inside anyway. Really, with Amelia Chase, one never knew.

He walked the perimeter of the hut until he came to the cabin's lone window—or where a window was once located, to be more precise. Beneath the window was a stack of fallen logs, recently disturbed.

He peered inside, though it took a few moments for his eyes to adjust to the shady interior. Cracks and chips in the walls allowed pinpoints of light to penetrate the shadows, and several large holes in the fusty, thatched roof allowed in large, concentrated beams of light.

One such beam highlighted the remains of two wooden rocking chairs and the edge of what MacLeod knew to be a three-legged table. They'd brought the table in quite a few months ago when they'd used this place to detain a suspect in their investigation.

And a second ray of light illuminated the sleeping form of Amelia Chase. MacLeod was admittedly somewhat surprised to see her there, lying on the floor, tucked into a tight ball for warmth. He felt a moment's pity for the lass, for last night must have been devilishly cold.

At the same time, he felt a spark of admiration upon seeing her safe. She'd evidently escaped her captors; it was impossible not to approve.

And utterly impossible not to acknowledge the sense of relief he felt, knowing she was unharmed.

He decided to forgo following her method of gaining entry to the shack, climbing through the window frame. Besides, his shoulders would never fit. Rather, he picked up a hammer hidden in the weeds, kept there for just such a purpose, and walked back to the front of the cottage to begin 'unlocking' the front door.

Of course, the noise he made pulling the planks of wood off the front of the cabin was enough to wake Amelia.

"Who's there? I'll have you know I have a really, really big dog in here with me. With big vicious teeth. He's asleep now, but I can wake him at a moment's notice. And I have a big gun. And I know how to use it. Not to mention I expect my husband to return any moment now. He's a big, strapping man. A highlander. Ever hear of one of those?"

He chuckled to himself. "No, I've never heard of one of those. Is he verra big?"

Silence.

After a few moments when she still didn't reply, he paused in his task and asked, "Mrs. Chase?"

"Yes?"

Her voice sounded subdued and he shook his head, wondering at her sudden reticence. He wouldn't press her. For the moment, opening the door was his priority. "Nothing."

A few minutes later, MacLeod finished removing the outer wooden 'locks' and pulled the heavy oak door out of its opening. He had just set it against the outer wall of the cottage when a fire ball of petite woman ducked beneath the inner 'locks' and flew out of the cabin straight into him, literally knocking him on his arse. Which was something, considering his size.

And of course, she went down with him.

He was somewhat taken aback by her behavior.

For a moment, words...thoughts...actions...failed him. She was just *there* hanging on while he lay on his back looking down at her spread across his chest. His arms remained out-stretched as he was not entirely sure what to do with them. Hug her back? Push her off?

"Mrs. Chase?"

"*Mmph*," came some sort of muffled response. She had her face buried in his chest and her arms around his waist. The burst of heat from her breath caused goosebumps to lift on his neck and the fine hairs on his arm to stand on end.

"What happened, lass?"

"*Mm...mmph.*"

Another muffled blast of heat. She squeezed him tighter and shook her head.

"Mrs. Chase...?"

"*Mmm...mm...mmmm!*"

Och, there was nothing for it. He laid his head back on the ground, lifted his eyes to the blue skies overhead, and after a quick exhalation of breath, wrapped both his arms around her and returned her embrace.

God, she felt damn good, lying there in his arms.

HE WAS NEAR TO GOING NUMB BY THE TIME SHE ROLLED HERSELF OFF him and sat up, surreptitiously swiping her eyes. He pretended not to notice.

When she finally looked at him, her eyes were guarded and wary—nothing like the confident, boisterous woman he'd come to know. He declined to remark upon her uncharacteristic behavior, and instead, helped her up and asked, "What happened, lass?"

His voice was gentle as he could make it, considering he wanted nothing more than to chase Kelly down and pound the man's face into the dirt with his fists.

He stood there, as patient as a man like him could be, while she cleared her throat and let forth a small cough. He still held her arms, gripping her beneath her elbows, reluctant to let her go.

Eventually, she looked up at him, her eyes still shielded. "It was Kelly." Her voice was raspy and soft, but she continued on anyway. "He climbed in through the library window and abducted me. He...he drugged me!" Each word she said was louder than the previous.

Ultimately, she pulled out of his arms and paced the ground in agitation, but she'd stop and glare at him after every few words as if he were responsible for what happened.

"He. Drugged. Me!" She punctuated each word with a fist to her opposite hand.

He smiled inwardly at the return of her fire. Her earlier vulnerability was so ill-suited to the woman he knew, it made him uncomfortable to witness it, and at the same time fired a fierce need within him to protect her with his life.

She winced, utterly unaware of his internal turmoil, and resumed more quietly, her voice a touch above a whisper. "He said he had no choice. When I came to, he and I were traveling by carriage. He never told me our destination. And if you're wondering why my voice sounds funny, it's because I've been talking nonstop for hours trying to annoy the stuffing out of him."

Och, it would have taken her hours to annoy Kelly; he was far too easy going and it took an enormous effort to aggravate that man. Well, at least, the Kelly he thought he knew.

For MacLeod, even ten minutes sounded like a nightmare, for he loved all things quiet and he viciously guarded his own solitude.

Still, he smiled at her determination, though he daren't let her see it. She was...*prickly*...at the moment and he needed to hear her tale. If she'd stop pacing and stick to the point, he'd have it.

"Unfortunately, the man has the patience of a saint, and my attempts to anger him bore no fruit. Eventually, though, we stopped to make camp," she resumed talking and walking in circles. "I walked off to take care of my...well, you know..."

He watched her, giving her time to complete the point she was obviously trying to make. At the same time, she was utterly unaware he had the incredible urge to grab her shoulders and hold her still. Now that the sense of urgency regarding her safety had eased, his habitual impatience had returned in force. He wasn't annoyed with her, per se, but more to the point that he wanted them to be on their way so he could hunt down Kelly right now, not standing here talking in a field by the side of a dilapidated hut.

He embraced his cantankerousness like an old, worn coat, familiar and comfortable.

He also had the nigh uncontrollable urge to hit something. Hard. Preferably Kelly. Yet there was nothing he could do about it now.

"You know..." She pointed to the ground while turning beet red.

He crossed his arms and stared at her. Surely, after standing completely naked before him, kissing him to within an inch of his life until he thought his cock was going to explode in his kilt like a green lad—surely after all that, she wasn't embarrassed to say she needed to take a piss?

But then again, he'd known quite well how mercurial her moods could be and how very much she was like her brother in that respect.

Dansbury could change moods, seemingly with the drop of a hat or the wave of his hand.

Aye, they were definitely related.

"You're going to make me say it, aren't you?"

He said nothing.

"To the ladies' retiring room...?"

He nearly laughed at the imagery that invoked. A ladies' retiring room in the woods? Obviously, he wasn't quite as impatient and irritated as he'd thought.

She shook her head and continued, "Anyway, I stumbled upon some mushrooms I recognized. I knew that when they are brewed in a tea, they are tasteless and will put a man to sleep for hours."

She smiled, seemingly at the memory of her successful daring.

"You drugged them?" He was genuinely surprised. Despite the questions to Kelly's allegiance, the man was a trained spy and a good one, at that. To think this spitfire of a woman had gotten the best of the man was...*interesting.*

"Why, yes. I did." She paused midstride and finally (finally!) smiled at him. The sun followed suit and lit up the clearing they were standing in.

She continued. "Once they were asleep, I managed to free myself from my bonds, then—"

"Wait," he interrupted, "you were bound and able to get out of your ties?"

"Well, don't act so surprised, MacLeod. It's not above my huckle-berry..." She sighed when he arched his brow as he looked at her with some confusion. Such an odd choice of words. "Yes, it really wasn't that difficult."

She watched him a moment, possibly searching for his approval, so he urged her to continue. "Go on."

"They'd left the horses in their traces, presumably in case they needed a fast getaway. Anyway, I certainly wasn't going to look a gift horse..." She snorted.

He showed her his favorite impatient look as she snorted and chuckled over her pun.

She cleared her throat. "Yes, well...so I drove the carriage, then—"

"You *drove* the carriage?"

Amelia stopped and put her hands on her hips in exasperation. "Look, you seem to want me to get to the point, but you do realize that if you continue to interrupt me, it will make the telling take that much longer?"

"Aye, I ken. Go on." Dammit, she did make an excellent point.

"Well, a few miles up the road, I had the good fortune to stumble upon a man and his very, very pregnant wife. They were stranded, with a wagon that had an irreparable broken wheel. So I offered them a trade they couldn't refuse—the carriage for their donkey. He really was a nice man, but I couldn't imagine..." His growl got her attention

She scowled at him in return. "Right. I figured if Kelly and his man came to, they'd continue tracking the carriage right on to town, buying me time to ride across country on Horace."

"Horace?"

"The donkey. They called him Bruce, but he didn't look like a Bruce to me. Of course, that was when I still thought he was a horse."

"You mistook a donkey—"

"Look, it was dark and I was tired and marginally scared, it was an honest mistake. Anyway, I stumbled upon the hut, and here I am." She smiled and held her arms wide, pleased with herself.

"Where's...Horace?"

She broke eye contact and spoke to the ground. "I let him go," she mumbled.

"You let him go?" Just when he was beginning to admire her fortitude, she proved she was completely mad.

She crossed her arms and glared at him. "Do you always repeat what people say?"

"Only you."

"Oh." She looked contrite for but a moment, then looked him over, her lips pursed. "Well, I thought it would be best not to advertise my presence here."

"But you don't know where here is."

"Actually, I do." She smiled with knowing. "The farmer mentioned this was Stonebridge Park. I had hoped to find the house, but when I came upon this shack, it was so late and cold, I thought not to take my chances stumbling around in the dark. Figured I'd wake up and look for the house in the morning. I assumed it wouldn't be too far for me to walk."

"Stonebridge Park is upwards of a thousand acres."

"Oh."

"Yes. The house is no less than ten miles north west of here."

"Oh. Well," she said brightly, "I suppose it all worked out in the end, so no foul. I guess you want to find Kelly's camp and see if they're still there?"

"No."

"No?"

"No. They'll be long gone. Even if they aren't, there's not a lot I can do without the right kind of supplies or additional men." Not to mention Dansbury would kill him if he put Amelia's life at risk to pursue Kelly.

He would never put Amelia's life at risk to pursue the man, traitor or no. The thought had him rubbing absentmindedly at his chest.

Besides, they'd discussed this with the duke before setting out. Dansbury had essentially commanded that Mrs. Chase be the priority. If it were a possibility, they'd bring Kelly in, finally, but otherwise they were to leave off until Amelia Chase was safe and completely out of harm's way...

For once, *he'd* agreed, which was somewhat out of character for him. It'd certainly surprised both the duke and Dansbury.

Hell, they weren't the only ones.

"Oh. Well, good. I have no interest in seeing that pribbling, clay-brained pignut anyway. Good riddance, I say. I wash my hands of him." She slapped her hands together as if she was literally brushing Kelly from her the palms of her hands.

He would never own up to almost laughing out loud. Pribbling, clay-brained pignut? She must be a fan of Shakespeare.

"So, then, where are we going?" she asked.

"Greenwood Park."

"And where is that?"

"Several days' ride north east."

"All right. Is there a problem with going to Stonebridge Park? It is much closer..."

"Yes."

"Might I inquire as to what that problem is?"

"No."

"No?" she asked, unable to hide the incredulity in her voice.

He paused to look at her. All right, so maybe he wore his favorite glare?

She tried a different tactic. "Do I have any say in this?"

He shook his head, but lest she question his resolve, he added, "No. Now, let's go."

He started in the direction of his horse, Amelia followed on his heels.

"Now, just you wait a minute, MacLeod. What about my brother?" she argued from behind.

"I'll let him know ye're safe."

"You'll let him know?" She sounded astonished and angry. "Won't he be joining us at Greenwood Park?"

He turned his head to look back at her, so she could see the gravity behind his answer. "No."

She stopped and placed her hands on her hips. "I'm sorry, but I'm not a fan of this plan. I came here to see my brother, and I demand you take me to him."

He turned to fully face her. "You demand it?"

"Yes."

"Like it or no'—too bad."

She stomped her foot. "No. No, MacLeod. *Too bad* is not an acceptable response, you big weedy, idle-headed, minnow. You do not get to decide, you oversized brute, you villainous, earth-vexing, lout."

Not acceptable, eh? Idle-headed, minnow? Weedy? Earth-vexing? MacLeod relished what he was about to do next.

He ignored her astonished protests as he wrapped one arm around her back and tucked his other beneath her knees, then he lifted her high off the ground as he marched her over to his horse, carrying her like a babe.

Oversized brute, eh? He'd show her oversized brute.

"MacLeod, you big ox, put me down and stop manhandling me this minute. I am not going anywhere until we come to terms on this."

He carried on, completely unconcerned about her protests.

He set her down once they reached his horse, though he was still unprepared to hear her arguments. She didn't have enough information about the situation they were in to make the best choices. Besides, she'd proven more than once that her preferences were questionable, at best.

He shot her a warning glance to convince her not to be a pain in his arse. "This is no' a committee, and we are no' putting this to a vote."

"Why not?"

Och, the lass was determined to be one anyway.

And he didn't answer her. Instead, he crossed his arms across his chest and glared at her. Perhaps he could intimidate her into submission without the need for an argument. They didn't have time for a delightful row. They needed to be underway, now, and he wanted her cooperation, for once, without argument. *Was that too much to ask?*

Apparently, so. She mimicked his stance, which surprised him, and he had to fight not to reveal the surge of admiration he felt. But despite her bravado, she had to know she didn't have a choice. He had the advantage.

"MacLeod. Whether I like or not, I realize I need you at the moment. I have no way out of here save for by my own two feet."

He wanted to grin at her concession; he was a little smug. He settled with a stern look that told her she had best remember that going forward.

"But I also know you are an honorable man, and I'm not putting a finger on that horse until we come to an agreement. Therefore, I have the advantage in truth."

Dammit, she was too clever by half.

MacLeod looked up and skimmed the sky, searching for patience, before glancing back down at Amelia. "Look, Mrs. Chase. I will no' hesitate to bodily pick you up and place ye on ma horse. But in the interest of my own peace, I will explain to you the situation, since you seem unwilling to attend to it: you were kidnapped out of an aristocrat's home. Clearly, you have men after you. Dangerous men. And they will no' give up." He stepped forward and regarded her upturned face. She looked back at him earnestly, her emotions alive and easily readable in her expressive eyes. Och, he had to concentrate to remain firm with her.

"Further, I gave your brother, my closest friend, my word that I will keep you safe, and I do no' take that responsibility lightly. You are in a foreign country. You do no' know your way aboot."

He leaned down. He was practically nose to nose with her now. His voice softened and slowed. "Now, I am the only man you can trust, the only...man..." he paused as a burst of emotion forced his heart to feel like it was tumbling about in his chest. He swallowed a lump in his throat and took a deep breath. "...the only man who can keep you safe from those who will not hesitate to harm you." He nearly choked on the word *harm*, but there was more. "They will kill you should they decide to do so."

The thought that he and he alone was there to keep her safe was both a blessing and a curse.

Her eyes widened and she licked her lips. The movement caught his attention, and suddenly he wanted nothing more in this hellish, miserable, unfair world than to kiss those full, red lips once again. He leaned in closer, an involuntary response to her siren's call.

But she backed away and her expression—which had, for a moment, clearly returned his desire—shuttered before brightening. She wore a smile like he'd never seen on another and probably never would. "Why, MacLeod, I believe that is the most you've said to me in one breath since I met you." She patted his arm. "We're making progress. I believe by the time I'm through with you, you'll be talking to strangers on the street."

He took her flippancy as acquiescence. God, she was exactly like Dansbury. And her glib tone adequately doused his ill-timed desire. "Come on," he growled.

She hid her smile as easily as a thief could stow a stolen coin in their pocket, and it almost felt as if he were the victim of some theft, as if someone had stolen her smile and her light from him.

He shook off such thoughts and looked at her expressive face. After a moment, he was convinced she finally understood the danger she was in and *that's* what mattered.

She pursed her lips, but he didn't miss her sigh of surrender. "Fine. But I don't like it, and I'm really starting to not like you."

"Guid." He placed his hands on her waist to lift her up.

"And while we're on this journey together, I expect to hear an apology or ten from you—sooner rather than later, I might add—for the numerous times you refused to believe I was Dansbury's sister."

Aw, hell. She was no' going to let him forget that, was she? Could he blame her?

As MacLeod climbed up behind her, he couldn't help but remark, "What, you're not going to beg me to take you to see Dansbury again?"

She sighed and all but mumbled her response, "Truth be told, I could use a bit of quiet."

He was genuinely surprised. He thought she thrived on being around people. Lots of people. "Really?"

She turned to look back at him and said with a world-weary sigh, "MacLeod...shut up and take me to the safest place you know, all right?"

"Aye." He chuckled to himself. Thankfully she was seated before him and couldn't see the smile that fell awkwardly upon his face.

"Where were you, MacLeod?" Amelia sat before him on his horse, but he heard a suggestion of hurt in her voice all the same. He only just stopped himself from leaning down and placing a kiss on the crown of her head, which was categorically unlike him...or at least, unlike the *him* of the last five years.

Still, he owed her the truth. He was aware that she'd been briefed on his mission by Aunt Harriet, to a point, so he decided to tell her. "Initially, I was on the hunt for Kelly, the man you just escaped from."

She snorted sarcastically. "Obviously, that didn't work out so well."

He didn't take offense to her observation. It was the truth, for all that it rankled.

"Aye. But not long after, I was pulled off the mission. Even I don't understand why, but it's not my business to argue with a direct order. Besides, I trust Stonebridge, and there are very few people I trust." But, by God, he didn't have to like the decision, especially now.

He didn't know why he was being so forthright with her. She made it easy to open up, practically pulled this stuff right out of him as if she owned his damn mouth. Perhaps it helped somewhat that she was sitting before him on his horse and not watching him while he spoke.

"And after?" she prompted.

His hands inadvertently tightened on the reins. "I had to go to my estate for a spell."

She half turned in the saddle before him. "Is this the same estate we're headed to?"

Unfortunately. He looked away, pretending to take in the scenery. "Aye."

It was unfortunate because it meant she would learn all his secrets. He would be bare before her, and she didn't even know it. Further, she didn't realize the power she would wield with that knowledge, nor did she understand, yet, the sacrifice he was making to keep her safe.

And he could only hope that, in the end, she would never use that information against him, for she could kill him with it as sure as putting a knife through his heart.

Yet, even realizing all that, he was still willing to take her to his home, and he did so without hesitation nor question.

Damn.

She was silent for a moment, and he happily gave her that time, though it frightened him a little. What thoughts were going through her mind now and would he continue to answer her questions so readily? He was half afraid to find out what she was thinking and more than a little eager to know, which was a new feeling for him. Further, he hated that he couldn't watch her expressive face while she was off in her mind and wasn't that pure lunacy? Yet knowing that didn't change his desire to do so.

Eventually, she asked. "Where *are* we headed, by the by?"

"Scotland."

"Really!? To the Highlands?" He couldn't miss the note of excitement in her voice; she practically bounced in the saddle with anticipation.

"Nae." God, to say no still pained him, even after all these years. "My place is just over the border."

She slumped for just a moment, but perked back up right away—just like Dansbury. "I've never been to Scotland, of course, but I've wanted to visit. What about your parents? Are they nearby? Will they be in residence?"

"Nae."

"Oh. My condolences."

He laughed, once. Sarcastically. "Oh, they're very much alive," at least last he'd heard, "but they don't live nearby," *They* live in the Highlands, on the Isle of Skye. His true home, the land of his heart. "and will not be visiting." MacLeod cleared his throat. "We are estranged."

He didn't know why he added that last bit. He supposed he knew she'd learn the truth eventually.

"Why?"

Of course, she would ask, and he answered vaguely, not quite prepared for *that* conversation. She'd better understand why later, after she met the people, his true family, who lived with him. "Let's just say we disagreed on something verra important and leave it at that, aye?" He softened his tone and added, "You'll understand soon enough. lass."

And at that, he spurred his horse into a faster pace, hoping she would understand that this little tête-à-tête was finished.

He'd handed her enough of his soul for today.

Chapter Sixteen

Later That Afternoon: The Noisy Bird Pub & Inn

I t was unusually warm for this time of year. MacLeod wiped his brow with a length of linen as he stepped off the road and up onto the pavement, the movement causing a blast of fresh air to swirl up his legs and cooling his...

Aye, thank God for kilts...traditionally worn.

MacLeod opened the door to The Noisy Bird Pub & Inn and stepped inside, pausing to allow his eyes to adjust to the dim interior. He'd left Amelia here while he took care of posting a letter to Dansbury with word of his sister.

It was quiet inside the inn, which was odd, considering...

The low light made seeing difficult, but gave one the illusion that the air was much cooler than it was. MacLeod unerringly looked to the table where he'd left Amelia Chase sitting with a drink and a bowl of shepherd's pie.

And of course, she wasn't there.

Is this a habit of hers? Can she no' help herself?

MacLeod approached the innkeeper, currently at work wiping

down the main bar. "The American woman that was seated across the way...where is she?"

"Oh, ya mean Mrs. Chase?" At MacLeod's nod, he added, "Fine woman. Fine woman, indeed."

MacLeod didn't agree or deny it, but simply waited for the man to continue with what little patience he could muster given the circumstances. When waiting produced no results, he crossed his massive arms across his chest, a habit he seemed to need to employ more and more often of late.

The innkeeper got the message. "Right—let's see. She spoke with the Preacher Hayworth for a spell, then Pat, the post man. Erm, let's see, then there was James, the costermonger. Shirley, one of the Hughes' milkmaids. Jayne, another one..." The barkeeper's voice drifted off as he ticked off person after person. MacLeod was surprised, though he shouldn't have been. "Aha! I've got it. She left with Angus, the butcher, who needed help with a critter who kept pestering him for bones. A dog, I think."

Finally. "When did she leave?"

"Hmmmm. Good question."

MacLeod wanted to shake the man, who appeared lost in thought counting the minutes now.

"I'd say ten, no, twenty minutes ago. Aye, that's it. Twenty-five minutes ago, give or take five or ten minutes."

MacLeod thanked the man, then turned on his heel and left, destination: Angus the butcher. He'd find it himself; it'd probably take more time to listen to the barkeep give directions than it would for him to stumble upon it on his own. The town was only little.

Five minutes later, the bell over the door of the butcher's shop chimed in greeting as MacLeod walked inside. The place smelled disagreeably of blood and meat.

And once again, all was quiet, dammit.

A short, balding man with a bloodied apron appeared from the back, wiping his hands on the backside of his trousers as he sidled over to the counter. "Can I help ye?"

"I'm looking for Mrs. Chase."

"Oh, yea, Mrs. Chase. A fine woman. A fine woman, indeed."

MacLeod went straight to folding his arms across his chest and glaring the man down.

"Right—she was here, but a house maid from that big house on the hill, the Stevens' house, arrived in desperate need of some assistance. Let's see...she wanted..."

MacLeod didn't wait around for him to finish. It didn't matter *why*, he just needed to find *her*.

Ten minutes later, MacLeod was at the servant's entrance to the Stevens' House. A house maid answered the door.

Her eyes widened to the size of a dinner plates, and her jaw dropped open as she looked him up and down from the bottom of his kilt to the top of his head and said, "Cor..."

"I'm looking for Mrs. Chase."

"Cor..."

"Loud woman, about yae high." He held up his hand a few inches below his shoulder.

"Cor..."

"Do you speak English?"

The maid nodded her head yes, but said, "Nay."

"Well, which is it?"

The maid shook her head no, and said, "Aye."

Exasperated would be a mild description for what he was beginning to feel by this point. Hell, this entire day was turning into a comedy of errors—or a tragedy—he wasn't quite sure which.

"Which way did she go? Did she leave with someone?" he tried again.

"Butler..."

"Thank you." MacLeod left without another word and walked around to the front of the house. The door opened before he had a chance to knock on the door, the butler standing in the frame stiff and formal, his pretentious nose practically touching the sky.

"May I help you, sir?" said the manservant, in typical *butler-esque* fashion.

"I'm looking for Mrs. Amelia Chase."

The butler raised his brow and took in MacLeod's appearance. Clearly, the man wasn't sure whether it was safe to answer.

This time, MacLeod decided to try a new approach. "She's ma wife."

Right away, the butler's bland façade turned into a scowl of disgust, and he lifted his nose higher in the air, if possible. The man sniffed once, then attempted to close the door in MacLeod's face, but MacLeod placed his big booted foot in the doorway, foiling his attempt.

"She told you she was a widow, didn't she?"

The butler nodded once.

Of course, she did. MacLeod sighed and shook his head in exasperation, his fingers rubbing the bridge of his nose as he felt the beginnings of a headache coming on. He wasn't sure if he wanted to laugh or bellow to the sky in frustration. *Of course*, this man knew Amelia was a widow. She'd probably told everyone she met here today her entire life's history.

There was nothing for it. When he found her, he was going to kill her. She needn't worry about Kelly and his men.

MacLeod pleaded with the butler. Man to man. "Look, mon, I need to find her. It's important. Verra important."

The next step was to lift the butler by the velvet lapels of his coat, part of his ridiculously formal livery, and force an answer of him. In truth, MacLeod hated resorting to physical violence when a person was only doing his job. In fact, in other circumstances, he might admire the butler's fortitude in the face of an obviously angry and frustrated man. But MacLeod was beginning to grow alarmed over his inability to catch up with Amelia, which meant he was willing to bend his own rules a little in this exceptional circumstance.

Fortunately, he didn't have to resort to that.

"She left with George, the blacksmith." The butler all but spat out the words before he slammed the door in MacLeod's face, successfully this time.

Yet strangely enough, MacLeod's first thought was: *Is everyone in this town known by their occupation?*

MacLeod turned, shaking his head, and jogged down the front steps.

The blacksmith, Amelia?

Five. Hours. Later. MacLeod had visited the blacksmith, a carpenter, a shepherd, the local priest, a mum of five, the post office, and six —count them, six—different women of questionable reputation. He suspected that covered the entire population of the small town.

Now, he was back to where he started: The Noisy Bird Pub & Inn, and he was equally furious and anxious, both at Amelia Chase and at the unavoidable flair of suspicion he harbored over her unexpected and lengthy absence.

Not once did he suspect she might actually be in trouble.

MacLeod walked inside and was practically assaulted by Amelia the minute he stepped through the doorway.

"There you are, you big wayward, tardy-gaited, oaf! Where have you been, MacLeod?"

Chapter Seventeen

MacLeod glared at her, anger apparent in every line of his face. He stepped forward, she stepped back. "MacLeod..." She held her hand up in warning. To stay him.

Of course, he ignored it.

He continued walking toward her, staring her down, while she continued retreating, unsure of the fury that burned in his gaze. She could have sworn she'd seen relief cross his face when he'd spotted her across the room. Now? Not so much.

The back of her legs hit a chair, so she sat and looked up—and up —at MacLeod and all his towering and vibrant ferocity.

But he said nothing. And without any sort of warning whatsoever, he bent over and picked up her chair.

With her in it.

"MacLeod, you oversized, rough-hewn ox. Put me down? What did I do this time?" Oh, she could think of any number of replies to *that* question, but still, "What could I possibly have done to make you angry? I haven't seen you since this morning..."

He didn't respond. Not a single, solitary word. He simply marched up the stairs carrying her via chair as if he weren't burdened with the weight of it all.

"MacLeod, I mean it. If I kick you..."

"...you will fall doon the stairs." He finished for her.

She crossed her arms, uninterested in confirming the truth of that.

Still, MacLeod reached the second-floor landing and set her down, before he whirled on her, leaning over her and bracing his arms on the back of her chair, effectively trapping her in her seat. "Mrs. Chase. Do ye have to talk to everyone ye meet?"

Well, that was unexpected. And completely unfair. "Don't be silly, MacLeod. There are quite a few people I didn't talk to today."

"Name one."

She folded her arms across her chest and tapped her foot. How to answer? She couldn't possibly tell him the truth.

She decided to see how he liked audacious defiance with his dose of preposterousness. She smiled. "Now how could I possibly know who I didn't speak to, when I didn't speak to them? I cannot be expected to know everyone's name. I've never been here before in my life."

MacLeod practically threw his hands up in the air and spun on his heel. Of course, he didn't actually toss up his hands. *That* would be far too much animation for a man like MacLeod, but she read the desire to do so in his actions just the same. Instead, he ran a hand through his hair and down his face before he spun back around, a blazing inferno in his eyes and perhaps a touch of frustration...and maybe, just maybe, a wee tinge of fear.

She spoke first. "Look, I had to do something. I cannot possibly sit around doing nothing all day but wait for you to return. You were gone for half an hour." That sounded like a reasonable enough excuse.

It was close enough to the truth. Somewhat.

"I wasna gone for more than ten minutes." He argued.

"Well, it felt like half an hour."

"I'm sure it did...to you."

She narrowed her eyes. "Now what is that supposed to mean? Are you making a joke or being mean?"

"Take your pick, woman." He turned and began marching up the hall, clearly expecting her to follow.

Amelia wanted to stick her tongue out at his back like a child, but she didn't, more's the pity. Instead, she stood and followed him, "All right. I choose..." She paused as if giving the matter serious considera-tion. He stopped and turned his head part way to the side as if listening for her answer. She suppressed the involuntary smile of sweet success. But she did poke him in the back as she said, "I choose to take it as a joke. Your fierce demeanor is all a façade. I know it. You were worried about me, and it has made you cross."

"Believe whatever ye want," he muttered.

"Thanks, MacLeod, I will. Now, where have you been, you didn't say?"

He whirled on her again, which was unexpected and caught her off guard. She couldn't help but take a step back. He backed her into the wall, his face inches from hers. "Where have I been? Where have *I* been? Where *haven't* I been? I've been tracking you doon, following in the wake of yer glorious and very openly vocal generosity All. Damn. Day."

"So?" Really, he was put out by her being kind? For endeavoring to not be alone? For looking out for herself, just in case. Which was far closer to the actual truth. She thought of it as one of Amelia Chase's Rules of Survival: Always have a backup plan.

Of course, he couldn't know that.

"So? So?!..." He stepped back and rubbed at his head again. "Do you no' recall our conversation this morning? About your safety and the men chasing you?" He faced her again and pointed a finger her way as if to emphasize his point. "In fact, when I left you here, I made it plainly clear that you were to remain inconspicuous, in the corner, head doon, arse in the chair...."

"I wasn't born in the woods to be scared by an owl, MacLeod."

He looked at her strangely for a moment, probably trying to piece together what she'd said. Or perhaps suppressing a laugh. She could have sworn his lips twitched.

"MacLeod. I know Kelly is, on the surface, up to no good."

"On the surface?"

"Yes, but honestly, I've met some truly malevolent, wicked, kick a baby or a dog before they helped someone men before, and Kelly is not that kind of man."

"How do you know? How do you know what a truly evil man looks like?"

She lifted her chin. This conversation was headed down a path she would not travel. He couldn't know; he didn't need to know her sense of self-preservation was a fixed part of her personality. She couldn't not act on it. "It's none of your business."

"None of my—! You practically told the entire town your life story, but when I speak to you it's 'none of my business'?"

She remained stubbornly mute at that. Now was not the time to open up about her past.

He evidently gave up. "Did you even stay seated for more than a minute after I left? Never mind, Mrs. Chase, never mind." MacLeod sighed as if exasperated by a child and pinched the bridge of his nose as he closed his eyes, frustration screaming from every inch of his form. "Look. Ye donna have to help the entire town, ye ken?"

He threw his hand down with an irritated sigh and turned to continue their march down the narrow hall toward their rented rooms.

She smiled at his retreating back, relieved for the change of subject, though somewhat guilty for playing the fool to his concern. She knew he worried about her. She knew he was only trying to help.

Unfortunately for him, he didn't know her. Not really. "Oh, MacLeod, you really were worried about me, weren't you? That's what all this is really about, isn't it?" Possibly he just didn't like that she'd disobeyed him, but she wasn't about to suggest so.

She could have sworn she heard him growl in response before he spun around and confronted her once again. "Aren't you being a bit ridiculous?"

She smiled. "Why yes! Yes, I am!"

His frown deepened, if it could be believed. "Why?"

"Because you don't react the way you're supposed to." Which wasn't precisely the truth. Oh, she'd made a living off of charming men, bending them to her will. It was how she survived. And she was admittedly somewhat flummoxed by the fact that her charms did not affect MacLeod as they did other men.

He smirked. "You mean I don't fall at your feet at the first sight of your witty charm and coy looks." Then he spun around again before she could respond.

She smiled, and it was a genuine one. Was it possible he was not as immune as he seemed? "You think me witty?" She touched a finger to her chin. "Hmmm...I can work with witty."

Right away, Amelia realized it was in her best interest not to take this—game? thing?—any further; he was at the end of his patience. She didn't need to see his face to know it; she could see it in the way his shoulders tensed and his fists clenched. He suddenly seemed to grow an extra foot taller and three feet wider.

Yet she couldn't help herself. This man made her want to poke at him until he exploded. Maybe if he did, she would figure him out.

"If I didn't know any better, I'd say you needed a lover, MacLeod."

MacLeod laughed, a sarcastic sound with no pretense at mirth. "And how would you know?"

"Ha! Asks the man with a perpetual scowl. You, a man so full of passion and physicality, crave an outlet, a safe place to unburden your soul.

He stopped and spun on her. "I see." He stepped close, crowding her once more. He looked her over once, then asked, "And are you offering yourself up for the position?"

Amelia lifted her head. She shrugged, but said, "N-Not, precisely, but it doesn't change the fact that you do."

Yes, stuttering, a fine example of her not allowing him to see how he disturbed her. Ladies and gentlemen, I present to you, Exhibit A... Amelia snorted to herself.

MacLeod reached around her, his hands braced against the wall, caging her in. He leaned in close and whispered. "Och, lass. I'm a cold-hearted bastard, or hadn't you heard? The last time I took a lover, I looked her in the eye as she was hanged for her crimes and didn't feel a single moment's remorse for her demise."

Amelia swallowed the sudden lump in her throat, but maintained her bravado. She hadn't known. *My God, MacLeod.* To him, she said, "Well, then, I suggest you haven't found the right kind of lover."

He stared at her lips then. For a moment, maybe ten. Then he abruptly turned and stormed off once again.

Amelia sucked in a deep breath, her thoughts flying in a thousand different directions. No remorse for his ex-lover's demise? Like hell, she saw the depths of despair beneath his cloak of anger and disinterest. The man might fool himself, but he did not fool her. Not about that.

He felt with an intensity she'd never seen in a man before.

And yea, she knew she was being deliberately provoking, but she was determined that if she remained perpetually cheerful, charming, and appeared somewhat naïve—besides steering him away from her own uncomfortable truths—some of her good optimism would eventually, *hopefully*, rub off on this man. He needed it.

"Are you coming?" he called out from some ways down the hall.

"Coming," she called back and pushed away from the wall to follow him.

Dash it all, they both needed it.

MACLEOD PULLED A KEY OUT OF HIS SPORRAN AND OPENED THE LAST door on the left, then stepped aside to allow her to enter ahead of him.

She lifted her chin and marched around his over-sized, over-muscled bulk, unintentionally brushing his chest with her shoulder in the process. Blast! The doorway was far narrower than was average, she was quite convinced of that fact.

To her delight, she heard him suck in a swift breath of air in response.

Ha!

After practically burying himself into the wall behind him to prevent such an occurrence, she felt a peculiar joy in knowing he was still affected by her touch, innocent though it were.

Unwanted attraction often proved quite useful, when necessary.

Though after the bath...and that kiss...all those months ago, it was somewhat ridiculous to even question his attraction to her.

Still, she was relieved to see evidence the fire was still there. She didn't want to be the only one to find her gaze wandering where it oughtn't.

Did that make her a naughty woman? A touch impish, perhaps?

Amelia shook off her musings and stepped fully inside the room, taking time to note her surroundings. The room was surprisingly light, bright, and clean. The walls were whitewashed and the bed linens similarly blanched—surprisingly bright, in fact—for such a small, remote inn. What little furniture the room boasted was absent any sign of dust, and the floors and hearth were swept clean.

There was no fire burning in the hearth yet, but the room scarcely needed it for the south facing window allowed in an overabundance of light. That, coupled with the white linens and walls, made the room feel bright, warm, and cheerful.

It suited her well.

The room even smelled clean, the subtle hint of fresh oranges, pine, cinnamon, and cloves infused the very air, as if she might find a bowl of said plants hiding amidst the furnishings. To her, the space smelled of the outdoors, without the threat of bugs. She took in a deep breath and closed her eyes, committing the scent to memory. When she opened them again, she discovered MacLeod standing before her, watching her and wearing the strangest expression upon his face. But it was his eyes that made her breath catch, for his eyes were all but burning with emotion.

Amelia threw him a quick smile and looked away, oddly discomfited by his countenance, for his expression suggested a depth of emotion that was fearsome, dark, and complex...and barely contained.

Physical attraction was one thing. What she saw now was something else entirely.

She could never forget the glimpse of that physical hunger that lurked beneath his surface. His kiss was still burned in her memory, like a brand. She had relived that kiss in significant detail every damn day since it happened.

She touched her fingers to her lips as they tingled with the memory of it. She shrugged off the remembrance with some difficulty and asked, "S-so you managed to procure a room. Is, erm, is this one mine..." She *nearly* gulped. "...or yours?" Her voice was falsely cheerful, tension pulled at the edges of her smile.

And she swore her heart held its next beat while she awaited his answer.

"Ours."

Amelia's heart skipped its next *two* beats at the raw sound of his voice as he choked out that single word. Such a small word, but in this context, it carried considerable import.

Ours.

And in that moment, she was relieved her back was toward him, for her face burned hotter than any noon day sun shining down upon rosy, upturned cheeks. She felt overheated and hypersensitive everywhere—behind her neck, beneath her arms.

Between her legs.

She swallowed and hoped it was as silent as she had intended. She fanned her face quickly, then looked back over her shoulder at him and suspected it wasn't. Heat seemed to arc between them, suddenly changing the very makeup of the air they breathed.

Once more, they were back to that night. The bath. The kiss.

She took in another deep breath, pasted an overly large smile across her face, and sat on the bed. She bounced a couple of times, testing the quality of the mattress. Like a coward, she no longer found it possible to look him in the eye. She felt abnormally—for *her,* anyway—shy of a sudden.

Amelia Chase: Slayer of Men, indeed.

Over the course of the last few months, she'd vowed to forget that kiss. The hunger. The uncontrollable need that flared to life between them. To see it rekindle so easily was upsetting, despite all her bold pronouncements of him requiring a lover.

He'd left her behind, dash it all. She wanted to hold on to her bitterness over that fact with both hands, to shut out the desire that knocked around inside her, desperately trying to make itself known. To take control.

Amelia tried to refocus on the here and now.

Oh, yes. The bed was surprisingly comfortable. The mattress was firm, its ropes pulled taut.

Realistically, however, it was not nearly big enough for them both. She might be reasonably short, but MacLeod was a huge man. She suspected he was longer than the bed and nearly as wide in the shoulders. She peeked up at him, and had to fight the urge to swallow, again, lest he hear it with his overly acute hearing or note the telltale flexing of her throat.

Her eyes caught on his lips, firm and full. She knew from experience they were soft, incongruent for a man so hard.

"Nae." He denied in a growling, brusque voice.

She jumped and her eyes leapt to find his.

She hadn't asked him anything, yet she knew precisely what he meant: they couldn't share the bed. Which was right. Proper. Exactly what she wanted him to say, or at least, what she was supposed to want him to say. It was to be expected, but frighteningly enough, she didn't quite know how she felt about that gruff *nae*; her emotions were confused and completely contrary to what she should be feeling: relief. Instead, she wanted to beg him to stay, to take her in his arms and kiss her until her toes curled and she melted in a puddle on the bedding, which he was thoroughly capable of doing and doing well.

She looked away, no longer able to bear his scrutiny, for it affected her in so many unexpected ways. She wasn't ready. Despite all her preparations for their reunion, she couldn't do this.

Between her own observations and private conversations with Lady Beatryce and Aunt Harriett, she suspected MacLeod was a complex man, though possibly broken beneath the surface. He'd been hurt, deeply, by people he should have been able to trust, and she suspected it was the reason for his, sometimes callous, demeanor, and yet he had unfathomable depths. She was desperate to search those depths, but afraid to do so all the same. What would she discover about herself in his all-knowing eyes?

Yes, she knew she affected him. She'd forced a few cracks here and there in his carefully cultivated armor.

Amelia turned away and smoothed her hand across the quilt, the fibers soft beneath her fingers. She continued in this manner until her hand began to feel numb to all sensation; she was determined not to look at him and see the longing lurking in his expressive eyes.

Still, the tension in the room continued to escalate.

She flinched when the door slammed, screaming his departure.

She flung out her arms and fell back across the bed with a deep sigh, only now realizing that she'd held her breath.

She was alone. At last. She was relieved! Never mind her racing heart and heated cheeks disagreed with the sentiment.

Oh God, Amelia. This is hard. It might be too hard.

On A Farm: Two Towns Over, or 20 Miles as the Crow Flies

Kelly and his driver dismounted their respective horses and eyed the out of place carriage sitting in the middle of a wheat field to the right of a farm house two miles outside of the town of Burrwich. It certainly looked like his missing conveyance.

Damn.

He shook his head. He was both irritated and impressed by Mrs. Chase's ability to abscond so thoroughly. He'd certainly underestimated her capabilities.

Kelly walked up the steps to the main cottage and rapped on the front door while pasting on his most amiable smile.

He waited.

And waited.

Dammit, if she were escaping out the back door...

Kelly had barely finished the thought before he was bounding down the steps and around to the back of the house.

He came to a halt as he came upon an unexpected sight—the farmer and his very pregnant wife were playing ole Venus's game, right outside amongst the beets and barley.

"Well, ahem, pardon my intrusion." He winked at the farmer. "I'll just take myself back to the front door and see ye when yer finished up here, then."

He turned on his heel and left, shaking his head with a smile and a laugh.

Ah, lucky farmer.

Half an hour later, the farmer came strolling around the side of the house, a whistling a merry tune. He sported a wide grin and nary a blush.

Kelly recognized a kindred spirit when he saw one.

"My name's Kelly. Are you Mr. Jones?"

"Yes, that's me. How do you do, Mr. Kelly?"

"Fine, fine. I came out on account of your interesting addition to the right field over there—the one with the traveling carriage sat out in the middle. It looks familiar, you see. I believe the previous owner may have been my cousin, Mrs. Amelia Chase. We've been searching for her for a few days now, when she didn't show up at the house as planned."

The farmer's grin fell; his face gone serious with concern. "Well, that is interesting. The previous owner of that carriage is...er, *was*... Mrs. Chase. She traded it for our donkey, Ole Bruce, when she came upon me and the missus stranded on the side of the road. She offered the swap, so I could get my Mary back to Town seeing as she couldn't ride Bruce and the wagon was undrivable, what with a broken wheel and all. So Mrs. Chase left on Ole Bruce and I took me Mary home in the carriage."

Kelly searched the farmer's eyes for the veracity in his words.

"It's the honest to God truth, I tell ya. We didn't steal it, if that's what you're thinking..." The man suddenly looked fearful. He removed his dusty hat and began twisting it in his hands.

"Oh, no, no. I didn't think that for a moment. I'm merely surprised, that's all." Kelly was quick to reassure the man.

Though now, it was the farmer's turn to look suspicious.

"Did Mrs. Chase happen to say where she was headed?" Kelly asked.

Wary now, the farmer said, "She said she was a guest of the duke, over the hill there. Though it 'twere strange as she'd been headed in the opposite direction from the Park and she told a mighty fanciful tale in the process. Summat about a bet, good-natured ribbing, and the duke's peculiar friends."

Kelly laughed. "That sounds like our Amelia, all right."

The farmer laughed, too, though one could detect a thread of strain amidst the sound. "I suppose you'll be wanting the carriage returned to you now..."

"Oh, no. Keep it. You've come by it honestly, I'm sure. Never let it be said that a Kelly, or a Chase, went back on their word."

The farmer released his breath, clearly relieved.

"Thank you for your help, Mr. Jones. We'll talk to the duke, perhaps he'll know where she's gone." *Damn. Her trail was cold.*

Chapter Eighteen

Two Days Later: On the Road to Scotland

I t was the brightest day in English history, or it felt that way. MacLeod had slept very little the night before and the sun seemed to mock that fact, all but aiming its rays purposefully and unerringly into his bleary, gritty, sleep-deprived eyes.

Earlier that morning, he'd managed to procure a horse for Amelia. Thank God one had been available. Fortunately, the owner had not recognized the desperation behind his request to purchase it, never once aware of just how far MacLeod had been willing to go to secure said mount—regardless of its state of health. Hell, the mare could have had only three legs, razor sharp teeth, a hunched back, and one red eye, and he *still* would have traded the shirt off his back to acquire it.

He'd lost almost an entire night's sleep over the persistent imagery of spending the rest of their trip to Greenwood Park on the back of his horse with Amelia Chase fit snuggly between his thighs. His cock twiched at the memory, damned uncooperative bastard.

Thankfully, the horse was young and in relatively good shape, the mare more than up to the task of carrying her all the way to Greenwood Park. And, mercifully, his shirt wasn't required to finalize the transaction.

Amelia was pleased with the filly, of course. She'd already named her Winnie.

"You know, MacLeod, I think we've reached a new level of friendship, indeed I do." She began, patting her horse gently as if speaking to Winnie and not him.

He looked straight ahead and trained his ears on the steady sound of their horses clopping down the unpaved road. He wanted to argue against the idea they'd reached any sort of friendship at all, which was ridiculous and just him being contrary, but he was out of sorts this morning. First for his lack of sleep and second because he wanted nothing more than to pull her back onto his horse, settling her between his legs and in his arms before him. How quickly he had grown used to riding with her there.

But he thought it was prudent not to speak, much less argue the point. It certainly wasn't *friendship* that occupied his mind when he allowed his thoughts to wander.

Clop. Clop. Clop.

"So, I think we should start calling each other by our given names. I mean, we're traveling the countryside together and will be for some time. And honestly, I'm rather tired of you referring to me as Mrs. Chase...even with that delicious Scottish brogue of yours."

"No," he barked, his response immediate. The word *delicious* from her lips caused all sorts of inappropriate images to flash through his mind. He did not need to revisit such thoughts again, not after yesterday's renewed connection in the bedroom and an entire night sleeping upright by the fireside of a drafty old inn.

She sighed as if she'd expected that'd be his response. She *should* have expected it; he was a man who was quite simple to understand. He never padded his words nor spoke in riddles.

"Come on, Alaistair," she prodded.

Blast and damn! A small flame ignited in the general area of his heart when the sound of his first name tumbled from her lips. It took his breath away, for no one had called him by his first name in five years. No one since...hell, no one since Alain.

And only Alain ever did.

He refused to acknowledge his traitorous ex-fiancée.

His heart raced wildly with a startling onslaught of emotion. He fisted his hands and screwed up his face in anger to mask the pain that flared, similar to the pain that always hovered beneath the surface of his skin after bearing such betrayal and all the consequences from it.

Oh, Alain.

He glared over at *Mrs. Chase*. Little could she know his scowling façade was, in reality, him pleading with her not to continue. Dammit, last night he'd have sworn she was angry at him.

Now, she seemed to be brimming with joy. Och, he didn't know which end was up with this woman.

Just. Like. Dansbury. How had he missed it?

"Oh, don't look at me like that, Alaistair. I'm a perfectly progressive woman and an American, and I say it's senseless to hold to propriety in this instance."

He didn't answer her. He couldn't. A lump the size of his fist seemed to have formed in his throat, and she didn't even know it. He returned to watching the distant horizon ahead of them, his neck protesting the strain of muscles that were pulled taut with strong emotion, the wind causing his eyes to water.

"In case you cannot recall it, my first name is Amelia."

Swallow.

Oh, he knew her first name, all right. Of course, e*veryone* in the last two towns probably knew her by her first name.

But that wasn't why he did.

"Some people call me Amy. Others call me Mellie. I'm fine with either one if Amelia doesn't suit. Amelia is longer and I know you to be quite sparing with your words, my mute friend." She chuckled, seemingly pleased with her attempt at humor.

"Mel."

Damn, it just slipped out. Och, pray God she'd missed it.

He peeked over at her and caught her gaze as she grinned from ear to ear, surpassing the sun with her brilliance. "Of course, Mel. It suits us..." She blushed as she added, "It suits you. And I like it. Certainly, no one's ever called me Mel before."

Och, what was she doing to him? Really? Mel?

THEY TRAVELLED IN BLESSED PEACE FOR ANOTHER HALF AN HOUR after his inadvisable suggestion he call her Mel. He supposed he'd surprised her with his compliance to her proposal, which kept her mind pre-occupied with her own thoughts. So, there were benefits to his mistake, after all, for he was in no mood to converse today.

They rounded a sharp bend in the road and came upon a farmer with his cart stuck deep in a rut.

"Hello, good man." Mel called out to the farmer, who was currently working a shovel into the mud gripping one of his rear wheels. The man paused to lean on his shovel and wipe the sweat from his brow with a dirty sleeve while he grinned over such a cheerful greeting.

"Good morn to you, ma'am. Sir."

"And to you. It looks like you're in a spot of trouble there. Might we assist you?"

"Aye, I could use a pair of strong arms to help me get me wagon unmired from this muck."

"Mel..." he warned. He spoke low, so only she could hear.

She ignored him. "Well, it just so happens I have a set of muscles here you can borrow." She chuckled as she gestured in his direction.

He growled in response to her offer of his *muscles*, but rather than argue the point, he dismounted from his horse and walked over to assist the stranded man. It was a wasted effort to argue with her at this point, and the sooner they were on their way, the sooner he could toss her over his knee for deliberately ignoring his commands. What part of 'Talk to no one. People are after you. We need to make haste' did she not understand?

Never mind that he would never in a million years do such a thing as hurt her, physically.

"So might we have the pleasure of your name, good sir?" Mel called out to the farmer.

"My name's Spencer, ma'am. John Spencer."

"How to you do? My name is Mrs. Chase and this man is Lord MacLeod..."

The man nodded his head to MacLeod, "Milord."

"We're on our way south. Or will be, soon enough," Mel continued.

They were headed north, but MacLeod did not correct her. It seemed she carried some sense to know not to tell this man everything.

"Do you live near here?" she continued.

"Aye, about five miles further up the road and on the right. I live there with the missus and me five young boys."

"How delightful. I bet you see all sorts of travelers on this road."

"Actually, not many, ma'am. We're pretty self-sufficient here, with nothing much but sheep and farmland to be seen. We've barely a town, just a small public house and a church."

As he listened to Mel and the farmer chat, MacLeod dismounted and walked over to assess the stuck carriage, yet in the back of his mind, he couldn't help but feel irritated by her reckless behavior. Sure, she'd misled the man as to their travel plans, but now they were chatting like old friends over tea. He couldn't understand how she failed to understand the seriousness of their situation. His unambiguous warnings from his *'dangerous men are after you, trust no one'* speech should feature prominently behind her every waking decision. Yet she conveniently seemed to forget his counsel whenever it suited her to do so.

Like now.

For certain, they would be addressing this problem in the very near future. His hand itched to give her a good spanking...

"You might want to fit a large branch behind that left wheel." Came a bit of unsolicited advice from behind him in an all too familiar, smoky voice which had recently begun to haunt his dreams. Unwelcome, sensual, erotic dreams. When she spoke unexpectedly and out of sight like that, his mind always delivered him directly to the last inappropriate dream he'd had of her.

Dreams he could not banish no matter how hard he tried.

"Yes, my lady, I have a board in the back of my cart here that should do the trick," answered the farmer, all smiles.

MacLeod climbed into the carriage and retrieved said board; he'd do anything to keep his mind focused on the task at hand and not dwell at the oft exasperating woman behind him.

MacLeod bent to place the board. He was wedging it in when he heard her suggest, "I'd turn it the other way if I were you." He gritted his teeth and carried on with *his* plan.

Just as he'd moved to wedge his foot behind the board to stabilize it, he heard, "I'd place your foot on the end of the board to keep it in place, if I were you."

"Och, Mrs. Chase, if you wanted to help, you could very easily dismount and assist." he snapped, then called to the driver. "Aye, give it a go."

The driver laughed and shook his head before he turned and yelled, "Yah," just as MacLeod noticed a pair of slender arms reach up to push on the back of the carriage...

"Stop!" he yelled, but it was too late. The carriage lurched forward at the same time Mel was reaching for it.

What happened next was inevitable.

Amelia Chase lost her balance and landed face first in the mud.

KELLY OPENED THE NOTE HE FOUND BENEATH THE DOOR OF HIS rented room and held it to the light of the lantern next to his bed.

Black Irish,

    I have information you may find of great use. You might consider making your way to the Bull and Finch...with haste.

        — THE PUPPET MASTER

Black Irish was the code name he only used through his work for the Crown. Very, very few people knew it.

So the Puppet Master was seeking him out? Wanting to talk directly to him? Interesting.

The man was clearly playing some sort of game.

The man knew everything. In fact, Kelly would swear the man knew more than the Crown about what went on in the Kingdom. Hell, he would swear the man knew more than the entire team of agents he worked with, including the Duke of Stonebridge, which had to annoy the hell out of the duke.

This man had eyes and ears everywhere.

In fact, Kelly wouldn't be surprised if the man even knew all the players working within the Society and was simply playing with them all, pitting them against each other. He was a mercenary at the very least.

And Kelly was sure every one of Stonebridge's agents used him as a source, probably under different code names.

Through personal experience, Kelly knew that the Puppet Master was a man who understated everything. Kelly could no more avoid going to the Bull and Finch than he could walk around without trousers in a London ballroom. He'd just have to make a quick trip over and see what his old *friend* had to say.

Though more likely he'd be meeting with an associate, rather than the man himself. And he'd send a woman, as usual. The man seemed to understand Kelly was far more forthcoming with women than men.

Kelly smiled at the prospect.

Chapter Nineteen

"**M**el!" MacLeod scooped her out of the mud and set her gently on the back of the cart they'd just freed. The owner was there almost immediately, reaching out to hand him a relatively clean towel he'd fetched from out of the back of the wagon. MacLeod took it with a gruff, "Thanks," and began to wipe away the mud on Mel's face.

She was silent, for once.

He wiped her delicate forehead, her rosy cheeks, her stubbornly pointed chin, her sharp brow. His actions slowed as he revealed more and more of her soft, sun-kissed skin, along with her host of adorable, brown freckles.

He'd spent long hours counting those freckles, in his dreams.

He took one last swipe at her proud nose and then paused, his hands braced on either side of her legs. She looked back at him, her eyes at first soft and sad; then she searched his, looking for who knew what.

The entire world seemed to pause as she explored the depths of his soul. Then she smiled, a soft sweet smile, and it brought out his old disused one in return.

Then, as if choreographed by God himself, they laughed. Together.

Hers unfettered; his rough around the edges from neglect. Without thinking about his actions, he pressed his forehead to hers, his heart light for the first time in years.

Five years, to be exact.

It had been at least that long since he'd last laughed, a genuine, heartfelt chuckle of built up emotion, freed from its confines at last.

He wanted to stay there forever like that, the moment was so perfect.

She leaned back and peered up into his eyes. "What in the blazes was that sound? Did you just *laugh*, MacLeod?" she teased.

He simply smiled.

Aye, he'd laughed. Out loud. And he owed it all to the charm of this crazy, kind, mad ball of fire before him...who might very well exactly what he needed.

But was he ready?

Hours Later

Och, Mel. She was far too friendly for her own good. When they turned a bend in the road and he spied another carriage up ahead, stalled upon the side of the road, he reached over and pulled on her mare's reins before she had a chance to hail the occupants.

"Mel. You cannae stop to help everyone you meet along the way."

"I haven't."

"Ye have."

"I have *not*."

He held up his hand to count off her transgressions. "First, it was the stranded delivery driver, the butcher, then the maid, then the lost butler, the blacksmith, the shepherd, and now who knows what lies in that carriage up ahead? And I canna fathom how these people seem to make their way into your path. I've no' seen so many people in need of help in ma life. Ye're like a magnet for..." his voice caught, "...lost souls."

"Maybe you've just never noticed before?"

"Well, maybe you should start noticing less?"

"Why? I mean, what is wrong with helping people in need? Look, MacLeod, this is me. This is who I am. I am capable; it is wrong for me not to help those who cannot help themselves."

"That's fine in the normal course of things, but most of those people did not truly need your help."

"So?"

"So?"

"Yes, so. What is so wrong with taking the time to help others? It's fine, MacLeod, really."

"It is not fine when there are men after us."

She laughed. She genuinely laughed. "Do you honestly think Kelly is still going to come after me? I hardly think so, and we've seen no evidence to support his continued pursuit since we started making our way to Greenwood Park. Upon further reflection, I think he was only half-heartedly carrying out his orders. I don't think he really intended me harm."

"How can you be so naïve?"

"Ha! I am hardly naïve, darling."

For a moment, her eyes took on a haunted look. There was darkness in her past. Experiences she had buried deep and refused to discuss. He both wanted to know what she'd seen and wanted to run from it as fast as he could go.

Instead, he came out with the inanest response anyone could possibly utter. "But you're Dansbury's sister." Why that should make a difference, he didn't know. It sounded good, anyway.

Actually, it didn't. It sounded idiotic, to tell the truth.

Amelia waved her hand in the air. "But I didn't know that until recently, so that hardly signifies."

He reached for her reins again. She had him wound up in knots and he knew it. Hell, she probably knew it. "You are far too trusting, Mel."

She turned to look at him, her face grave now. "I'd rather have the courage to believe in the innate goodness of humankind than to be diminished by my doubt in it. Honestly, I cannot live in a world like that—a bleak world where trust doesn't exist. Even if misplaced trust kills me."

MacLeod felt broken inside once more when he heard the pity within her words, but he had to make her see. Misplaced trust could kill. Very much so. He settled on, "I don't have the luxury of living with that sort of optimism. It would be a gamble with more than my own life to do so."

"Pity, that." She appeared genuinely sad about it.

Then, without further ado, she lifted her nose, turned her attention toward the unidentified carriage, cupped her hands to her mouth, and called out, "Hallo up ahead! Are you in need of some assistance?"

Och, she was going to be the death of him.

At the Same Time: The Stevens' House

Ciarán Kelly loved women. *All* women.

Big women, small women, tall women, petite women. Buxom, slender. Blonde, Ginger. Rich women, poor women.

Strong women, even weak women.

He genuinely loved them all. The way they spoke. The way they walked. The way they laughed and smiled. The way they cried, kissed, and batted their eyes.

The way they made love...

No matter what reason he had for being with a woman, he cherished them all. Though at times—and some might call it distasteful—he charmed them into spilling their confidences. Normally, in the name of the Crown.

It almost made him the male equivalent of a whore.

Hell, it did make him a whore. A man-whore.

Alas, he was good at it. At this. Good at charming. Good at sex. Good at making a woman voice her deepest, darkest secrets; he loved them too much, and they responded in kind.

Was it wrong to enjoy a woman's company for a spell, so long as the feeling was mutual?

He never harmed a woman to get at her secrets, he merely applied a healthy, hefty measure of charm. Generally, Mrs. Chase notwithstanding. *That* was an extenuating circumstance.

A soft moan brought his attention back to the woman before him and her long, beautiful back—so soft and feminine. He felt a trace of guilt for allowing his mind to wander away from her.

This woman, Millie was her name, was no different from so many others. She was pretty in the way he found all women, softer around the edges than a man, with a smile to remind him of sweeter times.

Right away, she'd wanted him, and he returned the sentiment. She even wanted to have him the *way* she had him, with him riding her from behind.

Not his preferred way to make love, but alas, who was he to deny a woman her desires?

Kelly took a deep breath, the smell of sex and flowers carried on the breeze, the wind ruffling his hair. The woman he made love to started to shift off sync with his rhythm, and Kelly leaned forward to croon softly in her ear.

"Hold on. Tighter." Kelly stroked the maid's back as he spoke, caressing her with the barest touch.

The maid shifted her grip on the tree before her and held on as best she could.

"Aye, that's it Millie...so good, *bean álainn...*"

"Cor...I...luv...Irish brogue...mmm..." Her broken words in her delightfully soft accent trailed off on a drawn-out moan.

Kelly shuttered his eyes as he continued to love her. He literally couldn't watch his cock as he slid in and out of her warm, wet sheath... or it'd all be over too soon. And that would be selfish; she needed her pleasure, too.

His hips continued their rhythm, moving in and out, in and out, and he tried desperately to focus on Millie. On this warm, willing woman.

But anxiety kept tugging at his mind. Again. Pushing against his concentration and dragging his mind off to a thousand other thoughts and images.

And before he knew it, his mind fixed on a memory of *her*, of his

Charlotte, and he nearly lost his stride *and* his erection. Just like that. Just like he did every time *she* danced across his mind.

He shied away from her memory. Charlotte was lost to him forever, permanently out of his reach. He disciplined his mind to focus on the woman with him now.

This woman, who coincidentally had spoken to both Mrs. Chase and MacLeod and whom the Puppet Master had suggested he find, knew something. Hell, the entire town, particularly the servants, would be gossiping about the unexpected visitors and what everyone knew of their plans. And this woman was a servant.

So perhaps not so coincidental after all.

He refused to evaluate whether he was a bad man for doing this because in truth, he'd enjoy his time with her whether she eventually told him everything or nothing at all.

But ultimately, they always talked.

The maid moaned again and Kelly zeroed in on her and her pleasure.

Her moans became shorter, louder, and more frequent as she neared her crisis. Ahh, God he loved the sound of it, always so beautiful.

All too soon, she began to climax around him, her warm sheath squeezing every inch of his cock. "Ah, that's it, Millie. Let it go. Let it all go."

As the spasms gripping him began to subside, he picked up his pace as he raced to his own finish, pulling out with plenty of time and using his fist to finish himself off.

He would not risk a child being born a bastard.

The maid held on to her tree as she caught her breath, her eyes closed. After a few moments, she turned and flopped to the ground, her bare bottom upon the grass and a giggle upon her lips. Kelly buttoned his trousers and lowered himself to the ground beside her. He leaned back on one arm, all casual and open, and watched her a moment as she fiddled with her dress and looked out over field of wild-flowers behind the Stevens' home.

He could easily sit back and simply enjoy the warm weather, but he hadn't the time. It was a sincere shame.

Kelly sat up, leaned in, and spoke softly near her ear, "So lass, what makes such a charming lady giggle so?"

"Oh, Mr. Kelly, you are a fine bloke as I ever saw, you are." She batted him away, but he didn't budge.

"Ah, ma lass, surely a woman in your position meets many an interesting man. I hardly believe you haven't seen finer or bigger men than I."

"Cor, I must admit I did meet a big giant of a man...'twere only a few days ago. I swear his arms were as wide as the trunk of this tree."

He gave her a disbelieving look. "You jest."

She raised her hand. "Honest to God. He frightened me to death, he did. So much so I couldn't get me mouth to work anymore than saying, 'Cor' or summat." She giggled again at the memory.

"Indeed?"

"Cor, yes. He looked to be a rough and ready brute."

"Rough and ready? A man so big and rough as that? Why in the world would a man like that have need to speak to someone at such a respectable house as this?"

"Cor...well..."

Kelly leaned back on his arm again, his most charming smile firmly in place, and relaxed as the maid told him everything he needed to know. He watched her soft, pouty mouth as she formed the words that apprised him of everything she knew of MacLeod and Mrs. Chase.

Meanwhile, in the back of his mind, the beginnings of a plan began to take shape because there was one thing that was absolutely clear:

He was catching up to them.

Chapter Twenty

The Next Day: Still Traveling

M acLeod and Amelia rounded a bend in the road and pulled to an unexpected stop. A large portion of the trunk of a tree blocked the road. MacLeod pulled on his reins, prepared to go around.

"You cannot just leave it there, Alaistair. What would someone traveling in a carriage do?" What would she do if she were fleeing in a carriage and came upon something like this? Her seemingly selfless actions often had an ulterior, perfectly *non*selfless motive. She was always looking out for number one, growing up an orphan and on the run from one's *crimes* tended to do that to a person.

MacLeod sighed in response.

Well, that was too bad, they couldn't leave a tree blocking the road when it was within their power to move it. MacLeod was a big man. Surely, he could see to it?

He guided their horses off the road and proceeded to dismount, his movements jerky and forced. Amelia smiled to herself. He would do as she asked even though he didn't want to. He hardly put up a fight, in fact. It was the tiniest bit endearing.

He tied the reins to a nearby branch and removed his gloves. Then he removed his coat and she tried desperately not to stare as he peeled the garment from his body. But what a magnificent body it was, all brawn and hard. She knew what it was like to be crushed in those massive arms, delightfully so.

Once finished, he tossed his jacket over his saddle and went to work on his waistcoat, his eyes now locked on her—the entire time. Was he warning her, daring her, or just letting her know he was angry? She couldn't tell. All of the above?

Regardless of what that look meant, his actions had her squirming in her saddle as more and more of his body was revealed to her hungry gaze.

When he began to loosen his cravat, her mouth turned dry.

Still, he never looked away. His eyes, locked with hers, daring her to look.

And she did. Oh God, did she ever.

Finally, after throwing the cravat on top of the growing pile of clothing on the back of his horse, he rolled up his sleeves while he turned to face their wooden obstacle.

It was only then she could finally breathe.

After looking over the situation for a few moments, he stepped forward toward one end of the tree and positioned himself with his legs braced apart.

But as he bent down to grab ahold of the log, she yelled out, "Stop!"

MacLeod stood and brushed his hands together, purposefully, as if he had all the time in the world. Then, he took of his hat to run his hand through his hair once before replacing it on his head. He took his time about it, his movements slow and deliberate.

He turned to her, his face stoic, but Amelia felt his ire—and perhaps a touch of exasperation—burning just beneath the surface. "What nou?" His tone was clipped.

"You should check for snakes. Who knows how long that tree has been lying there?"

MacLeod shook his head and looked away, his gaze settling upon some unknown point in the distance. He seemed to do that an awful lot lately.

"Mel." She almost didn't hear him with his face turned to the wind. "There will no' be snakes beneath this log."

Winnie danced a bit in place as Amelia tugged a bit on the reins; like her rider, Winnie was ready for battle. "You don't know that."

"Aye, A do."

"No, you don't."

"Mrs. Chase, do you see the branches towards the other end of the tree?"

"Yes..."

"How do they look to you?"

"Green and large and—"

"Green'll do. And what do you think that means?"

"That the tree only recently fell?"

"Aye. Good. No snakes, ye ken?"

"Aye...erm, I mean yes."

MacLeod bent down again. Amelia couldn't help but mutter beneath her breath. "Don't say I didn't warn you."

MacLeod dropped his head for a moment, and she could have sworn she heard him growl beneath his breath in response. Or was he laughing? He seemed to do the growling bit an awful lot...around her, at any rate.

She was struck completely mute by the sight of his shirt pulled tight across his expansive shoulders. The next thing she knew, she was imagining all sorts of naughty thoughts while staring at those massive shoulders. She imagined running her hands along the breadth of them, tracing the outline of his muscles with her fingers. She pictured the tension there as he reacted *fiercely* to her touch. She fancied he called her his pet name in that delightful, gruff brogue of his.

"Shite..." MacLeod interjected, interrupting her pleasurable reverie. He dropped his end of the tree as if it were on fire and grabbed a hold of his left hand. He stood stock still, his back to her, his shoulders tense.

Amelia slid down from their horse and rushed over to MacLeod, her ire lit like a spark to kindling. "You churlish, beef-witted lout. What did I tell you?" She grabbed at his hand, but he held it high above her head and then brought it around behind his back. "You were bit, weren't you?"

He glowered at her, but said nothing.

"Scowling at me doesn't change the fact that you were wrong and that you are bit. Let me take a look."

"Nae."

"Aye, you fool."

MacLeod searched her eyes and must have accurately read the determination there, for he sighed and reluctantly thrust out his hand. She could see the two perfectly placed punctures in the beefy part of his palm.

Amelia knew exactly what she had to do.

She pulled his hand to her face, and opened her mouth. But before her lips met his palm, he jerked his hand from her grasped. "What are ye doing, lass?"

"I'm going to suck out the poison, you silly man, what else?"

"You doona need to do that."

"I do."

"You doona."

"Listen here, MacLeod, growing up in America, I know a thing or two about snake bites, and I know that when a snake has bitten you, you must suck out the poison. Now do hurry MacLeod, time is of the essence."

"Yes, well, in England, our snakes are no' poisonous, so it doesnae matter, ye ken?"

She worried her brow and stared at him to ascertain the truth of his assertion. "Are you sure?"

MacLeod growled (again!) and turned to storm off toward his horse.

His contention simply wasn't good enough for her. "Well, bully for you, MacLeod, but I'm not taking any chances." She grabbed at his arm. "Give me your dashed hand, you oversized..." He turned and scowled at her, anger blazing in his eyes. She smoothed her tone in response, as one might with an injured animal one was trying to soothe, and smiled, with a blush and an *innocent* flutter of her lashes. "...fellow."

He practically snarled at her, as if he was an animal, but he thrust out his hand in acquiescence. She grabbed ahold of it and gave him a warning look to cooperate, then looked down at the two tell-tale punctures in his hand. They really were quite small; one could almost miss them if one wasn't looking.

But after all her incessant nagging, as she brought his hand to her mouth, the *intimacy* of her actions became acutely transparent.

At that precise moment, the entire world and everything in it seemed to slow, apart from her heart, for it—that contrary, disagreeable, unthinking organ—began to race.

His hand, just there before her, was large—oh, so much bigger than her own—and rough; the hands of a man who had seen plenty of hard work in his life.

She inhaled in steady, measured breaths, desperate to slow her racing pulse. What she got for her efforts was the complex scent of his very essence, the subtle hint of which sprang from his palm like a smoking candle.

His was an intricate aroma made up of the smell of leather from his gloves and a distinctive scent she'd come to associate specifically with MacLeod, an earthy note that brought to mind the trees in the forest and the soil beneath her feet—a clean and practical scent.

His skin was hot, so much warmer than hers; she could feel the heat emanating from him as she drew his hand near. She had the almost irresistible urge to cradle her cheek in his palm and soothe her wind-chapped cheeks there.

Then, there were his fingers; they were long and broad and strong, so *capable* of work, of strength, of pleasure...

She glanced up into his eyes, as she bent to touch her lips to his palm, determined to see to the task she'd fought so hard to perform.

She was taken aback by what she saw there. His pupils were dilated and sharp with desire. He had zeroed in on her mouth as if she wielded a veritable weapon.

Regardless of the obvious danger, she ignored all the signs she should stop. Instead, she carried on, inching his palm ever closer to her mouth.

He hissed in a quick breath the moment her lips touched his scorching hot skin and her heart jumped in time with the sound.

She closed her eyes then, suddenly unable to do what she needed to do. She was completely overwhelmed by the surge of emotion that flooded her, sensations she'd never, ever felt before with such intensity. She felt weightless and dizzy and warm all over. She squeezed her thighs together, for she tingled and ached in the very heart of her womanly center.

She couldn't stop. She wanted more, so much more.

She touched her tongue to the center of his palm, no longer thinking of snake bites and poison, no longer thinking of anything but him and his skin and his touch.

MacLeod let out an unmistakable warning, "Mel..."

Amelia looked up and was taken aback by the portent in his blazing green eyes. He looked *raw*. He looked *hungry*. He looked *determined*. The emotions swirling in his gaze were almost frightening in their intensity.

Yet she touched her tongue to his palm again anyway proving she wasn't afraid of his fire.

That was the final straw; like the snap of a leather strap pulled too taut, he growled one last time like the beast he was before he ripped his hand free and grabbed a hold of her, his lips descending to hers with unerring accuracy.

Oh, sweet God!

He demanded. He conquered. He assaulted every one of her senses.

His lips were soft, yet commanding and fierce. He reached in for a hard kiss, then pulled back. He turned his head and charged in again, then pulled back once more. Their kiss was a dance and a tease and a force all in one.

He paused in his assault and pleaded, "Oh God, Mel...open up for me, lass."

And when she did, his lips and tongue plunged inside, invading her soul.

Right then and there, he claimed her. All of her.

He refashioned her into someone utterly new.

Oh, God. In the end—the very end—she would never be the same.

She'd already changed.

At the Same Time

"We'll take her when they stop for the night, most likely here. Until then, we'll keep an eye out for them from this vantage point here." Kelly leaned over a crude map of the area as he pointed to the area in question with his knife.

It had taken a lot of interrogation and hard riding to catch up to MacLeod and Mrs. Chase. Kelly suspected he had Mrs. Chase to thank for their success. He'd have to remember to express his *gratitude*.

"What's a vantage point?" asked a small, lanky kid with two few teeth and even fewer brain cells in his head. Kelly tried to hide his exasperation. The men he had to work with were thick. It made him miss working with gruff, hard-nosed MacLeod. The man may have been stiff, but he was also brilliant.

On a positive note, MacLeod and Mrs. Chase were almost within reach; in fact, he would have her as his guest once again before the next day was through.

He rolled up the map and ignored the kid's ignorant question. "I have one more person to speak to, then we'll meet back here in an hour. Be ready to go then. We have at least an hour's worth of hard riding ahead."

The men were all snickering quietly before a particularly foolish man spoke up and related what they were all thinking. "Does this *informant* have plump titties, too? More 'n a man can hold with his bare hands?"

A few whistles, lewd comments, and loud guffaws followed that remark, all of which had Kelly seeing red. He grabbed the loose-lipped man and shoved him against the wall by his throat. "Don't. Disrespect. The women."

The man tried to swallow; his false bravado lost through his penis as he pissed his pants. "I—I—I ain't disrespectin' nothin'," he stammered. Then he *tried* to turn his head to spit on the floor to vouch for his oath.

The point was moot; his answer wasn't the correct one.

One punch to the face was all it took to knock the blighter out.

God, he'd be glad when this was all over.

Chapter Twenty-One

The Next Day: More Dusty Roads

Amelia and MacLeod rode in absolute silence, each lost to their own thoughts. For MacLeod, he would normally be pleased with their mutually agreed upon quiet, regardless of the reason behind it.

But this time, his own thoughts were wholly unsettled.

It'd started with the look in her eyes as she'd brought his hand to her mouth, setting off a swirling heat which began in the pit of his stomach. Her eyes flashed, and the churning had intensified, a maelstrom springing to life in storm-tossed seas.

The feel of her lips to his palm had brought forth another surge of emotion, a flood of passion which seemed to undulate beneath his skin, heaving like giant waves, surging and crashing and surging again as he fought with absolute desperation to rein in his wild desire.

He'd given her fair warning should she continue, his self-control hanging by a thread.

She'd continued anyway, and the resulting kiss had been...staggering. Life-altering. Unforgettable.

Even now, in the morning light of the next day, he craved her. He wanted nothing more than to kiss her again. And again. And again. His hands itched to pull her from her horse and onto his lap so he could lay claim to her pouty lips while his horse wandered where it will. To hell with bad men and secret societies.

To hell with responsibilities.

To hell with his friendship with her brother.

But, alas, these were lines he would not cross. He would never forget his responsibilities nor betray his friend, whose trust he valued immeasurably. It was that thought that kept him from taking things further than a kiss yesterday.

It was that thought which stayed his hand today.

If he wanted her, truly wanted her, he would have to marry her. There was no other way. But could he? Did he want to? Was he even ready?

Could he trust her?

Despite his confidence in his own honor, he understood everything had changed. When they parted—and they would indeed go their separate ways—he would not be the same man he was before; her very being would leave its mark upon his soul. Hell, it already had. It was her kindness. Her ability to laugh so readily. Hell, her ability to make *him* laugh. It was her wit, her zest for life, her bravery. She made him want to be a little more carefree, to rediscover the man he'd been before treachery had taken his brother from him.

But he simply didn't know if he could.

The sound of an animal wailing sliced through his turbulent thoughts, and he instinctively reached for his *sgian dubh*. He pulled his horse to a stop, his stallion's ears flickering and turned toward the source of the sound. MacLeod scanned the trees to his left as his horse danced and pawed the ground.

He couldn't see anything, but he suspected it was a fox. A faint shifting sound had him speaking without once taking his eyes off the forest before him. "Doona even think aboot it, Mel."

He heard her huff of breath, an obvious sign of her displeasure, and he interrupted her before she had a chance to begin her rebuttal, "I've told ye before, ye canna stop to help everyone you meet. That definitely includes wild animals, *especially* foxes, and don't say we've set a precedent because we already picked up the cat."

"But we left him with the farmer," she refuted, as if that made any difference whatsoever.

"And then there was the bird..."

"But we left him with the owner of that public house in the last town."

He shook his head with exasperation as he attempted to ignore the pleading in her eyes. He knew she had the power to sway his mind, to make him reject sound logic.

He continued making his case, "And for the life of me, I canna fathom how you managed to convince the publican to take it, even though I heard it all with my own ears. But, Mel, a fox?"

Mel smiled as if she'd won and turned in her saddle to dismount.

"Doona even think about it, or I will tie you up and throw you over that horse's arse like a saddlebag for the rest of the journey."

She hesitated for only a moment before she slid to the ground with a grin and began picking her way through the brush at the side of the road, one hand holding her horse's reins, the other lifting her skirts.

Och, she was never going to heed his warnings.

"MacLeod, you really need to reconsider your approach to people."

"Is that so?" he called as he dismounted to follow her.

"Yes. Every time we stop at an Inn, you put us in a private room and growl at anyone who enters."

"We're meant to be in hiding; it's for your own safety." He sounded like a petulant child. They were doing a piss poor job of hiding, unless he pretended they were hiding in plain sight. He would never own up to the fact she had him completely wrapped around her dainty little fingers.

But she did. And he knew it.

Worse, she likely did, too. Their journey to check on an injured fox only proved the point.

"If I believed that were the only reason, I'd let this go, MacLeod, but I don't. And we both know it's the truth."

He wouldn't own up to her accusations. He wouldn't!

"You cannot be rude to everyone you meet and expect people to meet your lofty expectations—"

"That is the most—"

A shot rang out, the sound jarring them out of their argument.

"Mel, get doon now!"

Amelia's horse jumped, spooked, then pranced and whinnied with obvious agitation. "I can't. Oh, God, Alistair, my horse, she's bleeding!"

MacLeod ran up alongside Mel and tossed her onto his horse, then climbed up behind her. If her horse was lame, leaving Mel to ride her own put them all at risk. Unless he could asses the seriousness of her horse's injury, which he couldn't with madmen and criminals having caught up to them, this was how it would be.

MacLeod let go of Winnie's reins and headed off at a gallop through the brush at the side of the road.

"MacLeod, we cannot leave Winnie!"

"She'll only slow us down." he yelled over the wind.

Amelia looked over his shoulder, sadness and regret evident in her eyes.

"Lass, Kelly will no' hurt the horse."

"How can you be so sure?"

"I know the mon."

"So you say, but could you have predicted he would turn out to be a traitor?"

She had a point, but he couldn't explain it. He, of all people, would never leave a horse behind if he thought Kelly would harm it. Horses were too valuable, and if the horse were seriously lame, she'd have to be put down, anyway.

He wasn't idiotic enough to point this out, though surely she had to know it.

Together they raced over stone fences and across fields, around shrubs and through the brush. No more shots were fired, but he did hear the occasional shout from the men attempting to follow them. There was more than one in pursuit.

Regardless, MacLeod wasn't worried; he was the best horseman of anyone on the team, including Kelly. He could outrace them even with his unexpected passenger.

Ten minutes later, they made it to the tree line of a dense forest. He slowed his horse and carefully picked his way between the trees. Once safely hidden within cover of the forest, he turned to check on the status of their pursuers. There was no sign of them, no sight or sound to be heard.

Mel was uncharacteristically silent and had been since they first dashed away, leaving her horse behind.

She turned back to look at him, and he touched his finger to her face, lifting her chin. "Lass, are ye all right?"

Amelia nodded but still didn't speak, her eyes downcast. That worried him more than any physical injury might have. "Lass, look at me."

She complied, and he saw the anxiety in her expressive eyes. Eyes he had come to enjoy watching—reading—as she revealed every thought in her mind through their gold-flecked depths.

"Lass, Winnie will be all right, I promise ye."

Amelia nodded once more, then laid her head on his shoulder, unable—or possibly unwilling—to look him in the eyes any longer.

It would be easier to tear out his own heart than to figure out how to deal with this. He would give his left arm to fix it now, though he had to be satisfied with the knowledge that he would see her horse returned to her. Sooner than she could possibly realize, for he recognized this wood.

Aye, they had crossed over onto his own land the minute they'd passed the tree line.

MacLeod waited another ten minutes before he was satisfied they'd lost their pursuers and could safely carry on. To be sure, he walked them along the very edge of the forest in case they had to jump into hiding with little warning.

They were only twenty minutes away now; less than half an hour to find a way to pull Mel out of her misery.

Seeing as how she was Dansbury's sister and how she seemed to share some of his same characteristics, he considered how Dansbury usually broke out of one of his rare moods. It seldom took much effort.

Mel was clearly similar in that regard.

"Mel, look at me." Maybe now that they weren't running for their lives, he would convince her that Winnie was safe. "I know you're worried about Winnie, but you needn't be. I know where we are, we're on my lands. I'll have a man out to retrieve her the moment we arrive."

Amelia smiled, the feel of it not dissimilar from the sun peeking out from behind a thick cloud. "Do you mean it?"

His eyes softened. He touched his palm to her cheek. "Lass, do I ever say things I don't mean?"

Amelia laughed. It was at moments like this he saw her resemblance to her brother. Dansbury had an easy-going temperament as well. The man could be stark raving mad one minute, then carefree and relaxed in the next.

"Truth."

Amelia touched one hand to his arm. "Thank you, MacLeod."

MacLeod touched his forehead to hers once again. "Och, Mel, what are ye doin' ta me?"

Chapter Twenty-Two

Thirty Minutes Later: Greenwood Castle, Scotland

"*This* is your home?"

"Aye."

Greenwood Park was not what Amelia Chase had expected. She was not precisely sure what she had expected, but it was certainly not this quirky, magnificent, but barely capable of keeping the rain out, medieval castle.

Zounds! MacLeod lived in a castle. One that would benefit from one or two minor major repairs, but still, a *castle*.

The uneven walls, the crenellated towers, the MOAT, the small, narrow slits used by medieval archers which probably had a name but she had no idea what it was, the crumbly, moss-covered stones...it was all spectacular, marvelous, breathtaking, awe-inspiring. *Och*, as MacLeod liked to say, she simply didn't have enough words. She couldn't wait to explore every inch of it.

And there was a drawbridge! Yes, it had a blasted drawbridge!

This place had better have a suit of armor, medieval weapons, and some hidden passages, too, or she'd be quite let down.

Oh, and a dungeon. This place *definitely* required a dungeon.

Amelia closed her wide-open mouth as soon as she realized MacLeod was watching her over her shoulder, his expression unreadable, possibly bemused. She straightened her spine, pursed her lips, and crossed her hands on her lap. "I'm sure it'll suffice," she replied, her nose firmly in the air and she, pretending to put on airs.

He snorted in response, and she nearly burst out laughing at the sound of it. He shook his head and looked away, but not before she caught the slight lift of his mouth, indicating a smile had dared to tug on his lips.

Together they pulled up in front of the castle, and she waited while he dismounted, tied his horse to a post placed there for such a purpose, and turned to help her down.

She couldn't stop her groan as she slid off the beast, allowing MacLeod to do all the work of her dismount.

Her arse hurt, dammit. She and her backside would be quite happy if she never sat in a saddle ever again.

Once standing, she hobbled up the stairs. With MacLeod's assistance, of course.

She shot him a disgruntled look as they took the stairs one at a time, and she realized *he* walked normally as if he hadn't been riding a horse for four days straight. At the very least, he should pretend to be in at least a little discomfort.

She was chafed between her legs and had to walk with them spread wide to avoid them rubbing together. She felt like her thighs were on fire, they stung so badly.

It was not ladylike, to say the least, and she began right then to think seriously about placing the blame for her discomfort squarely on his broad shoulders.

The massive oak door opened as they finally reached the top step, and a friendly-looking, elderly man stood there with a wide, toothy grin. His clothes were informal and wrinkled, but in good repair. He wore a loose-fitting Jacobite shirt and a blue and green kilt like MacLeod's, which ended less than an inch above two knobby knees. He wore woolen socks, though one was pulled high to just below his knee and the other sagged a bit in the middle and clung to his leg mid-calf. He had a profusion of wild white hair as white as the clouds in the sky, and all of it scattered and sticking out in every direction as if he'd tried to cuddle up to a lightning bolt. His build was stocky, his nose prominent and hooked, and he was rather short, only a few inches above her diminutive height. But the most interesting bit was his face —it was weathered and wrinkled, but alive and animated, and his eyes were lit with abundant kindness.

Amelia liked him on sight. This was certainly no stuffy, English butler.

"Och, Master Alaistair, welcome home." He said, his love for his gruff lord evident in his very demeanor.

"Mac. This is Mel, erm, this is Mrs. Amelia Chase."

Amelia stepped forward and reached out to shake his gnarled hand. Mac clasped her proffered hand in both of his, but looked at MacLeod with a knowing grin.

MacLeod shrugged his shoulders and looked away as he said, "Och, She's American." As if being American explained everything.

Aye, as MacLeod would say, she supposed it did.

Mac turned back to her, a curious gleam in his eye. "Is she, then? Well, welcome to Greenwood Park Mrs. Chase the American," he said as he continued to shake her hand with both of his. He winked, and his eyes held an extra twinkle that hadn't been present quite so obviously before.

She looked over at MacLeod with a smirk and replied, "Why thank you...Mr. Mac."

"Ah lass, jus' call me Mac. We are quite informal here, for truth we are."

"Why thank you, *Mac*. And you can call me Mel; it's what the big silent ox over there calls me," she said as she gestured toward MacLeod.

Mac was obviously surprised by her revelation, but covered his shock with an even toothier grin, if it could be believed.

Amelia smiled like a cat with a canary and added, "And I think we will get a long quiet well, you and I. Quite well, indeed."

"Och, to be sure, lass. To be sure."

At that, Amelia slid her hand into Mac's elbow and turned him toward the house as she stepped inside on his arm. "So Mac, tell me about this magnificent castle."

They left MacLeod alone on the front stoop.

KELLY MOANED. ONE OF THE IDIOT THUGS WORKING WITH HIM HAD managed to clip him with his shot. His own man. It was a simple graze upon the arm, but at times, even the smallest scratch could be painful if cut across the skin just so. As this one was.

He'd have to call for Megan downstairs to tend to him for he probably required a stich or two. The thought left a smile upon his face, despite his *failure* to capture his quarry.

A knock on the door interrupted his musings upon the very accommodating redhead down below.

"Come in."

A footman in unfamiliar livery entered bearing a note. Kelly stood and grasped the letter, ignoring the footman, who simply turned about and left, as he opened and began to read:

Irish,

We need to meet. Himself is most displeased. You are to ride to Carlisle with all due haste. Present yourself at the Hairy Goose Inn five miles west of the city by sunrise tomorrow.

— X

Evening, The Same Day

When Amelia came down for dinner that evening, she expected to be taken to some colossal medieval dining room with a table to sit sixty, possibly with a fireplace large enough to fit four MacLeods standing shoulder to shoulder within the firebox.

Instead, she was taken to the kitchens, which suited her just fine. She honestly preferred intimate and cozy over vast and cold.

Its fireplace wasn't quite tall enough to fit a standing MacLeod, but it would fit about ten MacLeod's bent over at the waist and standing side by side!

And there were two of them. Two fireplaces, that was. It must have been something to see in medieval times when it was new, not like it was now, darkened with over three hundred fifty years of soot and grime.

To her surprise, MacLeod was already seated at the head of a small dining table. To his right was an empty seat, presumably hers. Mac was next to the empty chair to the right. She nodded her head in his direction when she saw he noticed her, and he winked in return.

An older woman, "Mrs. Mac" as she was introduced earlier—the housekeeper, organizer of maids, and head cook, basically the woman who did it all and held this place together with her more than capable hands (they got along famously)—sat across from Mac, her back to Amelia.

To MacLeod's left, with his back to her, as well, was a man with short reddish hair sitting in a wheeled chair. She, admittedly, was surprised. She hadn't realized anyone else of note to the family resided here in MacLeod's castle.

She stepped further into the room, and MacLeod stood with alacrity, his simple wooden chair scraping the stone floor and echoing off the stone walls, his face tight and focused.

Mac, on the other hand, stood with more care, slowly and with some difficulty as he was getting on in years. *He* wore a large grin planted firmly across his face, his white hair still in wild disarray. She was beginning to suspect it stayed that way all the time. Even directly after a combing.

The man in the wheeled chair couldn't stand, of course, but he did turn back to look at her.

And Amelia's stomach dropped into her feet as she met familiar green eyes.

She unconsciously stepped forward and might have stumbled as if literally tripping over said stomach. She honestly didn't know, as surprised as she was. For there, in a chair designed for people unable to walk, was a man who was the exact image of MacLeod.

His twin.

Not a parent. Not a son. Nor a cousin or nephew.

A brother, an identical twin brother.

He didn't speak, and of course, he couldn't stand.

After her initial surprise passed, she quickly noted that there were, in fact, some subtle differences between the two men. The brother so closely resembled MacLeod, a stranger would have difficulty telling them apart, yet upon further reflection, she could see that his face did not wear the hard edges characterized by MacLeod's focused intensity. The brother's face was soft and open, speaking of a relative innocence by comparison.

"Mrs. Chase." said MacLeod.

"MacLeod." she returned.

He held his hand to her as if beckoning her to his side, and oddly enough, she placed herself there, by his side, as if the action were the most natural thing in the world to do. She turned to face MacLeod's brother, a genuine smile upon her lips.

"Mrs. Chase, may I introduce to you my brother, *Alain*..."

MacLeod's voice softened when he spoke his brother's name, the sound almost a whisper with far too much emotion tumbling out alongside the word. She heard love in those two syllables, and more. Heartbreak. But far worse, despair.

She waited a moment for him to speak, but he only smiled back at her. So she said, "It's a pleasure to meet you, Alain."

MacLeod leaned down and spoke quietly in her ear, his breath warm and sending shivers through her body. She looked up to him, caught the look in his eyes as he said, "Lass, he canna speak."

Chapter Twenty-Three

T he bottom fell out of her world.

Or at least, it felt as if it had. God. Just when she thought she had it all figured out, this.

Oh, MacLeod.

She'd caught one glimpse. One stupid infinitesimal glimpse into his eyes a mere moment after he'd introduced her to his brother, and what she saw there ripped a hole in the fabric of her reality. For one fleeting moment in time, MacLeod looked broken and *exposed*.

She could scarcely conceive of a world in which a man like MacLeod could be vulnerable. It was all wrong, as if she'd woken up to find the sky painted green and the grass blue, and pigs flying about with wings of glass. It made her desperate to soothe and support him. To be his friend, his steady rock. To fix him, putting everything to rights as it should be.

MacLeod's vulnerability was gone in an instant, replaced by the stalwart man she'd come to know and respect.

God, what must it be like to have a twin you couldn't speak to? Or share jokes with? There would be no discussing the hideous waistcoat he might have received for Christmas from some senile aunt, nor whether the latest news from France was accurate or a bundle of lies made up by the government.

They couldn't talk about that fish that got away. Or what they should get their mother for her birthday.

They could no longer do all the things that siblings, particularly twins, do.

MacLeod helped Amelia to the only vacant seat at the table. She was relieved for the distraction as she was at a complete loss for words while her mind spun about, flitting from one thought to the next and never latching on to any one thing for more than a moment.

Her lips felt like cracked earth, so she reached for a glass of water and drank in great big gulps until she'd banished the sticky dryness from her mouth.

In the midst of a million other random thoughts were a jumble of competing emotions. She wanted to wail; she wanted to scream. God, she even wanted to laugh. *How crazy was that?*

She wanted to reach across the table and punch MacLeod in the nose for being so enigmatic and tight-lipped about himself, about his life.

Who would blame her? He'd never—not one single time—even hinted at a brother, especially a twin brother. And certainly not one with some level of disability. It made her fully aware she knew very little about Alaistair MacLeod, and that fact bothered her to such a degree she wanted to excuse herself from the table so she could hide in her room and examine her feelings from every angle, poking and prodding them until she'd explicated them all to death in her mind.

She and MacLeod had been through so much, had spent so many days together—*months,* even.

And the most ridiculous thing about it all? She was a damned hypocrite, for all that.

Aye, as MacLeod would say, *crazy.*

Once MacLeod returned to his seat, he reached for the platter of roast beef before him and began to carve off slices of meat. There were no footmen on hand to perform the task—or even to serve them at all, for that matter.

Thank You, God.

She'd always felt uncomfortable in the past when seated at a table with servants to cater to her every desire, and every single time she'd felt the pressing need to talk to them rather than ignore them as everyone expected her to do.

MacLeod turned to his brother, and with a voice so soft she'd have thought it came from someone else had she not been watching him speak, asked his brother, "Would you care for some meat, Alain?"

His brother studied *her* while he nodded his head and answered, "Yes."

But I thought...?

"*Yes* is the only word he can say." MacLeod bit off as if he'd read her mind.

She looked at MacLeod and frowned at his obvious change in tone. He was surly now, like a wounded animal.

Yes, exactly like a wounded, vulnerable animal.

She heard a swift thump, followed by a grunt from MacLeod, who looked sharply at his brother before turning back to her and offering, "My apologies, Mrs. Chase. I did not mean to speak so disagreeably," in a much more congenial tone.

Amelia looked to Alain, who gifted her with a very charismatic smile and a wink.

A *wink*.

That small gesture stunned her absolutely. Amelia blinked, it was all she could manage for a moment. She swallowed the newly formed lump in her throat and returned his grin with one of her own.

"Och, so tell us, Mel, have you enjoyed your visit to our shores?" inquired Mac while everyone saw to passing around the remaining side dishes, filling their own plates as desired.

Amelia ladled a spoonful of peas on her plate. "It has certainly been interesting, thank you for asking."

"Go on with ya," said Mrs. Mac, her name was Mairi, then added, "You've been travelin' with this here silent beast, I'd say interestin' is a wee bit of an understatement, if ye ask me." Then, she laughed loudly, a long drawn out guffaw that spoke of confidence and a carefree disposition, clapping her hands in glee.

Amelia couldn't help but smile and revert to form. She passed the peas to MacLeod. "Well, let's just say that I firmly believe his brutishness is all a cover. He's really a big ole softy. I'm rather convinced he'd prefer to be wearing pastels with lace and dancing in drawing rooms in gold knee breeches if he could have his way." She winked at Alain.

Alain laughed out loud, catching everyone off guard for a moment. For two ticks of a clock, one might have heard a pin drop. Then, as quick as if someone had snapped their fingers, they all joined in with companionable laughter.

Well, everyone except MacLeod.

MacLeod finished ladling a spoonful of peas on his plate then asked his brother, "Peas, Alain?"

There was the soft tone again.

Alain said, "Y-yes," but shook his head no.

To that, MacLeod said, "Of course." He stood and brought the bowl of peas over to Mairi.

Chapter Twenty-Four

Later that Night: MacLeod's Study

Amelia threw open the door to MacLeod's study, slammed it shut again, and strode across the room as if she owned the place, which didn't surprise him. He could finally admit it; he found her confidence attractive.

She was captivating in her fury, so much so that he didn't stand upon her entry into the room—and didn't even notice that he hadn't until she was all the way across the room. By then, it was too late and fortunately, she didn't really care.

When she reached his desk, she threw her hands on her hips and said, "You didn't tell me you had a brother," in a tone that was quite accusatory.

He almost laughed at the flash of fire in her eyes. Almost. Instead, he ignored her outburst, picked up the top letter from the pile of mail on this desk, and proceeded to open it as he said, "Och, there's a lengthy list of things I've not told ye, Mel."

He eyed her briefly when she reached forward, placing two small fists on his desk. She bent low over said fists, looking him square in the face. "Such as?"

He didn't look at her when he said, "I was engaged once."

That remark was met with silence. He looked up just as she collapsed into a chair. No graceful seat. A full-on collapse, her face stunned.

Eventually, she asked, "How long?"

"Five years ago."

She tapped her fingers on the arm of her chair, having regained some of her shocked composure. "And where is she now?"

"Dead."

Amelia's hand flew to her throat and she swallowed. "I see."

He looked at her then, the devil pricking his temper. "Nae. You don't. Her name was Delilah, and she was a traitor. A traitor to England." He didn't add, *and to me*. "In case you were wondering what kind of man you're dealing with—in case you were thinking you could reform me—I'll have you know I watched her hang, completely unmoved by her pleas for a pardon."

A million thoughts seemed to flit across her face. She appeared confused for a moment, and she frowned. He wanted to ask her what she was thinking, but he wouldn't. He couldn't.

He didn't want to admit, even to himself, he was afraid to know. That he wanted to take back what he'd just acknowledged lest she judge him and find him lacking, which was absurd.

Amelia stood and leaned over the desk once more. "So, now you're cross with me again?"

He looked back to his letter. "Nae."

And it was the truth. He wasn't. Not really. He felt edgy of a sudden. Like his shirt was too tight and everything around him was just *off*. He hated the feeling. Like any man, it made him grumpy. He decided to throw himself into work to distance himself from his discomfiting feelings.

Feelings he was loathe to review. He wouldn't...at least, not yet.

Rubbish. That was an utter lie; he'd thought of her ceaselessly since the moment they met. And when he wasn't dreaming about fucking her senseless, or simply caressing her until she fell asleep in his arms, he was thinking about every single emotion she wrenched from his soul, all with apparent ease and all without his consent.

His response clearly did not please Mel, for she let out a *"Humph,"* and rounded his desk. When she reached him, she stepped between his seated self and his work, pulled the letter from his hands and tossed it behind her, then leaned back against the desk, blocking him from his pile of correspondence. She crossed her arms and tapped out a melody with her dainty, yet impatient, foot.

He looked down so she wouldn't see his smile, and his gaze stayed pinned there until he had his revealing grin under control. Once he was able, he explored her stance from her tapping toe all the way up to her sentimental gaze. He saw compassion there. At least it did not feel like pity.

When their eyes met, they stared at each other for a long, drawn out moment. Her foot slowed, then ceased its incessant tapping altogether. In fact, everything seemed to still as if the world held its breath, waiting. A thousand words flew between them without either one of them making a sound.

She called to him, this strange and difficult woman, with her American ways and her open smile.

Without saying a word, he spread his legs wide, her legs between his knees, caging her. He slid forward in his chair and pinned her to the desk as he wrapped his arms around her waist and rested his head against her stomach, his cheek cradled by warm woman and pillowed by the softness of her feminine body.

He felt her fingers in his hair.

He closed his eyes, feeling as if the world had finally shifted back to normal. A world which had truly ceased to be normal five long years ago.

Now, this incomprehensible, open, determined, bright-eyed woman had stepped in and turned him inside out. She forced him to see her. To think of her. To know her, despite his ever-present desire to distance himself from others, especially women.

Particularly from women who were sister to one of the few people he called friend. Because honestly, he didn't trust himself to keep her happy should they decide to make something more of this—thing— between them. If they did, he would have to marry her, of course. But he just didn't know if he could ever trust her—or anyone, for that matter—enough to *keep* them content, for eventually, that distrust would eat away at their relationship and with it would come misery for them both.

Then, Dansbury would kill him in truth and rightfully so.

"Do you want to talk about it?" she asked.

"Nae." He meant it. Besides, when did men ever want to talk about it? He hoped she didn't press him, for he now knew she had the power to make him confess even his darkest secrets. His deepest desires.

And honestly, there were no words to be said, no words he *could* say. Right now, her arms were simply comfort for a man starved for affection.

He was truly ravenous for it.

And it wasn't long before her soothing, supportive embrace wasn't enough.

It might have been a shift of his arm or a twitch of her knee as she adjusted her position, but whatever the cause, he slowly became aware of her curves—voluptuous lines and edges that flared and contracted. She was a heady combination of sensual beauty and fierce independence. Och, she fit him just right. On top of all of that, there was her warmth and her womanly scent. Together they painted a complete picture that accurately described everything he'd ever desired in a lass.

God, he should have predicted this end. How many nights had he woken to tangled sheets as he recovered from a heated dream involving him and this very woman in his bed? Still, he ignored the danger of her temptation, though perhaps it was intentional on his part as he daren't acknowledge his guilt.

It no longer mattered. He was gone.

To a point.

He turned his head and kissed her stomach, a light but lingering kiss that whispered of a need he'd buried deep for a very long time.

Dare he acknowledge it? Dare he allow his need for this woman to overcome his fears of distrust? This was his friend's *sister.*

He felt her fingers tighten in his hair as she pulled him closer, an unspoken approval of his actions.

He accepted her tacit consent and stood then, slow and steady. As he did, he skimmed his hands up her sides, feeling his way, learning her shape so he could remember it in the future when he was once again alone. He framed her breasts, then continued up and over her shoulders and gently, ever so gently, caressed the sides of her bare neck.

God, her skin was so soft...

He cupped her cheeks, cradling her face as if he could capture her essence in the palm of his hand.

She reached up and touched her fingers to his and her eyes—*oh, her eyes*—he could have fallen into their depths and resided there for an eternity. He saw in those dark orbs an endless well of longing.

It was his last thought before the dam broke, and he claimed her lips with his own.

Passion exploded, ignited by their kiss and fueled by the pent-up desire that had been rekindled and building for days. Months, even. His lips explored hers, learning once again their full, plump shape and their sweet, addicting taste. He rediscovered the corners of her mouth, the full pillow of her bottom lip, the defined edges of her upper. She opened to him and he dove in, his tongue greeting hers and stroking— no, dancing—in a tangle of burning want.

She moaned as her hands tousled in his hair at the back of his neck, her fingers driving him wild and urging him higher. His hands left her face and wandered down and around her waist until he could lift her up on his desk. He laid her back, scattering his papers and mail to the floor as she descended, a reckless, desperate response.

She settled back on the soft inset leather of his desktop, and he studied her a moment, committing every detail to memory as he prepared to worship this woman who had somehow managed to coax her way into his life.

He had Mel laid before him: his desk, her shrine. How often had this scene played out in his dreams?

Far too many times to recount.

He knelt before her, humbled by her—her perseverance, her wit, her passion. Slowly, she sat up on her elbows to watch as he ran his hands up her quivering legs, lifting her skirts along the way.

"Doona move."

She rubbed her foot along his arm and smirked, then blew him a kiss.

He smiled. He couldn't help it. For one moment, he read astonishment in her eyes.

Were they truly so rare, those moments when he shared a smile with her?

Too soon, she returned his smile with her own and laid back, spreading her legs as she went, opening herself to him. A gift he would cherish for the rest of his miserable, lonely life.

He continued working her dress up, higher and higher, kissing a path up her legs along the way as he followed the edge of her dress with his lips. He caressed her lightly in between kisses, raising gooseflesh on her curvy limbs. He heard her laugh and felt her squirm, and he realized she was ticklish, his touch almost too much for her to bear.

He tormented her further, kissing and nipping, but never enough to make her pull completely away.

Finally, he neared the pinnacle. His aim, her core.

Scandalous woman. She wore no drawers; nothing impeded his way towards his goal. He inhaled slowly, taking in the smell of her arousal

Her arousal for *him*.

He dove in. His tongue found her pulsing nub while his fingers unerringly found and filled her sopping wet core.

Oh, God, she tasted divine. Sweet and salty and one hundred percent ambrosia.

He feasted. Relentlessly. Like a man starved for food. He licked with the tip of his tongue, then sucked, then licked and sucked some more. All the while thrusting his fingers in and out, then quirking his finger just so to hit that spot deep inside, the one that had her arching her back in an urgent, desperate plea for more. She whimpered now, no longer able to restrain the vocal manifestation of her need.

It made his cock jump with every burst of her erotic song. Again, with every thrust of his finger. His hips moved of their own accord, mimicking the rhythm he set.

All too soon, her whimpers became faster, higher, and he knew she was near. He latched onto her nub, sucking hard while she tensed for one heart-stopping moment...

...and then toppled over the edge with a raw moan that sent fire racing down his spine. On and on, he suckled her as she bucked helplessly against the leather, her legs tightening around his neck until he thought she'd break his damn neck.

Her fingernails bit into his scalp and it was all he could do not to join her in release. Still, he carried on tonging her pearl, dragging out her orgasm until the sensations became too tense, and she pushed at his head.

He pulled back, slowly, the smell of her sex lingering in his nose. He closed his eyes. *Ah, nectar of the Gods, indeed.* He would never forget her smell, her unique taste. For the rest of his life, it would color his dreams.

He helped her to sit up and straighten her skirts. Their eyes met and they laughed as they observed the obvious mess of each other's hair, a result of their wandering fingers.

She turned shy of a sudden, which was a bizarre demeanor for such a bold woman. "Can I...?" She looked toward his kilt, tented with his barely leashed desire. He knew what she was asking.

He pulled her close and cupped her face, looking deep into her eyes. "Nae, lass. No' yet. I need...I need more time."

He did. He wasn't ready. This was a gift for her. For bringing light into this life once more.

Besides, taking it further meant the connection would be too deep, more personal. He wouldn't be able to pull back—to guard himself—once they crossed that line.

Even now, it may already be too late.

Chapter Twenty-Five

Morning, A Few Days Later: The Back Gardens, Greenwood Park

Amelia lounged back, propped up by her elbows, across a tartan blanket laid out over a lush field of grass, her face lifted toward the sun. She could feel the heat of its rays as they kissed her skin. She took a deep breath, the air fragrant and fresh, and tried her damned best to capture a sense of inner peace off the gently blowing breeze. She trained her ears and could just make out the rustle of leaves from distant trees and the sounds of birds singing amidst their branches. That and the drone of a distant bee added to the idyllic setting, reminding her that, like it or not, life carried on, despite what troubles might haunt a person's soul.

Truly, it was a glorious day to be outside, and she would look to any casual observer as if she were utterly at peace in her repose. And it all would have been thoroughly perfect if other, weightier matters didn't persistently tug at the back of her mind. Harmony was an elusive myth that teased her, riding out of reach on the wind. The thought of it brought a few light tears to her eyes.

How long had it been?

Amelia shook her head and squeezed her eyes tight. For one perfect moment, she *would* forget...or at least, pretend to do so.

Amelia took a second, deep breath. Oh, to capture one more nugget of tranquility before reality intruded, that was all she wanted. Really, how long had it been since she'd felt so safe, despite everything she knew to be going on outside these grounds? Five years? Ten?

Had she ever?

Lord Sharpe had claimed she could trust MacLeod. And she did; there was no question about it.

On top of all that, memories of MacLeod—a man so thoroughly stoic, yet passionate in the heat of his love-making—taunted her. His touch had sizzled across her skin, making her feel boldly sensual and beautiful. Despite the decadent desire she had seen in his eyes and felt in the heated glide of his hands, he remained quite untouchable. Still, there was *something* drawing them together, an attraction neither of them could deny.

This morning, Amelia had Alain for company while MacLeod attended to business of some sort or other. Regardless of his difficulty communicating, Alain was an absolute delight to be around. At times, they sat in companionable silence, with not an awkward moment to be felt between them. Never mind that inside, she valiantly fought the intrusion of unwanted memories.

At other times, she had more than enough to say for them both. Of course.

Though the atmosphere was sublime, *this* morning more than her own troubles imposed upon her thoughts.

Amelia glanced over at Alain, so like his brother in looks. He, too, had raised his head toward the sun. He might have favored his brother exactly were it not for his easy-going manner and slighter build, having not walked for some time. Still, his legs were strong for a man bound to his chair, which was an odd notion, considering.

She wanted desperately to ask him about it, though it was deemed by anyone with any sense of propriety to be rude to enquire. Would he take offense at her boldness if she were to do so, anyway? MacLeod certainly would. But somehow, she didn't think Alain would.

Even though she was somewhat hesitant to broach the subject, she couldn't resist, her curiosity, as usual, getting the best of her.

"All right, Alain. I have a question I've been meaning to ask you." She picked at her blanket as she spoke, the action betraying some of her discomfort at asking so personal a question.

She chanced a glimpse at Alain. He looked down at her, his brow raised in question and an easy smile on his face, encouraging her to continue. "I've noticed you have some strength in your legs? Was it me or did you not kick MacLeod under the table at dinner the other night?"

Alain held up both his hands as if to say *guilty as charged* and said, "Yes," followed by a laugh.

Interesting.

Amelia rolled onto her stomach and rested her chin in her hands, his positive response giving her the courage to be bold. "As I thought. So, can you walk? If only a little?"

Alain shrugged.

"Having that sort of strength implies you can, at least physically..." she hedged.

Alain shrugged again.

"Would you be willing to try...for me?"

Alain studied her for a moment, and Amelia held her breath while she awaited his decision. It seemed an eternity passed before he cracked a smile and dipped his head, only once, but a definite yes.

"Really?!" she all but squealed with delight. As she'd fretted over this puzzle last night, she'd hoped beyond anything that he'd agree to try. As it was, she could already feel tears welling in her eyes at the thought of this man succeeding in such an endeavor. Sometimes she was such a watering pot.

Amelia jumped up, excitement and more than a little hope lifting her heart. She didn't know whether she was more excited to see Alain succeed, or to see the hope in MacLeod's eye when he learned of Alain's success.

She watched as Alain released his footrests so they would be out of the way. She loved that there was no hesitation in him once he'd made up his mind. How alike MacLeod in that respect.

Once stowed, he looked at her intently before pointing to the wheels beside him. She followed his gaze and heard him say, "Yes?"

Guessing his intent, she asked, "Do you want me to hold the chair steady for you while you stand?"

He smiled once more, pleased, and dipped his head with an obvious, "Yes."

"Oh, all right, then." Amelia stepped before him, rather than behind. "I'll stand before you like so, thus if you feel the need to steady yourself, you can grasp my shoulders or my arm as needed." She braced her legs in case he required to do just that.

Alain nodded, and his look turned serious as he concentrated on the task ahead of him. Amelia's heart raced with anticipation. She imagined the joy she'd see on MacLeod's face when he finally saw his brother stand again. She closed her eyes, briefly, and prayed with all her might that this would work, a lone tear escaping down her cheek at the thought.

She always did wonder at her propensity to become teary when she was happy, or in the grip of strong emotion.

Alain began to slide forward, his feet searching for purchase on the stone walk. He shuffled them a bit before finding the precise way he preferred.

Amelia watched his feet until they stilled, then she looked up, square into his eyes. "Ready?"

He nodded, not a single hint of hesitation furrowed his brow.

"Right then, on three?"

He nodded again.

"One..."

He gripped the arms of his chair right behind where hers held onto this chair for dear life.

"Two..."

He scooted a bit further, his jaw clenched and determined, so remarkably like his brother's.

"Three!"

Alain, though shaky and slow, pushed himself up and out of his seat. He took the time to secure his legs, and for a moment, she thought he would fall back, but then he lightly touched one hand to her shoulder and with a renewed surge, steadied himself completely.

They stood there for several minutes, his smile as bright as the cloudless noonday sky. Hers matched his equally, she was sure. He was doing it! He was standing, his touch only light and there purely for reassurance.

She smiled at him, tears of joy welling up in her eyes. "Oh, Alain, you did it!" She crooked her head, wondering at his ability to do so on his first try.

Amelia twisted her lips with a knowing smile, "You've been practicing, haven't you?"

He shrugged, but then nodded, a twinkle brightening his eye. Right then and there, she was almost overwhelmed by this man's courage and strength. That he could smile and remain so confident and easy-going despite his disadvantages was humbling.

And more than a little curious. "Had you planned to show Alaistair soon?"

He scowled a moment, but nodded anyway. She was confused by this; why would he hesitate to show his brother what he could do?

If he had been practicing, perhaps he could do far more than she'd first considered. "Do you think you could take a few steps forward for me?"

Alain hesitated, but for only a moment, his gaze on the ground. He looked up at her and nodded once, his confidence secure.

"All right, then. On three again?"

Once more, he gave her his habitual single nod, coupled with a gentle squeeze to her arms. This time he held on to her, lightly—almost reverently—with both hands. She held onto his waist in return, as if they were preparing to waltz, rather than seeing whether this man could walk. If only.

Amelia locked eyes with him, focused. "Great. On three, we'll take two steps—you forward, me back. One...two..."

Alain made to slide his foot forward.

"...thr—"

"No!"

Her count was interrupted by an absolute roar of fury from across the green.

Chapter Twenty-Six

MacLeod roared as he bolted across the lawn, but he was too far away and far too late. He watched helplessly as Alain tried to take his first step and then, as predicted, came tumbling down on top of Mel, both of them landing in a heap upon the rigid stones beneath them.

Stones that could crack a man's skull in a matter of seconds.

MacLeod leapt over a hedge in his path as he raced the shortest distance to his brother and his...Mel, barely breaking his stride and never slowing in the least. It felt like it took half an hour to reach them, though in reality he was there in a matter of seconds.

What were they thinking?

He reached for Alain first, who was on top, and as gently as possible, lifted him and set him in his chair using his foot to hold the chair in place so it wouldn't roll away from them. Fear commanded his muscles, making him stronger than ever.

Still, he took a moment to lean down and look his brother in the eye, his voice far steadier than he felt. "Are you all right, Alain?"

His brother clenched his jaw, his own frustration and anger apparent, but he nodded his head once.

MacLeod, relieved, touched his hand to his brother's cheek, a light scrape the only evidence of the mishap.

He turned to face Amelia who was still lying on the ground, watching, a wary frown upon her face.

After quickly ascertaining she was in perfect health, he saw red as he reached down to help her up. "What in the hell do you think you are doing, Mrs. Chase?"

His voice was raw as feelings of rage and fear warred for prominence.

Of course, she wasn't cowed by his roar. No, of course, not. Not his Mel. She stood toe to toe with him, fists on her hips and anger sparking from her eyes.

"It should be obvious what I was doing; I was helping your brother to walk."

"Aye, I could see that much. But once more, you demonstrate your inability to make sound decisions. Are you mad? Alain is far larger than you. This ground is uneven. How could you even think to do something so reckless, so careless?" His fear and anger had him lashing out, his normal reticence lost to emotional warfare.

She crossed her arms. "Well, someone had to see to it."

He was taken aback by the accusation coloring her tone. "What in the hell is that supposed to mean?"

She jabbed her finger in his chest. "It means I think that if you had honestly tried, if you'd honestly *allowed* it, your brother would be walking now, completely on his own. He has the strength for it."

She couldn't have stunned him more completely if she'd punched him with one of her balled up fists. Still, fury won. "First, it takes more than physical strength to manage walking."

"Sure, but do you even let him try?"

For a moment, no one spoke. Her accusations hung in the air, a dark cloud stinging him with truth.

Unfortunately, anger made a mess of a man's reason, and he refused to acknowledge her direct hit. Instead, he leaned forward, they were nose to nose now, and in a voice that vibrated with rage, he dared her, "What are you implying, Mrs. Chase?"

She took a moment to consider her response; she seemed far more sensible than he at the moment, though he shied away from acknowl-edging the truth of it.

Eventually, she said, "I'm not implying anything. I'm telling you that you need to quit trying so damn hard to keep him safe." He must have expressed his shock at her intuition for she added, "Aye, I've been watching you two for days now and talking with the staff, which I know you don't like. And before you get all bent out of shape, they respect you and love you, which at the moment I can scarcely under-stand why. Still, it didn't take a genius to figure it all out."

Her insight did nothing to calm his rage, yet all he could manage was, "You doona know what in the hell you're talking about."

"Don't I?"

The stared at each other in silence, each one holding on to their ire with a stubbornness more unshakeable than an ornery mule.

Out of nowhere she blurted out, "I want you to take me to my brother."

He jerked as if she'd slapped him. It almost felt like she had. At the very least, it felt like a punch to his gut; he nearly doubled over in pain. He held his ground while his mind raced through all manner of irra-tional thoughts. *She wants to leave me? She doesn't feel safe here?*

Ultimately, one word, one thought, rose above all the melee and refused to be ignored.

No.

It didn't matter why, just, *no.*

He said it aloud as well. "No. I won't allow it." He crossed his arms to signal his immovable conviction.

"You...you won't *allow* it?" her eyes rounded with surprise and disbelief.

He might've been in the wrong with his outright refusal, but the tickle of fear, the irrational sense of loss that accompanied the thought of her leaving, stayed his tongue like a vise, despite how angry he was with her at the moment. He refused to admit he'd erred, even to himself.

Now he'd decreed his command, his anger subsided somewhat, yet in its place was something he hadn't felt in years: heart-stopping fear. Fear for the safety of those he held dearest. Fear for Alain.

Fear for her.

It made him unreasonable. He knew it.

He didn't care.

"Aye, I forbid you to contact him. You are not allowed to step one foot outside of this castle until I deem it safe."

He might have gone too far. Still, he refused to rescind his decree.

She glared at him, a frightening mix of anger and sadness. She stormed off, taking his heart, his pride, and perhaps all his good sense with her.

He watched her walk away, too stubborn, too ornery, too prideful—and too resolved—to call her back.

He felt a tap on his shoulder.

Surprised, he turned around to see his brother standing on his own.

Even more astonishing was the sight of Alain, the one person he held closest to his heart, as he drew back his fist...

...and punched him right in the face.

Chapter Twenty-Seven

Later that Day: In the Kitchens

"MacLeod is a nobcock. An artless, hasty-witted, scut."
Whack.

Mrs. Mac laughed as Amelia devoted herself to the task of chopping carrots for dinner. They were supposed to be having beef stew...if Amelia didn't ruin the vegetables, of course.

Whack.

By all appearances, Mel was preparing root vegetables for the stew, but in her mind, she was hacking away at one ornery Highlander.

Unfortunately, in her manic *enthusiasm*, she was making an utter mess of said vegetables; they'd end up with mashed carrots and mushy potatoes at this rate.

Regardless, Mrs. Mac did not chastise her for her zeal, and instead, commiserated with the sentiment. "Och, he can be at that, lass. He can be at that."

Amelia looked up, gripping her knife and brandishing it about as she spoke. "Sometimes, I want nothing more than to punch him in the nose." She punctuated her threat with a jab of her fist, then a mighty *whack* as she returned to her task.

Mrs. Mac chuckled with a smile. "Aye, lass, I'm sure ye do."

Whack.

"Who does he think he is? He's effectively holding me captive against my will."

Whack. Whack.

"Och, lass...ye ken he wouldn't do such a thing if he didnae have reason?"

Whack.

"No, Mrs. Mac. I don't. Because he doesn't confide in me about anything." *Whack.* "Besides, I'm a woman grown. I have been on my own for many, many years and lived to tell about it. I don't need his brand of protection." *Did she?*

Whack. Whack. Whack.

In her state of anger? No, she didn't.

Mrs. Mac put her hands to her hips, her stirring spoon still in one hand, and stared at her. "If ye truly believed that, then why are you still here?"

Whack. Whack. Whack. Whack.

Amelia threw down her knife after that last attack on the vegetables. Then sat back and considered the cook's pointed question. Why didn't she leave? Because she was afraid? Yes and no. This was as good a place as any to hide from her troubles, but she was a survivor. She would survive on her own. She could also go to Viscount Sharpe or Dansbury, if she so desired. She could find a way.

So if that wasn't it, why?

Because she didn't truly believe her own accusations. Because he was hurting, inside, and she understood that pain; she'd been there before. Because he didn't trust easily, and she understood that, too. Because they had kindred souls, both having faced hardships many would never in their life experience and couldn't fully comprehend— and because of *that*, until she explored this connection between them fully, she would stay.

But she couldn't explain all that to the cook. So Amelia ignored the pointed question.

One look at Mrs. Mac, and she suspected she didn't need to answer her anyway. Cook already suspected the truth. Instead, she returned to discussing MacLeod's faults.

She picked up her cleaver. "Doesn't he realize I might be more understanding if he would simply learn to trust me, to tell me what is going on? No, don't answer that. But doesn't he realize that over-protecting—not only me, but his brother, too—is wrong? It's stifling. It makes one feel like a child. It's practically asking for us to rebel. I don't take too kindly to a man who feels he has the right to tell me what to do, to deny me access to my family."

Whack.

Mrs. Mac simply *mmm'd* in response, a telling remark despite the lack of specific words to define her thoughts on the matter. Amelia had to hold still so as not to squirm in her seat with guilt.

She had no reason to fear her own culpability.

Fed up, Amelia threw her knife down on the table once again and turned on her stool to face the cook. "But why, Mrs. Mac? I mean, why is he this way?" She thought she understood, but she wanted to hear confirmation from someone who knew him better and who loved him anyway.

The cook sighed, and answered her, all the while continuing to stir the stew. "Och, lass. Alaistair is an intensely private man. Ye must ken that by now."

Amelia snorted. "Oh, I know it, I do. And funnily enough, I even understand. To a point." That was a little disingenuous. She understood it, a lot.

Mrs. Mac ceased stirring the pot and turned to stare at her, really stare. "Do ye lass? Do ye truly?"

Undeterred, Amelia responded honestly. She waved her hands as she spoke, as she was wont to do when she was passionate about something. "Yes, I do. He is the most remarkable man I've ever met. I can see this, even though he likes to keep that side of him buried deep. Even though he likes to posture and command—all to keep us safe, mind, and too overprotected for our own good."

Mrs. Mac turned back to her pot and let loose another chuckle. "Aye, ye've the right of it, lassie. The man puts everyone else before his own needs, too."

And like that it fully clicked for her. MacLeod was afraid. Afraid if he didn't protect everyone he loved, he would lose them. Like he almost lost Alain.

Amelia stood and joined Mrs. Mac at the fireplace, leaning against the brick surround and rubbing her arms for comfort. "The truth is, I find myself wanting nothing more than to reveal that side of him, the man few people have the good fortune to see. Strangely enough, at the same time, I want it all to myself, which is not...*me*. Does that make any sense?"

Mrs. Mac threw her a knowing smile. "Aye, it does." Then her face dropped, her kind eyes turned serious, "But lass, ye must be careful. Alaistair is not an easy man to care for. Not since...the accident. He—"

Amelia held up her hand. "Mrs. Mac...don't. I don't think...I mean..." Amelia sighed, her thoughts confused and chaotic, her emotions fighting with her head over this stubborn, ridiculous man. "Am I right? Isn't this all a façade? A cover for a deeply caring man?" Never mind she was now back-stepping, contrary to her rant against him.

Mrs. Mac shook her head. "Aye. I know the truth of what ye speak. I've known the lad for a long time now. When he loves, it is profound. Unfortunately, he has a streak of stubbornness worse than an old ass to go along with it. But know this, if you betray him, he will never, ever forgive you."

That's what I'm afraid of.

"But..." and Mrs. Mac smiled, a pleased, hopeful twist of her lips, "...I'm thinking ye may be exactly what he needs."

But was she? She had plenty of her own secrets. Would MacLeod find her past a betrayal?

Unfortunately, Mel already knew the answer.

MacLeod stepped back into the darkened corridor outside the kitchen, ashamed of himself for eavesdropping, and for the truth they spoke of his faults. He even understood their feelings on the matter.

Regardless, he could not let go. He couldn't put them at risk, vulnerable to his enemies. In his line of work, the people he cared for were at risk. *Always* there was risk. Alain's disability was living proof of that. It was why he was so secretive; it was just to protect his own selfish heart from betrayal.

And if anything were to happen to either of them, he wouldn't survive it this time. He knew this. He couldn't bear the pain again.

Chapter Twenty-Eight

Two Days Later

Amelia walked the first floor of MacLeod's castle with a spring in her step despite her apparent captivity and her unreserved frustration with the master of this magnificent abode. Today, she was pushing Alain in a wheeled chair. He was a charming, enjoyable companion, much more so than his moody, churlish brother. Alain gestured magnanimously to every tapestry, painting, odd nook, or statue they passed as if to regale her with the history and its purpose here—without words, of course.

There wasn't a lot to see, in truth. All the walls were stone, as were the crooked and uneven floors making up the meandering halls. Every room was cool and drafty apart from the plush, red carpeted runner that flowed down the center of every hall.

She joined in Alain's impromptu fun, remarking with astonishment as she pretended to 'hear' him tell her all about whatever artifact or architectural feature was in view at the moment.

They laughed and laughed.

Bemused, she realized she was likely his perfect companion, for she had no trouble carrying on both sides of their conversation, requiring minimal input from him. It certainly seemed to suit them both just fine.

And it was quickly becoming clear Alain was fully aware of everything going on around him. Perhaps more so than any of the rest of them, with his watchful eyes and astute listening. She supposed one became more attuned to their surroundings when one's mind wasn't occupied by thinking of what to say next.

Certainly, Alain paid attention.

They came upon a particularly boring stretch of the hall, devoid of anything in the way of ornamentation save for the torches lining the walls for light. With nothing to remark upon, Amelia introduced another question that had been circling in her mind since they met. "Alain. I do apologize for being so nosy, but your brother...well, he's not much for opening up about his life and the people in it." They both laughed at this. "But I must ask...have you always been chair bound and unable to speak?"

"Yes," Alain shook his head no. Obviously, he meant no, though he was unable to say the right words.

If he weren't such a lively man, her heart would break right open for him. What must it feel like to know the words you want to say but not be able to say them? It must be frustrating, indeed. *God*, that had to be an understatement. She tried to imagine it and failed; it was too much.

And per Mr. Stubbs, Alain's nurse, Alain suffered the same problem with writing.

It was a testament to Alain's character that he maintained such a jovial disposition in the face of his challenges.

"I wish there was a way for you to tell me what happened."

Alain pointed to his head in an unmistakable sign of a gun at his temple.

"You were shot?"

"Yes." Alain nodded in confirmation.

Amelia walked on in stunned silence a moment, a thousand questions coming to mind. She reached the end of the hall and made to turn left, but Alain reached back and brushed her hand, before pointing to the right.

"All right, if that's what you want, then." She chuckled as she changed course.

"So I presume you were shot in the head and ever since you have been bound to your chair and unable to speak what is on your mind?"

"Yes," he confirmed.

"So, let's see, what happened to get you shot, then? Hmmm...were you fighting a duel over a lady's honor?"

Alain chuckled. "Yes." He shook his head no.

"No? Well, then...I know! You were captaining a ship...a pirate ship...and you were hit by a stray bullet while plundering another merchant ship for its bounty." She giggled between words, his good nature contagious.

Alain laughed harder. "Y-Yes..." he said, but shook his head no and wiped at his eyes.

"Not that either, eh? Well, then. Let's see... You were rescuing a damsel in distress who was captured by a pirate king!"

They both were laughing in fits and giggles now. Well, at least she was. Alain's laugh, while good natured, was still heartier. Healthy and full. "Yes." Again, he shook his head no.

"Well, phooey. Ooh! It was a spy mission gone terribly wrong."

This time Alain did not laugh. He spoke, though his tone was the most subdued she'd heard from him since they met. "Yes."

Of course.

All of the sudden she knew, or at least she could imagine. MacLeod was involved. He had to be, for hadn't Lord Sharpe told her MacLeod was a spy?

Did he carry some measure of guilt in his heart? Is that what tempered his demeanor and weighted his words?

Oh God, what a burden to carry upon one's shoulders!

She walked on in silence, her and Alain both content to tend to their own thoughts for the moment. Her steps echoed against the stone walls, while his chair squeaked a chorus of mousy chirps with each rotation of the wheels. Theirs were the only sounds now, a solemn tune for their thoughtful qualms.

She was brought back to the present when Alain's hand brushed hers once more. He pointed to a closed door to the right.

"You want to go in here?"

"Yes?" This time his tone was different, as if he were asking a question and not confirming her statement. She gathered this must mean she was half right.

"You want me to go in, but without you?" she hedged.

Alain smiled then, and said "Yes," with absolute conviction.

"I see." And just as she began to wonder about how she would ever find her way back here through this maze of a castle, because she certainly wasn't going to go in and just leave Alain sitting out in the hall, Alain's nurse came walking around the corner with suspiciously perfect timing.

"Mr. Stubbs, hello." She smiled as he neared.

He was a tall and broad, dark man, who hailed from Manchester, though his family was originally from Africa. He still spoke with a harsh Northern accent, but he wore a genuine smile and had the brightest teeth one might ever see; a full set appeared in a magnificent pearlescent display whenever he opened his mouth. He had a kind demeanor which put her immediately at ease, the kind of soothing presence that was the hallmark of all the best nurses.

Mr. Stubbs was strong and capable, able to carry Alain if the occasion required it, and he was genuinely affectionate and careful with his charge. Respectful, even.

Likewise, Alain seemed satisfied with his nurse, who appeared most times to be more friend than servant.

"Mrs. Chase, Lord MacLeod," said Mr. Stubbs in greeting.

Hearing Alain called MacLeod was startling. But she supposed it was technically correct, it was just strange hearing Alaistair's name on someone else after so many months of just knowing one MacLeod.

"Mr. Stubbs, you are just the man I needed to see."

Mr. Stubbs smiled at that. "Oh, is milord not holding up his end of the conversation again?" he joked.

Alain, who had leaned on his hand, propped on the arm of his chair, smiled at the good-natured jest.

She placed her hands on Alain's shoulders. "On the contrary, I'm afraid Alain might have grown weary of the sound of my voice. I do tend to carry on so."

They all laughed at that, while Alain began rubbing at his ears as if to soothe the pain.

"Lord MacLeod, are you ready to return to your rooms then, old friend?" asked Mr. Stubbs.

"Yes." A definite yes, that.

"See? I told you. He seems intent on me seeing this room, but says he doesn't want to go inside himself." Strangely, Alain tensed beneath her hands.

Mr. Stubbs glanced over her shoulder at the door, his eyes widening ever so slightly before he looked to his charge.

"Milord, she cannot. You know he wouldn't like—"

Alain, somewhat agitated, maintained his desire. "Yes," he interrupted, his tone commanding and firm.

Amelia looked to the unassuming door, curious now as to what lay behind it. It was a grand, dark-stained oak door that appeared to be in rather good repair apart from a touch of rust around the latch.

Mr. Stubbs sighed. A reluctant acquiescence, if she'd ever heard one.

Amelia moved to stand before Alain. "I guess I'll see you later, then. Thank you for a lovely morning. I enjoyed it immensely." She was determined to see this room now, and was reluctant to give the well-meaning nurse a chance to talk her or Alain out of it.

Amelia held out her hand. Alain took it, but rather than give her hand a shake as she'd intended with her American ways, he pulled her hand to his lips to kiss her knuckles with effortless gallantry, smiling all the while.

"Yes," he said in agreement.

Mr. Stubbs looked as if he would say something, but thought better of it.

"Mr. Stubbs?"

"It is nothing, my lady. Just...take care."

"Of course. I'll see you later, then?"

"I look forward to it."

She watched the men as they walked off down the hall, a frown on her face.

What an odd conversation.

Chapter Twenty-Nine

A melia turned toward the closed door, more curious than ever.

And that was saying something considering she was far too nosy for her own good at the best of times.

But Alain clearly wanted her to see this room, and see it, she would, even though she was now a touch concerned about whether it was safe for her to walk through that door.

Would it change her life? Anger someone? MacLeod, perhaps? Ha! Probably.

Well, it mattered not, she simply had to see for herself. Sure, it was the kind of decision that had brought her trouble in the past; she knew it and embraced it.

Amelia engaged the latch and shoved at the door, which was unlocked but somewhat stiff from infrequent use. The door scarcely moved with her first push, only enough to expose a small gap between the door and its frame, but it was enough to show the room behind glowed with a brilliant light.

The edges of the door appeared to glow white, a bright contrast from the dark hall and the even darker door. After prowling the dim halls of this castle for the better part of an hour, it almost hurt to look at it. Still, Amelia continued to push at the door, slowly increasing the gap and revealing a larger and larger beam of sunlight. She could clearly see dust motes dancing in the rays, stirred up from her efforts with the door.

Eventually, she opened enough of a gap to squeeze through and into the room beyond.

The room was certainly bright—so much so, she had to shade her eyes until they adjusted to the change.

The first thing she noticed were the eight large windows standing sentry on the far, south facing wall—the obvious source of the over-abundant light in the room. She followed the line of windows, realizing that the room was long and curved, presenting almost like a gallery of sorts.

Or a gallery in truth, for as she stepped further into the room, Amelia could see that it was filled to the brim with art in various mediums. Paintings—some oils, some watercolors. Sculptures in both clay and marble. Silver figures. Brass figures. So much talent, hanging from every wall and covering every surface.

Hundreds of paintings lined the walls, in some cases the canvases were simply leaning against the wall on the floor, eight pieces thick. There were wooden tables covered in splattered white linen every-where, most of them jutting out from the wall opposite the windows, creating short aisles with their precise positioning. There were at least fifteen small corridors in all, or thereabouts. And on the tables were various sculptures, mostly of animals.

She followed the room by walking along the windows, her eye like a child in a sweet shop unable to stop to look at any one thing for too long—there was simply too much to see. She wanted to touch every critter represented in clay and marble, sometimes silver and cooper. She wanted to stare at every painting for hours, while she made sense of the scenes and the emotions they conveyed. The room, the sight of it all, was both shocking and an absolute marvel all at once.

As she passed the fourth window, she was startled to spy MacLeod at the far end, standing before a work table wearing a threadbare kilt and an old shirt, all of it covered in various colors of paint and what appeared to be dried clay.

He wore no cravat, and his shirt was missing a few of the top buttons. It hung loosely revealing a small sampling of his chest. His kilt had threads dangling around the bottom hem, along with larger strips from being ripped at some point in the past.

And upon his nose, perched there quite unexpectedly, were a pair of spectacles. He stood frozen in place, paused in the act wiping his hands on a length of linen, his head dipped so he could watch her from above the top of the rims of his glasses.

She licked her lips. *Goodness.* She never realized she would find a pair of glasses so—alluring.

It didn't take a genius to fit the pieces together. "Are these...yours? You've done this? All of this?"

Her question seemed to spur him to action for he resumed wiping his hands on the cloth, cleaning them of bits of clay. "I dabble, aye."

The man was amusing. Dabble was quite an understatement.

She broke eye contact, suddenly aware of the intimacy of her trespass upon his private domain. Uninvited.

This place—it was so personal. These were not pieces of art on display in the public rooms of his home. This was his studio.

Her eyes landed on a large bed against the wall off to the side, untidied, but inviting and very *present* in the space. The swirl of emotions dancing around inside her mind began a faster jig at the sight.

She jerked her eyes away, though they landed right back on him. He'd turned away and was hanging his cloth on a bar at the end of a nearby workbench.

She hadn't seen him for more than a few scarce moments since their argument on the lawn two days ago. It was as if he had gone into hiding, leaving their quarrel open and unresolved.

He turned to face her and against her will, her focus dropped to his lips. She recalled—for probably the thousandth time in as many seconds—all the erotic things those he could do with those lips.

He could glide them across her skin with reverence before he kissed her tenderly on her neck, on her shoulder, or on her cheek. He could form them into soft pillows or into intractable, hot iron as his mouth danced with hers, demanding or coaxing per his will. He could brand her as his while he traced the line of her legs, her thighs.

And he could bring her to the height of ecstasy as he stroked and caressed her core while she lay there, writhing in heat across the surface of his desk.

She felt a telltale surge of moisture between her legs as the memory resurfaced in surprisingly acute detail.

No, not surprising, really, considering how many times she'd relieved the entire event since then. And *oh God*, she was more than ready to do *that* with him again. And again. Oh, how effectively could they make use of the bed so conveniently available...

But he wasn't ready; he'd said as much that day with no sign since then to suggest he'd changed his mind.

Amelia jerked away and turned her back on him, lest she give him no choice in the matter. Dash it all, she needed to say something, else she'd climb his body right there in the middle of his workspace, his preferences be damned.

Amelia squared her shoulders and looked around the room with more than a little respect. She was awed by his talent and intrigued at this latest glimpse into MacLeod's hidden depths. He never ceased to surprise her.

Her eye caught on a painting of a London scene. She walked over for a closer look. Oh, yes, she knew it was London from the familiar buildings making up the skyline in the background. But this was not the usual landscape committed to canvass by the average London artist. This work, like the man, was dark and gritty, the mood brooding. The street in the scene was clearly in a very poor part of town, possibly St. Giles. The cobbles were dirty and puddled, soiled with rivers of filth running along the edge of the lane. Beggars in ragged clothes squatted in front of dilapidated houses, most too poor and downtrodden to even look up at passersby in the hopes of a little charity. Many of the homeless were young, clearly children, who should have been playing and smiling, but who instead carried the weight of a thousand lives in their eyes.

His colors were muted and unsaturated except for a weed, a thistle caught in a sunbeam. It stood tall and almost reached for the sky. Its colors, from the leaves to the flower, were vibrant and brilliant amidst all the grey and dirt.

But it was clear that the weed was only moments away from being trampled by the careless step of a man in a kilt, walking with his head turned to the side, not looking where he was going.

And no one else on the street appeared aware of the impending doom.

There was no question the man in the painting was MacLeod. A self-portrait of a broken man.

She wanted to weep for him. Weep for this man who cared so much—too much—and shared so little. What must it be like to be gifted with the love of a man like that? It made her heart yearn for even a small taste.

Amelia was barely able to breathe for the thought of it.

She turned around and peered in his eyes, eyes which held their usual intensity, but with perhaps a tinge of worry and a hint of doubt.

She hated to see that. She never wanted to see it again.

She knew her eyes were bright with the threat of tears. She reached up to touch his face as the first tear fell.

"MacLeod, I..."

MacLeod covered her hand with his, closed his eyes, and leaned into her caress, effectively halting whatever she had intended to say. Hell, she no longer knew.

When he spoke, it was barely a whisper. "Mel. I'm sorry. Though it pains me to say this, everything in me screams in protest, I want ye ta ken: Ye can leave if ye want to. I will take you to Dansbury, if that is your wish."

She was floored. And honored. And pained to hear this. She suspected she knew what it cost him to offer her her freedom.

She studied the crease across his forehead, the tight squeeze of his eyes, his firm but gentle grip on her hand. The signs were there, whispering—no, exclaiming—his need, his *desperate* need, for companionship and affection, for someone simply to confide in. How long had it been? How long since he'd opened his heart to another?

She stood to the tips of her toes, sliding her hand around to the back of his neck, and pulled him down for a kiss; her answer to his offer of freedom.

The moment her lips touched his, she saw fireworks flash in the darkness behind her eyes. His lips were soft and hot. His breath smelled of MacLeod, warm with a hint of spice and a touch of mint. His beard was somewhat rough against her skin and it all colluded to enhance her essential need to taste him more fully.

She licked his lips, and he opened his mouth on a groan.

The touch of his tongue felt like home.

His hands wrapped around her back and pulled her close; her heart sung at the feeling. This was right.

His warmth enveloped her, secured her. She needed him, and she knew that he, in turn, needed her, too. And oh, God, how she wanted him to need her!

It was at once too much and not enough. And she knew, at that moment, she wanted to remain in this very spot, in his oh-so-capable arms, for a lifetime. Might as well set out a table and a bed and mark it with a grave, for she was never, ever leaving.

MacLeod shifted and Amelia could feel his arousal through her clothes as his hard cock slid against her stomach, unfettered as it was beneath loose folds of wool. Without giving a thought to whether she should, Amelia reached down and lifted the edge of his kilt, exposing him to the heated air about them.

"Mel..."

"Shhhh...let me..." It was all she could manage before she slipped to her knees. She kept her eyes on his almost as though she was afraid to see the proof of his desire. To see longing in a man who felt as deeply as Alaistair MacLeod was...daunting.

And, oh, did he want her. His eyes burned hot with desire and his hands shook with ravenous need. His breath sawed in and out as if he'd run the length of a race track for hours, never breaking stride to rest.

Still, she never broke eye contact as she unerringly slipped his hard-throbbing cock into her mouth.

"Oh, God," he ground out, one big hand sliding around to cup the back of her head.

Amelia whole-heartedly concurred. His eyes burned hotter, if possible—his craving, his *need* almost painful in its intensity. His head tilted back on a wave of desire so intense, she felt the echoing throb in his cock with a flair of hardness, a twitch of desire.

She sucked him then, and an answering pool of wetness surged between her legs. His pleasure, hers.

Both his hands came around to cradle her face, gently, reverently. And his thighs, which she squeezed with both her hands, the better to hold herself in place, twitched with restraint as he tried desperately not to thrust into her mouth.

"Mel...God, Mel..."

He murmured her name like a benediction with each suck, and her heart leapt knowing this man was so completely undone by her own hand, her mouth.

Before too long, she felt him harden to solid rock and knew that his crisis neared. He was no longer able to keep from pulsing his hips. His hands squeezed and relaxed repeatedly, cradled around her head, but never forcing her to continue.

She reached up to cup his balls and he stilled, but then tried to pull back.

She wouldn't allow it. All too quickly, she grabbed ahold of his ass and pulled him tight to her mouth as his cock erupted down her throat. It was a magnificent release and indicative of days of pent up passion and she was thrilled to be the one who brought him to completion.

The King George Tavern: Near Carlisle, England

Kelly was led to a private room by a giant ogre of a man with small, beady eyes and no visible teeth, not a typical drawing room dandy, to be sure. Once inside, Kelly studied the room and its lone occupant.

It was obvious the room was normally bare of ornament, utilitarian and sparse. Nevertheless, the man sitting in a chair by the hearth had arrived with a surfeit of his own personal luxuries, which blanketed the room's practical features like an ill-fitting mask. Gold-threaded cloths were draped over one of the inn's battered dining tables, another swathed a crude side table by the hearth. More gold-threaded and heavily tasseled cushions were precisely positioned upon a wooden bench and a rickety, three-legged stool situated by the fire. Underneath it all, a thick, Aubusson carpet covered the floor at the man's feet but couldn't completely hide the scrapes of over two hundred years of chairs and boots being dragged across bare wooden floors that peeked out from beneath it like unraveled threads of wool.

The man waiting for him wore gloves and formal wear. He was meticulously combed and clean shaven, yet he strove to appear relaxed as he sat back in an overstuffed chair likely brought with him in a second wagon for just such a purpose.

Kelly briefly wondered if the man supplied his own bed as well. Certainly, he had brought his own linens.

When the man finally spoke, his voice rasped and grated like a hundred-year-old man who'd been smoking for decades, certainly not the booming voice Kelly remembered from his youth. It was jarringly at odds with the man's assiduous toilet.

"I'm beginning to think you have no desire to succeed. If I didn't know any better, I would question your loyalty to our cause." The old man wasted no time with social pleasantries.

If only he could tell the man what he *really* thought.

Kelly's jaw tightened, the only outward sign of his anger. "I am still your man."

"That certainly remains to be seen. I don't understand how an insignificant American woman managed to escape one such as you, a master spy? I find your explanation of the events leading up to her escape suspect and utterly fantastical." The man studied the gold-rimmed glass in his hand while he spoke. The amber liquid within glowed, catching sparks of light from the fire as he turned it this way and that.

Kelly smiled. When he spoke, his voice was a smooth as the scotch he knew the man sipped from his monogrammed glass. "Do you really think I would put everything on the line here to save the life of one American?"

"Well, it certainly made me question your reputed capabilities, if not your loyalty."

"The tart got lucky."

The man sneered. "Tart? That's an interesting descriptor. Did you seduce her? Or perhaps she seduced you?"

"Neither. She's not my type."

"Too much like you, then?"

"Ha. Perhaps." Tired of the direction of this conversation, Kelly crossed the ridiculous carpet and relaxed against the wall beside the fire. There were no other chairs in the room save for the bench at the table, else Kelly would have sat, invitation or not, putting them both on an even level. He put his hands in his pockets, sending an unmistakable message of confidence and untroubled calm. "But enough with this line of questioning. Despite the unfavorable outcome, my actions have met with some success. Dansbury has certainly taken note."

"I don't see how you can see this as anything but a failure! Absolutely, Dansbury has taken note and is now on guard and out for vengeance."

"Ah, but that can work to our advantage, don't you see? He'll be after me now with nothing but retaliation in mind, which means we can lead him where we want him to go."

The man smiled a cold, calculating smile. "Indeed, we can, which is precisely why you're here."

Chapter Thirty

Late the Next Day

Mel followed a well-worn path with an eye out for an older barn further afield from the stables. Or in Cook's words, 'that wretched, well-loved ancient pile of scrap wood what's known as the Hospital.'

Yes, she was on the hunt for MacLeod. At the 'Hospital'. She supposed she would find out what that meant, precisely, when she found it. Also, per Cook, she would know it when she saw 'that woefully misbegotten but favorite of all places' place...*er*...it.

Amelia hadn't seen MacLeod since yesterday's *assignation* in his art studio. She suspected he was avoiding her while waging an inner battle between his honor, misguided though it was, and his attraction. Well, she was prepared to settle his dilemma once and for all.

But, obviously, she needed to find him first.

After speaking with Cook for half an hour this morning, Amelia had finally worn the woman down and gotten her to confess where she might find MacLeod and the general location of the afore-described 'Hospital', which Amelia, if she were as 'fortunate as a pack of hounds in an untended kitchen' might find some distance away from the main stables. Then, Cook had sent Amelia on her way with a basket of bread and cheese, a full bottle of wine, and a promise to keep any 'good-for-nothing, nosy visitors' at bay.

Had she mentioned she really liked MacLeod's cook?

Now, after walking for at least twenty minutes—minimum—after passing the stables, Amelia finally found what she was thought was the 'Hospital', or what remained of it, at the base of a small hill on the far side of a field of wildflowers.

It was definitely an old barn, or used to be. It appeared as if it had been built sometime in the last century, or earlier, and had clearly seen better days. At the very least, it qualified as ancient. The wood was rotting and colored a weathered gray. By contrast, the roof appeared to be wholly intact. At least it looked as if the building would keep the rain off one's head.

Though perhaps not the wind.

Numerous pieces of siding hung at odd angles and the path leading up to the front door was...well, *well-worn* was apt and a touch of an understatement. Needless to say, Mel took her time to pick her way down the uneven path leading to the front door.

Mel stopped before the barn's faded, red door and blew out her breath. A mere moment to gather her wits was unquestionably warranted. Amelia had never backed away from a challenge in her life, and Alaistair MacLeod constituted a challenge. There was nothing for it. Amelia rolled up her sleeves (figuratively), lifted her chin (literally), shifted her basket of goods to her left arm (she was right-handed), and reached for the rusty circular door pull, grabbing it securely with both hands.

Suspecting a door this large would as be stubbornly difficult to open as its owner, she pulled at it with all her might, her basket bumping her leg awkwardly.

All too quickly, the door gave way quite soundlessly and worse, unexpectedly, and...

...She fell on her backside for all her efforts.

It seemed the large faux-derelict door opened quite easily after all. *Well.*

Amelia blew her hair out of her eyes and glared at the offending door. It hung open on smooth, sturdy, probably well-oiled, hinges. Of course.

Drat it!

She awkwardly scrambled to her feet.

After brushing her hands together and smoothing her skirts, Amelia patted at her hopelessly failing coiffure all the while looking about to see if anyone had noticed her decent. It was never too late to ascertain if there were any witnesses to one's mishaps.

Nearby, a mare with a mouthful of hay watched and chewed, showing as much interest as a person seeking wonder in drying paint.

She patted her hair once more and called out, "A fine day we're having."

In response, the mare bent down in search of more food.

Pppth.

Turning her back on the mare, Amelia looked about for her lunch and found it nearby, upright and entirely intact. *Thank God.* She retrieved it, then strode purposely for the now open doorway and stepped inside.

The interior was remarkably bright due to the presence of what seemed like a hundred or more candles lit along the central corridor. Fortunately, there was no obvious signs of hay to make such illumination a potential fire hazard.

As she pulled the door closed once again, Mel heard a distinctive Scottish brogue shout out in the distance, "Doona you even dare—" This was followed by a strange chirping noise.

Well, it seemed Cook was right; MacLeod was there after all.

Amelia took care to step quietly down the main corridor, determined not to alert him to her presence until she was ready. She wasn't afraid, not really. She was feeling quite feisty, truth be told. Feisty, but cautious. She just wanted a moment or two to see him utterly at ease before alerting him to her presence. That was all.

She could see his shadow moving about in the distance. He was in a little alcove off to the left of the main aisle.

When she reached the niche, she carefully peered around the corner, only to witness something she never would have believed possible: MacLeod, shirtless, tending to and comforting, with profoundly gentle hands, no less, a fox.

As she approached the table, he spared her a quick glance and an almost shy smile, then carried on attempting to bandage the fox's leg.

She stopped across from him and set her hands gently upon the table. "Is that my fox?"

He peeked up at her once again. "Aye," came his gruff reply. He looked down once more; one hand now cupped the fox's head and the other held the new binding in place. "Will you...?"

Amelia reached for the excess bandaging and began tying off the makeshift dressing. "Why? I mean, How?" She didn't quite know where to start.

"I sent my man for him when we arrived."

He ignored the why. She suspected she knew why, though he would never admit it. Not yet, at any rate. But the very idea made her heart leap.

When she finished tying of the cotton strip, Amelia looked up to find him staring at her. His eyes spoke a thousand words he might never say. Best of all, he didn't need to speak. Somehow, someway, they'd reached a point where words were unnecessary.

And suddenly, everything fell into place. Him. Her. Them. Oh, yes, *them*. She—*oh, tarnation*—she loved this man. She loved the way he was reserved in speech. The way he protected his friends, his family. The way he loved his brother fiercely. The way he was closed to most people but burned hot beneath the surface with physical, raw strength, oh-so-tightly leashed. He was *everything*.

And altogether impossible.

Tears threatened, but she willed them away. Impossible was for another day.

The fox chirped then, an adorable sound like a child at play, and they both burst out laughing. MacLeod lifted the fox and carried him over to an empty stall, placing him on a tiny pallet of blankets in the corner. Amelia followed and watched, mesmerized by his gentle handling of the injured creature. The fox licked MacLeod's hand and once more Amelia had to fight back tears.

When had she turned into such a watering pot? Was this what love did to a woman?

MacLeod stood then and turned to her. "Mel..." his voice was so soft when he spoke. It compelled her to look him in the eye and right then and there, she tumbled over the edge in love with him all over again. For what she read there, vulnerability over being found to be so tenderhearted towards this fox coupled with a flash of defensiveness, possibly in the event she chided him for it (knowing how many men were sensitive to that sort of thing), was too compelling, too lovely, too endearing to ignore; it made her heart surge with love.

She leaned up at the same moment he looked down, and their lips met, the kiss instantly pulling her out of reality and into a world where only the two of them existed. An Eden of such beauty and volume that it could never be contained in this earthly realm. She ached for it all to be real, for them to be able to forget reality—with its unsure future of spies and brothers and traitorous friends—and simply be with each other.

The kiss quickly turned passionate. Flames ignited her to the point where nothing with this man could ever possibly be wrong. Her hands slid up his chest while his slid down her back and cupped her arse. Oh, how glorious to feel the warmth of his hands through her dress, caressing and comforting her bottom.

He pulled her tightly against him and she could feel the strength of his erection as it pressed against her abdomen.

The fox yelped again, reminding Amelia of where they were. Certainly, no place for a rendezvous. She stepped out of his arms and glanced up, expecting him to be laughing with her at the untimely interruption.

Instead the air around them crackled. He took a step forward. She retreated one step back. His eyes flashed with raw heat and desire as he stalked her with predatory intent.

Her heart galloped, enjoying this new game of cat and mouse.

He stepped forward again. And again. Walking now. Closing the distance. Still she retreated until her back hit the wall of the stall across the way. He stopped inches before her, his breathing hard as if he'd run a marathon, not walked across an abandoned stable.

Slowly and with infinite care, he reached up and pulled out one of her remaining hairpins. Then another and another, until her hair fell loose and free. She watched him and stood utterly still while he saw to his task. He spoke not a word as he undressed her, focused in that intense way of his on his mission. As if this was his sole duty in life.

She could have left at any moment. Fled him and his passionate intensity. She knew that. But she wanted this. Wanted him.

Tomorrow was another day.

Macleod reached both his hands into her hair and massaged her scalp. It felt wonderful, still she kept watching him, reading the emotions he didn't bother to hide as they flitted across his face. Desire. Awe. Respect. Love.

It all humbled her, yet made her heart soar.

Slowly, he leaned forward and whispered, "Turn around, *a ghràidh*."

She did as he bade, bracing both hands against the wall as he began to undo the buttons at her back. As her dress loosened, she could feel her skin becoming more and more sensitized to his touch. She tried not to squirm as his fingers brushed her back once, twice, thrice. Too soon, she couldn't bear it, and she began to squirm in earnest. And laugh. And scream.

She heard him chuckle behind her, then he leaned forward and held his hands firmly (thank God) on her shoulders as he whispered, "Ticklish, are we?"

Such a tease. "Y-y-yes. Very."

She shivered once again.

"Good," he said on a long exhale. Right in her ear. Intentionally so.

She squirmed away and spun around. "You did that on purpose."

There was laughter in his eyes as he raised both hands and said, "Guilty as charged."

She narrowed her eyes then and he responded as if he'd read her mind, "Just so ye ken...I'm not ticklish."

Amelia arched one brow, "Oh, no?" letting the sarcasm in her tone say in no uncertain terms that she didn't believe him for one single minute.

"Nae."

She stepped forward, the aggressor now. He stepped back.

She wasn't having that, so she launched herself at him. They fell onto a bed tucked on the far side of the wall. She didn't even know it was there, yet she couldn't complain for she found herself straddling his stomach on a bed of soft ticking.

His eyes widened and dropped to her chest. In her enthusiasm, she'd lost her dress down to her waist. Underneath she'd worn no corset, no chemise.

So she might have anticipated this moment beforehand. Amelia Chase: Seducer of recalcitrant men.

She took pure delight in watching his eyes widen at the sight of her bare breasts hanging before his face. He licked his lips.

It made her feel wanted. Powerful. She felt a resurgence of lust hum through her body, and her nipples puckered tight with her awareness.

MacLeod lifted his head, intent on a distended nipple. His fingers pressed into her back, gripping her, conveying the power of his desire, and she arched just as his lips made contact. He suckled sharply, and an answering spasm trailed by a surge of wetness followed between her legs. It felt like there was a direct link between her nipple and her core that he, and only he, could operate.

"Oh, God." She couldn't help it. Her breasts had never felt so sensitive before, so heavy.

MacLeod released her nipple, blowing on the wetted tip, then found the other one and began to suckle once again.

For a moment, she allowed herself to bask in the glory of his attentions. It felt too good. Too delicious. Too much.

"No," she said, and he looked up and into her eyes, though he kept his lips latched firmly on her nipple. She read the smile there as a twinkle in his eye. "I...mmmm...had a point...to make, damn you..."

It took all her effort, but she reached for his sides and put every bit of her will behind tickling the man beneath her.

Yes, tickling.

MacLeod released her on a startled laugh and bucked uncontrollably.

"Not ticklish, eh, MacLeod?" She knew it; she wanted to raise her fist in the air and celebrate her victory.

"Nooo..." he howled with laughter a moment more, then he

growled and flipped them both over. He gripped both her hands in one of his and held them above her head. She was well and truly caught.

And she didn't mind one bit.

His breathing was furious now, heavy, and his eyes, though still holding traces of mirth, were heavy lidded as he traced her every curve. His hips thrust subtly, suggestively, in small rhythmic surges. Slowly, mimicking the act that would soon follow.

His kilt had ridden up and she felt the hard ridge of his erection as it slid against her leg, so hot and heavy. It jumped when his gaze settled on her breasts once again.

"I love your breasts, *mo chridhe*." He suckled her once. "I could feast on them, on you, for hours." He took another taste.

He slid his hands down her arms and sat back, his kilt tented by his undeniable erection. They both glanced at it; it was impossible to miss. He glanced at her with a smile and a shrug before starting the process of slowly and painstakingly unwinding his woolen tartan.

Amelia couldn't look away, mesmerized by this unveiling. Sure, she'd seen him before in all his glory, but this time—*this* time she would have it all, and thus everything was new once more.

She grew impatient as her arousal grew. She wanted to scream at him to hurry. She glared at him, telling him in no uncertain terms that he was taking too long. He noticed, for his gaze never left hers. With a smile, he slowed his speed even more. Bastard.

So she knocked his hands away and tore at his kilt. He laughed and stood up on his knees, assisting her with her efforts.

She yanked the kilt away as fast as she could and tossed it to the ground. Out of sight out of mind.

But who cared? There was MacLeod, all six and a half feet of furred muscle, bared to her view in all his masculine glory. His erection jutted out before him, magnificent in size, and, without further thought, she reached for it, intent on wrapping her hands around his length. She wanted to taste him again, to watch as he was overcome by his own passion and desire.

Instead, he backed away, only a hairsbreadth out of reach, "Oh no, my love, not yet. First, we must finish ridding you of this dress. I want nothing between us when we finally make love."

For a brief moment, Amelia closed her eyes committing his words, his actions to memory. Then she looked him square and said, "Do it." There was nothing left to say.

He removed her dress and tossed it aside as carelessly as she'd thrown his kilt. He sat back on his heels and studied every inch of her body. She didn't squirm, rather she reveled in his review, for she knew the sight of her was mesmerizing to him. Appreciated. Rather, she wanted to stretch and purr like a cat, thrilled and satisfied to see him drowning in their mutual desire.

Unexpectedly, he leaned forward and touched his forehead to hers. His breathing was erratic, his breath a hot brand on her neck and chest. "Mel...I need you. I-I have wanted this for so long. I'm no' sure I can go slow. I..."

Amelia grabbed him behind the head, capturing his attention. "Then don't."

And just like they were of one mind, they were of one body; she spread her legs as he thrust unerringly into her core. She felt branded, so full. By his second thrust, she was coming. Her feet were on fire as she soared to the heavens.

He thrust again. And again. Harder. Faster. And with each glide of his hard cock, she spasmed once more. It was miraculous. It was ecstasy.

It was love.

Still he continued. Again. Again. Again. And Again. He stiffened and his cock hardened and lengthened inside her to unbelievable proportions. On a roar of "Mel!" he came, flooding her with his love, his essence.

He remained that way—pushed tight to her core, his eyes closed, sweat on his brow, and his breathing heavy—for long minutes before he finally rolled to the side and pulled her on top of him, collapsing into a boneless heap.

Amelia could do nothing more than go along with him. She felt adrift in post-coital pleasure with the occasional aftershock pulsing between her legs.

Within minutes they were both sound asleep.

Chapter Thirty-One

The Next Day: The Back Gardens

Alistair MacLeod sighed contentedly as he lay on his back in a field of grass and wildflowers. Amelia was tucked tightly into the crook of his arm. This afternoon they were both enjoying the unseasonably warm and unusually bright weather by watching the clouds roll by on a perfect canvas of bright blue. Per Mel, cloud-watching was something she'd often enjoyed as a young girl, and she was delighted to find him amenable to joining her in the pastime. It had been a long time since he'd indulged; he'd forgotten what it felt like to be so carefree.

Aye, a very long time.

Amelia pointed to a large cluster of fluffy clouds. "I think that one resembles a dragon with his wings spread wide."

MacLeod squinted and stared at the cloud in question. "Nae. I see a mama fox with a couple of cubs frolicking about."

Amelia sat up and looked down at him. "A mama fox? Truly?"

"Aye."

Amelia studied him for a moment. MacLeod simply returned her gaze. She pursed her lips then and asked, "Speaking of foxes. Why did you send a man to rescue my fox?"

MacLeod looked back to the sky and considered her question carefully. When he spoke, he did so while looking heavenward. "Animals don't betray you."

Amelia plucked and pulled at his shirt, nonchalant like, but he could have sworn she'd stiffened the tiniest bit.

Nevertheless, she rested her chin on his chest and asked, "Tell me about her."

MacLeod sighed, both pleased and irritated she could understand him so easily. "I had known Delilah for many years. Since we were children. She wasn't from Scotland originally, but she moved to the Isle of Skye when she was verra young and lived there most of her life."

MacLeod looked at Amelia; her face was so full of concern. He couldn't help but reach up and tuck a stray strand of hair behind her ear before he continued. "We were engaged to be married." He shrugged. "It seemed to make sense. I thought I loved her, but she betrayed me." MacLeod swallowed hard. "It was she who led the men to Alain the night he was shot..."

She didn't say anything, just joined him in allowing the emotions that statement brought forth to settle around them both. At least she didn't offer him pity.

It also allowed him to continue. "Alain almost died that night. He was shot in the head. As you know, it caused a significant amount of damage to his brain. It was months before he recovered and we understood the full impact of his injury; it was a miracle he didn't die. But Alain, who was my father's heir being the oldest twin, was clearly no longer capable of handling those duties, so they fell to me. I never wanted it, of course, but would have done my duty. And was preparing to do so. But then I learned my parents' plans for Alain. They wanted to commit him to Bedlam..." He heard Amelia's gasp of horror, but carried on. "...to hide him from society, so they didn't have to deal with his disabilities. But I wasn't having it. Alain is my brother, my twin. There was no way in hell I was going to allow him to die a slow death, tucked away in a dank, dark cell in Bedlam. So I took Alain and left, making my own way. I would care for him; I had the funds of my own, and well, here we are. I haven't spoken to nor seen my parents since."

Amelia clenched her hands into fists, gripping his shirt with fierce intensity. "Oh, God, Alaistair..."

MacLeod pulled her down and kissed her on the forehead. "Shh... it's all right. It was five years ago now, and Delilah is long gone. She was hanged for her crimes, a fitting end for a traitor. I cannot deny that it has impacted my life. As you know, I don't trust easily. As for my parents? They weren't the most loving of parents, and I have made peace with our estrangement. I have people around me whom I do trust, though it doesn't come to me easily."

Amelia seemed intent on the ties of his shirt when she asked, "I understand now, why honesty and trustworthiness is so important to you; I would feel the same way in your shoes. But what if you were in trouble...like life or death sort of trouble...and little white lies would offer you protection?"

MacLeod chuckled. "Obviously, in my line of work, I cannot argue against the value of deceit. My survival depends upon it."

"Hmmm," was all she said, and before he knew what was what, her fingers were drifting down, headed nonchalant like for his sides.

But he wasn't fooled for a minute. He knew right away what she was about. "Mel," he growled a warning.

"What?" She tried to sound all innocent. It wasn't working.

"Doona even think it, you ken?"

"Think what, Alaistair, you big fustilarian?" Again, the innocent ploy while her fingers walked unerringly down.

"Woman..."

And then she did it. She dove in for the tickle.

"Amelia Jayne Chase," he choked out between laughs. "I'll have you know I'm quicker than I look for a big fustilarian."

"But not as quick as me." She teased and before he knew what she was about, she was holding up his kilt pin."

He laughed. "Wherever did you learn a trick light that?"

"Acting school?"

"Acting school? This wouldn't happen to be one of those little while lies we were just discussing, now would it?" he asked, one brow raised. Perhaps a touch of distrust colored the tone behind his teasing words.

And she noticed; her smile faded. "Alaistair, I meant nothing by it."

Suspicious flared, but he suppressed the impulsive feeling and he felt like an absolute cad for it, which brought forth all his usual fears of ever having a normal relationship with a woman. She'd done nothing, truly.

Just terrified him.

And now he'd ruined a perfectly fine morning.

Fucking hell. Would he ever outrun his past?

MacLeod shoved that thought away and pulled her back into his arms. Her expression was unreadable and wasn't that a first? "God, Mel. I'm so sorry. I don't...I...." He released a long breath. "Just that. I'm sorry."

Hell, he had to try or he'd never leave his past behind.

Five years was entirely too long to wait to fix this. How miserable would he be in five more?

Chapter Thirty-Two

The Next Day

The Duke of Stonebridge's arrival was as unwanted as a tax collector, a necessary evil but deuced inconvenient even at the best of times.

MacLeod ignored the tightening in his gut that portended bad news from his longtime friend and braced himself with a smile. He leaned back in his chair and propped his booted feet on his desk, both hands tucked behind his head.

A few minutes later, Stonebridge walked through the study door, the picture of a perfect mess, a frustrated scowl etched upon his brow. It was a surprising state for a man who wasn't often dressed less than impeccably.

The duke all but stopped in his tracks when they locked eyes, his mouth dropping open in surprise.

"MacLeod?"

MacLeod nodded. "Duke..."

Stonebridge let loose a startled smile then. He seemed surprised, but pleasantly so. "It's good to see you so..."

"Not myself?"

"I was going to say happy, my friend. Life appears to be agreeing with you."

"Aye, so it is."

Stonebridge stared a few more minutes, appearing somewhat incredulous before taking a seat before the desk.

Fortunately, the duke knew better than to inquire as to the cause of such unexpected contentment. Sure, MacLeod may be happy, but he hadn't changed that much. He still fiercely guarded his privacy. "So what brings you here, Duke?"

The duke began a staccato rhythm on the arm of his chair with one long finger, a longtime habit he'd never quite managed to break. "It's Dansbury. He's gone rogue looking for Kelly, and I need to pull him back."

MacLeod dropped his feet to the floor and leaned forward, resting his elbows on his desk. "Och, can you blame him?"

"Of course not, but that is irrelevant. You must realize this situation is greater than personal vendettas."

"Personal vendettas? Might I remind you Kelly made it personal when he betrayed his colleagues and abducted the mon's sister!"

"I haven't forgotten, and I understand what you're saying, friend. But Dansbury is too angry to see reason at the moment, and even if his anger is justified, he cannot go off half-cocked chasing down Kelly and acting on pure emotion. You of all people know this. Hell, *he* knows this."

"Aye, yet if Kelly were standing here right now, I'd rip the man's head from his shoulders without a second thought and still sleep like a baby tonight because I'm quite sure *my emotions* would feel damn guid about finding satisfaction in his death." So maybe that was an exaggeration. Sure, he still, after everything, thought the man would never hurt a woman...and the duke agreed; they'd discussed this at length before...but Kelly had still put them all through hell. And was possibly —probably—a traitor.

"Which is precisely why I'm glad you're here and not chasing the man down, too."

"So why exactly are you here, then?"

"I need to question Mrs. Chase."

"No."

"No?"

"Did I stutter?" So much for his previous good mood.

Stonebridge stood then, aggression oozing from him in palpable waves, which gave MacLeod pause. The unflappable Duke of Stonebridge was not a man to react with physical violence.

"Damn you, MacLeod, you are better than this."

Nor did he usually color his words with emotion.

"Och, better than *what*? Better than a traitor and a lying bastard? Aye."

"Better than a man who would let emotion cloud his judgement. Better than a man who would accuse a friend of treachery before he had all the facts. Better than all of that."

"Are ye truly trying to convince me that Kelly might have reasons for doing what he did?"

"No…"

"Guid."

"…but that's precisely my point, we don't have all the facts."

"And this is a problem, how?"

Stonebridge glanced away. "It's complicated."

MacLeod slammed his fists on the table and stood now, too. "Och, you unbelievable bastard. Considering everything that's happened: the secrets, the lies, the treason—are you telling me you're still holding out on me? Are you withholding the full truth?"

"MacLeod, don't do this. You know better than—how long have we worked together, known each other? You know it is I who is ultimately responsible for everything and everyone on this team and that I take that responsibility seriously. I am the sole person here who every damn day must make the hard decisions that might put you or someone else's life in danger. People I love's lives in the path of real danger. So yes, I have my secrets, and if I feel it necessary they remain secret, I will keep them so."

"Right. I could have sworn you mentioned the word 'team' in that load of tripe you just spewed, but go ahead and keep your secrets. Just know that in doing so, you will always keep a wall up between you and every man on your team by making it painstakingly clear that you do not trust our judgement. So you know what? I'll go get Mrs. Chase and you'll see she has nothing to hide and nothing to share that I didn't already recount in my last report."

"Thank you."

Ten minutes later, Mel whirled in to the office. Right away, MacLeod's heart felt relieved in a way that was difficult to put into words. They shared a brief, knowing look before he began the introductions.

"Stonebridge, may I introduce you to Dansbury's sister, Mrs. Amelia Chase of America? Mrs. Chase, this is His Grace, Philip Langtry, the Duke of Stonebridge."

With a wry grin, Mel curtsied. MacLeod almost laughed. A curtsey? Though the proper response, he didn't know she had it in her to do so.

"Your Grace."

"Mrs. Chase, a pleasure. You seem to be recovered and doing well after your ordeal."

"But of course, that errant, beetle-headed, codpiece didn't stand a chance."

The duke laughed, though his laughter sounded strained to MacLeod's ears. "Good. Please have a seat."

Mel sat, followed by the men, but not before MacLeod shot Stonebridge a warning look to watch himself. Not that he thought Mel couldn't handle things just fine, but the Duke of Stonebridge was not a man to be taken lightly; he was head of their team for good reason.

"Mrs. Chase," began Stonebridge, "I'm not sure what you've been told, but I'm here to ask you some questions about your abduction."

"Of course."

"MacLeod has already recounted the basics, so I'm only going to ask you pointed questions."

Amelia sat back and relaxed into the chair. She appeared utterly at ease and ready to take on the Duke of Stonebridge. "Shoot."

MacLeod smiled his approval and sat back to watch the show, fiercely proud of her strength. She was going to put the duke on his head, and he was looking forward to watching the show.

Stonebridge did not yet realize this, and if he didn't know any better, and he knew his friend quite well, he would say that he was setting Mel up. It was in the way he sat so tense, with tension apparent in his jaw. Mel could take care of herself, but for the first time, MacLeod felt a spark of distrust in the form of a tingle skate down his spine.

The duke pierced her with his gaze, though his words were all conciliatory. "First of all, now that you've had more time to consider everything that happened..."

Amelia grinned, a cheeky smile. "You mean, now that I am no longer a hysterical, simpering miss..."

"I never said that."

"You didn't need to. But it's what many men in your position think of women in their mind."

The duke remained unruffled. "It's perfectly natural for anyone, myself included, to overlook details while our emotions are in a heightened state of—"

"And before you do suggest it, I'll have you know I've never been hysterical or simpering a day in my life."

The duke and Mel eyed each other then, sizing each other up for what was shaping up to be an entertaining confrontation.

After a moment's pause, the duke smiled and said, "Well, that's good to know. Americans are rather notoriously robust."

Mel dipped her head in acceptance of the compliment.

"Let me ask you this, then: did you ever feel as if your life was in danger while with Mr. Kelly?"

"No."

The duke quirked one brow. "You seem fairly confident of that."

Amelia shrugged and spread her hands wide. "I'm good at reading people. No, I excel at it."

"I see." The duke leaned forward. "And how did you come by that skill?"

MacLeod, taking exception to the tone of Stonebridge's voice, sat forward in his own chair and crossed his arms. He kept his council but was ready to intercede should the situation call for it.

Mel cocked her head as if reconsidering her opponent. "As an orphan, one is forced to learn many skills not found in your typical London drawing room. It's necessary for survival. Even in America."

The duke smiled, his tone deceptively calm, but MacLeod saw right through his false charm. "I see. So your recent escape from a skilled agent was a bit more than just pure luck?"

MacLeod launched to his feet, knocking over his chair in the process. "Look here, Duke. I doona think I like the tone of yer voice, and the current direction of this line of questioning. I don't see the point to it."

The duke looked at Mel as he answered. "And I don't like putting the lives of my agents on the line for someone I know so little about."

"Goddamn it, Duke." MacLeod prepared to leap over the desk.

"Alaistair, it's all right," came Mel's subdued reply, which startled him enough that he turned toward her.

She sat there for a moment, all color leeched from her face, with her hands clasped, one thumb worrying the other. After a minute, she glanced at him, the briefest of looks, then turned to face the duke. "You know, don't you?"

"More than you would like, I suspect. But not nearly enough."

Mel looked to him, tears welling in her eyes. MacLeod's blood pounded in his ears.

No. Just, no.

He wanted to turn back the clock. He wanted to flee the room. Already, he could feel the twin sensations of anger and betrayal seeping into his mind though she hadn't yet said a word. He almost cried out for her not to speak. If he could prevent her from saying anything, they could carry on as if nothing had changed.

But already everything had changed, and he knew it would be bad. All the many times he doubted this woman came hurtling back to the forefront of his mind like a recurring nightmare. He both didn't want to hear this and couldn't stop from desiring the truth, at last.

Even if it meant learning about another betrayal by yet another woman.

Damn it!

MacLeod turned his back to look out the window, one hand pulling through his hair. Still, he listened to every word and watched with scrutiny her reflection mirrored in the panes of glass. She spoke to his back.

"Even as a young child, I was gifted with a certain amount of charm and wit. It quickly became all too apparent that people, especially men, treated me differently because of it. Still, there wasn't enough charm in the world to find me a set of parents who were willing to adopt me.

"So eventually, I grew up and learned first-hand how cruel the world can be. Would you believe how often men, powerful wealthy men, dumped their bastards at the orphanage with only a token payment and a good riddance to the rubbish? Nearly every damn day. Those men, those greedy bastards, cared not one whit for owning up to the responsibilities of their actions. Hell, most of the time, they couldn't even be bothered to do the deed themselves, rather they sent a footman or a maid in cover of night and left them on our stoop. And there was nothing anyone would or could do to stop it.

"So I did my part, to make them pay. I learned how to move amongst society. How to adopt different personalities, change my appearance. And I took what they owed and gave it all to the orphanage, anonymously of course."

MacLeod spun around then, fury getting the best of him. "So you became a two-bit thief? A confidence artist? A trickster?"

Mel lifted her chin in defiance.

"Och, doon tell me ye're a regular modern-day Robin Hood, is that how you see yourself?"

"Yes, actually, I do.

"God, I canna believe this."

Stonebridge interrupted. "So what happened next?"

"I was ready to quit. I'd been at this for several years, and it's not an easy life to live. You have no friends. Not to mention you're forever looking over your shoulder. But then I was tempted with one last...*job*. One particularly nasty man had done the tried to have one of his murdered, but the boy was taken to the orphanage instead.

"Everything started off normally—was going extremely well, in fact —but then everything went wrong. It was all a set up. A trap to catch me. Apparently, I'd angered the wrong men. Before I knew what was about, I was framed and arrested for a murder I didn't commit, and the power behind this was so big, they'd forgone any sort of trial, found me guilty, and scheduled me to hang in a matter of days."

MacLeod turned at that. Shock, fear, anger, amazement, devastation…a full plethora of emotions exploded in his mind. She'd been days away from being hanged.

Hanged.

"Out of nowhere a man who calls himself Spyder contacted me. He said he could get me out of jail, but that I needed to be prepared to do something for him in return. I didn't want another job, but I definitely didn't want to be hanged for a crime I didn't commit, and it was painfully clear there would not be a fair trial nor chance to prove my innocence. So, I accepted his terms."

MacLeod and Stonebridge shared a glance. *Spyder!*

MacLeod asked his own question then. "What exactly did Spyder ask ye to do?"

"He told me I had to leave America. That it was no longer safe for me there. And to find Dansbury and tell him he's my brother."

No.

MacLeod clenched his fists and gritted his teeth, barely able to utter the question that had to be asked. "So, are you, Mel? Are you Dansbury's sister?"

Amelia glanced at her hands once more, her shoulders drooped in resignation.

He slammed his fists on the desk. "Answer the damn question."

She jumped up and looked him in the eyes then. "No! No, all right? I am not!" She spun around and ran out of the room on a sob.

Chapter Thirty-Three

Later That Afternoon, Time Enough for Calmer Heads to Prevail:
MacLeod's Provisional Barnyard Animal Sanctuary

Composed once again, Amelia stepped into MacLeod's makeshift animal hospital, suspecting she would find him here of all places.

She was right.

She wasn't silent when she approached, preferring to approach him boldly with nothing to hide. Still, she was dismayed by the obvious stiffening of his shoulders.

Dismayed but not discouraged.

"MacLeod…"

He pounded the worktable he was standing at. "You're nothing but a thief, a two-bit hustler. A liar."

She lifted her chin in indignation. "I am not." Though she expected his anger, it was still upsetting to hear his harsh words. Still, she hid it well.

He spun around, slicing his hand through the air. "Och, you might as well be."

Amelia clenched her fists and stomped her foot. "I will not hang my head in shame anymore!"

The man snorted in response. Snorted!

"Look, MacLeod, I did what I had to survive and to help others who aren't as lucky as me. I'm sorry if that doesn't fit with your worldview."

"My worldview? Mine? Mel, the world says I'm right. People don't take from others that which doesn't belong to them. They go to gaol when they do. As you did."

"Ha! Tell that to the men that left their bastard children with nothing!"

MacLeod turned his back on her, and her anger exploded into fury. She marched around to stand before him, unwilling to be ignored. When she caught the look in his eyes, everything clicked into place. "Oh, you are a good liar, too, aren't you? This isn't about me playing Robin Hood to a handful of orphans, is it?"

He didn't respond, close-mouthed once more. A muscle ticked in his jaw and fury blazed in his eyes.

"This is all about you. You feel betrayed by me, is that it? And you don't trust me."

He glared at her, still mute.

"Look, MacLeod, I did not set out to betray you for nefarious reasons. I needed a safe place to go. I took advantage, I admit it. But I never intended any harm."

He broke his silence at last and pointed his finger off toward some unknown distant place. "How can I believe a word you say when my friend is out there tearing apart the countryside trying to find your abductor? He should be enjoying his new wife, instead. For all I know, you and Kelly planned all this. It seems I have every right to distrust ye. Were you ever even married? Is Mrs. Chase even your real name?"

Amelia shook her head, incredulous. After all they shared, he had zero faith in her. None. "I admit I was never married. It was a convenient lie to make it easier for me to move around your country. My name is Amelia Chase, my true name. But this really isn't about me, is it? This is about Delilah."

"It isnae, but if the shoe fits..."

Amelia slammed her fist into his chest. "I am not her! If you cannot see the difference, then fuck you!"

She intended to strike him again, her despair getting the better of her restraint, but he caught her fist midair. Then, he bent down then, glaring into her face, anger rolling off him in giant waves. His voice was quietly lethal when he spoke. "The only difference I see is Delilah had a calculating look in her eye I refused to acknowledge. But you? You hide it better but that just makes you a better liar."

And then he pulled her close and kissed her. It was a kiss of anger, fury. But wasn't anger the other side of the coin to passion?

Whatever the reason, their shared fury melted into lust, inciting their mutual passion.

She hiked up her skirts and climbed his body, unable to get close enough. He was like a furnace, his body hot and hard. It was like her very soul caught fire.

MacLeod cupped her ass and hoisted her higher, then spun around and slammed her into the wall. Not enough to hurt her, but enough to press her tight into his hard body, providing the perfect amount of pressure. Right where they both needed it.

She kissed him, tearing at his hair, while he pulled up the edge of his kilt.

Then he was there, hot and hard, pushing into her wet sheath.

She screamed as she climaxed instantly.

"Oh, God, yes, Mel!"

Her core squeezed his invading shaft while he pumped up into her, harder, faster. Racing his way to his own finish. Each glide of his hard cock brushed her sensitized insides, sending a tingle of pleasure pulsing through her body. Already, she was fast on her way to another orgasm and oh, God, it was almost too much; she'd never felt this way before.

He grunted now, as he pumped on and on. The sounds of his exertions, his rapid breathing, the sound of his body slapping against hers, ratcheted her lust impossibly higher. She squeezed her eyes and saw stars as they came together in an explosion of power and passion.

Afterwards, they remained locked that way, their heads together, their breathing sawing in and out of their lungs as they floated back down to earth. She clung to him, afraid to let go. Afraid if she did, he would be gone from her life for good.

After a moment, his breathing slowed and in a whispered warning, he said, "This changes nothing."

Then, he let her go.

Chapter Thirty-Four

The Next Morning

MacLeod sorted through the papers on his desk, sorting his correspondence ahead of his departure in a few hours.

He and Stonebridge were headed out to find Dansbury.

The duke walked in, his attire perfectly crisp and back to normal. "You look like hell, MacLeod."

"Fook you, Duke."

"Ah," was his only response.

MacLeod didn't care what the man thought of his returned ill-humor. Besides, the reasons were obvious to anyone with half a brain.

"I'm nearly ready—"

He broke off when Amelia walked into to the room unannounced.

"You're leaving?" she asked.

He crossed his arms and glared at her. She walked in anyway, her chin high. He hated that he admired her for not being cowed by his surly attitude.

The duke stood. "I'll leave."

"Nae. There's no' need," he said. To Mrs. Chase, he added, "Aye, I'm leaving."

"Where are you going?"

He simply glared at her. As if he would tell her anything.

She turned to Stonebridge.

The duke answered, ever the mannered lord. "I'm afraid that's classified, Mrs. Chase."

She looked back at MacLeod. "Take me with you."

"Hell, no."

"I might be of use to you."

"Nae."

She glanced at the duke once more, briefly, then back at him. "MacLeod, don't leave like this. I don't want to end it this way."

"I doona fooking care."

"You don't mean that."

"Aye, I do. And there's something else. I expect you to be gone from here when I return."

Her face paled. He didn't care. He *didn't*. Never mind his soul felt like it had burst wide open when he said those words. He would not take them back. He would not be made a fool again. He lost everything the last time. He wouldn't lose it all again, not for the likes of her.

She turned then and marched out the door. He was, in a way, surprised. She usually needed to have the last word, but not this time, and it was all wrong.

It didn't matter. They were through.

He didn't know how long he stared at the empty doorway. Suddenly, the duke stood before him. "That was cold, man. Even for you."

He snorted, a brave façade to be sure, and turned back to resume his packing. "If there's one thing I know, Duke, it's that Amelia Chase will be fine."

"Did you not hear the part about her nearly being hanged?" he countered.

"Aye. But she wasn't, was she?"

Stonebridge shook his head then and turned to leave. MacLeod watched him go, then finally allowed his face to fall. Hell.

Damn.

He turned then and picked up the brass paperweight from his desk and threw it at the wall and roared in righteous anger.

Damn you, Mel. Damn you!

Chapter Thirty-Five

Two Days Later: Greenwood Park...Still

MacLeod left two days before. Two dark and dismal days before. Unbeknownst to him, Amelia Chase was still in residence in his home.

Ha! Take that, MacLeod!

Amelia thumbed her nose at—no one, actually. The idea of MacLeod?—and paced around the man's library one more time before settling in with a cup of tea on a lovely tartaned settee by the fire.

Aye, as MacLeod would say, she was still here, living in his home, eating his food, joking with the servants, taking walks with his brother, and all but wasting away in self-pity, which was not the norm for Amelia Chase.

But these weren't her normal circumstances.

She hadn't left because, quite frankly, she wasn't quite sure where to go. She didn't know how to get in touch with Spyder. Dansbury wasn't around, and even if he were, he was no longer an option for obvious reasons. The same with Lady Beatryce and Aunt Harriett. They probably would not want to see the likes of her *ever* again.

Dash it all; she'd never felt more alone in her life.

Sure, as a child she was an orphan. But there were plenty of other children around in the same boat as she. It made for a sort of family through commonality. But now? Now, she had no one.

She'd *thought* she'd had MacLeod.

Amelia swiped away the tears she swore she wouldn't shed and punched the pillow next to her before picking up her cup and taking another sip of tea. Honestly, what she really needed was something a bit stronger than tea.

Dammit.

She didn't survive her life—the orphanage, bad men who tossed their children away like so much rubbish, and a too-close-for-comfort almost hanging—only to be brought low by a too-deeply-feeling, brute of a man with trust issues.

Honestly, Amelia had half a mind to disobey MacLeod and remain here, in his home, forever. Or at least until he physically threw her out.

Would he do that? Actually throw her out on her arse?

He was a physical man, but he'd never harmed her. Not really.

And she didn't believe he would hurt her, either. At least not bodily. Oh, she had no doubt he was furious and confident he *thought* he didn't want to see her ever again.

And his words could cut like a knife—damn...

But what did she want? Was she ready to give up on him? Should she obey his demand to leave?

Her dismal musings were interrupted by a rap on the door, followed by the familiar shuffling step of MacLeod's man about house, Mac.

"Good evening, miss. There's a gentleman here to see you. A Viscount Sharpe? Shall I show him in?"

"Oh, thank you, Jesus. Yes, Mac, yes. Show him in."

A few moments later, the man she knew as Spyder, walked through the library doors with a confident, broad stride. He was dressed to the nines yet again, complete with rings adorning every finger and a silver tipped cane he obviously didn't need.

"Good morning, Mrs. Chase."

"Is it? Good, I mean?"

That gave him pause. "Ah. Trouble in paradise?"

She snorted. "You could say that." Surely, he could tell by her pale skin and reddened eyes.

Spyder tilted his head and gave her an odd look as he passed, headed for the matching settee opposite her. He gestured to the seat and asked, "May I?"

Amelia waved the question away. "Of course."

Spyder sat deep into the settee with an innate grace he was clearly born to, then crossed his legs, one arm resting on the side and the other propped up by his walking stick. He looked her over once more. "Well, perhaps not everyone is having a good morning at this precise moment, but for you? Aren't you happy now? You finally have a family; I'd have thought you'd be a little bit more enthusiastic toward your change in circumstance."

"Change in circumstance? What do you mean? Nothing's changed that I can see."

"But you have a family now. A brother. An aunt."

"You mean a pretend brother."

"Now, where in the world would you get that idea?"

Her heart dropped with those ten words. *What did he mean? What did he mean!* "You told me to tell Dansbury he's my brother. I assumed, based on our past association, that this was another role to play, a cover. Was I wrong?"

"My dear Amelia Chase, but you are his sister. Truly, you are. That is why I went to such lengths to save you."

At those fateful words, Amelia laughed. And laughed. And laughed some more. She sounded like a maniac. She was bowled over, hands across her stomach, unable to sit up straight laughing. My God, the irony. She almost couldn't stand it.

Spyder smiled and seemed willing to allow her her moment of insanity. "I hate to interrupt your amusement, darling, but I came here for a purpose. Well, a purpose other than correcting your incorrect assumptions."

Amelia held up one finger in the universal sign of *give me a minute* while she pulled herself together.

After another minute or so, she finally said, "A-all right." *Snort* "I'm ready."

Wearing a bemused smile, Spyder asked, "Am I correct in understanding MacLeod and Stonebridge left Scotland two days ago?"

"Well, they left here two days ago. Whether they're still in Scotland, I couldn't tell you. MacLeod and I weren't exactly on speaking terms when he left."

"And do you know why they left?"

"I do, actually. They left to find Dansbury, who is chasing down Kelly."

"Then we haven't a moment to lose, love. They're walking into a trap."

Chapter Thirty-Six

Four Days Later: The Rusty Hook Tavern, Blackpool

F our days later, MacLeod and Stonebridge entered the Rusty Hook Tavern near the sandy beaches of the little hamlet town of Blackpool. Through a thick haze of smoke, they spotted their quarry seated at a table nursing a pint of ale. Both men were surprised to see he was alone.

As they approached, Dansbury kicked out one of the two empty chairs at his table. "How did you find me?"

Stonebridge remained standing, his hands on his hips, and said, "Believe me. You don't really want to know. Rest assured it wasn't easy. We've been on the road for six days."

Dansbury toasted them their success and took a healthy swig of his ale. "In all honesty, it matters not. I dispatched a note two days ago that would have brought you here, at any rate. You're only a few days early, is all."

"Where's Lady Beatryce?" asked MacLeod, convinced she was somewhere nearby.

Dansbury cracked a smile at the question and glanced at the ceiling. "She's upstairs."

Of course. While he and Stonebridge were tracking him down, concerned he'd gone off half-cocked, Dansbury was settled here having a grand old time with his new wife.

Stonebridge shook his head and scanned the room. "Is there someplace private we can talk? We have matters to discuss."

"Nothing, save for the rooms above. But trust me, I've been watching these people for days. They're not interested in anything we have to say. We won't be bothered."

MacLeod picked one of the vacant chairs and sat.

Stonebridge did the same and got right to the point. "I assume Kelly is here."

Dansbury nodded his head. "Yes. In fact, he's been staying at this hotel; I've seen him myself."

MacLeod was genuinely surprised.

Stonebridge appeared relieved. "I must commend you for your restraint. I'm thankful we didn't arrive to find you in gaol for murder."

"Ha! *Please.* Had I acted on my impulses, my friend, I wouldn't have been caught. You know this."

The duke shrugged. "I suppose I do."

"Och, so what have you learned?" This from MacLeod who was irritable from days in the saddle and a lack of sleep.

Not to mention beautiful liars.

Dansbury took another sip of his ale and smiled at MacLeod. "Ah, moody as ever, MacLeod? Someone been ruffling your feathers?"

Before MacLeod could respond, likely with a regrettable remark, Stonebridge interceded. "That's a question best left for another day."

Dansbury threw MacLeod a curious look, then proceeded to brief them on what he knew. "Kelly is in Blackpool as are several suspected members of the Society. Kelly has a room here. The others have just left and are en route to Liverpool and a ship docked there. An ex-war ship I might add, the *HMS Nightingale.*"

They both froze at that tidbit of information. A Royal Navy ship in use by the Society? And not a small ship, at that. The HMS Nightingale was over 175 feet in length and more than 50 feet in width with six floors.

"Did you recognize anyone? The man in charge?" asked Stonebridge.

"Unfortunately, no. I believe he was here, but I have no proof. I cannot imagine them going through all this trouble—the ship, the meeting locations, the secrecy—if he weren't."

"Do you have a plan?" asked Stonebridge.

"I do. We wrap up here, then head to Liverpool and search the ship."

MacLeod barely refrained from groaning out loud. Liverpool meant crowds.

"And Kelly?"

Dansbury fiddled with a small knife he held in his hands. "We leave him for now."

Stonebridge smiled, obviously pleased. MacLeod wasn't so magnanimous, but he understood. Despite everything, those men in charge were the priority.

MacLeod stood. "Guid. Let's end this."

"Hold up there, my friend. I believe we have something to discuss."

MacLeod crossed his arms, a defensive move at best, and remained standing. "Such as?"

"My sister. I believe I left you in charge of her welfare. So I must ask, is she here, and if not, where is she?"

"Don't answer that," interjected the duke.

Dansbury turned to Stonebridge. "Why not? I have a right to know. This man assured me he would guarantee her safety." Dansbury turned back to MacLeod and narrowed his eyes. "She is safe, isn't she? You haven't hurt her?"

It was on the tip of his tongue to tell Dansbury he'd fucked her then kicked her out of his home for being a lying thief. It was essentially the truth.

But he feared everyone would see right through him should he do so, and then they would all know he'd been brought low by a woman once more. That he'd fallen and was finding it damn difficult to pull himself back up.

Instead, he said, "I'm going for a walk," which brought forth a few curses from both Stonebridge and Dansbury.

Still, he turned to go, leaving Stonebridge to manage Dansbury's wrath.

Aye. Better Stonebridge than he. Else he risked saying something that would forever destroy his friendship with one of the few people he considered a friend.

MACLEOD WALKED OUT OF THE RUSTY HOOK TAVERN AMID A SWIRL of angry shouts and heavy cursing. So be it. He knew what was at stake. He would be ready, but for the moment, he was unsettled and needed to walk off his frustration. Hopefully, a walk along Blackpool's sandy stretch of beach would be just the thing.

He wasn't so senseless as to not realize the source of his ill-humor. He'd thought of nothing else for six days. Mrs. Amelia Chase. Bold. Beautiful. Absolute Trouble. Just as he'd suspected that first time he'd seen her across a crowded inn.

And ever since that fateful day some four months past, she'd consumed his waking thoughts with regular occurrence. But not all those thoughts were good, rational, or hell, even *sane*. Just persistent.

MacLeod stepped out onto the sand and headed south, dismayed by the number of people present to take in the waters and salty air. He couldn't walk a straight line without sidestepping a bather or hard-working servant. Frustrated, MacLeod looked further ahead. To his consternation, what he saw was more of the same. People, pets, and servants everywhere.

A group of people parted ways and his entire world came crashing to a halt.

For there she was: Amelia Chase. Still bold. Still beautiful. Still trouble. But a damn sight to see. His first instinct was to crack a smile, a telling and unwanted predisposition.

Then reality set in. Mrs. Chase's presence in Blackpool meant nothing *but* absolute trouble. For her to even know where to find him —because there was no way this was a coincidence—suggested she colluded with the enemy. The thought threatened to break him.

God, if he'd had any doubt about her culpability—to which he'd never admit—she'd dashed those thoughts completely.

And still he wanted to wrap his arms around her and kiss her senseless; she was a sight for sore eyes.

Bugger.

Before he knew it, she was standing before him. The same smile. The same light in her eyes. The same confident presence.

"MacLeod." A gust of wind blew her hair into her face. His fingers itched to brush the loose strands away. Instead he crossed his arms, the better to keep his hands to himself.

She watched the motion, a look of apprehension crossed her face but a moment, then she met his gaze with a worried frown. She hesitated, which was quite unlike her.

He had no such reservation. "You might as well spit it out. Every moment you hesitate, I become further convinced your presence here is not a coincidence."

"But of course, it's not. I came here to find you."

Damn, that was precisely what he didn't want to hear.

"Right. So how did you manage it this time? Dumb luck? Another anonymous, bullshit message?"

She held up her hand to halt his barrage of questions. "Look, MacLeod. You're angry. I get it. So why don't you practice your usual stoic silence and give me a chance to tell you?"

He dipped his head in acquiescence. The truth did sometimes bite.

"Spyder led me to you."

MacLeod looked up and scanned his surroundings. "Spyder? He's here?"

"Yes and no."

"Of course." He didn't try to hide his exasperation.

"He's here, you see, but you won't find him. Not if he doesn't want to be found."

"Ah. Such faith in my capabilities."

She shook her head in obvious exasperation. "Spyder isn't important right now."

"I beg to differ. There's quite a few people aboot who would relish a chance to speak to Spyder. Why, we've more of an interest in apprehending him than you."

She ignored his purposeful barb. Like a child, he wanted to yell at her to fight back. He knew she had it in her to slay him with nothing more than words. Instead, she said, "We came to warn you that you're walking into a trap."

"Is that all?"

"You don't believe me?"

"Quite honestly, I don't know what to believe anymore. All I hear are words colored with lies. Everything you say is suspect at this point and with good reason."

"Why would I risk coming here if it wasn't important? Risk your wrath? Risk capture? I wouldn't have unless I thought you were in real danger. Please, MacLeod, please consider what I'm saying."

"I'll take it under advisement, I'm sure." Which she correctly understood to mean he wouldn't heed her words at all.

She reached out and grabbed his arms. "MacLeod, please don't. Just because I'm a damn good actress, and just because I've done the things I've done, doesn't mean I'm not scared or unsure or just plain cracked up sometimes. Please hear me. I-I love you."

Och, she burned him with her words, with her touch. His eyes locked with hers, mirror expressions of shock and heated attraction arched between them. He clenched his fists lest he throw her over his shoulder and haul her away. And in that moment, he nearly hated himself for still harboring that desire. For her. For them.

For a life that never actually existed, for it was all a lie.

"Well, that's foolish."

Mel tightened her grip. Her voice cracked when she pleaded, "MacLeod..."

It nearly killed him to respond, but he broke free of her grip then and said, "Jus' go," and walked away, a furious ache in his chest that he feared would haunt him for the rest of his days.

Chapter Thirty-Seven

That Night: The Shores of Blackpool

Alaistair MacLeod dug his feet further into the sand while he watched moonlit waves crash upon the shore. The tide was coming in, but he had a few hours or more before the cold water reached him where he sat upon the sandy coast of Blackpool.

He took another swig from his bottle of rum; the bulk of it he'd already downed in less than an hour. It tasted like water now, but that mattered not. It was getting the job done and quite well.

Aye, he was as drunk as he'd ever been, so drunk he hardly felt the cold air as it blew in off the sea. Still, the drink wouldn't scrub the unwanted memory of Amelia Chase from his brain.

Damn it.

He didn't want to remember the feel of her. The taste of her. He didn't want to see her smiles when he closed his eyes, nor hear her laugh and especially not her lies when all was quiet. He just wanted her gone so he could move on.

He took another mouthful of rum, then wiped his mouth upon his sleeve. Aye, he was one of those unlucky bastards who never forgot a thing, no matter how much he drank.

MacLeod glanced left, then right. As desired, not a soul could be found on the beach now. It was late enough, which was the point. Unlike so many other men, when MacLeod was drunk, he grew *less* talkative, more introspective. Which meant he definitely didn't want an audience about attempting to commiserate.

No singing, laughing, boasting, dancing on the table tops, or rioting for Alaistair MacLeod. No pouring out his soul. For MacLeod, being drunk meant he pondered the meaning of life. His life. His brother's. Anyone who meant anything to him was a possibility for reflective consideration.

Hell, sometimes even absolute strangers danced across his mind.

What he wouldn't give to be carefree, to allow drink to loosen his tongue and relax his mind. Then maybe, just maybe, all this shit with Amelia Chase wouldn't hurt so goddamn much.

A seagull burst on the scene searching for food. He watched as it hopped around on the sand to his right, his obnoxious chirp a plea for a handout.

"Och, go on with you, bird. I've no' got a thing save for my drink." He followed his threat with a mouthful of rum. The bird cocked its head as if it was contemplating having a taste of his drink.

Just then, someone grabbed ahold of his shoulder, using him for balance so they could join him on the sand. "What are you drinking, my friend?" came a familiar voice.

MacLeod looked left to discover Danbury settling in next to him, his knees already tucked to his chest while he tossed a handful of pebbles, one after another, towards the sea. Damn, it was good thing Stonebridge had given him the evening off, for he certainly wasn't in the most observant frame of mind; he hadn't even heard the man approach.

"Rum." he answered eventually. And in that one word, even he could make out the slight slurring of his speech.

Aye, he was very, very drunk.

Dansbury chuckled. "MacLeod, the Scottish Pirate." He elbowed him in the arm. "Arghhh..."

MacLeod shrugged. "It's what was available."

Dansbury tossed another pebble. "Oh, I'm sure."

MacLeod shrugged again and took another swig. "Even better, it's getting' the job done." *Hardly.*

"Oh, that I can see for myself."

For a moment, the two of them sat in silence. MacLeod watching Dansbury toss his pebbles while downing mouthfuls of watery rum at irregular intervals.

Eventually, he had to ask, "Did you have a point to joining me this night?"

Dansbury dusted his hands together, having thrown the last rock. "Stonebridge told me about Amelia."

"Ah." *Of course.* MacLeod wasn't sure he wanted this conversation, but he was also sure he'd never talk Dansbury into dropping the subject. When the man had something to say, he had to say it.

Still, he waited for Dansbury to continue. It didn't take him long; the man always had been the talkative sort. "I don't know why Amelia thinks she's not my sister."

MacLeod jerked his gaze to Dansbury, the man's statement catching him off guard. It was not at all what he expected him to say.

"But I can assure you of one thing, my friend. Amelia Chase is very much my sister."

What the hell? "How do you know?"

"Spyder."

MacLeod shook his head. "No."

Now it was Dansbury's turn to shrug. "He submitted proof. Irrefutable proof."

MacLeod continued shaking his head in denial. "But that makes no sense. Why not tell her the truth? Or if he had, why did she tell us she wasn't?"

Dansbury shook his head as well. "I can only guess. Until I speak with Amelia..." his voice trailed off.

MacLeod propped his arms on his raised knees and tossed the remains of a fallen leaf he'd been decimating to the ground. "It matters not. She's still a—"

Dansbury grabbed his sleeve, his expression fierce. "I'm warning you now, take care of your words, MacLeod. We are friends, but that woman is my sister. Do you hear? I will not sit idly by and listen to you disparage her, friend or no."

MacLeod shook off Dansbury's hold and wisely bit his tongue. Oh, he had much he wanted to say, but for the sake of friendship...

On impulse, MacLeod tilted his head back and roared his frustration to the sky. It was a loud, primal scream. His feathered companion took flight.

God, it felt damn good to let go like that, like that scream had been bottled up inside him for years. Decades, even.

He turned to look at his friend, expecting to find the man looking at him as if he were crazy. Instead, Dansbury grinned, then tossed one arm around his shoulders. "My God, man. You love her."

MacLeod snorted and looked away from his friend's smiling face. "If this is love, I want no part of it."

Dansbury shook his head. MacLeod detected a hint of pity behind the action. "At the risk of meeting your ham-sized fists, I'm only going to say this once. You're drunk enough, so I'm not so worried, but, Amelia Chase is not Delilah Brooks."

MacLeod chuckled, but he wasn't laughing. He picked up a nearby pebble that had escaped Dansbury's fingers and flung it toward the sea. "Funny you should say that, Cliff. She said the same damn thing."

Chapter Thirty-Eight

One Week Later: Ye Hole in Ye Wall Public House, Liverpool

Seven days later, MacLeod, Stonebridge, and Dansbury reconnected at *Ye Hole in Ye Wall*, a public house on Hackins Hey in Liverpool, several streets away from the waterfront. Their ultimate destination was the *HMS Nightingale*, which they suspected had been commandeered by alleged members of the Society for the Purification of England. MacLeod had just confirmed that the ship was currently moored at Salthouse Dock on the River Mersey.

With more than eighty thousand people calling Liverpool home, *Ye Hole in Ye Wall* was quite overwhelmed with patrons. MacLeod dodged rowdy and unruly drunks as he edged around tables crowded with regulars and sailors alike, the tables' scuffed wooden tops sticky with ale and gin. Indeed, the smell of stale beer and unwashed bodies permeated the air, even masking the usual maritime smells from the nearby docks.

Eventually, he found the rest of his team in the back, two men seated in a dark corner quietly sipping their ale and watching the crowd with pretend disinterest. He recognized Dansbury and Stonebridge, though both men were dressed commonly so as not to draw

notice to their station nor be recognized by an unexpected acquaintance. He didn't see Lady Beatryce at present, which wasn't a surprise
seeing as how the house did not serve women. And even though Lady
Beatryce was not averse to wearing trousers, she, like Amelia Chase,
was unmistakably a woman.

Bloody hell, why think of her now?

MacLeod shook off that thought and pushed through two patrons
loudly singing a colorful ditty. Though he despised crowds, he understood the purpose for meeting in such a public place; the noise and
boisterous activity would provide adequate cover which was far more
important than his own discomfort.

MacLeod took a seat and an ale was immediately set before him, its
frothy head overflowing the glass. He wasted no time on pleasantries.
"She's moored at Salthouse Dock. The crew have been given a full
week's shore leave."

"Perfect," replied Stonebridge.

"They have few guards, if any. By all appearances, the ship looks
abandoned. So far, I've seen no sign of the officers, which is deuced
odd." MacLeod had arrived two days before the rest to establish
surveillance.

Stonebridge pulled out a folded paper and flattened it on the table
before them. MacLeod had seen numerous like it pasted about town.
Its title read, "Earl of Liverpool in Towne! Gross spending of public
funds ensues!" and included a picture of five extremely fat lords and
ladies with Everton toffee puffing up their cheeks and hanging out of
their mouths while they bowed on bended knees before a youthful
Prime Minister. "As I'm sure you have noticed, the Prime Minister
arrived in town four days ago. Tonight, he will be attending a party at
the home of the Marquess of Hastings as the guest of honor. The men
we hunt would not dare miss such a gathering."

Stonebridge glanced to MacLeod once more.

"I've managed to board the ship both nights, but haven't come
close to combing through all of it." MacLeod shrugged. "It's a bloody
large boat."

Stonebridge smiled. "I imagine so. Did you find any hard
evidence?"

"Some. But circumstantial, at best."

Dansbury spoke up then. "I suggest we board tonight. With four of us there and the crew on leave, we can broaden our search and cover the remainder while they're away. Then we can surprise the officers when they return from the party."

"Four of us?"

"Lady Bea. She won't be denied." Dansbury answered with a grin.

The duke raised one brow in question.

"She's more than capable." Dansbury answered his unspoken question.

The duke, had he been the type, might have rolled his eyes at this. Instead he simply said, "We'll meet outside the Duke's Dock Warehouse at dark, the southern side of the building."

MacLeod hunched into his coat. The breeze off the water was bitterly cold this evening, stinging his eyes and nose with its frosty bite. And this time, he had not been drinking copious amounts of alcohol to stave off the piercing wind; no liquid heat burned in his gut to help shield him against the penetrating chill. Despite the late hour, sailors and businessmen hustled up and down the wharf, mostly intent on their personal destinations and away from the ships floating on the water, though conversation was constant. A laugh here, an argument there, an occasional offer from a prostitute, there was no peaceful solitude to be found in a place such as this.

Despite all the bluster, he heard the shrill call of gulls in the distance and the muffled clang of a buoy's bell as it mutely tolled the pattern of incoming waves.

A sudden gust of wind caused him to shiver and brought the smell of briny sea. A tornado of cotton circled around his booted feet. MacLeod tucked tighter into the doorway in which he stood, his nose tucked into his scarf, while he waited for the rest of his team to arrive.

MacLeod stretched his cold, cramping fingers, then tightened them into fists. Two knuckles cracked for his efforts.

He was getting too old for this shite.

MacLeod looked over at Stonebridge, who stood beside him in quiet contemplation, seemingly impervious to the icy weather. Lady Beatryce and Dansbury had yet to arrive, having been tasked with ensuring the *HMS Nightingale* was suitably vacant so they could board.

MacLeod had the impulse to ask about Grace, the duke's new wife, but he bit off the urge, somewhat surprised by the maudlin thoughts hounding him to do so. Besides, the current atmosphere was decidedly not conducive to general conversation. Instead, he turned his attention to the people as they passed; most were working men and somewhat destitute, based on the state of their clothes. Liverpool had such a strong financial center, rivaling even London these days, but clearly these men were not a part of it.

Time passed all too slowly. Then, twenty minutes later, Dansbury and Lady Beatryce finally arrived and gave the all clear.

Despite their precautions, MacLeod couldn't help but wonder about Amelia's plea that they were walking into a trap. How accurate was her information? Could she be trusted?

And how would Kelly play into all this? After hours in the saddle and numerous conversations with Dansbury and Stonebridge, he struggled to paint Kelly a full-fledged traitor despite all evidence to suggest so.

Ten minutes later, all four of them were on board and searching the ship in absolute silence. Each was assigned a different floor, for the ship was huge. They were looking for proof, anything concrete to tie these men with the Society for the Purification of England, though even circumstantial evidence would be welcome.

MacLeod was on the lowest level, searching the kitchens, of all things. He didn't really expect to find anything, but one never knew. They would leave no stone unturned.

MacLeod methodically searched every nook and cranny, every pot and pan, every cupboard and every drawer of the galley. He found evidence, though it was circumstantial at best; every plate, glass, and piece of silver was stamped or etched with the logo for the Society for the Purification of England.

What boastful arseholes. They clearly weren't afraid to flaunt their allegiances.

Next, MacLeod made his way into one of the aft cargo holds and was surprised to find it reasonably bare, apart from half a dozen barrels surrounding the room. MacLeod looked inside the nearest vat and discovered it filled to the brim with gunpowder, which was deuced odd.

After checking all the barrels were filled with the same, MacLeod checked his watch and realized it was past time to reconvene with the others. He jogged out of the room and climbed the ladder, taking the rungs two at a time. Once on deck, he headed straight for the others.

Stonebridge spoke first. "I found nothing in my search." He looked to Dansbury. "You?"

Dansbury shook his head. "Not a thing."

Lady Beatryce had kept watch on deck.

They all looked to MacLeod. MacLeod tossed a napkin to the Duke. "All the dinnerware, flatware, glasses, and linens are either stamped, embossed, or embroidered with the Society logo."

Stonebridge shook out the napkin and studied it with a grim look.

"But that's not the most interesting discovery. The aft cargo hold is empty of any supplies save for a half dozen kegs of black powder. I haven't checked the forward hold, but I think we should; it's not accessible from where I was searching."

The duke nodded his head. "Agreed."

This time the three men headed to the front of the ship and down another set of stairs to get to the forward hold.

The situation was the same. Barrels of powder lined the outer walls of the room.

The duke stood in the middle of the room, looking about. "I don't get it. Did you not find any supplies in the kitchens besides tableware?"

MacLeod shook his head. "No."

Stonebridge looked to Dansbury. "You say these men having been living on the boat? Have you seen any supplies coming or going?

"Yes, by all accounts there were regular supplies coming and going, enough to provide for fifteen men. But why would they empty the boat?"

"They might if they knew we were coming," suggested MacLeod.

Grim faced, Stonebridge looked to his men. "We need to leave."

"Aye." MacLeod agreed, an uneasy feeling unsettling him.

"Something's not right," Dansbury said at the same time.

The three men climbed the ladder to the surface and raced to the ladder leading down to the boarding ramp, Dansbury in the lead and Stonebridge bringing up the rear. Dansbury whistled to Lady Beatryce who, donned in trousers and a waistcoat and boots, caught up with them. "What's the matter?" she asked.

Dansbury was about to answer, one foot poised to step on the top rung of the ladder, when a man called out. "Leaving so soon, Duke?"

Everyone spun about and looked aft, all eyes landing on the man standing on the poop deck. Moonlight glinted off the unmistakable barrel of a gun, which appeared to be pointed straight at Stonebridge.

A second man opened the blind of a lantern, illuminating the area above the helm where both men stood. A second gun was trained on MacLeod.

Several more lights blinked on behind them from the fore of the ship.

Goddamn, they knew we were coming.

"Lord Foster, so kind of you to welcome us," answered the duke as calmly as if commenting on the weather.

Lord Foster nodded in response. "Had we known you were coming, we might have been better prepared for your arrival."

The duke looked around and laughed. "I believe it's fairly safe to say you knew we were coming."

Lord Foster shrugged. "Perhaps." He turned to look at Lady Beatryce. "Lord Dansbury. Tsk, tsk. Bringing your lady on a mission, placing her life in danger? How liberal."

It was Lady Beatryce who answered the taunt. "This *lady* can handle herself." Dansbury simply stood back and crossed his arms, a smug smile and an obvious look of pride firmly in place; he was clearly confident in her skills

There was a slight pause, Lord Foster clearly hadn't expected that. He turned his attention to Dansbury, "You should have taken care of Kelly when you had the chance."

Dansbury muffled a curse. The implication in that statement obvious to them all: they'd been betrayed once again.

Lord Foster looked to MacLeod. "Alaistair MacLeod. Should have listened to your lady friend, aye?"

MacLeod spit on the deck. "Fook you." Not polished or charming, but perfectly clear and straight to the point.

He could have sworn he saw the duke's shoulders shake from a sudden burst of laughter, and he certainly heard Lady B and Dansbury doing so.

"So, Lord Foster, what is your plan? What do you hope to achieve this night? You cannot possibly believe you will come out of all this unscathed." said Stonebridge.

The man rocked on his heels, clasped his hands behind his back, and began to pace. "Ah, I take it we won't be able to convince you to join our cause, then?"

Dansbury snorted. "What gave it away?"

Lord Foster paused for but a moment. "I assumed you could be reasoned with."

The duke shook his head in apparent exasperation. "What part of my character suggested I would ever entertain such a thing? Do I seem like the traitorous kind to you?"

"Every man has his price."

"Not this man."

Lord Foster touched his fingers to the bridge of his nose as if a headache threatened. MacLeod was happy to oblige. The traitor sighed and continued, "Ah, I see."

"I should hope so," added Dansbury.

"Well, I'm afraid, then, that I have bad news for you all. Either you join us, or you all have to die." Without warning, Lord Foster turned to the man holding the lantern. "Shoot the big one, Mr. O'Connor, then toss the others into the brig."

Lord Foster turned his back on them all then, but paused in the act of walking away. "Bring Lady Beatryce to me."

"You bastard!" shouted Dansbury.

MacLeod dove for the deck just as a shot rang out, embedding itself in the deck behind him.

He rolled as soon as he hit the ground, but not before another bullet hit him square in the chest.

A woman screamed in the distance as MacLeod jerked once, shaken by the impact. As he began to lose his hold on consciousness, he heard the unmistakable sound of another shot, followed by the sound of breaking glass.

MacLeod smiled. All hell was breaking loose.

Chapter Thirty-Nine

Chaos erupted on the deck of the *HMS Nightingale*.

Amelia Chase had shot a man, possibly killed him. And she could not care less. Hell, she *hoped* she'd killed him, that bastard who'd shot MacLeod.

Unfortunately, as the man had collapsed to the deck, his lantern had smashed to the ground, spreading flames and whale oil all about, ultimately setting fire to the poop deck and the nearby mizzenmast.

So perhaps *unfortunately* was an understatement that did not accurately reflect the situation at hand.

The fire was a concern. It put all their lives in further danger, obviously. And it was quickly spreading, the whale oil an effective fuel for burning. Still, despite the danger, Amelia recognized that it proved a useful distraction as she ran, for in the wake of bedlam no one paid her any mind.

Amelia fell to her knees beside MacLeod as people clamored and shouted all around her.

"MacLeod, darling. Wake up! Oh, please, please be all right," she yelled as she reached for him.

Amelia clasped his familiar face between her hands. He breathed still, his cheeks warm and flush with life. Amelia let out loud gasp of relief.

MacLeod let out a soft moan, then slowly opened his big, beautiful green eyes. His lashes were ridiculously long for such a large man, and his eyes glinted with fire, a reflection of the flames climbing the sails behind her. So beautiful, yet utterly reflective of the exigency of their situation.

The ship was burning! And shouts and shrill screams seemed to echo from every direction while random gunshots and small explosive sounds peppered the air in haphazard bursts of noise creating quite a deafening racket, but most importantly, MacLeod was alive!

"Speak to me, darling. Can you get up? We must go," she yelled, urgency taking over her temporary relief.

"Aye." MacLeod tapped his chest, a dull thump sounded. "Cuirass. Still hurts like hell, though."

Amelia briefly touched her forehead to his and let out a soft laugh, relieved. He'd heeded her warning. She clamored to her feet and helped him to his.

He was unsteady but a moment, then his training took over. "Lass, we need to go now. There are barrels of black powder below."

MacLeod grabbed her wrist and turned toward the stairs that would lead them to the lower levels and the gangplank, but Amelia resisted his advance as she remembered what she'd discovered in the brig far below.

Or rather whom.

"Wait! MacLeod—it's Kelly." She pulled on his arms, begging him to listen. "He's in the brig, badly beaten. You must save him. He'll die otherwise."

"Fook!"

MacLeod ran one hand through is hair and spun around in frustration, then he grabbed her by both arms, "All right, but you must go, now. Get yerself to safety. I'll take care of Kelly…"

Amelia shook her head in denial. "But you'll need me. I know it."

MacLeod cupped her cheeks and brushed away the tears she didn't even realize were falling. "Lass, you must go. I canna worry about ye as well…"

Just then, Dansbury, Lady Beatryce, and Stonebridge appeared on deck, the three of them running towards them, obviously bent on securing their friend.

Both Dansbury and Stonebridge wore twin expressions of relief on seeing MacLeod on his feet.

"Let's go!" shouted Dansbury as he ran and gestured towards the stairs that would lead them to the gangplank below. He slid to a halt beside them when neither Amelia nor MacLeod made a move.

Lady Beatryce carried on.

MacLeod thrust Amelia into his Dansbury's arms and yelled, "Get Mel to safety, now. I have to get to Kelly!"

Dansbury nodded once, his grip on her arm secure. The duke said, "I'll go with you," to MacLeod.

MacLeod touched his hand once more to Amelia's face, a goodbye of sorts, then turned around and ran for the forestairs. Amelia watched until he disappeared before she reluctantly allowed Dansbury to drag her aft and off the ship. Every instinct screamed at her to stay with MacLeod. Yet, she knew if she stayed he would worry, which would help none of them in the end.

Practical as always, despite every irrational emotion pounding in her head to be otherwise.

But once on the dock, Amelia could not be persuaded to go any further. Practicality only took her so far. She had to clap eyes on MacLeod. She simply had to. For some inexplicable reason, she felt like her staying there, watching and waiting, would help him. Ridiculous, to be sure, but it mattered not.

Dansbury saw Lady Beatryce off, yet he stayed behind with Amelia. He didn't even try to convince her to leave, prudent of him.

Ten minutes felt like an hour. In that time, the ship had become a raging inferno. Flames slithered up all three masts and licked up the walls supporting the poop deck.

Another five minutes and the first of five different Fire Brigades arrived. Horses pulled huge fire engines, each manned by seven to ten men. Within minutes, they had lined up in a row alongside the ship and began furiously pumping water through the hoses. Their efforts seemed futile, a flame lit by whale oil was quite difficult to put out even with five hoses pumping continuous water. They worked valiantly, none the less.

And still there was no sign of MacLeod.

Amelia was drenched with the water that seemed to spray in every direction while she desperately sought to see, her eyes hardly straying from the top of the gangplank so far above.

Still, nothing.

Bells rang, men shouted as they ran to and fro, her face burned from the heat of fifty foot flames, and the stench of burning wood filled her nose. Amelia ignored it all, her fingers clasped and twisting in her skirts before her. She felt helpless. Out of control.

In her head, she chanted, *Please, please, please. Hurry, MacLeod. Come back to me, darling. Please, Please, Please,* over and over again while her eyes bored a hole in the top of that gangplank.

Dansbury shouted, his arm pointing high over her shoulder, "There!"

Up on the deck, so far up above, three men backlit by a wall of fire stood at the railing. The two men on either side were obviously carrying the third between them.

She recognized MacLeod at once as the man standing to the left.

Her heart leapt with fear. Their way out must have been blocked. It appeared the duke and MacLeod were tying a rope around Kelly...

Oh God, they were going to climb down the hard way.

For a few moments, nothing happened. It was apparent the men— Stonebridge and MacLeod, at least—were arguing. Amelia wanted to rail at them to hurry, but she dared not distract them. Though if they didn't begin their descent very soon, she was going to climb up and toss them all over herself and leave the fire brigade to clean up the mess of their remains on the dock afterward.

After what seemed like minutes and was probably only seconds, they came to an obvious agreement.

Stonebridge began his descent first.

Dansbury whispered over her shoulder, "Stonebridge will descend first, then MacLeod will lower Kelly to him."

His explanation made everything worse. Would they even have enough time? She wanted to roar her frustration, Demand MacLeod descend first, but she knew it was for the best even if she didn't like the decision.

Stonebridge had just touched his feet to the dock when MacLeod began to gently lower Kelly.

She wanted to yell, *Toss him over! No time for care!*

Her heart raced. Time ticked away faster than normal. Eventually, she couldn't stop herself from yelling, "Hurry up, damn you!"

It was the last thing she said before the first explosion rocked the very ground beneath her.

Chapter Forty

ansbury shoved Amelia to the ground behind a stack of crates and covered her with his body while the entire world shattered around them.

The crates toppled over them, creating a shelter of sorts, as she laid curled up beneath Dansbury, her knees scraped raw.

All she could think of was MacLeod.

Boom!

Another explosion rumbled the very air, brightly exploding through the cracks in the cover surrounding her, then dimmed once more. Though shadows flickered and danced in her vision, evidence of still more fire raging without. Dansbury grunted above her, his breathing rapid and harsh.

Amelia covered her ears and waited, though every instinct in her screamed, *Get up! Find MacLeod!*

Boom.

A third explosion sounded, and the noise seemed quieter now, more distant, though she suspected the ringing in her ears meant the sound was simply muffled through the reaction in her own body from the previous assault on her senses.

Acrid smoke filled her nostrils, the smell of burning wood taking on a more pungent, darker aroma.

Boom. Boom.

Two more explosions sounded in rapid succession and Dansbury grunted once again.

In total, five separate explosions shook the ground, the sound of the blasts still echoed loudly in her ears.

They waited and waited for what seemed like hours before Dansbury began to dig them out of their makeshift shelter. Eventually, she stepped out of their pile of rubble, shocked they had even survived, and into a world that seemed to have turned into hell, though the sounds were muffled through her throbbing ears.

Dansbury hugged her to him, an unexpected reaction that lifted her heart with joy. Then, he pushed her back and checked her all over, asking, "Are you hurt?"

"No. I'm fine. Well, perhaps my ears are ringing a bit."

Dansbury wiped a smudge from her nose. "Ah, that's to be expected. You'll recover in a day or two. Let's search for the others, shall we?"

Together they turned toward the destruction. At first, there was nothing to see; the very air was heavy with black smoke. One or two areas were lit by fires, though they were smaller now than the soaring fifty foot flames from before.

As if summed by her prayers, the wind picked up and cleared away much of the smoke. What was left was thorough destruction.

"MacLeod!" she screamed in horror.

There was no way he survived. She knew that. It simply wasn't possible. She would search until she knew for certain, one way or another. She searched the face of every man who passed as she ran to the edge of the dock. There wasn't much of the hull of the *HMS Nightingale* left and what was there was rapidly sinking beneath the surface. Wood sizzled as smoldering beams were swallowed by the sea.

Still, Amelia searched the water valiantly, looking for any sign of MacLeod.

"Stonebridge!" Dansbury shouted the duke's name just before

Amelia saw a man, his clothes singed and his shirt bloody and blackened, stumble into view. Dansbury ran to him, Amelia on his heels.

"Bloody hell, I feel awful." Came the duke's unexpected reply.

Amelia grabbed him by what remained of his shirt as he wobbled in place, one question on her mind. "Have you seen MacLeod?"

Stonebridge shook his head, and Amelia released him, her eyes returning to scan the black waters of the sea. A man nearby shouted, and Amelia turned to see that one of the warehouses behind her had ignited, its interior filled with cotton.

"Oh, God, that'll go up quickly."

Amelia, more mercenary in her thoughts said, "Hopefully not too quickly, we can use the light." All she cared about was finding MacLeod.

Indeed, the flames from the warehouse lit up the sea, making it easier for her to see.

All at once, she thought she saw something. A rounded shape on a scrap of flotsam. Could it be? She didn't want to sound an alarm precipitously, but was it he...? Precious hope flared in her chest.

Amelia began to pull off her undergarments. She needed to reduce the weight of her clothes, just in case. It was slow going, for she didn't want to take her eyes from the hunched over shape floating in the distance.

"Allow me." Dansbury appeared before her, a knife in his hands, and she nodded her head once before seeking out the source of her excitement once again. Cool air bathed her legs as Dansbury cut through her skirts, shortening them indecently. But she didn't care, and quite honestly she secretly loved how Dansbury never questioned her resolve, reasoning, or capability. How practical and so not overprotective like so many other men.

"Done."

As soon as the words left his lips, she ran and dove into the icy water.

She broke the surface thirty yards out, her shoes heavy and disgusting on her feet. They'd be ruined for sure if she even managed to keep them on as she swam.

She didn't care.

She surfaced and found her target another two hundred yards before her and that was all that mattered.

Her heart raced as she became more and more confident she'd found him. It gave her the surge of adrenaline she needed to carry on.

She lost one shoe after fifty yards.

And the other another fifty yards after that.

It seemed to take an hour. Her lungs felt like they were going to burst in her chest.

Eventually, she was within yards of his life raft and that was when she knew without a doubt.

It was he. MacLeod.

She laughed, then started crying immediately. Sobbing, actually, as she stroked. She had never known such joy as that moment. Never felt such relief.

She reached him, and still she sobbed. His head was bloody. His eyes were closed. But he groaned and it was the sweetest sound she'd ever heard.

She held on to him then, thrilled to feel his chest expand on a ragged breath. She sobbed once again when he said, his voice gruff from smoke said, "Aya lass, aren't you a sight for sore eyes?"

Then he let out a soft snore.

Chapter Forty-One

Two Days Later: The Home of Some Nameless Nob, Liverpool

Two days later, Stonebridge, Dansbury, Lady Beatryce, MacLeod, and Amelia Chase reconvened at the home of some nameless nob, MacLeod couldn't quite remember who, to debrief and to try to make sense of the fallout of their run in with the Secret Society for the Purification of England.

MacLeod crossed the threshold into the library, his head an aching, throbbing mess. He had stitches at his temple and on his chin and the scattered remnants of burns on his arms and face, none of them particularly severe. He might have a scar or two in the end to show for his efforts. In all, he was a damned lucky bastard.

And good God, how many times had he absentmindedly rubbed his chin before remembering the stitches in place there? His burning jaw said at least one time too many. Och, he'd done it a dozen times at the very least.

Though he'd prepared himself for the sight of her, he nearly stumbled when Amelia Chase stood upon his entry into the room. She was a sight for a starving man. He wanted nothing more than to pull her in his arms and hold her tight, melting in the heat of her embrace.

He'd felt far too cold and edgy in recent days. He missed her, aye, he did.

But Dansbury, damn the man, had kept her out of his reach while he recovered from his injuries.

It was probably a good thing.

It gave him plenty of time to think, but not enough time to reach any conclusions. In his defense, the pain in his head from the slight concussion didn't lend itself to thinking too hard about anything.

"Good. We're all here," began Stonebridge, "We'll start with Mrs. Chase; she has few things to share."

Amelia looked at MacLeod while she spoke. "Lord Foster was not the man you seek."

"Was?" MacLeod interrupted.

Dansbury spoke up, an unmistakable sense of pride colored his tone. "Lady Beatryce took care of that problem before we left the ship."

Lady Beatryce shrugged and answered, "He tried to take things a little too far, so I slit his throat."

"Ahem, I didn't hear that." interrupted Stonebridge, "Continue, Mrs. Chase."

Amelia dipped her head at the duke. "Thank you, Your Grace. Like I said, Lord Foster was not the man you seek."

MacLeod interrupted again. "How do you know this? And don't say..."

Amelia looked like she wanted to take off his head, judging by the glare she threw him. Still, she answered, "Spyder."

"Bloody hell, of course. But let me ask all of you. Why do you trust this man so much? What proof does he offer? And how the hell does he know?" asked MacLeod.

The duke answered, "I've had contact with the man myself. Far more limited, though. You'll have to trust me; he's given me sufficient evidence to believe he speaks the truth. His motives, however, are questionable. This man is a person of interest I'd like to speak with myself." The duke gave Mrs. Chase his trademark raised brow, the question there obvious to them all.

MacLeod looked Amelia in the eye as he asked his next question,

"Aye, and do we all trust *her*?"

Amelia gasped in outrage. Aye, he was a bastard to the bone.

But what he didn't expect was Dansbury, who had shoved him against the wall practically before he'd finished asking his question.

"That is my sister you're besmirching with your backhanded accusations, and I won't stand for it, you bastard."

"Get off me, friend." MacLeod broke Dansbury's hold, but didn't shove him away. The man had every right to be angry. "I had to ask."

"But that's where you are wrong. You didn't have to ask. You, my friend, simply didn't think."

"So are you claiming her as your sister, then? You believe Spyder?"

"Oh, I know she's my sister, you twat. First off, she fits. Here," Dansbury touched his heart. "Besides, Aunt Harriett confirmed the truth. She's the spitting image of my Aunt Gertrude in her youth. Aunt Gertrude is a woman who was ostracized from the family in her twenties. I never met her, but Harriett has a portrait of her at Bloomfield Place. There's no question; the resemblance is remarkable." Dansbury turned and walked over to Amelia, settling his arm around her and pulling her in tight to his side. "But even without all of that, she would be welcome in my home. I absolutely claim her as my sister."

MacLeod, his voice gruff with emotion, said, "You're an honorable man, Dansbury, but—"

Dansbury lifted his chin and so did Amelia, effectively cutting off what he was about to say. The familial resemblance between them was there for all to see.

And it was a good thing he didn't finish what he was going to say for he knew he was digging himself a very big hole he might never crawl out of with his cutting words. He needed to return to bed. To get well. To get over the hurt and betrayal which still lingered in his heart like a persistent cough, causing him to say things he oughtn't, despite the fact that he knew he had to let it all go. He needed to forgive. Himself. Amelia.

He needed to forgive and forget.

The duke, as efficient as ever, interjected here. "Now that we have that settled, we have another piece of business to attend to: Kelly. We were unable to find him after the explosion. We believe he's fallen."

Chapter Forty-Two

Two Weeks Later: Greenwood Castle, Scotland

Alaistair grumbled, "Enter," at his manservant's knock. Mac walked in, or marched, more like, anger apparent in his every step. Mac didn't even blanch at his unkempt state, MacLeod having not shaved nor hardly combed his hair in two weeks. Not since he let Amelia Chase walk out of his life.

His shirt was opened, the sleeves rolled and wrinkled, and he wore his studio kilt, complete with bits of dried paint and clay, even though he was not in his studio but, rather, working on estate business in his study.

He didn't even have on shoes.

"Is that a message for me?" inquired MacLeod.

Mac's only answer was a grunt.

MacLeod supposed that was livid for *Yes, you bastard*.

Mac placed the letter on his desk, turned on his heel, and marched out the way he came in—silent and angry. They were all furious with him. His brother. His cook. His dinners were cold, breakfast practically nonexistent. And no one made any pretense of joining him for a meal. Or a conversation. Or even a walk outside. It was as if he lived completely alone.

MacLeod stared at the letter as if it were a snake about to bite.

He didn't want to touch it.

He returned to his work; the bills had to be paid.

He only glanced at the note six—no seven, truthfully—times in the next half hour.

Still, he ignored it.

It couldn't be important.

Curious, he picked it up. A feminine script addressed the envelope, the location Bloomfield Park, the home of Dansbury's aunt, Lady Harriett Ross.

MacLeod dropped the letter as if burned by it.

No, it couldn't be from her...from Amelia?

MacLeod returned to his work.

He glanced at it once. Twice.

Eventually he threw down his quill and ripped it open, his eyes devouring the words before him in a matter of moments:

Alaistair...dearest,

Thank you, dear husband, for allowing me to take time to visit with my long lost brother, you ridiculous, confused man. It was very kind of you to agree to such a long...separation.

While you are being so thoughtful and helpful, would you kindly see to the forwarding of my luggage? You see, I left behind quite a few items in my rooms at Greenwood Park...

My heart being one of them.

My love, another.

Seriously, Alaistair...I miss you, so terribly much. I know we've had our troubles. I understand the value you place in trust, and I'm unbelievably sorry to have broken that with you.

Would I do it all over again if I could?

Yes, certainly...but in the same fashion as before. For you see, everything I am...and everything I did...led me to you.

And I wouldn't have it any other way.

Anyway, I look forward to seeing you at my debut ball in London.

I know, I know, not a chance! But I remain ever hopeful that you will find your way back to me in time. If only to return my things.

Until then, safe travels, my love.

I Remain...

Affectionately Yours, etc.

— AMELIA

MacLeod closed his eyes, briefly, then read the post script:

P.S. Thank you for the adventure, the laughs. I forgive you, old man...you bumbling, pig-headed old flap-dragon.

Alaistair MacLeod dropped her letter, then rubbed at the ache in his chest, a constant pain that hadn't left since he'd parted ways with Amelia Chase two weeks prior.

For long moments, he simply looked off into the distance, his sight not focusing on any one thing. He saw nothing but a future of bleak darkness and despair.

Then he felt a spark. Was it hope? At first, it was as a small kernel of light deep in his chest. Then slowly, and persistently, it grew.

In his mind's eye, he saw Amelia. He saw her smile. He heard her laugh. He felt her caress. He remembered the worry in her eyes. Her fear for *him*.

And just like that, hope exploded inside him. Hope and optimism and sun and everything that represented all those things. Oh, God—he loved her! He loved her like no other woman before her. And she loved him, too. He knew this with every fiber of his being, not just because of her words on the peace of foolscap before him, but through her actions, her emotions, her smile, her laughing eyes.

And he knew exactly what he had to do to make it right.

Chapter Forty-Three

Four Weeks Later: The Ballroom, Dansbury House, London

It was to be her debut to society. Everyone who was anyone was here to meet the long-lost sister of the Marquess of Dansbury, Lady Amelia Ross. As expected, the new name took some getting used to, but in a way, having this new identifier was a way to *be* someone new, someone else. A chance to reshape herself, to shed her past and begin again. Here. Complete with a shiny new family. And so, she would accept the changes, even if such changes didn't fit her quite so well...yet.

The Dansbury Ballroom all but glittered in the light of a thousand candles. Drapes of shimmering silver framed the five French doors leading to the rear piazza. An ice sculpture the size of a small pony, but in the shape of a five-pointed reindeer stood amid two tables of silver dishes filled with all manner of food and drink. The reindeer? It was a joke between her and Dansbury. She still couldn't believe he'd done it.

Oh, everything sparkled and shined. So did Dansbury, for that matter, in his dark purple waistcoat shot with silver thread. And Amelia, too, was wrapped in velvet, silk, and diamonds from head to toe, all in deep plum, her favorite color.

And yet she would have given the tiara off her head to be in Scotland. In Greenwood Park, to be perfectly precise. And wasn't that the dumbest thing in the world to think at a time like this?

Sure, she'd enjoyed getting to know Aunt Harriett. Dansbury was an utter lark. Even Lady Beatryce was a pleasure to be around; there was much to admire and appreciate in an equally strong woman despite their vastly different upbringings.

Yet one man stubbornly refused to leave her thoughts despite her every attempt to eradicate him from her mind, though she hoped beyond all belief that he would answer her summons and find her here at long last.

Alaistair MacLeod.

She looked for him wherever she went, which was patently ridiculous. He hated society, refused to participate in it. He wouldn't be caught dead at a society ball unless it was absolutely required of him to do so, meaning it was life or death and part of his job.

Even then, he'd try to get someone else to do it. She understood men who kept to themselves.

Dash it all! They'd said everything they had to say to each other. And unbecomingly, she'd practically begged. Begged him to take her. To admit he loved her.

She would not make such a fool of herself again. If that man couldn't see her worth, he didn't deserve her.

But it was oh-so-much more difficult to oust the man from her mind, her soul, despite every intention to do so.

"Lady Ross, may I have this dance?" A gentleman by the name of Baron Smythe, introduced to her earlier, addressed her. She almost laughed out loud. Every time someone called her that, she looked for Aunt Harriett. God, it was odd answering to a new name. She would never get used to it, she was quite sure.

Still, she behaved as instructed and curtsied, "Of course."

And wouldn't you know it, after taking their places on the dance floor, the orchestra began playing the first chords of a waltz? A gasp was heard around the crowd, followed by the whispered giggles of a dozen debutantes who'd come back to town from their country estates for just such an opportunity. The waltz was still quite blushingly scandalous, but not so much that one's reputation would be completely destroyed by dancing it.

Amelia Chase colored, which was not a common occurrence for her. She'd had rather silly dreams of dancing this dance for the first time with MacLeod, which she'd suddenly, unwillingly recalled.

Baron Smythe clearly took it as a sign of her innocence and naiveté —ha!—based on the smug smile he wore before taking her right hand in his. He placed his cold left hand upon her waist, as was appropriate, and she had to force herself not to shy away.

And then they were off. To hell.

Within four steps, he'd trampled her toes twice. Her beautiful plum dancing slippers wouldn't survive this dance, much less the night.

"Apologies, my lady."

"No worries, my lord."

See? Perfectly courteous.

So their conversation was a bit stilted. Still, Amelia tried her best to paste on a brilliant smile and go with the flow of the music. Perhaps if she didn't make eye contact, Baron Smythe wouldn't feel the need to speak.

Amelia winced—having one's foot trampled more than a dozen times during a single song tended to cause such a reaction—and they came to a complete stop, though the song was far from over.

"May I cut in?" came a familiar brogue.

It should have been a dream; MacLeod wouldn't come here and make a scene, surely. Only, she felt itchy as the entire room stared her way. Even the musicians had stopped playing.

She could see Dansbury over the baron's shoulder, a wide grin on his face.

"Now, see here—" sputtered Baron Smythe.

"Let me rephrase that," came that delightful brogue once again, "Move along, lad. This dance is mine."

The baron sputtered once, then dropped her hand and marched off, his posture stiff.

Then, before she knew it, Alaistair MacLeod stood before her, dressed formally in a cravat, waistcoat, and a familiar blue and green kilt.

He'd never looked so wonderful.

He looked equal parts sheepish and nervous before he said, "Hiya, Mel." Still, he slid his hands down her arms and grasped her hands. His were warm. She could feel that even through his formal gloves.

For a moment, she simply stood there, somewhat dumbstruck. She didn't know what to say or what to think. Even though she all but invited him to this party, she'd expected him to either decline completely, or more truthfully, contact her before *now*, four whole weeks later.

In the next moment, she was angry. For everything. For making her wait. For taking too long to make up his mind. Even for interrupting her stupid dance with the baron, even though her toes had been in utter misery, and she let him know it. And she had to get it all off her chest before they could move on. He had been a bastard. She needed him to know it. "You stubborn man. You paunchy, tickle-brained, malt-worm."

"Paunchy?"

"All right, not paunchy. But wayward, definitely. And folly-fallen."

"Aye. I'm an imbecile."

"Yes, yes you are, and a—"

"Coward."

"Why yes, yes, you are, and a—"

"Blind nincompoop, a hideous slug-toed thief of hearts, a goatish, clay-brained dewberry."

"Yes, yes, and yes." She almost—*almost*—laughed. In fact, she had to look down at her trampled shoes to pull together her composure. Eventually, she looked back up and glared at him. He looked suitably chastised, but not quite enough.

Ah, but she could fix that; she knew precisely how. "You know what? Wait right here. Don't you move a muscle. I will be right back."

She left him standing on the dance floor. She knew what she was after, had heard stories of its role in the lives of her family and friends and this time, it was her turn to use it. She knew precisely where it was, in fact.

She was only gone for a few moments.

When she returned to the ballroom, MacLeod was still standing where she'd left him, the crowd blatantly watching with delighted expectation. Even the musicians were waiting, their instruments by their sides. No one pretended not to be waiting to see what she would do.

Well, they would see it all—an absolute eyeful.

For she walked right up to Alaistair MacLeod and bashed him over the head with Aunt Harriett's Umbrella.

The Umbrella.

Dansbury, Aunt Harriett, Lady Beatryce, and the Duke and Duchess of Stonebridge began clapping at once.

The rest of the crowd, with bewildered looks about them, joined in. Who would dare to not follow the lead of the Duke of Stonebridge?

MacLeod blushed. *Blushed!*

"Do you know what, Alaistair MacLeod?" She had to yell to be heard over the roar of the applause, and their laughter at MacLeod's expense.

He leaned down, "What?"

"You love me, you stupid man."

He smiled. It was a smile not a single person in that room had ever seen on the face of Alistair MacLeod. It was an ear-splitting grin that lit up his face. The room fell silent at the sight and every soul heard him when he said, "God knows I do, Mel."

One might have heard a pin drop. He wasn't finished. "Don't you know? I'm a better man when I'm with you. You bring the light into my life I need to see. I love ye, Mel, I love you something fierce."

She was crying then, dumb, stupid, fat, blobby tears. Full on down her face and onto the velvet nap of her décolletage.

She didn't care.

She put her hand to her mouth, the better to stifle the sob threatening.

Then MacLeod fell to his knee, and she couldn't stop the sobs from coming. "Mel...marry me, please."

She grabbed his head and touched her forehead to his, but between gasping air and unladylike sobs said, "Of course, you silly man. And it's about bloody time, too."

Epilogue

Six Months Later: Upstairs, the Garrick Inn, Stratford-upon-Avon, Warwickshire

Amelia lifted her chin, faced the door in question: #27, threw her reticule to the floor, and dropped to her knees, setting her right eye to the key hole.

Yes, she was Amelia Chase:

- Married lady
- newly-minted-spy-extraordinaire (for real, this time)
- Independent American Expat (by choice)

...and a woman who *still* peeked through key holes.

But only when the occasion called for it, of course.

Unfortunately, *this* keyhole was no more cooperative than the last. Only vague shadows decorated the room's interior despite a window whose curtains were tied back allowing the moon's white rays to reflect an abstract version of the window and its nine panes on the floor across the middle of the room. But otherwise, nothing.

When sight failed her, Amelia tried listening, yet as before, all was silent within. Eventually, Amelia leaned back on her heels, frustrated. Again.

Men. Why did they always have to be so difficult?

Amelia clenched her fist in mock outrage, gently cursing the man within with one shaken fist, then leaned forward again, trying once more to see anything useful—at all—through the blasted key hole. Goodness, just a hint would suffice.

She held absolutely still.

She was one with silence, her breathing *slooooow*...

And steady...

And calm...

If she strained to listen, she might hear...

...*Creak*...

A nearby floorboard groaned under pressure...

Then a wisp of warm air wafted across her ear, sending a shiver up her spine, just before a deep, gravelly voice with a delicious, thrilling, familiar, and more than welcome Scottish brogue said, "What the hell do ye think ye're doin', Mrs. MacLeod?"

Amelia smiled, then jumped.

Despite history repeating itself, he had clearly not expected her to jump. Amelia spun around, finding it terribly difficult to suppress her habitual smile. "What in the blazes do you think you are doing, MacLeod?" She covered her mouth with her hand to ineffectually hide her smile.

"What am *I* doing?" he queried, yet his voice held no trace of outrage. On the contrary, his brogue was warm and sultry. Quiet and slow.

"Yes. What are you doing? Don't you know better than to sneak up on a person when she is...when she is..." Amelia licked her lips and marked the answering flare of heat in his gentle green eyes. "...erm...concentrating?"

He snorted and stepped closer, crowding her space before the door, his eyes drawn to her wetted lips. "Och, is that what you were doing?"

His gaze pinned her in place, searching for...something.

Amelia reached down and felt around for her reticule, her gaze never leaving his. "Well, what else would I be doing?"

His eyes followed her movement.

Eventually, she managed to gain purchase on her bag and stood once more.

Alaistair moved in closer, his cheeks brushing hers, his nose dipping into her neck as he whispered, "It looked to me like you were..." She closed her eyes as he drew in a long, slow breath, then continued, "...spying on the occupants of this room."

Amelia closed her eyes and choked back a moan. "Ridiculous." Her response was so soft, it barely qualified as a whisper.

MacLeod touched his forehead to hers and chuckled lightly, "So you weren't on your knees..." he punctuated that thought with a gentle thrust of his hips. "...just now...spying through that verra keyhole?"

A soft chuckle of her own burst forth and she smiled as she returned, "Well, that would be silly now, wouldn't it?" Amelia rubbed her hands up the sides of his arms, and wrapped them around his neck as she whispered, "My, you have quite the imagination, Alaistair MacLeod."

"Well, Mrs. MacLeod, why don't we revisit my room, and I can show you precisely how active my imagination can be?"

"But..."

"It's all right, tonight's assignment was a practice run, anyhow."

"What?!" MacLeod, luckily, ducked as she swatted at him with her reticule. "Truly?"

"Och, aye." He laughed, full and loud, a sound many who'd known him over the past five years would discredit had they not seen him do the like on numerous occasions since he married her.

However, this time, she did not find him funny in the least.

She practically chased him back to his room, swatting at his head with her reticule.

Did she mention she had a book inside?

Before they turned the last corner, she clocked him good, and when she stopped to check to see if he was seriously hurt, he grabbed her and threw her over his shoulder, laughing all the way to his room.

Bastard.

THE DUKE OF STONEBRIDGE TWIRLED HIS LADY AROUND AND PULLED her close. "Grace, darling, let's forgo the rest of this party and head upstairs." He waggled his eyebrows in suggestive invitation, if not a comical one.

"But Ambrose, these are our guests. Our party. In our home—"

"So? No one will care. The bulk of them are soused, anyway. The rest are too busy gossiping and playing the marriage mart game to care about an old married man and his lady."

Grace laughed and lit up the room with her brilliant smile.

"My lady."

A click of booted heels followed by "Your Grace," quelled whatever he would have said next. The duke sighed and turned to find a servant standing next to them bearing a silver tray with a note.

The duke acknowledged the man with a nod. "Gerard."

The man let out a small smile for the familiar acknowledgement and said, "An urgent message just arrived for you."

Stonebridge tucked his wife against his side and reached for the missive with his free hand. "Thank you, Gerard."

The butler bowed and walked away.

The duke looked to Grace. "Should I open it now?"

"Oh, go on then. It must be important or Gerard never would have interrupted."

"Quite so."

Stonebridge quickly opened the message and scanned the contents before handing it over to Grace. It read:

Duke,
  Kelly is alive.

— *SPYDER*

"Oh, thank God." Grace said, echoing the duke's sentiment perfectly.

The End

Next up - Ciarán Kelly's story: What the Rake Remembers

About the Author

Amy Quinton writes humorous historicals...with heat from her home in Summerville, SC. She lives with her husband, two boys, three cats (George, Astrid, and Toothless), and one dog (Bear). In her spare time, she likes to read, go camping, crochet/knit, read, hike—oh, who is she kidding, what spare time?

http://amyquinton.net

Sign up for her newsletter at:
https://app.mailerlite.com/webforms/landing/u4s4j6

f facebook.com/AmyElizabethQuinton

🐦 twitter.com/AmyQuinton

📷 instagram.com/quintonamy

ⓐ amazon.com/author/amyquinton

ⓟ pinterest.com/amyquɪɪ

ⓖ goodreads.com/amyquinton

BB bookbub.com/profile/amy-quinton

What the Duke Wants

Agents of Change, Book 1

http://bit.ly/whatthedukewants

England, 1814: She is from trade. He is a duke and an agent for the crown with a name to restore and a mystery to solve.

Miss Grace (ha!) Radclyffe is an oftentimes hilariously clumsy, 20 year-old orphan biding her time living with her uncle until she is old enough to come into her small inheritance. Much to her aunt's chagrin, she isn't:

- Reserved—not with her shocking! tendency to befriend the servants...
- Sophisticated—highly overrated if one cannot run around

barefoot outside...
- Graceful—she once flung her dinner into a duke's face... on accident, of course.

But she is:

- Practical—owning a fashion house is in her future; unless someone foils her plans...
- In love... maybe... perhaps... possibly...

The Duke of Stonebridge is a man with a tragic past. His father died mysteriously when he was 12 years old amid speculation that the old duke was 'involved' with another man. He must restore his family name, but on the eve of his engagement to the perfect debutante, he meets his betrothed's cousin, and his world is turned inside out... No matter, he is always:

- Logical—men who follow their hearts and not their heads are foolish...
- Reserved—his private life is nobody's business but his own...

And he isn't:

- Impulsive—it always leads to trouble...
- Charming—that's his best friend, the Marquess of Dansbury's, area of expertise...
- In love... maybe... perhaps... possibly...

Can he have what he wants and remain respectable? Can she trust him to be the man she needs?

What the Marquess Sees

Agents of Change, Book 2

http://bit.ly/whatthemarquesssees

England, 1814: He is a marquess and a spy with a woman to protect and an assassin to thwart. She is...not nice.

The Marquess of Dansbury is a strong, charismatic man living a charmed life, despite interacting with the dregs of society as an agent for the crown. His past isn't without tragedy, but he is too amiable to allow misfortune to mar his positive outlook on life. Until now...when he finds himself tasked with protecting the one woman he actively disdains, Lady Beatryce Beckett, from a deadly and all too insane assassin. No matter, he is always:

- Charming—though perhaps not around a certain lady...

- Laid-back—again, maybe not around a certain lady...
- And strong—especially around a certain lady...

And he isn't:

- Irrational—ever. Even around a certain lady...generally speaking...usually...
- Or in love...with a certain lady. Especially not that. Honest...

Lady Beatryce Beckett is mean. She ruins other women on purpose. She lies. She cheats. She even steals. She's fast. And she takes particular pleasure in provoking a certain marquess. In short, she'll do anything to get what she wants: Freedom from her abusive father. Much to everyone's vexation, she isn't:

- Reserved—with anyone, but especially with a certain marquess...
- Trusting—with anyone. Ever. Even with a certain charming marquess...
- Or a coward—especially around a certain marquess.

But she is:

- Strong—she's had to be...particularly around... need she really explain?
- Worthy... of love. Possibly.
- And in love...Wait, what?

It will take a special man to see the true woman beneath the surface...and a strong woman to allow him that glimpse. Can she teach him that his ruthless drive to seek justice isn't all that different from her determination to be free?

What the Rake Remembers

Agents of Change, Book 4

http://bit.ly/whattherakeremembers

England 1814:

Theirs was a forbidden love, but now...

Agent for the Crown, Ciaran Kelly, is an Irishman who loves women. *All* women. Big, small, buxom, slender, blonde, ginger, rich, poor—their features matter not. Fortunately, he was born with a silver tongue, enough wit and charisma to rival Claude Duvall, and an air of mystery, necessary to be an effective spy. In short, women love him. But after being branded a traitor and tortured by the very villains he's vowed to destroy, he's lost his memory and is left with only one person in the world he can—and must—depend upon...*and she despises the very air he breathes.*

No matter, he is:

- Confidently optimistic—she'll come around.
- Smooth-talking—beneficial when he makes her angry. And he will make her angry.
- And brilliant—useful, if only he could remember...

And he isn't:

- Impatient—there's always time. See also confidently optimistic above.
- Or afraid—of being in love. He's been there before.

Frederica Glyndŵr has matured since her father erased her from the family tree, tossing her to the streets of London with nothing more than her wits to aid her survival. What started out as a horrific journey towards female enslavement has ended up being the best possible thing to happen to her. She's learned to be a fighter, a thief, a stealthy observer, and a surprising revelation to any villain who happens along—they love to underestimate her. Everything is finally perfect. Until a disappointment from her past invades her life once more, threatening to expose her secrets. She's ready for a reckoning, but never forgiveness...*too bad he has no memory of their past.*

No matter, she is always:

- Prepared—a life lesson; she will never be caught ill-equipped again.
- And capable—she's proven *that* to herself time and again.

And she isn't:

- Sloppy—with the men they're after, this could mean the difference between life and death.
- Patient—normally not a positive trait, but time is of the essence. Bad men are coming.
- Or in love...or won't be if she could only retrieve her heart from the man who stole it.

As the enemy closes in and Kelly's mind begins to heal, he discovers just how deep his betrayal goes.

Can true love prevail over such sins?

Frederica can't speak for some sins, but she's damn sure it can't survive all secrets...

Also by Amy Quinton

How to Take Revenge on a Disloyal Scot

An Agents of Change short story

Love is... revenge? Because what else's a girl supposed to do when she learns the man she loves has found himself a bride?

The Umbrella Chronicles: George & Dorothea's Story *A short story, part of *Never Too Late*, A Bluestocking Belles Collection

St. Vincent's days as a bachelor in good standing are numbered.

The Umbrella Chronicles: James & Annie's Story *A short story, part of *Follow Your Star Home*, A Bluestocking Belles Holiday Collection

Prodigal duke seeks professional matchmaker for matrimonial assistance. Prefers foolproof plans

in 10 parts. Magical solutions accepted. Missteps likely.

The Umbrella Chronicles: John & Emma's Story *A short story, part of *Valentines from Bath*, A Bluestocking Belles Valentine's Day Collection

A serious-minded, scientific man of learning seeks a complex and chaotic practitioner of all things superstitious who will upend his well-ordered life.

Hoodwinked for the Holidays *A short story, part of the *Love in the Lowcountry: A Winter Holiday Collection, Volume 1*

Wanted: Ghost with good reviews for special holiday tour. Team Player a must. Matchmaking skills NOT required.

Coming February 2020:

The Umbrella Chronicles: Chester & Artemis's Story *A short story, part of *Fire & Frost*, a Bluestocking Belles Collection

Beastly duke seeks confident *any* woman who doesn't faint at the sight of his scars. Prefers not to leave the house to find her.

www.ingramcontent.com/pod-product-compliance
Lightning Source LLC
Chambersburg PA
CBHW072129250626
47159CB00007B/2617